Renquist pointed  her to come to him. Whi   d motionless, the dark   m, as though in the grip   from unpleasant narcotic   eft of her consciousness,   magenta to deep blue, frightened but also lethargically excited. Lost from reality and completely unable to translate what was happening to her, she was vacuously happy someone was bringing her the shadowy and mysterious drama so completely lacking in drab real life. . . . She would embrace her last moments with a previously unpracticed passion. She stood in front of him, stiff and unseeing, but then one level of control seemed to give way, and she sagged into Renquist with a confused sigh. "I don't understand."

Renquist caught her easily with his left arm, as though they were about to dance. His right hand slipped into the pocket of his leather jacket, closing around the smooth silver tube. "You never will."

"I don't mind."

The tube was out of his pocket, and he thumbed the button. The sharp steel spike slipped out. "I know."

MORE THAN MORTAL

MICK FARREN

TOR®

A TOM DOHERTY ASSOCIATES BOOK
NEW YORK

This is a work of fiction. All the characters and events portrayed in this book are either products of the author's imagination or are used fictitiously.

MORE THAN MORTAL

Copyright © 2001 by Mick Farren

All rights reserved, including the right to reproduce this book, or portions thereof, in any form.

A Tor Book
Published by Tom Doherty Associates, LLC
175 Fifth Avenue
New York, NY 10010

www.tor.com

Tor® is a registered trademark of Tom Doherty Associates, LLC.

ISBN: 0-765-34293-6
Library of Congress Catalog Card Number: 2001027529

First edition: August 2001
First mass market edition: April 2002

Printed in the United States of America

0 9 8 7 6 5 4 3 2 1

The candles had been made to a formula of her own devising, so rather than giving a soft orange-yellow light, their flames burned an electric blue. Columbine Dashwood had always embraced a passion for games with light and fire. Of the four primeval elements, fire fascinated her the most, even though she was forever denied the most elemental fire of all, the direct radiance of the sun. Perhaps that was the reason. For more than almost two and a half centuries Columbine Dashwood, by her very nature, had been confined to the night, restricted, on pain of her own total and agonizing destruction, to deliberately kindled fire and lights of artificial construct, except for the wax and wane and coldly bruised whiteness of the moon, the starlight and skyshine, the occasional forked lightning of a nocturnal storm, and, of course, that one time in the Western Islands when she had witnessed the aurora. Columbine was more familiar than anyone with the rich strata running through the very core of her character that fervently desired what she couldn't have. She actually admired this in herself. The perverse trait of personality was a guarantee of her existence always being interesting, although, at times it could also make her life frustrating and even dangerous.

The boy lay still, smoothly naked and knowingly vulnerable. He was scarcely more than a teenager, but over his time with her, he had learned a depravity beyond his years. His legs were pressed together, and his arms spread wide, at right angles to his body, like a supine crucifixion. One thin white hand gripped the corner of an embroidered Moorish cushion, while the fingers of the other twisted a fold in the burgundy satin sheet that covered the large circular bed. The third finger bore the ring, the one with the large single ruby in an elaborate art nouveau claw setting, which she had given him in the afterglow of their first night together in the cryptic and wafting luxury of her bedroom at the Priory. Like all the others who had been there before him, the boy loved her, and he wanted to be loved by her in return. His aura showed his breathlessly mixed emotions: anxiety and anticipation, but also a definite measure of fear. He wanted to be controlled and led by her, but part of him was apprehensive of where she was leading him. Already she had taken him to the edge of the sensual abyss, and to free fall well beyond. She knew he was aware that, sooner or later, she might conduct him to a place from which he would be unable to return. She had known from the beginning this was both what he desired and dreaded in almost equal proportions. This duality was a part of what had attracted her to him in the first place, along with the more mundane consideration that he also was possessed of a fey androgyny and the sensually geometric features of Michelangelo's *David,* albeit submissively softened.

Dashwood stood beside the bed, pushed back her long, pure white curls, and looked down at his face. One of the bed's tentlike draperies of the sheerest muslin gauze hung between them, softening the focus and rendering him even more idealized. "You are very beautiful."

Once, before her training had fully taken hold, he might have replied. Undoubtedly, some highly unoriginal flattery to the effect that she was even more beautiful, but he had soon learned she didn't need or even want him to speak. He lacked the intellect for any conversation she might crave. She required him silent, obedient, and objectified. She leaned forward, pushed aside the canopy, and lightly touched his smooth and completely hairless chest with her fingertips. She was as naked as he, and the blue light of the strange candles gave her death-pale skin an almost reptilian sheen. She smiled sadly and repeated herself. "Yes, my dear, you are so very beautiful."

As she lay down beside him, stretching in the dim chamber's interplay of light and shadow, her movements were sinuously nonhuman. But this was only as it should be. Columbine Dashwood was in no way human in anything but outward appearance. Of course, the boy didn't know that. Yet. His mind was always open to her, and she knew he considered her strange, but he was too infatuated with the ecstatic illusions she fed him to question the nature or origin of her strangeness. He sometimes wondered why she shunned the sun, but he dismissed it with a young and overwhelmed lover's carelessness as an eccentricity of vanity. His only half-formed theory was that maybe she had a complexion that burned rather than tanned. This would certainly be in line with prematured white hair. At times she found his lack of curiosity irksome, but she supposed it went hand in hand with his passivity, and if it hadn't been for his passivity, he never would have survived to keep her amused for so long.

She moved her body against his. Too bad he had to go. He was gorgeous, stupid, and infinitely malleable, the complete plaything—really all Columbine Dashwood had needed until this current situation had arisen.

Unfortunately, the imminent arrival of Victor Renquist
had changed all that. Playthings were extraneous. Her
long season of leisure was at an end, and to prolong him
made no sense. She must finish him this night. She allowed herself a single wistful sigh; humans wilted in
time, anyway, like roses from a transitory admirer. Hundreds like him had served briefly in her infinitely extended existence, and hundreds like him would serve in
the future.

The evening had started, at least for the boy, with
opium and a chilled white wine. When the crucial time
came, he would feel no pain. Respecting his devoted
service, she stroked his mind, intensifying his sensation
of being blissfully afloat. She kissed his throat, and he
groaned softly. At the same time, she slowly extended
her fangs, down from the twin cavities in her unusual
skull. She knew that many of the supposedly sophisticated kin had forgone their fangs and had them surgically removed. Defanging enjoyed an especial vogue
among her American cousins and also those in the Far
East, both cultures being so taken with cosmetic surgery.
They favored the small blade or steel spike, but Dashwood remained a staunch naturalist in the matter of the
kill.

When she struck, the boy felt almost nothing. The
penetration was so fast and smooth, he experienced only
mild surprise. She drank quickly so as not to prolong his
departure, and his strength ebbed with a sense of wondering bewilderment at all the last dying noises and the
darkening of the blue light. When his pulse ceased, Columbine's own body convulsed, and she let out two long,
soul-deep, heartfelt shudders. At the same time, the blue
candles guttered. Her being was permeated with climac-
tic power. Many of her kind might, at such a moment,
rise and moon-howl, but that suited neither Dashwood
nor English behavior. Concealed responses and near-
silent triumphs were long-maintained traditions, and
ones with which she had no intention of breaking.

She lay very still as the boy's stolen energy stilled and settled, her own trembling subsided, and her fangs involuntarily retracted. The tiny sounds of the old manor house, the small creakings and creepings, whispered around her, and outside, a breeze rustled the branches of the four-hundred-year-old oak. She raised herself on her arms and gazed at the body of the youth. If anything, in the pure whiteness of death, he was even more beautiful. Hair slightly tousled, ice-blue lips parted, and head a little turned, one hand stretched out, palm up, across the dark satin sheet like a tragic figure in a Pre-Raphaelite painting. She had fed neatly and with care. The wounds in his throat were small, and only a few drops of still-glistening blood spattered one of the multitude of damask pillows. She knew that with his passing, her protracted extravagance of indolence and hedonism was at an end. The lazy cocooned winter was about to explode into active and possibly violent spring. The secret that she had kept so long was, in one way or another, about to be revealed, and she would be compelled to deal with the consequences. The letter she had sent to Victor Renquist had already put the sequence of events in motion. No way remained to halt them.

She rose from the bed and slipped into a silk peignoir, at the same time calling out to the thralls. "Grendl, Bolingbroke, come to me now. I need the two of you to remove this empty thing to the furnace."

Immediately she remembered the ring. Ecstasy had made her careless, and she turned and eased it from the limp dead hand. Too fine a bauble to be consigned to the fire or stolen by servants. In any case, it made up part of a set, and she would doubtless use it again when the present dilemma had been addressed and resolved.

A tilting movement and then a slide forward brought Victor Renquist fully and watchfully awake. He could feel the reinforced flight case finally being unloaded. For the eleven hours it had taken to transport him from Los

Angeles to London, he had remained in a half-dream, enveloped in a darkness so total even his undead senses could see little except the faintest psychic fluctuations of his own enclosed aura. Some twenty minutes earlier, the jolt as the wheels of the aircraft touched the solidity of an English runway had interrupted his somber nosferatu introspection, but even at that point, he had still not fully given himself up to the consciousness of the moment. The real danger would not come until the ground crew began to unload the small corporate jet's cargo, of which the custom-crafted aluminum flight case was the primary item. Over his centuries of existence, Renquist had taught himself a very complete patience. Anticipating a threat when he could do absolutely nothing about it would be to subject himself to pointless stress.

In theory, no threat should exist. All necessary arrangements had been made, the correct bribes had been proffered and accepted but, humans being what they were, a random danger always remained that some unforeseen error would come to pass, the chance element of ever-assertive chaos, what they called Murphy's Law. The flight case had been designed to look as little like a coffin as possible, but its very dimensions—over six feet in length and some two and a half feet across—still hinted of funeral parlor. The diplomatic stickers liberally pasted to its exterior were supposed to prevent any unexpected opening of the case. In addition, the private airfield to the southwest of London had only a minimal representative presence of Her Majesty's Customs and Excise, which further reduced the chance of the case being unlocked for inspection and its strange contents being disclosed. The small jet's flight plan had been timed so the aircraft would land well after sunset, so at least an unwarranted intrusion would not expose him to sunlight and destruction in sudden and violent conflagration. Should he be discovered, however, he would still find himself subjected to what would undoubtedly be a barrage of unanswerable questions and perhaps a confinement from which he could free himself only with desperate and all too noticeable violence.

The flight case now tilted acutely, moving down what had to be a ramp, but Renquist was held firmly in place by the form-fitted foam rubber. A human would have quickly suffocated in such an enclosed and sealed environment, but Victor Renquist was easily able to compensate for the lack of air by adjusting his nosferatu metabolism. A jarring thud, followed by a regular and mechanical vibration, indicated the case and its occupant had been loaded onto a truck that was now moving away from the aircraft. Renquist allowed his mind to drop back into the semi-sleep in which he'd spent the flight across half the world. He knew he'd be awakened again when the ground transportation reached where it was going.

Even idly drifting in the labyrinth of his almost limitless memory, Renquist found he was still, to a degree, affected by his unseen surroundings. During the previous decade, his duties as Master of the nosferatu colony that had first made its home in Lower Manhattan, and now resided beside the Pacific Ocean in one of the more isolated canyons of the sprawling city of Los Angeles, had precluded all but the most pressing individual travel. He had journeyed once to New Orleans to act as a neutral adjudicator in a potentially messy bayou clan dispute. He had also, a few months earlier, been compelled to make a fast dash to Savannah, Georgia, in the selfsame corporate jet that had just brought him to the United Kingdom, to rescue some very ancient books that should in no way fall into the hands of humanity at large. Previously the tomes had been safe, part of a highly esoteric personal library belonging to a human who could be trusted in his isolated neurosis. After the man's exceedingly messy shotgun suicide, however, the collection, along with all the rest of his personal effects, was slated to be sold at auction by the IRS to cover the eccentric's outstanding back taxes; if that happened, the hand-lettered volumes, with their unique flamelike script, and the arcane and potentially dangerous information they contained could fall into literally anyone's hands. Thus Renquist was forced to make a night flight, commit burglary, and then hightail it back to California before he was caught by the sun.

Aside from these two excursions, the nosferatu colony had been more than enough of a disquieting handful to keep him tied closely to whichever of the two Residences was its home. More than two decades had passed since Renquist had left the continental United States, and it had been longer still since he had set foot on English soil. The last time had been during the so-called swinging sixties, when he had been drawn by the license and laxity of that Western cultural revolution of sex, drugs, and rock & roll. He had also been present for the World War II Nazi blitz when the toga-wearing Hermann Göring and his *Luftwaffe* had attempted, and failed, to bomb the population into submission. He had been in the city during the 1890s, at the time of both the fall of Oscar Wilde and the Jack the Ripper murders. Before that, some eight decades earlier, he'd enjoyed a passing acquaintance with Lord George Byron. At the end of the seventeenth century, he had been a witness to the Duke of Monmouth's ill-advised and swiftly defeated rebellion; but by far the longest time Renquist had spent in the British Isles was during the embattled reign of Elizabeth I, when he had provided dark, highly secret, and at times, scarcely believable services for Sir Francis Walsingham, the Queen's genius spymaster and a shadowy grey eminence of covert power.

Of course, by original birth, Renquist was technically himself an Englishman. Almost a thousand years ago, when the world had been so much more empty of men and the great forests still held sway in northern Europe, when bear and wild boar still thrived and deer crowded the thickets, he had been simply Victor of Redlands, the out-of-wedlock son of Roger, Earl of Cambray, and

Gwendoline the Saxon maid, turned loose to make his way in the world as a bastard, with only the horse, armor, and sword that were the sum payment of his father's considered debt of paternity. Despite these distant human origins, his arrival by no means represented any kind of homecoming. Perhaps he might have felt some ties to a homeland back in those ancient days of faded unreality, when he had been so young, so stupid, so human: roaming through France, England, and the Low Countries, hiring on with any lord, duke, or baron who would keep him supplied with food, drink, women, adventure, and the opportunity of pillage. Perhaps he might have felt like an Englishman in those troubled years at the start of the hideous idiocy that would become know as the Crusades. Soon after that, though, when only in his twenties, destiny had brought him under the influence of the hypnotic and frightening beautiful being known as the Great Lamia, the immensely powerful female nosferatu who changed him to what he now was. From that fateful day forth, temporal considerations like home and heritage had been consigned to an increasingly hazy past. The Great Lamia had transformed him, brought him across the mortal divide to join the somber ranks of the undead. He had crossed centuries and continents, the perpetual outcast and figure of fear except among others of his own kind, until the recall of his time as human was less than a dream.

Normally Renquist was able to mentally calculate time, almost to the second, without the aid of any timepiece, but for the long flight halfway across the world—and now the journey by road from the airfield into the city—he had tuned back his time perception, just as he had slowed his undead pulse and reduced his strange nosferatu respiration almost to nothing. An unawareness of time was the most complete protection against the boredom of all-enclosing darkness. Thus it came as a mild surprise when the truck carrying his container began making frequent short stops as though moving through reasonably heavy traffic, and he also became aware of the intrusion of minds of humans in massed numbers.

The plan had been a relatively simple one. The flight case in which he was concealed would be delivered to the Savoy Hotel in London's fashionable West End along with the rest of his more conventional luggage. A bribed bellhop would unlock the fastenings that held down the lid, but the man had been ordered to be sure and leave the room without looking inside. Once alone in his suite, Renquist would be able to emerge, shed his traveling clothes, dress for the outside world, leave the hotel, and merely reenter and register just like any much more natural new arrival. The strategy, far from earth-shatteringly complex, could never have been consummated without the Byzantine and globe-spanning network of contacts and the dossiers of human weakness and vulnerability Renquist scrupulously maintained for exactly such eventualities. The aircraft, the carefully timed schedule, the strangely explicit instructions, and the bribery and corruption required to ensure that those instructions were carried out to the letter, with no questions asked, were all a result of favors called in from men and women who owed Renquist either their liberty or their very lives—individuals whose dark secrets ranged from the bankrupting of huge corporations and small countries to deliberately and systematically feeding their heiress spouses coma-inducing doses of insulin or other medications. For the well-organized nosferatu, secret knowledge (and the threats it made possible) was as valuable as industrial diamonds, uncut cocaine, or hard currency.

The truck carrying his aluminum case-coffin came to a more decisive halt. Renquist could only assume that they had reached the delivery entrance of the Savoy. This was confirmed when the case was abruptly dragged to the rear of the vehicle, upended, and lowered. He was moving again, leaning at an angle close to vertical, as though being propelled on some kind of trolley. He was grateful that whatever human underling was overseeing the transfer strictly observed the prominently displayed THIS WAY UP stickers. He had no desire to make this final leg of his journey humiliatingly upside down. Headfirst might suit a bat, but never a nosferatu. Despite the weight of human folklore, the undead had nothing to do with the subfamily Desmodontidae except an occasional common predator rapport. Of course, he would expect nothing less than perfection in even the smallest details from the Savoy. It was, after all, one of London's most legendary and prestigious five-star hotels.

This inclined forward motion continued for a couple of minutes or more; then, after a series of bumps, it ceased and was replaced by a smoother upward one. He was in an elevator. His destination was close. After a second set of bumps, as the trolley was maneuvered out of the lift, the new, more muffled sound of its wheels told him he was now moving along a carpeted corridor. The trolley halted, a door was opened, and Renquist was moved into a room. The casket was lifted from the trolley and placed on the floor in a way that left Renquist lying flat on his back. One more operation, and his travel plan would be completed to perfection.

He heard a human voice. "All right, Sanji, old lad. You can go along. I've just got one more thing to do here."

One set of footsteps left the room, and moments later, he heard the click of the first of the fastenings on the case being unlocked. It was followed by the voice that had spoken before, this time talking to itself. "This is a fucking weird one, and no mistake."

The other fastenings were also unlocked, and then this human made his exit, closing the door behind him. Renquist waited a full thirty seconds and finally, with an almost embarrassing resemblance to the rising vampire in a cheap photoplay, he pushed open the lid of the case and stood up. He stepped from the box and looked

slowly round the suite. Again, his instructions had been
carried out to the letter. The rest of his luggage was
positioned beside the case, and thick metal foil had been
taped over all the windows so even the slightest hint of
sunlight was rigorously excluded. That a guest at the
hotel might obsessively demand the elimination of all
outside light might seem a little unusual, but the Savoy
was well accustomed to the unorthodox. Down the years,
the establishment had catered to the eccentricities of
such off-center luminaries as Sarah Bernhardt, Sergey
Diaghilev, the Duke and Duchess of Windsor, King Fa-
rouk, Salvador Dalí, Howard Hughes, Judy Garland, and
Elizabeth Taylor and Richard Burton to name but ten. It
was also a matter of public record that Elvis Presley had
demanded a similar sealing of the windows from his
hotels when he performed in Las Vegas or went on tour.
A slightly more conventional request by Renquist was
for the large jug of ice water—it had been placed by
unseen hands on the top of the suite's small bar.

When Renquist had assured himself that all else was
to his satisfaction, he picked up the jug and drank from
it in deep, wolflike drafts. It seemed, as he grew older,
that water became more and more important to his metabolism. He had no explanation for this and did not know
if the phenomenon was unique to himself or if it afflicted
all nosferatu who reached his advanced age. He, in fact,
had no way of knowing. Since the departure of the ancient Dietrich, he'd met absolutely no nosferatu as old
as he was.

After drinking, he dressed, but he took his time. He
was in a new city and felt it incumbent to present himself
with the optimum of grave good taste. A dark silk suit,
a navy shirt with a narrow black tie, and slightly pointed-
toe, Cuban-heeled boots seemed appropriate, topped off
with an almost ankle-length black trench coat, since it
never paid to trust the London weather. He considered
a wide-brimmed, slight dandified hat, but he was currently wearing his hair long with a slight curl. It hardly

suited a hat, and if it should get wet, so be it. It was
time for him to merge with the human population. He
considered taking the silver-topped cane that also served
as a sheath for the secreted blade of the finest and most
deadly Milan steel, but he decided a sword stick was
unacceptably flamboyant and probably surplus to his requirements.

Renquist was neither so naive nor so ill informed that
he stepped out into the London night expecting a Sher-
lock Holmes pea-soup fog. He was pleased to find he
had arrived on a pleasant, if slightly brisk, night and
decided, instead of going straight back into the Savoy to
register like a newly arrived guest who'd had his luggage
sent on in front of him, he would walk for a while and
get the feel of the city. London had changed a good deal
since he had last been there. To his eye, it had ceased
to be as individual and idiosyncratic as he recalled it. It
seemed to be succumbing to both the new European ho-
mogeneity and the overall multinational uniformity of
McDonald's, Sony, and Citicorp. He missed the Dick-
ensian intricacy he'd known in the days of Sir Henry
Irving; Lillie Langtry; Eddy, the Duke of Clarence; and
Mrs. Patrick Campbell—that same period when Bram
Stoker had caused such troublesome reverberations by
inventing the wholly fictional but uncomfortably too-
believable Count Dracula.

Aside from the Dracula anxiety, the 1890s had been
one of his favorite eras in the history of the ancient city,
but any nostalgia he might have had for the times past
wasn't sufficient to mar his enjoyment of strolling slowly
down the Strand, taking in the sights and sounds, the
store window displays, the marquees of the theaters, and,
most interesting of all, the vast international variety of
humanity who thronged the sidewalks. After being isolated in the relatively new and automobile-dominated
city of Los Angeles for so long, to be back in a metropolis where crowded streets lived and breathed, and pal-
pably dense history was layered beneath his feet was a

positive pleasure. He tuned back the mental auras of the passersby. He had no desire to eavesdrop on the details of their thoughts and feelings, and en masse, humans could be overwhelmingly intrusive on his undead perceptions.

He continued walking west until he was within sight of the circling traffic in Trafalgar Square, the cars, cabs, and red double-decker buses that orbited the tall monument to Admiral Horatio Nelson. Renquist looked up at the stone figure atop its narrow column, the surrounding pools and fountains, and the four guardian Edwin Landseer statues of couchant lions at the base. Nelson, the nation's great maritime hero, had destroyed Bonaparte's navy in 1805 but was shot down at his very moment of triumph. Poor Horatio. Renquist had never met the man, but the humans with whom he'd had contact on the staff of the Duke of Wellington had assured him the admiral had the ego of a pouter pigeon. What other reason could he have had for parading around the quarterdeck of his flagship, HMS *Victory*, in full dress uniform for all to see, complete with all his medals and insignia, including the Order of the Garter? He had presented too prime a target to any French sharpshooter, and it had been inevitable that one would nail him from the rigging.

By the time Renquist reached the intersection of the Strand and Trafalgar Square, he decided he'd walked enough. He was in no way fatigued—he just couldn't be totally comfortable relaxing and exploring the possibilities of the town until he had completed the process of checking into the Savoy and creating for himself a secure, if temporary, refuge. The cab rank of Charing Cross Station was just across the street, and Renquist decided he would ride the short distance back to the hotel and arrive in a wholly plausible manner, as though at the end of a long journey. A few rail travelers queued for the black London taxis, but cabs were coming and going in a continuous flow, and the fifth one up was his. Once inside, Renquist leaned toward the partition separating passenger and driver, and gave his instructions.

"The Savoy, please."

"You know you could walk that, don't you, mate?"

"I know, but right now I don't care to."

Renquist occupied himself through the short ride, idly inspecting the man's mind and finding nothing remarkable. The lower levels of the driver's concentration handled the vehicle and the surrounding traffic. The upper speculation was totally centered on later that evening, when he intended to talk his recently acquired lover, a twenty-two-year-old beautician, whose long legs and short skirts belied depressingly conventional sexual parameters, into some elaborate and slightly unorthodox carnal theatrics. The cabbie was at a loss to know what manner of response his suggestion would provoke. He hoped for eager acquiescence but feared angry outrage, her being so young and comparatively inexperienced. His dilemma held Renquist's attention for only a moment or two. The practices in question were hardly extreme, even by human standards, and hardly as uncommon as the driver appeared to believe. When Renquist paid him off in front of the Savoy, he tipped him overgenerously. This had always been his policy when he invaded the minds of servants without their knowledge.

At the Savoy's imposing reception desk, his business was transacted with professional fluidity. He registered under the name Victor John Renquist, using a Canadian passport in that name—one of the five that he carried with him hidden in his luggage. The letter of credit from the private bank in Brunei and the formal instruction as to where to send his bills caused the clerk a moment of pause. He had clearly never seen anything like it before, and he quickly disappeared to check with more senior management. His superior must obviously have set him straight, since the clerk hastily returned to treat Renquist with an even greater degree of respect than previously.

Only his final words after all formalities were complete took Renquist by surprise.

"Mr. Renquist, we have a letter for you."

"You do?"

"I believe it was delivered by a messenger earlier this evening."

The clerk handed Renquist a small beige envelope with just the two words *Victor Renquist* written on it in carefully formed calligraphy. Renquist turned the note slowly over in his hands and then slipped it into the inside pocket of his jacket unopened. "Thank you."

"Our pleasure, sir."

He walked thoughtfully away from the desk. Without having to open the envelope, he knew there would be a very different but equally meticulous calligraphy inside it; the flame-form script of the nosferatu Old Speech. Other letters in the same writing were upstairs among his papers, and their contents had brought him to England in the first place. He wasn't, however, about to open this fresh missive right away. He knew it represented a subtle form of tactical game-playing, and his response would be to ignore it until at least the following evening. He also had more pressing needs. His instinct was to hunt and feed after the confinement of his journey. He surveyed the lobby of the Savoy, and even there, he could see at least eight potential prey. He knew, however, that as a stranger in town, he must be circumspect. He would hunt, and he would feed—but not to the death.

Marieko Matsunaga watched with an absolute tranquillity as Columbine Dashwood reached the lupine pacing stage of impatience. Marieko's thin, almost boyish body was swathed in her favorite grey silk kimono decorated with the blue-crossed axe symbol of the Yarabachi, her limbs were folded into the physically complex and taxing *sinshu*, and she held the ceremonial lacquered mask on its slim ebony wand in front of her face. She knew that her detachment and perfect stillness would only serve to increase Columbine's self-generated frustration. It was a part of their long-played and perhaps infinitely continuing game. The acquisition of her impenetrable and armorlike geisha formality had not been without a terrible cost of time and pain, both as human and nosferatu, and she neither wanted to give it up nor, indeed, would she have been able to do so. She could not detach it from her character any more than she could rid herself of the elaborate tattoo of wild-eyed sea demons and Hokusai waves that ran all the way from her right wrist, up the full length of her arm, over her shoulder, and down on her tiny right breast, where it terminated in a tattooed carp with its mouth wide, as though in the act of taking a bite at the nipple. Both were permanent and irremovable, both inseparable and integrated parts of her personality.

Marieko never ceased to be amazed at how Columbine, after surviving more than two hundred years, could remain so overwhelmingly juvenile in her mercurial enthusiasms and inability to wait. Even on the most basic and bestial level, she was supposed to be a huntress and predator, but she never seemed to have acquired the capacity to bide her time, content in the knowledge that everything would ultimately come to her. Columbine had never mastered the technique of the silent cat interminably watching the mousehole. Marieko refused to allow herself to display such raw and unfiltered emotion. Such was a transgression to die for, and many of those with her training and background had done exactly that. Marieko also wouldn't permit herself to fall into the trap of immediately offering advice or instruction to her companion. Marieko knew much of Columbine's seeming capriciousness was far from spontaneous, a designed and deliberate girlish camouflage to disguise devious games fed by fully developed ambitions. Columbine might appear perversely immature, but beneath the facade, she was hard and determined, and more than capable at her own kind of control.

"He should have called by now."

Marieko didn't reply or even move, giving no indication she'd heard. Columbine hissed at her, a taunt of gratuitous fury. "Do you have to be so damned Oriental?"

The final remark all but tempted Marieko to react and respond in kind. Columbine was crossing a lot of lines. By one set of standards, merely entering the room qualified as an unwarranted interruption, but despite the escalating provocation, Marieko remained as still, silent, and expressionless as a work of art. The medium-size room on the second floor of Ravenkeep Priory had for years been looked on as Marieko's exclusive domain. The austere and almost antiseptic space of polished wood had been remodeled to a mathematic harmony with screens, a lowered ceiling, and false, backlit walls. The furnishings were minimal; a lacquered table supported carefully arranged decorative jars and bottles on its polished surface. The large rectangular sandbox waited so that she might slowly and elaborately rake its contents when in the mood for abstract creativity. A longer and narrower rectangle contained about seventy gallons of clear, pure water. Concealed speakers built into the sides of the tank caused ripple effects on the surface of the water. Right at that moment, they were playing a repeated, eighteen-note, sub-bass melodic figure, so low that it approached the limits of even nosferatu hearing, but in its time, the water in the container had vibrated to everything from Gustav Mahler to The Who. She had attempted to keep fish of various kinds in the tank, but all had succumbed to the damage of the vibrations and died. Now the only creature that lived there was a large, elderly, emerald-green frog who seemed able to survive any audio wave pattern and remain perfectly happy, provided it was fed a pellet of food every day. The koto she now very rarely played rested carefully positioned on its stand. Beyond these things, the only other artifact was the rush mat on which she had currently formed herself into the *sinshu*.

Under more normal circumstances, it would have been unthinkable for Columbine to enter the room while Marieko practiced her intricate disciplines. But, as Marieko well knew, these were not normal times. Victor Renquist was on his way to them, lured by Columbine's letters and a very partial account of Marieko's own discovery. The dice had been cast. Their plan was in motion. If it succeeded, they would be mistresses of an immense power. If it failed, it could well cost them their very existence, and Renquist was a crucial fulcrum for success. That his arrival in London should cause such overwhelming tension was only natural, and each member of the troika dealt with it in her own way. Marieko attempted to lose herself in the internal labyrinth of *sinshu*, while Columbine threw fits and trampled their personal protocols.

"Can't you put down that mask and speak?"

Marieko didn't immediately respond. Columbine was obviously having difficulty handling the situation without someone to talk to or, more accurately, someone to talk at, but she couldn't always have everything she wanted the moment she wanted it. Unfortunately, Columbine never saw it that way.

"Talk to me, damn it!"

Marieko finally took pity. She slowly lowered the mask and, with great care, disengaged herself from the *sinshu*. She stretched slowly but remained seated, her eyes still closed, letting her breathing return to its normal rate before she looked up at Columbine. Finally she stretched and flexed her fingers with their extended and perfectly varnished nails. "Hasn't everything possible been said already?"

"He's in London. I can feel it."

Marieko now rose to her feet, but again slowly, and with great care. Even for one of her long experience, the *sinshu* was an extreme physical trial. Legend insisted it went all the way back to the ancient days, when the shape-shifters still walked the night. She would have sat longer, but she didn't like Columbine standing over her. Relative positions of dominance in a troika of females needed to be matters of much sensitivity; careless physical psychology could easily abrade nerves. Again Columbine was exceeding the boundaries. When the two of them were on eye level, Marieko spoke briskly and not without irritation. "London is over a hundred miles away. You can't possibly sense him."

"It was the arrangement. His aeroplane landed hours ago."

"So?"

"So why hasn't he contacted us?"

"You know exactly why he hasn't contacted us."

Columbine grimaced. "Because he's Victor Renquist, the all-bloody-powerful, and he has decided to make me wait. As he has always made me wait."

"You can't still be venting resentment at a petty slight from two centuries ago."

"It wasn't a petty slight."

"Of course it was. He was already the notorious Renquist, and you were a freshly changed airhead. What did you think he'd do, bond with you as a hunting companion the first time he met you?"

"He led me to believe—"

"Oh, please."

Marieko decided Columbine was being far too self-indulgent, especially since the instigation and a good part of the authorship of the plan was hers. Although, with her superior and painstaking calligraphy, Marieko had been the one actually to write the letters dispatched by special courier to California; Columbine had, with equal attention to nuance and subtlety, devised the wording. The bait on the hook, so to speak. Marieko was well aware that Columbine, at heart, resented Renquist simply because he was Renquist. He was in all ways impeccable, never putting a foot wrong, but with a modesty second only to his secrecy. And yet, despite his efforts at concealment, his reputation grew and grew. Over the last few decades—and especially since he had become a Master of Colony—he apparently had done his best to lead a quiet and anonymous existence, but his more colorful and altruistic deeds, like removing the incriminating books from the DuMont Library or neutralizing Marcus De Reske and the Apogee in Los Angeles, had not only made him visible to his peers, but had also elevated his name to near legend. He was possibly the most powerful and respected nosferatu on the planet, unless, of course, there lurked others so much more powerful they could cloak their very existence. He was also held to be among the most knowledgeable and authoritative historians of their kind. Those were the reasons they needed him so badly in order to achieve their goal, but for Columbine to need anything from the male she saw as the purple betrayer of her first wild days of nosferatu romance angered her deeply. It wasn't rational, but it was Columbine.

"Where's Destry?"

"Destry will tell you the same thing."

"I just want to know where she is."

"Riding again."

Destry Maitland was the third of the troika, the final interlocking piece that enabled the three females to exist in the unusual, but not unique, hunting and survival bond.

"What's with her and that new bloody horse?"

"You know what's with her and the new horse. It's from the rarest of bloodlines. A familiarity with our kind is bred into its genes. That horse is her new pride and joy."

Columbine sniffed and scowled. "I've heard all about the thing's damned bloodlines. She's talked about nothing else since the beast was brought here."

"As I said, it's her new distraction."

Columbine pouted. "But does she have to ride it all the time?"

"She's bonding with the steed."

"Steed. Did you say *steed*, darling? Isn't that a trifle archaic?"

"Have you seen it? Have you examined its aura? It's definitely a steed."

"I don't loiter in stables."

"But you do loiter here disturbing me."

"Is that an indirect way of saying you want me to leave?"

"It's almost dawn, Columbine. My intention is to sleep."

"How can you sleep?"

"You should sleep yourself. Renquist will not make contact until nightfall."

"You don't think so?"

"He has to make it clear by his silence that he's not rushing to your summons. He will come in his own good time and not before."

"Damn his insolence."

"Sleep, Columbine. Conserve your strength."

Columbine pursed her lips and turned in the direction of the door, but not before emitting a final soft feline hiss. "We'll see about his own good time."

"I think I should go."

"It would probably be a good idea, in case your husband tries to call you."

"He won't call."

Renquist turned, faced the women who lay tousled on the ruined hotel bed, and nodded. "It will be dawn soon, and I need to sleep, I have a meeting later."

"I never fucked anybody in the Savoy before."

Renquist raised an eyebrow. The remark seemed hard to believe. Her body was as pornographically perfect as the best plastic surgery could make it, and tanned to an even bronze without any white areas created by swimsuits or underwear. She clearly spent much time in the sun, at the beach or poolside, in nude idleness. "Not even your husband?"

"He doesn't count."

Renquist slowly smiled. "Ah."

The woman scowled. "Don't *ah* me. I look on it as a form of virginity."

"But you didn't fuck me."

"I didn't?"

"Not in the strictest sense."

The woman blinked. She didn't have a clue what had happened to her. She was the Swedish trophy wife of a millionaire Venezuelan commodities speculator who had parked her at the Savoy while he went to Paris for three days. He name was Frieda, and she suspected the Venezuelan had a Parisian mistress. She had allowed herself to be picked up over cocktails by Renquist as a form of payback for the supposed marital infidelity, or at least that was what she thought. In reality, from the start of Renquist's first approach and overture, she'd had no choice in the matter whatsoever, but he wasn't about to let her know that. She frowned with the effort of focus through confusion. "It seemed to me like a very fine approximation."

"That is certainly true."

She crawled across the swirl of rumpled untucked sheets—paused for a long moment and then placed her bare feet on the floor and attempted to stand. "I'm not sure I can."

"Can what?"

"Stand." She stood swaying uncertainly. "Is it really dawn?"

"Not quite, but close."

"Let me look."

She stumbled in the direction of the nearest window. Renquist moved with nosferatu speed. "Don't—"

"Don't what?"

Instead of saying anything, Renquist steered her away from the curtains. He didn't want her to see that the drapes concealed foil and tape that blacked out the windows. "You've only got to make it down to the third floor."

"Are you trying to get rid of me?"

Of course he was trying to get rid of her, and for that she should be profoundly and mortally grateful. It was only his circumspection with regard to hunting in an unaccustomed environment that had saved her life.

"Discretion is the better part of passion."

The blonde Swede had at least started looking round for her clothes. She stopped and stared at him blearily. "I thought that was valor?"

"The same applies."

"So, passion is spent, and I am dismissed? Is that it?"

Renquist's expression was friendly but hard. He played the unashamed philanderer she imagined he was, the character she'd wanted when she'd first flirted with him down in the bar. "We both knew it was to be that way from the start, didn't we?"

"It's nice to pretend for a while."

"I don't think we have the time for pretense."

If Frieda did but know it, the entire night had been a pretense. The supposed passion she believed had left her satiated to the point of walking unsteadily had been largely chimeric—most of it completely in her own mind, with Renquist needing only to read her most covert fantasies to make them seemingly happen. The objective truth was he had only stared coldly as she lay on the wide bed of the room in the luxury hotel. She'd gasped and contorted, in the grip of mindbending and salacious illusion, while he watched with little more than an academic amusement at what he could achieve without laying so much as a hand on her. The mildest caress of her mind and memory raised sighs and shudders to full muscle spasms of repeated, wordlessly keening orgasm. Her hips twisted as she moaned and crooned in her native tongue and finally in no language at all. Her makeup ran as sweat beaded her face, and a fall of lust-tossed Nordic-blond hair half hid an expression of feral and greedy desire. When he decided the moment was appropriate, when she was totally beyond awareness of her surroundings, he sprang the small steel spike he always carried with him.

The coupling of the physical act of piercing her flesh with the roller coaster of sexual hallucination on which he had set her all but threatened both her life and sanity. As her lips shaped wordless obscene and ecstatic syllables, as her head thrashed from side to side, threatening to dislocate the vertebrae of her neck, he found he had to forcibly hold her down in order to feed, and he wondered if he had perhaps overdone the intensity of suggestion. Then he felt her energy gradually dwindle, and he knew that she was drifting toward death. He quickly removed his mouth from her throat, sealing the wound with a flick of his tongue, and moved back from her, out of her mind, allowing her to wake, shaking and completely disoriented but believing that she had just been through one of the most memorable physical encounters of her life.

Renquist reflected, as Frieda shakily dressed, how she would never be consciously aware of what had happened to her in this stranger's hotel suite, or in what grotesque and outlandish way she had been used. When she left the room and returned to her bright and social consumer world, she would have no inkling she had ever been the partial victim of a nosferatu, a creature she had always believed, in her material rationality, was a thing of myth, legend, and low-budget movie. Only the dreams to come might hint at what had passed between her and Renquist; the dreams would almost certainly haunt her sleep from then on, maybe to the end of her short human life.

She slipped on her shoes, fluffed her bed-tousled hair, and made a more determined move toward her exit. Renquist assumed she was going to the door, but instead she turned and went into the bathroom. He might have followed her, except the bathroom had mirrors that would necessitate specially created illusions of his reflected image. He heard the sound of running water and then rummaging in a purse. He assumed Frieda was in cosmetic repair. When she spoke, it was in disjointed phrases, as though she was distracted by the effort of applying lipstick or mascara. Her tone now had the acidic edge of someone beginning to view herself as a discarded sex object. "Didn't someone say the real reason men pay prostitutes is not to fuck them, but so they'll go away afterwards?" Frieda emerged from the bathroom with her trophy status fully restored. "I'd kiss you good-bye, but I've just done my makeup."

Renquist nodded. "I understand."

"I'll let myself out."

"Yes."

The door of the suite closed behind her, and she was gone. Renquist sighed and sat down on the bed, profoundly glad he wasn't human, and hadn't been for close to a thousand years. As a species, humans were so childishly complicated, with their lack of emotional logic and their erratic mood swings, especially where the ecstatic, erotic, and economic were concerned. Even though he'd fed, he hardly felt energized. The partial feeding had taken almost as much effort as it had generated, and he was more than ready to sleep away the dangerous daylight hours. At that precise instant, as though to confirm his original reserve that this solitary and impulsive journey to England had perhaps not been such a good idea, the telephone rang.

"Yes."

"Mr. Renquist?"

"Yes."

The Savoy operator's voice was unmistakable. Renquist had insisted his incoming calls be screened. "A Ms. Dashwood wishes to be put through."

Renquist smiled. Ahhh.

"Would you please give the lady my apologies? I can't speak to her right now, but take her number and tell her I will contact her. And ask for all the appropriate codes one needs to dial. The English telephone system has changed greatly since I was last here."

"I'll convey your message, sir."

"Thank you."

Columbine Dashwood—the dear girl was as impulsive as she had ever been. He would make her wait a little longer. Dawn was close, and he wanted nothing better than to retire. Columbine would wait until after sunset. Perhaps well after sunset. She could look on it as the penalty for making importunate telephone calls.

Renquist went to one of his trunks, extracted the large fur rug, and spread it over the hotel bed with a bullring flourish. He took the fur on all his travels; his one concession to a sense of continuity in the places that he slept. He drank another long draft of water and arranged himself to dream through the deadly sunlit day.

Columbine Dashwood surfaced from the dreamstate, but only by a major effort of will. Despite her protestations to Marieko and later to Destry, she had, in fact, slept. Indeed, she had slept deeply, but as she surfaced in the waking world, she knew sunset was still hours away. It wasn't her mixed emotions at being reunited after all this time with Victor Renquist forcing her to wake so frustratingly early, as her feline-uncharitable companions might have suggested. The dream had returned, vivid, intense, at greater length, and as disturbing as ever. For a while, after communication had been established with Renquist, the incessant nightmares had abated, but now the visions had returned with a vengeance. She sat up slowly on the circular bed of satin and velvet draperies, wafting gauze, and scattered Arabian cushions that was the central focus of the exotically cluttered room, but amid all the romantic and alien finery, her mood was as bleak as the dream. "Fuck. I swear I can't tolerate much more of this."

Anger forced bleakness aside. Columbine wanted to

scream out loud but knew that to do so would wake the
entire house. She didn't need the attention. Instead she
hugged her fury to herself, clasping her knees to her
chest with encircling arms as if to physically contain it.

"Did the dream have to come back today of all days?"

She was unsure which was the primary cause of her
vexation. Was it the return of the dream when she'd
believed she had it under control or the shame of challenged pride?

"Today of all days!"

How could she confront Victor, with all his superiority and perfect arrogance, when she must look so obviously hollow, hagridden, and drained by visions of
some stupid bloody ancient apocalypse? Or maybe what
upset her most was its ability to affect her. She maintained her shallow and petulant exterior, all the flouncing
silliness and headstrong caprice, as a lace-and-lavender
sheath for a rapier-steel will. Even before her Change,
she had grown to girlhood amid the dizzyingly multiple
social standards that allowed the English aristocracy of
the late eighteenth century to embrace both courtly manners and thug brutality. Epicene young fops who held
scented handkerchiefs to their noses when among the
common herd were also quite prepared to kill or maim
in violent duels with rapiers or pistols over the most
insignificant drunken trivia. Columbine's class hunted
with hounds and flogged their servants but could, at the
same time, smoke the finest East India Company opium
and write romantic sonnets as cloying as syrup. The
young ladies of her generation saw no paradox in private
conduct that employed the schooled and skilled depravity of the most costly harlot in Mayfair coupled with an
indecency of imagination to rival Donatien de Sade and
the simultaneous public social charade of fan-fluttering
virginal sensibility in which to blush, flutter, and swoon
were all expected tricks of the trade. In comparison to
the French, of course, the patrician English had been
relatively well behaved. The French aristos had so in-

dulged their unchecked libertinage that the common people had turned on them and dragged them to the guillotine.

The combination of such a human upbringing and the gift of remorseless nosferatu power had endowed Columbine with a mind of diamond hardness. No being would have ever dared to forcibly enter her mind while she was awake. That such a thing should happen while she slept was both unprecedented and disconcerting, and yet something, some entity, appeared freely able to penetrate her rest, to invade her dreamstate at will. The dreams caused her more distress than she cared to admit. In commonday parlance, they were starting to get to her, and she had begun to wonder just how long she could tolerate the constant and chronic interruption of her slumber patterns. She sincerely, if not too logically, hoped the arrival of Renquist might somehow diminish the nightmares' frequency and intensity. This tenuous hope also did nothing to improve her disposition. Columbine loathed Renquist, but, to be unmercifully honest with herself, she also desired him, if only to ultimately humble him and bring him to his knees. To be forced to manipulate him as a means to an end was irksome, but to secretly hope he might also prove the savior of her sanity was nothing short of humiliating.

She unclasped her knees and threw herself indignantly back amid the cushions, arms exasperatedly outflung, and stared up at the dark-mirror ceiling. She was not, of course, able to see her own reflection. The mirror had been installed so she could draw back the silk cover, and watch the humans as they contorted under her hands, her mind, and finally, her mouth and fangs. In the early stages of her more prolonged games, they might wonder and ask why their unbelievable paramour was invisible in the marbled glass, but when they did, she would either create an illusion, or if she was close to the point of revealing her true nature, she would merely laugh. "It's a magic mirror, my love. A special spell for your personal narcissism."

Usually, by that point, the pretty boys were so ensnared they'd believe and agree to anything. She wished she hadn't so flamboyantly renounced keeping a young man in attendance when they had agreed to the mission and the appeal to Renquist. At the time, she had decided a grail quest for unknown power required some nosferatu vow, a semblance of bizarre chastity, a resolve to forgo distractions by restricting her hunting to the fast and the practical. In this wide-awake afternoon, however, she found herself yearning for a smooth and vapid boy. If she couldn't sleep, she wanted to feed, but that was impossible. With no gilded youth in residence, she had to go outside to hunt, and outside, the English countryside was basking in a mellow early autumn sun. The leaves on the trees had yet to turn, but summer had definitely expired. Of course, more than two hundred years had passed since Columbine had seen the autumn sun, but she could sense enough to know how it was. Birds were singing, the grass was long with a scattering of poppies, the trees in the overgrown orchard were heavy with fruit, and the daytime servants, the ones she never saw, were at work in the house and in the Ravenkeep garden.

Ravenkeep Priory was an eclectic disturbance of architectural styles from a dozen different eras, attempts at alteration, and from the many different functions the structure had served through the centuries. The only attempt at any standardization was the late Victorian faux-Gothic arches, spires, and gargoyles added by Enoch Jarman, the Midlands munitions baron who had made the place a rural retreat from his dark and decidedly Satanic mills and foundries. The man had made gold-standard millions by supplying components for small arms and light artillery to the Empire-on-Which-the-Sun-Never-Set, but the effort had left him with an atrophied facility for the aesthetic. Large on money but small on taste, Enoch Jarman's efforts had only added to the confusion. Set in the lee of a low escarpment amid softly rolling woods and fields, some form of habitation or fortress had existed on the same site since prehistory, but the foundations for the presently enduring structure had been laid by Roger le Corbeau in the early twelfth century, when the Norman invaders were consolidating their hold on the Saxon underclass, and guerrilla bands like those of Robin of Huntington were maintaining a stubborn resistance in the deep forests.

The property had passed to the church, and simple Ravenkeep had become Ravenkeep Priory when the Baron Roger's childless, garishly degenerate, and poxridden great-grandson, Jerome le Corbeau, had, in a deathbed panic, bequeathed his estates to the church in the hope of escaping hellfire for a life of creatively abominable deviance. The Priory had remained in the hands of the clergy until the Priors were violently evicted by Henry VIII as part of his harshly hilarious Reformation and the inadvertently intelligent severance with Rome. Henry had awarded the estate, and the title that went with it, to a nondescript earl with few talents save butter-smooth flattery. Even that skill was depleted from the gene pool in a couple of more generations, and by the time of the Industrial Revolution, accumulated debts made sale to a nouveau upstart inevitable. The first plutocrat had been a Liverpool shipping baron in emotional need of a stately home, but when the Manchester Ship Canal bankrupted him, Ravenkeep passed briefly to a textile czar and finally to Jarman, the arms mogul.

Columbine would have been happy to boast how the Priory had been in her family for mortal generations, but in reality, the estate was a comparatively recent acquisition. It had fallen into her hands in the early 1920s, after she had come back from the human horror of the World War I trenches, where she had been known to British, French, and Germans alike as the Black Angel. Pausing only for an excursion to Moscow and a sanguine flirtation with early bolshevism, she had decided to return to England. Disappointed that man and nosferatu had not seemingly been created equal and that the Workers of the World were unlikely to thank her for her unorthodox assistance in freeing them from their chains, she switched sides and became an undead capitalist, resolving to surround herself with as much material security as she could. In addition to her political turnabout, she had also decided that a nosferatu who remained a rootless nomad for too long ran cumulative risks.

Columbine had contracted a mortal marriage to the arms mogul's grandson, the unfortunate Peregrin Jarman, who had been shell-shocked to the point of dementia on the Somme. By a certain synchronous irony, her brief husband had lost his reason on the same section of the Western Front where she had practiced her depredations. After leading him through a highly sedated wedding, she had maintained him in a state of blissful illusion while she slowly killed him. His death surprised no one, since he wasn't expected to survive his madness for very long. What did surprise the friends of the deceased was the rapidity with which the widow severed all ties, dropped the name of Jarman, returned to her maiden Dashwood, and surrounded herself with a set of the most unacceptable friends including the Aleister Crowley crowd, Tallulah Bankhead, Ezra Pound, Ayn Rand, and the ever-unpredictable Pauline Réage. Oswald Mosley had attempted to crash one of her parties, but she had turned the Blackshirt leader away. She had no time for human fascists and their petty bourgeois bullying. To the outside observer, Columbine appeared to be concealing herself behind a social smoke screen of scandal and depravity. And indeed she was.

The outbreak of World War II had changed everything at the Priory. The parties were killed off by blitz, shortage, and rationing, and the gilded boys went off to die, not in her arms, but in the Spitfires and Hurricanes of the RAF, and in tanks in the Libyan Desert. Although she knew it was irrational, she still harbored a certain vestigial patriotism for Old England, and she had arranged a private meeting with Churchill, at which she had offered the prime minister use of Ravenkeep by any research or planning group from a suitably outré sector of the war effort. Winston, unshockable, already familiar with the dossier on Nazi occult warfare, and willing to try anything, agreed with minimal persuasion. By way of a metaphysical bonus, Columbine had offered Churchill immortality, but he'd declined, pouring himself yet another serial brandy and rumbling that one life would probably prove more than enough. Very swiftly, she found herself playing hostess to a small and exceptionally strange task force commanded by Colonel the Duke de Richleau, who launched remorseless metaphysical attacks on the Nazis in general and Heinrich Himmler and Inner Order of the Black SS in particular. De Richleau and his people were tacitly aware of what Columbine really was, although, in a very English way; no one ever actually mentioned her being nosferatu. Her vampirism didn't bother them in the slightest, though. They and their endeavors were so deeply and ambiguously twisted, she hardly qualified as anything remarkable. In addition, de Richleau's team was special, and thus safe from her potential depredations. Had she victimized any of them, Churchill's personal goon squad, homicidal Old Etonians with old school ties and dead eyes, would have arrived immediately in large, unmarked cars and efficiently terminated her immortality with stake and mallet.

The cessation of hostilities found Columbine alone at the Priory. The ultra-secrecy of the de Richleau operation had endowed the house with a formidable unapproachability that lingered long after he and his people departed. This legacy suited her extremely well; she was able to hunt with a high level of impunity. Less than a year after the end of the War in the Pacific, Marieko had arrived, a nosferatu fugitive seeking a sister's right to sanctuary with one of her own. Marieko had been fleeing a deep and paranormal unpleasantness in the Far East. Columbine had never fully intruded into Marieko's secret past, but she had gleaned the general and somewhat intriguing impression of how the two American atomic detonations, in addition to vaporizing the city centers of Hiroshima and Nagasaki, had also spawned destructive manifestations in spheres far beyond the most sophisticated human awareness. Extradimensional nastiness had leaked, and somehow Marieko had been caught in the backwash and was forced to flee for her very existence by DC-3 and China Sea freighter, Greek tramp steamer and Orient-Express, and finally Channel ferry to the comparative and eventual safety of rural England.

For the remainder of the forties and most of the fifties, Columbine and Marieko had lived as hunting companions—as far as the local humans were concerned, an upper-class eccentric lesbian and her exotic Oriental companion, all very Sax Rohmer, and best kept at a safe distance. Destry had appeared in the early sixties, an undead Amazon adventuress who had grown tired of third-world voodoo colonels, CIA-backed warlords, the fall of empires, and all those postcolonial, machine-gun dictatorships with their one international hotel filled with spooks, KGB, arms profiteers, and adrenaline-addicted mercenaries. Columbine, Marieko, and Destry had decided to attempt a properly constituted nosferatu troika. At first, Columbine had been doubtful about the arrangement of three bonded females. Although she had known threesomes who had made the orchestration work, in too many cases it had been little more than a template for bickering and backbiting, with two picking on the remaining one in a cruelly rotating pecking order. They were lucky in that the early days of bonding had been fully occupied by their inadvertently becoming demigoddesses to a desperate Kali-worshiping human blood cult. For a while the role-playing had been both a fascinating anthropological study and a constant source of nourishment and amusement, but the existence of the cult had unavoidably come, story by story and rumor by rumor, to the notice of the local chief constable, and they had been forced to kill or disperse their devotees and then maintain a much lower profile, particularly with regard to their hunting.

Columbine, however, was not at that moment thinking of either her own past or the past of the house that was her longtime lair. The dreams dominated her thoughts. Over and over she had taken the logically deductive approach. She was certain the dreams that plagued her came from an external source. The content of the dreams seemed to indicate that whatever was routing, projecting, or otherwise broadcasting them had a fixation about a particular period in the human past. In the beginning, they were innocent enough, even a novelty; brief flashes of archaically dressed humans clustered in dark and candlelit ancient buildings or moving in green-day rural countryside. A harper by the fireplace, children on the greensward, lovers in cornfields or the fallen forest leaves beneath translucent sun-dappled trees. Slightly mawkish but definitely coherent glimpses of an unmistakably English locality, somewhere quite near to Ravenkeep, sometime in the fifth or sixth century of the Christian calendar. History had never been of immense interest to Columbine, but she guessed, by the seemingly Romanized clothing and artifacts, these humans existed sometime after the Romans had pulled their legions out of the British Isles, withdrawing to defend Rome itself against the encroaching barbarians.

At first the only puzzlement was why she was being granted such pointless camera-obscura vignettes of fifteen hundred years ago. At other times she had experienced dreams that could only be part of a common nosferatu memory, and she was a definite believer in the undead sharing some manner of universal mind, although others of her kind might argue with her. If that was the case, though, how could she account for the fact

that so many of the short vignettes took place in broad
daylight, a sight no nosferatu, no matter how ancient,
could ever have seen? The only sunshine dreams Columbine Dashwood ever experienced had their roots in
her own short life as a human, and as the years passed,
they had become increasingly few and far between. A
second problem was, when the characters in these
dreams spoke to each other, which they did quite regularly, she was completely unable to understand them or
even so much as recognize the language they were
speaking.

Columbine would never claim any facility for language. With their infinitely extended life span, some
nosferatu became almost obsessive about becoming as
widely fluent as possible. Marieko was one of these, although primarily knowledgeable in the inexplicable bab-
bling of Southeast Asia. Destry also had a smattering of
various Asian languages, as well as a basic Central Af-
rican pidgin, and, of course, there was always the almost
obscene command of tongues on which Victor-bloody-
Renquist so prided himself. She almost believed Renquist, dropped into the middle of the Amazon jungle,
would be conversant in the unique dialect of the very
first tribe he encountered. Columbine took the exact reverse approach, the traditional Anglo-Saxon view that
only some massive and primal error had rendered the
entire world unable to speak English. Despite her resistance to foreign verbs, nouns, and adjectives, she had,
over her two hundred years, motivated by both self-
protection and self-interest, picked up a smattering of
schoolgirl Latin, a reasonable command of German,
some bad French, and worse Italian. She could, however,
converse articulately in basic Russian. It had been a matter of survival in 1919 and 1920, before she returned to
England to wed the twitching and dysfunctional Peregrin.

Back in the early days when the dreams had been
pastoral, insignificant, and at times even pleasant, their

inhabitants had embraced, as far as she could tell, two forms of speech. One, exclusive to the ruling and the beautiful, seemed to Columbine an odd mixture of Spanish and Latin, while the rank and file yammered in a dialect akin to Welsh. The inexplicable and endless song of the harper in the one dream certainly sounded Druidic to her untrained ear, but she was so shamelessly ill educated that she found it hard to be precise, even with herself. Educated or not, though, she had been in no doubt that the unintelligibility of the languages was another indication that the source of the dreams was both external and other than nosferatu. Previously, when a dream she'd dreamed could only have emanated from another of her kind, she had always known what everyone was talking about. In these dreams participants either conversed in the Old Speech, which all of the newly undead seemed to receive with all the other alterations to their DNA, or an instant and seamless translation, consciously or unconsciously provided by the mind from which the vision originated.

Columbine had many times experienced dreams that could only have been an inadvertent print-through from Marieko in which Columbine found herself observing agonizing rituals in the black-vault dungeons of pitiless and inhuman shoguns, or hunting with the moon in the flawless pine forests at the foot of the symmetry of Mount Fuji. Such unavoidable intrusions on each other's dreamstates were quite natural when two females lived in such intimate proximity. In the same way, after Destry had joined them, she found herself riding on the side of a captured Sherman tank through cheering crowds in the subtropical midnight as Che Guevara liberated Santa Clara, or scrambling for the last DC-3 out of Léopoldville as the city fell to fire and small-arms slaughter. In every case, Columbine had been able to understand every word.

The next logical explanation was that the dreams were coming from a location rather than any individual. Columbine knew such things were possible. In her waking life, she had more than once observed the palest of psychic fires that remained, imprinted perhaps by either agony or ecstasy, or by the sheer weight of history, long after the individuals who had made that history had perished or fled. If such was the case, Ravenkeep itself had to be the prime suspect. The Devil only knew it had more than enough history. A settlement had almost certainly existed on the site in the fifth century, but that didn't explain why the dreams should so suddenly appear out of nowhere. She could think of no pivotal event or radical alteration to the structure that might have triggered a ceaseless stream of such powerful emanations.

When the dreams became increasingly grim and violent, the puzzle was less a game and more a problem that required a solution. She began to find herself in the middle of mercilessly bloody battles in which warriors afoot, armed with axes and spears and carrying bossed wooden shields, were ridden down by well-organized Roman-style cavalry. Murderous weapons designed to cut and pierce carved hideous wounds in human flesh, slicing bodies and severing limbs. The slaughter was relentless, with neither side willing to give ground in a madness of death-or-glory. The unswerving and formidable infantry made its appearance even more fearsome by the universal adoption of ridged helmets with metal faceplates, masked and anonymous, mouthless and with blank slits for eyes. Some were of plain hammered metal, but others were iron dominoes, fashioned into fantasy faces of incongruously blank and idealized beauty, or the ugly contortions of howling demons from the mythology of the Rhine river cliffs and the Germanic forests. Anyone facing these warriors was presented with a terrible illusion that they might be something other than men. Not that the opposing cavalry seemed to entertain many illusions. They performed and dressed in emulated memory of the cruel professionalism of their recently departed imperial masters. Helms were crested

with stiff horsehair, and red battle cloaks flowed behind
them over chain mail and bronze breastplates, and while
the enemy rushed in a haphazard, hacking and slaying
mob, they moved on command with the drilled precision
of turn and counterturn, tactics planned first to contain
and then to massacre from horseback.

These dreamstate conflicts always seemed to take
place in torrential rain with poor visibility. Men and
steaming horses, and the huge war dogs—free-ranging
mastiffs, heads higher than a man's waist, with wide
studded collars, slavering jaws, and even mail coats protecting their shoulders and ribs—all progressively
bogged down and stumbling in a sea of mud turning
crimson with the blood of the fallen. Columbine was
forced to wonder if she was actually seeing the same
battle over and over again. The conflict always came to
the same repetitive conclusion, another possible indication that she was, in fact, constantly viewing the same
fight. At first the horsemen, who Columbine assumed
were the military of the Romanized Britons, had mastery
of the field, and it seemed the fight could only go their
way. Then rain and mud would prove their undoing.
Horses slipped and foundered in the bloody quagmire,
and the tightly ordered formations disintegrated, ena-
bling the foot soldiers—she supposed a section of the
seaborne Saxon invaders of the time—to drag isolated
riders from their mounts and hack them to pieces.

A further paradox in the dreams was the way in which
Columbine was allowed to view them. She was observing everything through the eyes of a single individual
who, on one level, was supposedly present on the scene,
to the point of ducking and dodging thundering hooves
and berserk Saxon battle-axes, but playing no part in the
actual combat, wielding no mace, lance, or sword, and,
most perplexing of all, manifestly invisible to those present. The strange observer evidently sided with, or had
some relationship to, the mounted Britons, since, when
the survivors retreated in disorder, she found herself go-

ing with them and then later wandering aimlessly through the aftermath of conflict: the overchurned and rust-colored ground strewn with bodies of men and horses contorted in the agony of death or by postmortem rigor. Crows fed on the eyes of the corpses, and scarcely human scavengers foraged for what they could find amid the overturned carts, the discarded swords, broken spears, and shredded banners.

Of course, the escalating horror of the visions didn't disturb Columbine. She was no sensitive and impressionable human. Blood was her life. She was a killer herself. She had seen modern warfare firsthand, and in the context of the huntress. What she resented was her normally entertaining dreamstate becoming so relentlessly bleak. She was being monopolized by the daily repetition, and, worse than that, with this new phase of dreams she was being defeated in dream after dream, and experiencing all the emotional desolation of being repeatedly routed. It proved enervating, a debility that hung over into her waking days, leaving her fractious, dissatisfied, and drained of energy.

"If these damned visions aren't coming from here, where the hell are they coming from?"

She had begun to look further afield for a possible source. The nearest candidate, even more ancient than Ravenkeep, was the prehistoric burial mound and the broken circle of standing stones about twelve miles away at Morton Downs. Again, the same problem of the Priory came into play there: As far as Columbine knew, nothing had happened at Morton Downs that might cause visions of the fifth century to descend on her with the sunrise. Only by chance she discovered from Marieko that this was not the case.

"They've been excavating there for two or three weeks."

"Who's been excavating? Why didn't anyone tell me?"

Marieko had raised her already arched eyebrows. "I wasn't aware you were interested."

"Well, I am. Who is this *they* that's digging up the mound?"

"Some students from Wessex University."

"Students? Are they allowed to do that? Isn't it some kind of desecration?"

"I believe they're led by a Dr. Campion. He's apparently very well respected in his field."

At this point Columbine, who had previously kept quiet about the effects of the latest round of visions, gave up and told everything to Marieko and Destry. The dreams, the puzzlement, the damage to her sleep, and even how, in the last few days, the visions seemed to have slipped into a brand-new phase, showing bizarre rituals of fire, stimulants, and human copulation amid already ancient standing stones. At least a finger seemed to be pointing in the direction of the burial mound. The other two had, of course, known something was troubling Columbine, but in a troika, one didn't ask. Destry and Marieko were also well aware that Columbine was a virtuoso of deception and concealment, but Columbine didn't fool herself that they very often fell for her hoopla. What she counted on was their never being quite sure of the exact demarcation between truth and fiction, and that was where she kept her secrets. Thus her total candor in asking for their help and advice impressed them enough to take her completely seriously, and Marieko even offered to make a firsthand inspection of the mound.

Columbine had welcomed the offer. "You think I should go with you?"

Marieko thought about this. "No, it would be better if I went alone."

Marieko had never been one to delay, and the very same night she had left a little after midnight in the Ravenkeep Range Rover. Columbine knew Marieko's trip wasn't only motivated by her mysterious dreams. All

through her wanderings, when not obeying the natural
demands or coping with all the other shocks to which
her nosferatu flesh was heir, Marieko had maintained a
strong interest in human archeology. Under cover of the
night, she had observed the places where the short-lived
scrabbled in the dirt for physical pointers to their roots,
origins, and forgotten past, and was both amused and
appalled by their misconceptions and their deplorably
narrow perspectives when it came to their own history.
Time after time, they used the clues they grubbed from
the ground to prove humanity was the only sentient species ever to walk the Earth. Their vanity distorted any
scant reality of the past they might discover. Not that
Marieko was adverse to humanity wandering in an historical fog, unaware of the origins of its civilizations, or
how its very species came into being. The more they
floundered in a mass of confused hypotheses, contradic-
tory trivia, and legends entrenched as fact, the easier it
was for the nosferatu to operate among them without
detection.

As Marieko told it later, she had embarked on this
first reconnoiter expecting to find the sight deserted, but
for absolute safety, she had parked the truck a distance
from the roped-off area of the dig and continued on foot
across the short springy downland turf. A brisk breeze
had sprung up since the sun had set, and all round her,
Marieko had felt the busy stirrings and scuttlings of the
rural night. Somewhere she could feel an owl patiently
waiting on the routines of field mice. A distant flock of
black-face sheep stirred in their sleep, troubled by the
sense of a predator but were then calmed by an old alpha
ewe who reassured them this predator had no interest in
them. Before her perfect nosferatu night vision could
detect much more than a dark elongated mound at the
crest of a low hill, she perceived a faint but pervasive
vestigial aura radiating faintly from the first slit-trench
breach dug in the mound.

The flickering trace was of something not strictly

alive, neither nosferatu, nor human, nor animal, but far more positive than any residue or ancient imprinting. Marieko had covered the final hundred yards to the burial mound with the utmost caution. Alive but not alive? Or could it be a subtle and specialized lure for the curious? In the long and murderous hostilities between the Yarabachi and the Clan of Kenzu, a number of previously unknown and very dangerous entities had been loosed by both sides as uncontrolled weapons. She'd closely encountered two of the things, and those incidents had been enough to convince her there was definitely more in Heaven and Earth than was dreamed of in nosferatu or human philosophy. While some weapons simply ran amok in snarling frontal attack, others brought destruction, even to the highly wary, by stealth and subterfuge.

She reached the mound without any noticeable alteration in the aura or anything striking at her with paranormal tooth or claw. She had by this point begun to wonder if whatever might be the source of the aura was in a form of slumber, metabolic reduction, or hibernation. A certain slow pulse pattern in the aura tended to indicate as much. Convincing herself she wasn't walking into a trap, Marieko gave the excavation a cursory inspection and found Campion and his students had hardly begun to dig and were nowhere near breaking through into any inner chamber in or under the mound. The overwhelming temptation was, of course, to start digging herself. With just her bare hands and nosferatu strength, she could probably be into the inner chamber of the mound before dawn, but she knew to do so would alert the humans that something was amiss. She had also spent a great deal of time cultivating her flawless, four-inch, ivory fingernails, and one or more of them would undoubtedly be chipped or broken by such an endeavor.

Instead she took the rational if less dramatic course of returning to the Range Rover and driving back to the Priory as fast she could. Columbine and Destry were already waiting in the driveway when she arrived. As she parked the SUV and climbed from the driver's seat, even the unreadable Marieko couldn't keep the excitement out of her aura. Columbine had been as impatiently girlish as ever, all but bouncing up and down on the balls of her feet. "What did you find? What did you find? Was it something? Was there something there?"

Destry didn't make as much noise. Tall and commanding, with her broad-shouldered, long-legged athlete's body and mane of chestnut hair, Destry was more disciplined and self-contained, but her aura also revealed her curiosity. Marieko carefully closed the door, teasingly making the others contain their eagerness a few moments longer. "I went to Morton Downs. . . ."

"And?"

"And there is definitely something inside the burial mound."

"Something?"

"What something?"

Together, the three females walked back to the open front door and the angling serrated rectangle of light that illuminated the steps. Overhead, elongated tresses of pale, wind-driven clouds scudded across a blue-black sky, partially obscuring a yellow and waning moon and adding a perfect backdrop of external drama. As their shoes crunched on the raked gravel, Columbine and Destry interrogated Marieko.

"What do you mean, you don't know? You know everything." Destry, who was constantly impressed by Marieko's wealth of arcane knowledge, wasn't going to tolerate it failing at this crucial point.

"I know it wasn't human, and it seemed to be in some kind of extended sleep, but its aura was of a kind I've never seen before."

Destry halted. "Never?"

Marieko also stopped and hesitated. "Never . . . except . . ."

"Except what?"

"This is the most intangible of feelings. A theory almost without support. . . ."

"Yes, yes, we understand."

"I believe whatever is within the mound is not nosferatu, but it's somehow related. I think it's a distant kin."

"Not nosferatu?"

"No."

"Kin?"

Marieko's face was inscrutable, but her aura flickered with equal parts uncertainty and excitement over the potentially important discovery. "I believe that somewhere, ·in some ancient DNA, there exists a . . . link."

The idea opened such a wealth of possibilities that both Columbine and Destry were at a loss to frame the next question, which gave Marieko a chance to pause significantly before delivering her final observation and repeat her caveat: "Again, this is without any foundation except instinct—"

"We've already accepted the disclaimer." Columbine hated how with Marieko you inevitably had to wait.

"I suspect whatever is in the mound is immensely powerful."

"Powerful?"

Marieko repeated herself with added emphasis. "*Immensely powerful*. It was virtually inanimate, and the aura was little more than a flicker, yet it had a density."

Columbine wanted to ask more about the potential power of this thing, but Destry retreated to the practical. "This Dr. Campion and his humans, have they penetrated very far into the mound?"

Marieko shook her head. "No, not yet."

"Perhaps we should do some excavating of our own?"

Again Marieko shook her head. "I was tempted, but the humans would assume it was vandalism. The police could become involved, and I don't think we want that."

A thought occurred to Columbine. "Could Campion

and his delving students be in the process of waking whatever it is?"

Marieko had already considered this. "I doubt they know it, but I think it's a possibility. In fact, for all we know, the humans may have been unknowingly summoned to do exactly that."

Even in the comfort, not to say luxury, of the Savoy Hotel, Victor Renquist found he was unable to sleep. He lay flat on his back, in the traditional attitude of repose, legs together and arms across his chest, crossed at the wrists. He slowed his breathing until the black silk of his robe hardly whispered against the fur rug covering the hotel bed, but the best he could achieve was periods of semi-numb daze. The blackouts on the windows effectively cut the sound of the London traffic to a literal dull roar, but that couldn't possibly be the reason total and inert rest remained so elusive. After all, during his long existence, he had slept through air raids, artillery bombardments, and the sack and pillage of cities. He had slumbered in cellars while buildings burned above him and had shared desert caves with a multitude of bats and the keening of the wind across the dunes.

He wondered if this unaccustomed insomnia could somehow be caused by the long flight from California. Human travelers talked of a disorientation they glibly called *jet lag*, and he had once read a scientific paper on how the time-sense of even rudimentary creatures like bivalves could be confused by fast, long-distance journeys. A batch of oysters from Long Island Sound had been moved by transport plane to Lawrence, Kansas. Once relocated and settled in the laboratory tank that was their new home, they commenced, after a short period of adjustment, to open and close as though the Atlantic Ocean extended all the way to the Midwest and the tides behaved accordingly. Why such a bizarre study should be conducted in the first place had been something of a mystery to Renquist, but he had long since ceased to be surprised at the directions humans might be steered by their insatiable curiosity. Unfortunately, so few nosferatu practiced intercontinental air travel that little data was available to tell him whether he was suffering from some kindred reaction or this jet lag, and he resolved to keep mental notes on his sleeplessness. Sooner or later, the undead would have to come to grips with the jet age.

After about an hour, however, he discovered these spells of drifting were not without their own unique value. He found himself experiencing a new and, as far as he could recall, unique form of perception. For a being of Renquist's age to experience anything curious and original was such a singular novelty that he made no effort to control or thrust it from him. It also helped, of course, that the experience was far from unpleasant. The word *cozy* sprang to mind, and Renquist allowed himself to glide effortlessly with it. He might not be sleeping, but he was sufficiently relaxed to derive some recuperative benefit. Although the drifting perception was widespread and generalized, and lacked much in the way of precision, it delivered a fairly coherent, hypnovirtual view of the world in which he was now immersed. As during his earlier stroll down the Strand, he was again aware of both the psychic and material density of the Old World as close-packed modernity was layered on millennia of history. Although New York and some of the other cities on the Eastern Seaboard might come close, the United States as a whole seemed positively empty in comparison. Renquist wasn't sure which he actually preferred. Both had their attractions. As the strange demidreaming continued, he found a measure of specificity was possible, and he could exert a certain gentle direction without breaking the condition and returning to full waking. The odd perception also tended toward the two-dimensional. Humanity seemed spread around him like an ethereal and somewhat threadbare billiard table, except it had a distinct curve, perhaps conforming in its insubstantial way to the curve of the earth, or maybe to that of space-time itself.

His first tentative notion was to cast around for traces of other nosferatu, and no sooner had he entertained the idea than he began to notice tiny orange flecks amid the verdance of humans. Some were relatively close. The city of London apparently had its compliment of loners, but no concentration that might tell of a clan or colony. As soon as he could judge distance and direction, he observed a triple trace of tiny stars in the west he knew must be Columbine Dashwood and her two companions, the reason he was in London in the first place. Much farther away, far to the north, he finally spotted the kind of cluster that must represent a substantial community of the undead. Unless much had changed in the British Isles, it could only be the Fenrior of Fenrior who maintained his clan of vassals, henchmen, and bonded companions in the isolated and desolate grandeur of the Scottish Highlands. Renquist knew very little about Fenrior and his people beyond the epics and legends, which were both many and lurid but could not always be trusted. Most accounts seemed to agree that the Clan Fenrior was wild, uncouth, barbarous in the extreme, and conducted themselves as though they had yet to adjust to the sixteenth century, let alone the twenty-first. They reputedly depended on the old and violent blood ties of crag, glen, and tarn to preserve them from widespread human detection and retribution.

Renquist knew that if he was aware of the Fenrior, the Fenrior could well be aware of him, and he wondered how protocol might dictate he act toward them. They were, by all repute, immoderate in the cruelty with which they received strangers in their lands, and yet, by their numbers alone, they qualified as the primary community of nosferatu in Britain. He had been invited by Columbine Dashwood, and etiquette dictated that he must attend her first, but with her requested favor bestowed and his commission discharged, would it be expected of him to pay his formal respects to the Fenrior, or would it be far wiser to respect the privacy of these Scottish nosferatu beyond the Roman wall, not intrude, and leave them well alone?

As Renquist was drowsily contemplating how he should behave, he noticed a fleck of color to which he couldn't put a name, significantly close to the triple pin-points of Miss Dashwood and her friends. Now what was that? Renquist attempted to see more clearly, but as he did, the perception perversely vanished. The effort to focus had apparently broken the spell. Renquist sighed and ran fingers through the reassuringly familiar fur of the rug.

"No matter how we deceive or congratulate ourselves, the dreaming is never truly ours to command."

He was now aware, however, something was to hand that Columbine had neglected to mention in her letters.

On the very day following Marieko's visit to Morton Downs, Columbine's dreams had entered a new and highly disturbing phase—the one that would remain with her all the way through to the long day she waited for Renquist to make contact. One time and, mercifully, one time only, she had all but been dream-blinded by a flash that she knew by unexplained instinct was called the Fire in the West, although the same instinct refused to give up any further information or explanation of the horrendous and all-consuming flame. It certainly made no sense and seemed hardly to fit with what she knew of the sixth century. As she saw it from the point of view of her mysterious observing host, the explosion looked near-nuclear. The host had stood on a grassy hilltop at what seemed to be the moment of impact. Had the fire-ball first come from the sky? Columbine had entered the dream a fraction too late to be certain. Just in time, in fact, to be rendered sightless by the flash and all but choked by the stench of burned hair and singed clothing as a searing radiant heat swept over the hillside, scorching the grass and causing trees to ignite.

Multiple disasters struck her and her observer like a series of fast hammer blows. First the abominable light, then the heat, and then a shock wave with a sound like nothing she had ever experienced. A scream? A roar? A convulsion of the very earth? An extended thunderclap to herald the Doom of Everything? Finally the wind and a new shriek of universal doom. And yet she knew, again by weird instinct, that she was, in reality, a great distance from the true ground zero of the fiery destruction. In the middle of this off-the-scale violence, way out of both human and nosferatu proportion, she at least had confirmation of Marieko's theory that the thing through whose eyes she watched was massively powerful. He or she could remain standing when living trees were uprooted and swirled into the air and cattle flew like birds. His or her flesh could tolerate heat that scorched grass in an instant. Columbine also realized she was now freely assuming this observer was also the thing asleep in the mound; a long-jump of faith and connection to say the least.

The vision of the Fire in the West may only have shown itself a single time, but what followed was barely an improvement. Instead of peasants and sunshine, the rain and confusion of the battlefield, or the dank and bloody carrion plain that remained in its wake, she found herself in a twilight place of murky desolation where only the closest objects were visible in a choking fine-grain haze, chill but at the same time parched and gritty. Trees had been reduced to naked skeletons, with their bark chewed away, while the hillsides were bare of grass, and hedgerows were naked barbed-wire entanglements of dead brambles. Pale grey ash fell like dusty snow. Birds and animals seemed to be no more, save for hungry and combative rats and wolves. Haggard human survivors, mostly former warriors, with rust on their swords and mail, hollow-skull staring eyes, and weary leather falling away from their shields and helmets, tottered on the final cadaver legs of terminal starvation. Knights whose prized horses had been long since eaten, bowmen for whom no target presented itself, wagoners whose oxen had dropped beneath the yoke, and deserted kings of burned dominions; they all moved aimlessly through an occluded landscape where nothing was to be found except inevitable death. Only her host/observer manifested any real sense of purpose, and he or she seemed only to be seeking some specific if hard to find place of concealment in which to hide or maybe die like everyone else.

"This has to be stopped."

Unintelligible peasants and endless waterlogged battles were one thing, but Columbine drew the line at visions of an unknown apocalypse. As soon as the sun was below the horizon, she had assembled the others in the formal drawing room. "I'm not exaggerating. It was as though the world was ending."

Marieko thought about this, a single furrow appearing in her porcelain neo-geisha brow. "But it was still a vision of the past?"

"I think so."

"Not the present or the future?"

"It looked like the same period as all the other dreams except everything was dead or dying."

"So you don't think it was some kind of warning?"

"If you're asking me if I've suddenly turned into Edgar Cayce or Saint John the Divine, the answer is no. I don't think I'm having prophetic visions."

Destry was growing a little impatient. "Really, Columbine, are you telling us you have no idea what this might mean?"

"All I really know is that I didn't like it at all."

"So what do you want us to do? We decided we should wait."

Destry was absolutely correct. They had talked almost through the dawn, finally agreeing that their only option was to let Campion proceed with his excavation until more was revealed. After almost twelve hours of nonstop nightmare, Columbine had been more than ready for a radical revision of that idea. "If I have to keep seeing this shit every time I try to sleep, I'm going to lose my mind. I know you two don't have a high regard for it, but it's the only mind I've got, and I need it for thinking and getting me around."

"I still believe we should wait, and not do anything precipitate."

"But it's not you having the blasted dreams, is it, Destry? If I were human I could wash down a handful of Seconal with a shot of gin and sleep like a weary dog, but I'm not, and I've never encountered any drug or potion that could knock out one of us."

It had been Marieko who had given the very first momentum to what would become their plan. "I think we need the help of an expert."

"What are you talking about?"

"We would appear to have stumbled across something that is not only well beyond the sum total of our own collective knowledge and experience, but can also invade the dreams of one of us at will, leaving us powerless to stop it. I would suggest we need the help and advice of someone who is both highly knowledgeable and unable to resist a mystery."

"A nosferatu?"

"Of course."

"She would have to be extremely venerable but, at the same time, still retain a mental flexibility."

If inscrutability came in degrees, Marieko's expression achieved an unprecedented level of bland knowingness. "It wasn't a *she* I had in mind."

In an instant, Columbine had seen exactly where Marieko's logic was taking them. "No!"

"I know how you feel about Victor Renquist, my dear Columbine, but—"

"Never!"

"He has all the qualifications."

"He wouldn't come here."

Destry began to warm to what Marieko had set in motion. "I think he would. If he were to find out we'd happened across something very old with a nosferatu connection, he'd be here like a shot."

Marieko, cross-legged on her cushion, sat even straighter. "She's absolutely right."

Columbine had risen from her accustomed velvet wing chair, walked to a side table, and opened a pink-and-black art deco cigarette box. Smoking cigarettes was a habit she had picked up during her travels with Sir Richard Burton (the explorer, not the actor), when he had been on his way to become the first infidel to enter the holy city of Mecca. She had convinced herself that a cigarette lent a woman a distinct extra degree of authority. The principle applied to any elevation of rank from trollop to duchess. Since all the mortal fuss about cancer and secondhand smoke, it had become an even more powerful affectation, indicating, as it did, a certain devil-may-care, risk-taking ruthlessness. On a visit to a high-rise domination bordello in Tokyo's Roppongi district in the late 1980s, she had observed that the lace-, rubber-, and leather-clad mistress-sans all chain-smoked to stern and contemptuous effect. Right then, it wasn't authority she needed, and, of course, her nosferatu metabolism derived no pleasure or satisfaction—or harm, for that matter—from the process. It was a device she usually reserved for human company, but, right at that moment, she needed some manual ritual, a practiced distraction to cover her confusion. Of course, Marieko was right, damn her, but the idea of actually seeing Renquist after all this time was singularly disturbing. She flicked the matching table lighter, but it refused to catch, clearly out of fuel.

"Damn that Bolingbroke. Why can't he keep the lighters filled?"

Destry, who had remained standing through the conversation, took a lighter from the pocket of the bush shirt she wore over her usual jodhpurs and tight, high hunting boots. "Come here."

Columbine had moved to Destry. "He needs thrashing."

Destry flicked the Zippo she had managed to carry across a dozen war zones. "He enjoys the attention too much."

Columbine had inclined her head slightly and drawn on the cigarette, at the same time holding back stray ringlets so they wouldn't fall in the flame. "You know what would happen if Renquist came here? He'd try to turn us into the classic foursome. The male master and his three compliant concubines."

Destry and Marieko didn't seem to respond quite as quickly as Columbine would have expected. "Are you two out of your minds? Are you suggesting you might enjoy such an arrangement?"

Destry, realizing she'd been caught in a fleeting what-if reverie, quickly snapped her lighter shut and put it in her pocket. "Of course not. Would we live like this if we did?"

Marieko smiled with deceptive sweetness. "The presence of a male would, however, be a diversion."

Columbine had retorted angrily. "Then why don't you go the whole way and move in with Fenrior?"

"Rudeness is hardly appropriate."

Destry closed ranks with Marieko. "Really, Columbine, after all this time, the nonsense between you and Victor Renquist has to be primarily in your imagination. Even you have to agree you were very young and silly at the time, and he was, and still is, eight hundred years your senior. You've spent the passage of years enlarging and embroidering on the situation. He probably doesn't even remember you."

Despite herself, Columbine exhaled smoke and pouted. "He remembers me. I'll guarantee you that."

Marieko pressed their two-to-one advantage. "If you

could be objective for a moment, you would realize Renquist is exactly what we need."

"I don't want him here." But even as she spoke, Columbine knew her aura was giving her away. A part of her was subversively excited at the prospect of seeing Victor Renquist again.

"Be real, Columbine."

"You're the one who's complaining about the nightmares."

Destry glanced at Marieko. "Perhaps she thinks Renquist would be too much for her to handle. Perhaps she's afraid she'll turn into a simpering girl again at the sight of him."

Columbine knew she was being both teased and manipulated by the other two, but she couldn't stop herself from angrily reacting. "I am not afraid of Victor bloody Renquist."

Destry pressed home the advantage. "Then act your age, and let's make use of him."

Columbine wasn't quite ready to give in. "There must be another undead of the same stature."

"Name one."

Columbine cast around for a name. "I can't."

"No, of course you can't. So act your age, and let's make use of him."

Columbine was effectively outnumbered, but she couldn't surrender without one more turn of the wheel. "Very well, suppose we did manage to get Victor to come here. What then? If there is some potential power in the burial mound, wouldn't we be running the risk of him taking over whatever we might find there?"

"You think the three of us aren't a match for him?"

"No, I don't think that."

"So?"

"All right, all right, I don't want to see him, but if we can get his attention, I'll go along with it. I'm not so sure he's actually going to be that interested. He's fas-

cinated by nosferatu history, but he's also very circumspect, and protective of his colony."

Marieko made a Zen gesture indicating the great merit
of simplicity. "We send him a letter."

By the time the sun had begun to sink over the West
London suburbs, Renquist decided he had experienced
more than enough of this drifting but not sleeping and
resolved, as soon as he had the safety of twilight, to take
another walk out in the streets. He needed to move, to
stride and to swing his arms, and, after his own fashion,
to breathe in his new surroundings. Only after that, when
he returned to the Savoy, would he telephone Columbine
Dashwood. In the meantime, until the sun was down, he
would abandon these attempts at halfway rest and apply
himself to a final recap of what he knew so far about
the task at hand. He reached for the leather folder in
which he'd filed the paperwork relevant to the project,
unzipped it, and extracted the letters. The sequence of
correspondence and the way it had been couched bore
all the hallmarks of Columbine's style and operational
approach. She had always fancied herself as the seductive coquette, the incremental tease. Each letter had
given away a little at a time, never allowing him to know
more until he'd at least made some tentative commit-
ment of interest. He doubted, though, that Columbine
was the author of the letters in terms of physically creating them. Unless she had undergone a radical change
over the many years since he'd seen her, she was not
the kind to labor long and diligently at perfecting the
complicated calligraphy of the nosferatu. The flame
script, in scarlet ink on the handmade oriental writing
paper, had been drawn with a near-flawless dexterity and
what appeared to be an ultrafine 00 sable hair paintbrush.
The delivery by exclusive courier service had been the
icing on an already exquisite cake, and it was enough to
convince Renquist the whole presentation was a team
effort by the entire troika, and not just some strange,

out-of-the-night scheme devised by Columbine acting on
her own.

This made him a little more willing to take the information on face value. Columbine Dashwood, up to their
acrimonious predawn parting in Brussels, during the
grand ball on the eve of Waterloo, had never shown such
a capacity for detail. At the time, Renquist had been in
the highly covert employ of the Duke of Wellington, and
she had been the secretly undead darling of the Anglo-
Prussian alliance. She had challenged him to meet her
after the battle, but the tide of human events had intervened. He had never kept their rendezvous, and she'd
hated him for it ever since with all the ferocity of a
scorned female. Over the years, Columbine had made a
number of vengeful attempts to lure him into humiliating
or dangerous situations, but Renquist's instincts told him
the letters were not another of these. It was possible, of
course, that she had persuaded the entire troika to assist
her in another plot against him, but he thought it unlikely.

The first letter had merely hinted that she and the other
two women of her troika had come across some kind of
nosferatu artifact and perhaps a correspondence should
be initiated. His response had been politely interested,
but decidedly noncommittal. The second missive had fed
him a little more detail, clearly designed to tantalize. The
artifact, still unspecified, was seemingly entombed, beneath a prehistoric burial mound, presumably in the
countryside somewhere near the troika's residence. This
had both intrigued Renquist, as was intended, but also
caused him a measure of hesitation. Although England,
especially the counties in the southwest, was noted for
its wealth of prehistoric and Roman sites, the country
had always been exceptionally short on nosferatu in any
period with the exception of a few recent notables like
Sir Francis Varney, Barnabas Collins, or Lord Ruthven.
At no time had these islands supported a population of
the undead to compare with prehistoric India, the Third

Dynasty Egypt, China under the Shun, or eastern Europe at any time in the Christian era.

The British Isles were too ordered and contained to be the habitat of more than a handful of the undead. The population was too dense. The great forests had been all but completely felled in between the sixteenth and eighteenth century to build the men-o'-war of the formidable British navy. Since Renquist's mortality, the English had killed off their wolves, their bears, and their wild boar. The English countryside was a place of neat fields, measured acres, and a network of close interconnecting roads where hedgehogs were crushed under the tires of lorries and automobiles, and even the skylarks had been destroyed by pesticides. A few wild areas did remain, primarily the Highlands and Islands in the north of Scotland, but even these seem only to retain their untamed glory by a kind of national consent, as though they had a spurious permission to remain the way they once were because, in reality they could never really be domesticated. By strange irony, it was the highly tamed nature of the domestic United Kingdom that allowed the few like Columbine Dashwood and the Clan Fenrior to survive. No one bothered them, because absolutely no one believed in them.

The third letter had been somewhat more forthcoming. Apparently human archeologists were delving into the mound, and among their finds had been a tiny broken triangle of mica, assumed to be from a much larger sheet. The mica that carried a single but very clear character, the *nya* of the nosferatu flame script. This information had come close to fully convincing Renquist that the information being fed to him one bite at a time was genuine if maybe considerably less than complete. Any writing on mica had, by definition, to be very old indeed, dating back the full fifteen thousand years to the lost ages of the Nephilim, the Original Beings and Marduk Ra. Nowhere had mica been used as a print medium at any time since. It seemed all but impossible that such a fragment should turn up during a routine excavation of an English barrow, unless the mound had, maybe at some point after its original construction, been used as a place of concealment for some very old, very rare, and possibly priceless nosferatu relics. The suggestion in the letter was that Renquist should perhaps travel to England to investigate.

On this, Renquist had procrastinated for some time. He still considered the colony to be recovering its equilibrium following their hard-won victory over the Apogee cult. He had been loath to leave until the rest of the colony's members had repeatedly assured him, particularly Dahlia, Lupo, and Julia, they could get on very well without his obsessive, hands-on leadership. He had considered bringing Lupo with him, but to bring an escort resonated too strongly of packing muscle, and Lupo had "henchman/protector/bodyguard" written all over him. Born in the time of the Borgias and of the convoluted intrigue and skulduggery among the Italian city-states, Lupo was one of the few nosferatu who had ever exploited his undead attributes by actually marketing them to humans. For almost five hundred years, Lupo had been a nocturnal contract killer for popes, presidents, and prime ministers, captains of industry, bankers, beer barons, and racketeers. In more modern times, as his life continued to extend and extend, he had been content to assist Renquist in the organization and protection of the colony and to allow his fearsome-killer reputation to cool a little. This was not to say he didn't, from time to time, execute a commission for organized crime, who knew him as Joey Nightshade, or for the intelligence community, who claimed not to know him at all. He tended to be sought for the hits that were thought to be impossible, and he charged accordingly, which was a continuing boon to the colony's material liquidity. Lupo had old-fashioned principles and old-fashioned loyalties. He insisted on addressing Renquist as Don Victor, and for Renquist to show up with such an ancient and influential heavyweight at his shoulder would be too much like, as the humans put it, being "loaded for bear."

Julia had also expressed a desire to go with him, but since Julia Aschenbach always conducted herself strictly according to her own agenda, Renquist had turned her down flat. For him to so much as entertain the idea of traveling overseas with Julia was not asking, but pleading for trouble. Renquist often thought of Julia as a form of personal retribution. She was his own creation: a headstrong Berlin starlet from the National Socialist film industry whom he had brought through the Change mainly as a nasty parting gift for Joseph Goebbels. He had never expected her to survive, calculating that someone in the SS would know enough to drive a stake into her after she'd wreaked short but noticeable havoc. Quite the reverse proved true. Julia had not only survived, but had also honed herself into a remorseless cutting edge of Nordic steel, as some bastard undead conjunction of Marlene Dietrich and Niccoló Machiavelli. Ever since she had tracked down Renquist in the mid-sixties, she had alternated between challenging him, directly or by proxy, for the Mastery of the colony, or, since the destruction of his still sorely missed Cynara, by attempting to become his consort and pair-bonded hunting partner. Even by nosferatu standards, Julia was dangerous—definitely not a traveling companion he could trust to watch his back or act from mutual interest and common purpose. In addition, while Julia on her own was one thing, the idea that she might easily form an alliance against him with Columbine Dashwood and her two companions was very much another matter. That he might find himself pitted against four hostile and snarling females scarcely bore thinking about. If Renquist was going to travel at all, he would travel alone.

Renquist had become such a virtuoso of rational procrastination that it took a day or so to realize how, in his adamant resolve not to take Julia with him, he had already subconsciously decided he was leaving for England. His course was set; he just hadn't accepted it at a conscious level. The colony really could look after itself for a while. He was aware that he might possibly be walking into some form of trap or risky entanglement, but such was the chance he took whenever he answered any solicitation or enticement to leave the Residence. Such were the risks in the night-milieux of creatures like himself. Any nosferatu who didn't constantly expect the unexpected would never survive a decade—let alone a near-millennium. In the end, the temptation of the letters had proved just too intense. Both his own curiosity and fear of what these human scholars might discover were twin goads to which he couldn't help but respond. Renquist was very well aware that if the humans were to attempt to date and decipher such material, they could learn far more than was good for Renquist, Columbine Dashwood, or any of their kind.

Renquist had methodically begun reestablishing communications, calling in favors, implementing blackmail, and generally easing the way to the final and precise travel arrangements that had brought him to this comfortable suite in the Savoy. The preparation stage was behind him. He was now in a lull before the adventure began in earnest. A part of him, the ever-youthful heart-of-the-flame that still relished the excitement of a quest into the unknown, wanted to cease the game-playing and telephone immediately as the sun had set, but elder pride forbade this. He was Victor Renquist; it was fitting he should maintain a stern detachment. He would walk first, allow himself one more feel of the streets, and telephone on his return.

Chapter Two

Columbine jerked first, as though electricity had been fed directly into her undead spine, and then the phone rang. Marieko noted how the two occurrences had taken place in diametric opposition to what should have been their logical order. First Columbine jerked and then the double ring of the bell, as though she was experiencing a brief but nonetheless full premonition. Could Columbine sense the electrons or digital light pulses coming down the wire or fiber-optic cable? Marieko was unclear about the technical details of the Priory's phone service, but Columbine seemed suddenly able to anticipate it. As she reached for the receiver. Marieko intercepted her. "No."

"What do you mean, no?"

"Don't answer on the first ring. He's made you wait, so don't be overeager. In fact, let me get it."

Marieko reached past Columbine and picked up. "Hello."

A well-modulated male voice, almost without accent,

asked, "Could I please speak with Miss Columbine Dashwood?"

Columbine hissed at her. "Is it him?"

Marieko nodded. Only Victor Renquist could take such care that his voice revealed absolutely nothing. "Can I tell her who's calling?"

"My name is Renquist. Victor Renquist."

Marieko covered the mouthpiece with her hand and waited. Columbine tried to take the receiver, but Marieko swatted her away in dumb show. "For someone who's supposed to be an experienced game-player, you're acting like a teenager anticipating a first date." She spoke back into the phone. "I'm sorry, Victor, but Columbine isn't available right now. This is Marieko Matsunaga. Can I help you? I have as full a grasp of the relevant situation. I'm the one who actually wrote the letters."

"You have a very fine hand."

"Thank you."

"The realization of the flame-script was close to perfect."

Marieko inclined her head modestly. "I still make errors."

Renquist didn't continue the pleasantries, and came to the point. "I am now in London. I believe Miss Dashwood wants to meet with me."

"We all wish to meet you."

Columbine looked as though she were about to burst, but she contained herself sufficiently not to grab for the phone again.

"I'm staying at the Savoy. . . ."

"I know the Savoy very well."

"I don't know if you want to do this in London or . . ."

"It might be better if you came here. It would make possible an immediate inspection of the problem we outlined in our letters."

"That's probably the best plan."

"We would naturally send a car for you."

Renquist hesitated. Only for a fraction of a second, but long enough to convince Marieko his reactions were not as instant and impeccable as was generally believed. "No, there's no need to do that. I will arrange my own transport. It will give me greater flexibility."

Renquist was clearly protecting himself against any possible ambush or trickery. Marieko would have expected no less of him. "Do you intend to come tonight?"

"That was my intention. How long is the drive?"

"A little over two hours depending on the traffic."

"Then I could be there well before midnight."

"You will require directions. This place is a little remote."

"I actually know Ravenkeep."

"You do?

"From a very long time ago."

"The road system may have radically changed since then."

"It almost certainly has. You had better tell me the relevant roads and Motorways so I can relay them to my driver."

Marieko did nothing so gauche as giving Renquist time to reach for pen and paper. If he was as good as his reputation claimed, let him memorize what she told him. "You take the M4 out of London . . ."

Hardly pausing for breath, she recited the route from London to the Priory.

"All three of us look forward very much to seeing you, Victor-sama."

She hung up to find Columbine glaring at her.

"Why didn't you let me speak to him?"

Marieko's expression, as always, revealed nothing, although her aura hinted at a certain assertive satisfaction. "I would have thought that was obvious. By not allowing him to speak to you, he learned nothing of your prevailing mood or attitude, and he can speculate on the various possibilities as he travels down here. He made you wait, and now it's his turn to be marginally inconvenienced. The contest is surely one of balance and counterbalance, isn't it?"

The limousine was white, far too flamboyant, and Renquist was less than pleased. He didn't want to be mistaken for an entertainer. He supposed he should have given more specific instructions to the Savoy desk clerk, but did the man really imagine Renquist would require a vehicle so overtly ostentatious? The driver wore a grey double-breasted suit and matching peaked cap. The forepart of his mind was smooth with the professionalism of an upmarket service provider and colored by a distinct pride in the long list of the celebrated and notorious he had driven in his time. He had a ready repertoire of jokes and anecdotes should the client prove conversational, but also the ability to remain silent if need be, enclosed in his own thoughts and concentration. He also had a fairly comprehensive catalog of contacts for clients who not only required to be taken where they wanted to go, but also to avail themselves of sex, drugs, or other illegal, illicit, or merely bizarre distractions the city might offer.

Behind this anterior working facade, however, there burned a resentment as old and sullen as the English class system. The world, as he saw it, was arbitrarily divided into underlings, who drove, and the supposedly superior, who were driven, and this perpetually rankled. Having taken the brief measure of the human with whom he'd spend the next couple of hours, Renquist had little further interest. He had seen infinitely more brutal inequality in his time. A driver was a driver, and Renquist hoped the man wouldn't be presented with any occasion to rise higher than that. Renquist might have looked more deeply into the chauffeur's mind had its owner shown the slightest trace of rebellion or even of originality, but he detected no Red Flag rebel romance, no death on the barricades, no poet craving to be free. The chauffeur might have his resentments, but he also had a strong if spurious investment in the status quo, and he

truly believed in the gossip-column celebrity hierarchy
and his own minor place in it. For Renquist this made
him stereotypically dull.

The man clearly didn't know what to make of Renquist. He first assumed Renquist was an actor, but, by
the man's tabloid logic, if Renquist could afford to stay
at the Savoy and make use of a limousine service to take
him way out into the wilds of the countryside, the driver
should have been familiar with his face, and he wasn't.
The driver's second idea was that he might have been
one of the new breed of TV, sound-bite politicians, but
this also didn't seem to fly. Aside from the man's card-
index knowledge of famous and semifamous faces,
something didn't sit right. Sure, Renquist had the correct
assurance, the confidence of power, but somehow he carried it too well. These new politicians were good-
looking, but never this good-looking. They always
seemed to have some flaw or defect, and they never
looked him quite so unflinchingly in the eye. Just as they
didn't sport almost shoulder-length hair. Renquist was
almost tempted to smile. If only the chauffeur knew the
clear and unvarnished truth. That would surely give him
a story to tell, wherever chauffeurs gathered and told
their chauffeur stories. That was, of course, if he stopped
running long enough to ever tell the tale. Ah, humans.

The man held the door open. Renquist, as he stepped
into the low but ample rear of the car, repeated the instructions he'd been give over the phone. "We apparently take the M4 out of London . . ."

The driver nodded. He'd maybe absorbed about half
of what Renquist said, which wasn't bad for a mortal.
"You may have to refresh my memory as we go, sir."

"Don't worry, I'll see that we don't get lost."

The door closed behind him, and Renquist thought no
more about either the chauffeur or the less-than-
appropriate white limousine. They were merely a means
to the next item on the agenda.

                    *   *   *

"Keep still and focus, damn you, Grendl, or I swear I will have you beaten so badly you won't walk for a week."

Destry called from her dressing room. "Don't beat her before I've finished with her. I need her next."

Since time immemorial, the worthlessness of mirrors had created problems for nosferatu ladies of fashion. Columbine, Marieko, and Destry were far from the first to use the mind and vision of a maidservant thrall as a human looking glass when dressing or applying makeup. Of course, the mind of the thrall so used had to be under full and absolute control, still and functionally inanimate with his or her will completely subjugated and frozen— but wasn't that what thralls were all about? Psychological abasement and the surrender of the will and personality to a superior? Usually the commanding nosferatu promised or at least hinted at eventual immortality, but these were pledges rarely if ever kept. Both parties knew that to be used and exploited, to serve without question in return for just being in close and daily proximity to nosferatu was an end in itself for most thralls, whatever their hopes might be for an infinite future. The truth was that, in all but the rarest of cases, thralls, after a mortal life of servitude and subservience, made very poor nosferatu. Columbine always used Grendl or some other woman to be her mirror. Men could not be trusted. No matter how blanked and glazed they might be, they always tended to impose a measure of their own interpretation. They altered, flattered, and reflected what they desired rather than what truly was—very nice, but completely lacking in essential objectivity. Women were more ready to return the cruel truth and allow their mistress to make the crucial alterations.

Staring directly at herself through the immobile Grendl's mind, she finished applying a deep purple lipstick and mentally stepped back. "I'm still not sure this works. Maybe I should take a Polaroid. Does anyone know where the camera is?"

Again, it was Destry who answered. "I've got it here.
I'll trade it for Grendl."

The triad may not have been the first to use a thrall
to provide a psychic reflection, but they were possibly
the only ones who used Polaroid photographs as a check
and backup. The idea had been Columbine's, back when
Polaroid color film became readily available at the village shop. The idea never would have worked, however,
had not all three females been of that undead strain who
were able to produce a photographic image. Some nosferatu simply couldn't be photographed. Their image
failed to react with silver nitrate as anything but a
blurred, ectoplasmic apparition. Others might pose for
pictures, but if they wanted to fog the film, they could.
Like the original problem of the missing mirror reflection, this phenomenon had never been adequately explained to Columbine. Various nosferatu she'd met in
her travels had proffered theories, but never one that
completely satisfied her. It happened, therefore it was.
Maybe Victor had an explanation—although she might
not buy into his as a matter of principle.

No matter how Columbine, Marieko, or Destry might
later deny it, the imminent arrival of Victor Renquist had
created a swell of excitement in the paneled corridors of
Ravenkeep Priory. As the three women made their preparations, their auras left afterimages of flirtatious anticipation, which joined the wafting perfume and rustling
of fabric. Marieko had been right. A nosferatu male had
indeed not crossed their threshold in a long time, and no
matter how they might claim to be above such shallow
fancy, the prospect triggered an escalating indulgence of
vanity, cacophony, haste, and even a slight edge of hysteria. Columbine had really made the effort, perhaps
claiming her birthright from a more overdressed age:
after trying on a number of ensembles, she had settled
for a Versace extravaganza, unusual for the murdered
designer in that the ensemble eschewed what had been
his signature riot of color and was entirely black, a deco-

style creation of crustacean armor—layered sequins with an almost Elizabethan, face-framing collar of high spines webbed with black lace—but, at the same time, open to the navel and highly revealing. With her white ringleted hair and corpse-pale skin, the effect was one of total monochrome. To offset this, she slipped on the ruby ring she had so recently taken from the hand of the dead boy. She had also taken the matching necklace and pendant earrings from their velvet case. She took one more look through the eyes and mind of Grendl, adjusted the set of the necklace slightly, and was more or less satisfied.

"Take a photograph."

The thrall was so tightly controlled she raised the cheap Polaroid with slow and robotic arms. The flash left Columbine with retinal images, but as the small square print was ejected from the plastic base of the camera, she took it and waited impatiently for the image to appear. For a few moments she studied the picture; then she nodded and smiled. "Yes, indeed. That should help keep you off balance, Victor dear."

This was not to say Marieko and Destry hadn't made at least a comparable effort. Marieko had gone for an almost science-fiction glamour, in gold jeans of metallic leather, teetering platform shoes, and a scarlet chiffon blouse fastened only at the left shoulder so her right breast was exposed and the splendor of her tattoo-work was revealed to its full advantage. Destry, on the other hand, had opted for a somewhat more conservative look. A man's black tuxedo with satin lapels decorated with a diamond pin, in the shape of a Native American thunderbird, given to her by Fidel Castro during his exile in Mexico City before the revolution. To prevent an overly stern and masculine effect, she had mitigated it with very red, very high heels and matching lipstick that she now required Grendl to help her apply.

"Can I have both Grendl and the camera? You're not the only one who wants to create an effect."

Columbine snapped her fingers, raising a glimmer of

dull comprehension in the thrall. "Go to her."

As the dazed and round-shouldered servant shuffled drably away, Columbine realized the thought of going to all this trouble to captivate Victor should logically have made her very angry, but she found she was actually quite enjoying herself. They would weave their spell, and, once he fell under it, they'd ride him hard and put him away still sweating.

Initially Renquist paid little attention to the highway landscape through which the white limousine was passing. The expressways out of all major cities looked the same: stark blue-white lighting, blue or green exit signs with bold white lettering, lane reflectors that seemed to go on forever, neon advertising signs with familiar international logos. Essentially he could have been anywhere, Paris, Buenos Aires, Tokyo, or Newark—the minor local differences were too few to distinguish one twenty-first century conurbation from another. He passed the time by investigating the limousine's interior. In the small refrigerator of the mobile bar, he discovered, amid the beer, Coca-Cola, juices, and inevitable variety of mineral waters, a bottle of frozen Grey Goose vodka. Frozen vodka was an odd weakness of Renquist's, acquired in Saint Petersburg just before the fall of the Romanovs, and maintained for the past century. Although the alcohol had no real effect on his nosferatu metabolism, he enjoyed the shock of the chill raw spirit hitting the back of his throat and the distinct burn as it was absorbed into his system. Since he had time to kill, he selected one of the thoughtfully provided chilled glasses, filled it, and then downed the double shot in one swallow.

"Aaah."

Renquist could think of worse ways to commence an adventure. He repeated the ritual with the vodka and felt very much at ease with the immediate world. Whatever the future might bring, he was very content in the now.

Content enough, in fact, finally to turn his attention to the passing terrain beyond the car's windows. The suburban sprawl had diminished, and Renquist found he was looking at trees and fields, farm buildings, and scattered country houses, substantial within their own grounds. England had always impressed him with its neatly organized geography. He supposed it was inevitable. Social leveling, hastened ironically by the Black Death in the fourteenth century and the subsequent Peasants' Revolt, had begun far earlier in Britain than anywhere else in Europe, and to Renquist this was reflected in the very hedgerows and their smug containment of nature. The seeming confidence that all would endure, despite the global signs dictating otherwise; the romantic vision of country lanes and gathering lilacs, the surety that there would "always be an England," was maybe only possible to an island people who had once dominated half the world but had then been forced to relinquish their massive empire and sink into the quiet and somewhat grumpy nostalgia of a retired superpower.

Through all Renquist's long existence, England had somehow managed to keep its equilibrium. Crown, Church, nobility, and later Parliament had maintained a stability in which the opposing tensions actually remained in balance for most of the time. The king was restrained by the barons; the Church was kept down by the king but ensured that the barons never grew too powerful. Democracy also came early and cost Charles I his head, but, although it spared the entire aristocracy, it served to keep them circumspectly in line, and guaranteed, although they might throw up the odd Hellfire Club, Britain could never spawn an Elizabeth Bathory, a Vlad Tepes, a Gilles de Rais, or an Ivan the Terrible. With such comparative equanimity at home, the Brits could sail off in their ships, go about their legalized piracy and, with the flags flying and the old trade plying, rob the rest of the world blind in the name of Monarch and Empire. Should a potential psychotic aristo arise with a serious case of lustmord, he or she could be shipped off to a colony to take it out on the natives. England evolved a power structure that survived by shunning extremes. The worst crime was, according to Mrs. Patrick Campbell, "doing it in the street and frightening the horses." That was why they were still pissed that no one had caught Jack the Ripper. He had done it in the street and frightened the floozies.

Unfortunately, in all of those ages of British global wheeling and dealing, the Church of England—what Americans called Episcopalian—acquired too firm a grip on the pagan and the paranormal. While maybe not going to the extremes of their Protestant brethren in Germany and the Low Countries, or the Catholic Inquisition in Spain and France, as late as the 1600s, human superstition had been ruthlessly policed in rural England by sadistic witchfinders like Matthew Hopkins, who had, during his mobile puritan excess of hanging and butchery in the wake of the civil war between Cavaliers and Roundheads, destroyed several dozen genuine nosferatu without actually knowing it. The Church hadn't had it all its own way, however. As the empire had grown, even an island nation found it increasingly difficult to exclude the odd and the unnatural. Opium and sinister, Kali-worshipping, thuggee-committing stranglers slipped in from India via the docks of Liverpool and Limehouse, hashish and syphilis arrived from the Middle East, and a few groundbreaking nosferatu found natural cover among the fops, cultivated eccentrics, and intelligentsia of the Age of Reason, when Newtonian physics went hand in hand with the poetry of the Romantics and the secret machinations of the Illuminati. These bloodthirsty few had determinedly remained a powerful and exclusive clique, discouraging the fanged and ragtag migrants from eastern Europe. The English undead rarely frightened the horses, or the English humans, who couldn't quite bring themselves to seriously believe nosferatu really existed. Matters had comfortably remained that way right to the present day, although it would seem Columbine and her group had encountered trouble, were maybe at risk of detection, and, like so many Anglos before them, they looked to the USA for help.

As the route he took in bringing his American help diminished from a motorway to a simple winding blacktop, memories expanded in Renquist's consciousness in inverse proportion to the width of the carriageway. He had actually encountered Ravenkeep Priory twice before. The most recent occasion had been during World War II, when Duke de Richleau and his brilliantly demented team of specialists in the paranormal had waged rather successful occult warfare against Adolf Hitler. Renquist had been assigned by a cabal of even more distinguished nosferatu than himself to maintain covert observation on de Richleau, a mission that had been completely unknown to Columbine, cohabiting at the time with this rarefied task force. Although Renquist and his undead overlords had been in basic sympathy with the British battle against the Nazis, they had always considered de Richleau one of the most dangerous humans ever to walk the day. In his obscure but extensive field, the Duke appeared to know everything. He was certainly well aware of the existence of the nosferatu and was reputed to have a fairly comprehensive knowledge of their customs, habits, and at least some of their powers and limitations. Rumors even claimed he was able to pinpoint the Residences of a number of the major clans and colonies.

The surprise was that de Richleau had never acted on this information either for good or ill. He apparently failed to share most humans' extreme moral revulsion at the idea of blood-drinking night dwellers, and he simply accepted the undead as a fact of life, if such a semantic contradiction was indeed possible. He had never been tempted by the quasi-heroic role of vampire-hunter, but at the same time, he had never tried, as some had, to form an alliance between humans and nosferatu. Whether this was because he knew the undead were watching him or he simply thought in such abstract and altruistic terms that it never occurred to him was a matter of debate, but Renquist had always expected, sooner or later, de Richleau would somehow organize himself through the Change and seize his immortality. He would have welcomed the kinship of such a mind, but de Richleau never came across. He had staunchly retained his humanity and died in 1997 at the venerable age of ninety-three.

The first time Renquist had heard of Ravenkeep, it had yet to become a Priory. When still a hired sword-in-the-night, he had been offered hard human gold for the murder of Jerome le Corbeau, who had, by all accounts except his own, embezzled the collective ransom money for a number of Crusaders languishing in various dungeons and strongholds en route to the Holy Land. Renquist had even gone so far as to raise a band of human cutthroats to do the deed only to have the slaying canceled at the last minute. The worthless le Corbeau was so blighted with pox, he was already three parts insane and not expected to live for more than a few months, anyway. Those who had previously wanted him killed were more than happy to see him survive and suffer as physicians bled him, lanced his sores, and treated him with doses of arsenic and mercury.

Renquist had sunk so deep into remembrance he was actually a little startled when the driver lowered the partition and asked him for directions. "Where to now, sir? I think we're pretty close, but I'm not clear what to do at this crossroads."

Renquist leaned forward and pointed. "Go left, where it says Coldharbour Lane."

"Right you are, sir."

The limousine eased its way into the lefthand turn. On these narrow country lanes, the vehicle was proving even more ridiculous, seriously hampered by its excessive length, and Renquist couldn't avoid a sense of absurdity to be driving in such garishly flamboyant a conveyance through the open fields with their containing hedgerows and the small clusters of woodland with overhanging branches that turned the byways into leafy arboreal tunnels. He was also beginning to recognize sections of the landscape and was aware they were nearing Ravenkeep. The awareness, however, didn't stop him from failing to spot the gates to the estate until they were right on top of them. He quickly leaned forward and lowered the partition. "Stop. That was the place."

The time lag of instruction and reaction took the limo maybe fifty or so yards past the driveway before the driver brought it to a halt. He put the car in reverse and began to back up, but Renquist quickly stopped him. "Just pull over and park."

"I'll be all but blocking the road, sir."

"Put your flashers on, and don't worry about it. I doubt there will be any traffic."

The chauffeur did as he was told. "Whatever you say, sir."

The chauffeur was beginning to wonder if his passenger was a little crazy. Renquist decided the man needed at least a minimal explanation. "There's no cause for alarm. I'm quite sane. I just want to spring a little surprise on my friends."

Renquist observed a chill pass through the driver's aura as he momentarily wondered if his mind had been read but then dismissed the idea as impossible. Renquist smiled slightly and continued with his instructions. "I want you to remain here for twenty minutes, then drive up to the house and drop off my bags. I imagine a servant will be there to collect them."

"And you won't need me after that."

"I won't need you after that."

Renquist signed for the limousine and then handed the driver five twenty-pound notes. "Have a safe return journey."

"Thank you, sir." He pocketed the gratuity, reflecting

that Renquist tipped more like a gangster than any actor
or politician. "Thank you very much."

The chauffeur hesitated for a moment as though he
wanted to say something else. Renquist raised an eyebrow, although he already knew what troubled the man.
"Is there a problem?"

"Well . . ."

"Yes?"

"Are there likely to be dogs, sir?"

"Dogs?"

"Guard dogs or the like?"

The man had a phobia of large dogs. Understandable
insomuch as the driver, at around age ten, had been
mauled by a rottweiler and bore permanent scars on his
right thigh.

"No, my friend, no dogs." Renquist was sorely tempted
to tell the man that much worse dangers lurked at the
end of the driveway, but by necessity, he restrained the
desire to shock. "You have nothing to worry about."

"Thank you, sir."

Renquist left the car and walked toward the gates,
swinging his silver-topped cane. The imposing wrought-
iron gates, with their Victorian curlicues and threatening
rows of spikes, stood open wide. He imagined they were
normally kept closed and had been specifically opened
in anticipation of his arrival. The calm assurance that he
would drive up to the house like any mundane guest had
triggered the idea of taking Columbine and her friends
by surprise. A sudden flash of confusion would improve
his chance of learning more of the females' real motives
than if he behaved according to easy prediction. He
didn't expect a surprise entrance with a few psychic
fireworks to take them completely off guard, but he
might find that guard lowered at least in some measure.
He glanced up at the tall granite columns that supported
the gates and noted with a certain irrational satisfaction
that each was still topped with a large cast-iron raven.

During the Second World War, many such decorations had been removed and melted down to aid the war effort. Seemingly, the ravens, a Victorian interpretation of the ancient arms of the le Corbeau family, had been spared. A small gatekeeper's lodge stood just inside the gateway, but it was empty and all but derelict, with blind windows and a look of disuse. In complete contrast, light showed all over the great architecturally confused pile that was Ravenkeep itself. For a stately home inhabited by the undead, it seemed positively festive and inviting.

Renquist stepped through the gate and a concentric flicker of blue fire momentarily surrounded him but quickly faded and died. Had those inside been alerted, or had the paranormal warning been of too brief a duration? He couldn't be sure if his surprise was spoiled, but he pressed on. Directly, he was through the gates; he stepped off the driveway and walked on the grass verge so his footsteps made no sound. At the same time, he damped down his aura, embracing it so tightly it hardly showed. After centuries of practice, he could all but make himself invisible even to his own kind.

"Did something cross the threshold?"

Marieko and Columbine stood very still focusing all their concentration. "Nothing as large as a car. We would have heard a car."

Destry went to the window and parted the thick velvet drapes, just a small six-inch gap that allowed her to see outside. "There's nothing. No car coming up the drive."

"An aura?"

"Not that I can detect. I suppose someone could have walked through the gates, but I can't see or sense them."

"Victor Renquist wouldn't have walked here."

The troika had convened in the large drawing room, where all had been made ready for Renquist's arrival. The spacious room with its beamed ceiling, paneled walls, and thick Persian carpets covering the stained oak floor had originally been the banqueting hall when Rav-

enkeep was the stronghold of the le Corbeau family, and
legends recounted how the degenerate Jerome had used
it for a wide variety of diverting indoor atrocities. Later,
in its ecclesiastical days, it was the Priory's refectory.
After that it had returned to being a banqueting hall,
albeit more jovial and Elizabethan in style, and then,
finally, Enoch Jarman had attempted and largely failed
to turn it into a formal Victorian drawing room. Like
Ravenkeep itself, the room was an ill-matched conglom-
eration of architectural confusion, with an overall impression of an uneven and piecemeal lack of coherent
design, and this was not improved by the varied furnishings, objets d'art, and general nosferatu clutter that
had accumulated over the years the troika had been in
residence. The three females possessed far from kindred
tastes, and Destry's fondness for bold functional stark-
ness clashed wildly with Columbine's partiality to frill
and flounce that, in turn, fought with Marieko's precise
oriental exquisitry.

In anticipation of Renquist, and under Marieko's su-
pervision, the careful placing of candles and muted electric light had transformed the drawing room into a place
of comfortable shadows, disguising the worst of the clutter and the most glaring clashes of discrimination. A
roaring fire of aromatic pine logs blazed in the smoke-
blackened Elizabethan redbrick fireplace and lent it a
sense of venerable security. Not wishing to allow Marieko credit for the entire planning of the environment,
Columbine had ordered that one of her most singular
and prized works of art, the second, secret version of
Philip Burne-Jones's painting *A Vampire* be hung prominently over the fireplace. The well-known public version of the work had caused enough of a scandal when
first exhibited in 1897 for depicting a malevolent,
nosferatu-style female figure crouched over the body of
the dead or dying painter. Since the vampiress was unmistakably the actress Mrs. Patrick Campbell (the
woman seemed to be everywhere at the turn of the nine-

teenth and twentieth centuries) all of smart London assumed it was Burne-Jones's creative revenge for being
discarded by Campbell in favor of the sensual attentions
of the noted Shakespearean actor Johnston Forbes-
Robertson. What few of the capital's smart set knew,
however, was that Burne-Jones had completed a second
painting of almost identical composition, only this obscure version had Mrs. Campbell rendered revealingly
naked, and the discreet blood in the original was, in the
second and more vitriolic work, both explicit and lurid.
Columbine had acquired the painting from a decidedly
devious source shortly after Peregrin, her human husband, had died, and she hoped Renquist would be at least
marginally impressed by its unique and slanderous novelty.

Not that the troika, at this particular moment, entertained any thoughts about late Pre-Raphaelite art. The
painting was simply a background to the current concern. The built-in and natural nosferatu alarms had
sounded, and the three females wanted to know why.
Destry was convinced something had crossed the demarcation line at the gate, and yet no intruder could be
discerned on the grounds of Ravenkeep. The inexplicable frustration of the situation was a source of tension
and even over-the-shoulder apprehension. Columbine,
Marieko, and Destry had prepared long and hard for the
arrival of Victor Renquist, and now, at what had to be
the very last moment, a mysterious and unnerving
strangeness was insinuating its way into their plans. Columbine, with a certain level of denial, searched for an
answer in the realm of the mundane. "It could have just
been an animal, a fox or a badger."

Destry continued to peer through the curtains. "I don't
know. Maybe I should go outside and scan more thoroughly."

Marieko all but snapped. "Don't."

"Why not?"

"Because if Renquist is out there, it will only give the

impression we're anxious, even afraid of him."

"But I am anxious." Destry wasn't ashamed to admit it when something disturbed her.

"And you want him to know that?"

"Of course not."

Columbine sided with Marieko. "So come away from the window."

Destry didn't move. "I want to see if there's anything out there."

"You have a mind don't you? You don't have to use your eyes all the time. I mean, Destry, you're not a human."

Although it might well have changed a little in nearly sixty years, Renquist had once been intimately familiar with the layout of both the house and grounds of Ravenkeep Priory. Indeed, he had known them like the back of his hand in those wartime years when he'd been charged to silently observe de Richleau and ensure his team did nothing to threaten the well-being and survival of the undead in their occult assault on Nazism. The trees, in early autumn, still retaining their leaves, seemed taller and more lush than he remembered them, but that was fully to be expected over the course of some sixty years. Also some trees he thought he recalled appeared to be missing. Either, he guessed, felled, uprooted in storms, or fallen victim to the epidemic of Dutch elm disease that had destroyed so many magnificent trees a quarter of a century earlier. He was both surprised and gratified by how easily the details returned to mind and fitted into place like a self-arranging mental jigsaw. In the distance, to his left, he could see the sinister and crassly ugly Winged Victory statue, erected by Enoch Jarman in apparent celebration of warfare and the profits it generated, and beyond it, Renquist hoped, the geometrically formal rose garden still survived. When the famous Jarman rose collection was in bloom, even at night, the scent was all but intoxicating. To his right stood the decorative pointlessness of the folly, a Greco-Roman faux ruin, constructed during the eighteenth century when such things were all the rage, atop its own man-made grassy knoll, positioned to overlook the great lawn running down to the equally man-made lake.

A part of Renquist rather envied Columbine and her companions such a historic and imposing residence. His own colony's dwellings in New York and Los Angeles were both relatively humble in comparison to the monumental estate. The nosferatu realist, on the other hand, was well aware such reckless ostentation could be both a dead weight and a dangerous encumbrance. Places like Ravenkeep could be hard to leave. They created attachments of place and property that, like invisible shackles, could cause one to hesitate in a fatal moment when to flee and not look back was the only difference between continued immortality and oblivious destruction. Maybe in England, where humans still clung doggedly to an outmoded sense of class, such behavior might remain possible for a few more years, perhaps even a few more decades. Sooner or later, though, egalitarianism would come in one form or another and, with it, the dangerous curiosity of those who believed all were equal. Common sense alone dictated the avoidance of human curiosity should be a primary nosferatu motivation.

Renquist was surprised at the lack of precautions the Dashwood troika took to ensure their safety and anonymity. Once he had entered the gates, he had deemed it unwise to simply walk up the driveway to the front door. He had made a turn and followed the boundary wall for maybe twenty or thirty paces, on the lookout for the kind of silent, high-tech laser traps and buried, pressure-sensitive alarms he had ordered installed in the Residence in Los Angeles. Renquist knew he tended to be a trifle excessive in these things, not to mention the American love of gadgetry, but the total absence of any protection could only be judged a dangerous laxity. In all his searching, he detected nothing more than a sprung and rusted steel mantrap clearly set to catch Victorian poachers rather than any contemporary vampire hunter. Did Columbine really believe English cultural reserves would keep her out of harm's way forever, or had he been living too long in the USA with its left-over pioneer fetish for protecting home and hearth? Perhaps, but these women still seemed nonchalant to the point of negligence.

With no apparent technology to impede or give him away, Renquist headed for the house, but still by a deceptively circuitous course. His hoped-for objective was to enter the main building undetected and then appear among them, taking them completely by surprise, aura blazing in the most overwhelming display of psychic fireworks he could muster—and Renquist prided himself, with his infinitely varied experience, on being rather an expert at psychic fireworks. To this end, he skirted the trees that edged the smaller lawn at the front of the house. A red vixen, about her nocturnal fox-business, started at his approach and made off with almost as much stealth as Renquist himself. Moving from shadow to shadow and tree to tree, he could feel the soft vibrations of other nosferatu attempting to detect him, but he had his mind well enough concealed to know he was unobserved. The blue fire must have made the three females aware something had entered the gates, and now they were attempting to locate and identify that something. So far, they'd failed to nail him. He risked a momentary scan of his own, and immediately located three very undisguised and excited auras, gathered in what, if memory continued to serve, was the large drawing room of the house—the same imposing room with the dominating brick fireplace where de Richleau and his gang had brainstormed and strategized.

Animal auras were also visible way over on the other side of the rambling and haphazard structure. The stables; how fluently it all came back to him. Four horses and a half dozen hayloft cats. The well-fed and sleepy equine vibrations from three of the horses were completely unremarkable, but the fourth was something else entirely. A trace of hellish crimson in that horse's mind told him that it was a breed apart, an extreme rarity, one of a bloodline that he'd assumed had been extinct at least since the Great Slaughter of 1919, when countless nosferatu had perished in the aftermath of the Great War—and, along with them, a proud breed of arrogant chargers exclusive to the undead. This horse had night vision and a strange fire in its soul. It was undoubtedly from the original line created and bred by Pathan Gash (the Merciless and Eternal) in his Uzbek stronghold, where not even Timur the Lame dared interfere. The legendary butcher, also known as Tamerlane, may have sacked Delhi and taken Samarkand as his own, but he knew better than to mess with the undead Pathan Gash, and, for two uninterrupted centuries, his mares and stallions were supremely prized, and nosferatu horse traders with their gypsy thralls could name their own price for such animals.

Once upon a time, the huge black horses, with their unflagging strength and strange inbred affinity for the undead, had been ridden by nosferatu as far north as the Mongol steppes, all the way down through Persia to Turkey, and back up into the Balkans. Renquist had straddled a charger from the same bloodline in actions against the Turks, when he'd led a company of night-riding boyars, human but savage to the point of insanity, who tied red ribbons to the blades of their sabers and felt honorbound to hack to death any one of their number who came out of a fight, or even a minor skirmish, with his ribbon intact.

The horse in the Ravenkeep stable was both magnificent and unique, and Renquist was at a loss to know how these females might have obtained such a treasure. It clearly would not do to underestimate their potential resources. If they could get their cold white hands on a beast like this, they were well connected and highly capable. Also he had to see the horse. Let the women wait. He turned and made his way to the stables. He knew it wasn't a wise move, but he simply couldn't resist. Victor Renquist was rarely tempted to self-indulgence, but this was one time when he refused to deny himself. Entering the stable was like stepping back centuries, especially since his too-long sojourn in Los Angeles. The smell was the first thing that enveloped him—a unique blending of hay and leather, manure, saddle soap, wood varnish, and neat's-foot oil, but above all, the multitude of breathing secretions from the horses themselves. The bricks on which his boots made no sound must have been swabbed a hundred thousand times down the years. The oak beams above him that tied together roof and walls had been the roost of countless generations of pigeons and was coated with an almost geological patina of their droppings. Sleepy birds ruffled their feathers, and some even opened their eyes and blinked as he walked silently below, past the orderly tack room and the rows of stalls and loose boxes, but no pigeon cooed or fluttered in panic. Renquist was no threat to them. One horse whickered uneasily, but he quelled it with a thought. It was not the one he'd come to see. That masterpiece of horseflesh stood and regarded him through the half-barred door to the wide stall at the end of the row.

The horse was frankly curious. It knew him, and yet it didn't. Had the beast more reasoning capacity, it would have realized that it recognized the kind but not the individual. Horses are not logisticians, however, so it stood foursquare, wary, but in no way afraid. Its nostrils flared, but its eyes were fixed on the advancing nosferatu, black, deep, and unknowable eyes, as those of a shark when about to strike. In many respects, it was the same root unknowability that could, on an infinitely more sophisticated level, be found in the eyes of Renquist himself. The stallion's eyes were ringed with red rather than the white or yellow of more conventional horses. It moved its right foreleg as if in preparation to paw at the floor of its stall with one hoof, slowly and abstractedly, neither in panic or fury, just the uneasiness of perplexity. It recognized Renquist as undead, but the only other undead it had known were the three females of the troika and, before that, those who might have tended it at whatever farm, ranch, or stables whence it had come. To the horse, Renquist was an equine paradox, a familiar stranger.

"Steady now."

He approached the animal, an open hand extended. It tossed its head twice and then stretched its long neck forward, barely touching his palm with its black velvet muzzle. A brief nonverbal exchange occurred, but in the same instant, Renquist realized he had been exceedingly stupid and careless. In his admiration of the stallion, he had all but certainly given himself away to the three females.

Marieko's aura was a honed and searching razor. "Right then. Just a moment ago. Something. I'm certain."

"Where?"

"The stables."

"The stables?"

"I'm sure, but fleetingly."

Like two more probing, psychic spotlights, Columbine and Destry joined with Marieko, and their harmonic and united perception panned in the direction of the stables. "Where?"

Marieko concentrated, directing the search. Such was the true strength of the troika in time of threat or crisis. When need or desire drove, all three could operate as one. "As I said, it was fleeting."

"I'm getting nothing but the aura of Dormandu."

Columbine let out an exasperated hiss. "That damned horse is like a beacon. It radiates raw power. Even when Destry's riding, it almost swamps the fact that she's there on its back."

Marieko's perception suddenly halted in its searching

sweep. Where the faces of others frowned when thinking or perplexed, hers took on a distracted passivity. "It would be the perfect place to hide."

"Where?"

"Within the wild aura of the beast."

"If such a thing was done, it can only be Renquist."

"Or another nosferatu."

"A human would totally lack the understanding."

"If it is Renquist, why should he do such a thing?"

"As a test."

"A test?"

"Isn't existence little more than a series of tests?"

Renquist stepped swiftly beside the horse, as near as he could without unnerving the animal. He placed a calming hand on its neck and leaned his body against the stallion's shoulder. He'd let himself slip, and such carelessness was unforgivable. Although it was not his survival at stake—merely his ego and pride—he still wished to avoid discovery, and his only hope to evade it was to merge his own aura with the crude uncontrolled power of the horse. A surprise entry of the kind he wished to achieve was only credible if it worked. Premature discovery would reveal him as a fool playing a childish game, and the disadvantage at which it would put him with the three females was shameful beyond consideration. He had hoped to learn, but instead, he would be nothing more than a laughingstock. The intensity of the females' search was palpable, like a shudder running across the surface of his mind. He leaned closer to the horse for greater camouflage. He could feel its breathing and the beat of its heart. Both were moved rapid. The horse was growing increasingly uneasy at all the unaccustomed psychic traffic around it. Renquist wanted further to calm its anxiety, but to do so would be to effectively show himself.

He could, of course, quickly and easily be found if the females applied some fairly simple lateral thinking.

They were at present looking for him, and he was confusing them by merging his aura with that of the animal. If they merely reversed the process, and read the aura of the horse, they would immediately see him through the horse's eyes, and his flamboyant scheme, that he was now starting to regret, would be undone. He knew sooner or later the idea would occur to them. He didn't know Columbine's companions, but he knew her. She might be vain, shallow, and cruel, but she wasn't stupid. It was not quite time, though, to admit failure. If he just moved fast enough, he could still carry out his plan and avoid appearing the consummate idiot.

Speed was all he had left. He formed a mental picture in his mind: stable to scullery, kitchen to corridor, two more rooms, and into the drawing room. He perceived no locked doors to bar or delay his progress, and, hoping his memory served him correctly (and no structural alterations had occured since the time of de Richleau), he made his lightning move. With the fleet paranormal rapidity only a nosferatu could summon, he threw himself headlong on this hastily plotted course in exactly the direction of the three probing auras.

Neither Destry nor Marieko were particularly fond of the two crossed sabers mounted on the wall beside the fireplace, but Columbine insisted they hang there and not be removed. Almost two hundred years earlier, the swords had been used by rival admirers in duel. The confrontation had been notable, even at the time, for its slashing, no-quarter savagery, and also for how, within three days of the formal confrontation in the grey dawn of a mist-shrouded Richmond Park, both protagonists had been dead. The young Fitzroy Dudley, a captain in the tenth Hussars, and Lord Stockdale, known to his friends as Tiger, who had called out Dudley in the first place, had carved each other so badly both had died of their wounds scant hours apart. With neither becoming her new paramour and protector, Columbine had been

forced to seek consolation by being squired to the Prince
Regent's Pavilion in Brighton by the notorious Sir Harry
Deerpark, an amusing and degenerate libertine to whom,
in her human days, she had often turned when affairs of
the heart became altogether too much for her. Harry
Deerpark could be trusted never to fall in love and never
to fight duels over women. Columbine had been all of
sixteen at the time, but she already knew a certain tangible solace could be found in the arms of a man who
made it clear from the start he would never seriously
give a damn. Now she marched to the pair of blades and
selected the one within most easy reach. "Blast it to hell,
I'm going to the stables. I'm going to find out exactly
what's going on there and put a stop to it."

She turned with the heavy sword in hand, but before
she could take a step toward the door, a small but blinding star seemed to explode from the cosmos at the exact
center of the drawing room. For a nanosecond that
seemed like an eternity, Columbine ceased to subjec-
tively exist. The searing radiation was all-consuming,
and her personality was an indivisible part of it. The very
mathematics of her being were knocked off-line, and all
was dazzling diamond blindness. Then she returned to
herself as a falling spiral, a vast, spread nebula, or maybe
the interior of a neutron—macro or micro, it didn't matter. She twisted without will or power to stop herself
until the star coalesced in colors and flame of the visible
spectrum and way beyond, still flaring like a sun, but
Columbine was at least standing again in the drawing
room, on her own feet, the fatal saber still in her hand,
although dangling uselessly by her side. Gradually the
shining aura assumed the form of a winged humanoid,
a towering majesty of flaming demigod. It flexed like
some bird of prey, giving one final display of spread and
radiating pinions, with feathers of wild lightning, and
then the wings folded, the fire was extinguished, the
glare faded to nothing. Victor Renquist stood before

them, aside from the style of his dress, exactly as Columbine remembered him: tall in a dark overcoat, leaning nonchalantly on a silver-topped cane, the long curly hair, the young but gaunt features, and those ancient eyes that left no doubt they had seen most of what it was possible to see. The hard but full-lipped mouth curved into a smile of quietly demonic humor. *"Sorori in sanguinem."*

Columbine could feel herself turning grey and starting to physically quiver with undead anger. She was still sufficiently disoriented to be distanced from her surroundings and unable to speak, but she was completely capable of hatred, and right at that moment, she hated Victor Renquist more than she had ever hated him before—and perhaps more than she had hated any other being she had ever encountered. That he should stage such a gaudy and humiliating spectacle, the only purpose of which was to demonstrate his power and her weakness, reinforced everything she had ever loathed about him. And then he had the gall to address her as sister in blood in formal Latin. For some illogical reason, the Latin fanned her fury more violently than anything else. It was the conclusive mockery, the ultimate evidence of his overweening and insolent vanity, the final straw, the cherry on the poisoned sundae. The sword in her hand meant nothing to her, otherwise she might have run Renquist through right there and then. Instead she just stood and stared, and as the drawing room came more fully back into focus, she emitted a drawn-out hiss of pure soul-spite.

"How did you ever manage to survive for so long?"

Renquist laughed. "By never doing what's expected of me."

The laugh triggered a fresh surge of rage, distorting her senses all over again, but this time, the anger failed to render her immobile. Quite the reverse. Without conscious thought, she raised the saber and advanced on Renquist until the point was just inches from his chest. "I called you here for a purpose, Victor. I intended to make use of you, but I realize I detest you too much."

"So now you intend to put that sword through my heart?"

"I really have no choice, Victor. You've done enough. You're an unchanging monster, and you must finally cease."

Renquist's mockery diminished slightly. "You propose to destroy another nosferatu? Despite all the taboos and constraints?"

"You have invaded my mind and domain. I would be justified under the laws."

Marieko stepped forward with an authoritarian warning. "Columbine. This is madness. . . ."

Renquist raised a hand, indicating that Columbine was his problem and he would deal with her. "You'd do well to heed your friend, my dear. Think seriously about this."

"I don't need to think."

And so saying, she lunged at Renquist with all the speed, precision, and expertise of an experienced swordswoman, but somehow the blade never struck its mark. In a matador move, Renquist pivoted slightly at the hips and then, striking like a snake, grasped the steel eight or nine inches back from the point. The sword had been on display too long to be particularly sharp, but nonetheless, as he tightened his grip on the curved blade, it bite deeply into the flesh of his hand. His expression didn't change, though, even when, down the length of the weapon, Columbine could feel it's edge scrape on bone.

Not content with merely stopping her lunge, Renquist began slowly and deliberately to twist the sword. Columbine resisted as best she could, but she was no match for Renquist in any trial of pure strength. Her fingers could not retain their grip on the hilt. The guard pressed on her wrist, threatening to break it. The excalating pain was too much. The saber was wrenched from her hand. Renquist held the blade for a moment and looked deep into Columbine's eyes. Then he hurled the sword away from him so it clattered against the bricks of the fireplace.

"I'm really not so easily destroyed, my dear."

A furious sob rose in Columbine's chest, and she could do nothing to prevent its shameful escape. She wanted to look away, but couldn't. Renquist was drawing her in, and, no matter how she might deny it and hide behind a screen of fury, he had the power. "Damn you, Victor! Damn you!"

Renquist sighed and permitted himself a weary smile. "I've been damned beyond all memory."

Dark nosferatu blood was running down his right hand, dripping from his fingers and making irregular splatters on the three-hundred-year-old rug on which he stood. Without breaking eye contact, he raised his bleeding hand, wounded palm outward, reversing the direction of the flow so it trickled down his wrist, soaking the cuffs of his shirt and jacket.

Marieko felt the change instantly. Something old and savage was in the room. At the sight of Renquist's blood, an atavistic and transforming presence entered, and all culture and civilization faded like a cultivated chimera. Wild nosferatu faced each other in the firelight with a threatening, wolf-pack simplicity, three females and a male, and the male was bleeding. By untamed, unutterable, feral tradition, the females had two choices. They could submit, or they could take him down. They could seize tribute and drain him, or they could pay tribute and bow to his will. Columbine's eyes were huge and dark-rimmed. Renquist seemed to hold her in total trance. Destry's gaze was fixed on the bloody hand, and her breathing was becoming progressively deeper and slower. Marieko prided herself on being the most controlled of the troika, but even she could feel her rationality and composure being rapidly eroded by the most primal appetites. She, too, stared at the still-welling, deep burgundy blood, oft-desired and usually forbidden. She was gripped by the brutal, unnameable thirst. All undead secretly shared the craving, the taking of blood from their own kind, so much more to do with elemental power than with mere survival.

Destry's breathing stopped altogether, and Marieko knew she was holding her breath, preparing to spring. A final echo from Marieko's reasoning mind urgently reminded her they were millimeters from losing everything they had planned in one savage, snarling instant of forbidden gratification. Why didn't Renquist do something? He had precipitated all this. He had created the spectacle. He had to have known they were seeking him, and his psychic pyrotechnics would have a multifold effect on their open and questing minds. He had pushed Columbine into the abyss of violent and vengeful passion and then humbled her in front of her sisters in the troika. Now he seemed to be provoking them all to the mindless extremes of bestial excess by deliberately leading them into the temptation of his blood. Was he testing them, or had he, too, succumbed to a vampire insanity? Marieko's weakening voice of civilization managed a final whisper. "Isn't existence little more than a series of tests?"

Was that it? Renquist was leading them to the old and cruel precipice, risking himself to see if they could summon the mastery of themselves and step back in the final instant? Destry's sinews were bunching and tensing. Her fangs were extending. She was never going to step back. If anything was to be salvaged, Marieko had to stop this disastrous sequence of events, but she, too, was all but hypnotized by Renquist's bleeding hand. She was immobile, unable to speak. His appearance and the aftermath had been too fast, too unexpected, and too powerful. She was almost incapable of thought. She merely and starkly hungered.

Marieko was not a great believer in external rescues in the nick of time, so when a door to normality was opened at the far end of the room by the wholly mundane figure of the thrall-butler Bolingbroke, she could scarcely believe it was not just another symptom of the madness.

"Bolingbroke?"

The appearance of the human, even such a degraded creature as the troika's thrall, created an instant transformation.

"There is a chauffeur at the door, my ladies. . . ."

Renquist whirled round so his bloody hand was not visible to the man and, at the same time, whipped a black silk handkerchief from his breast pocket and wrapped it around the wound. Destry's fangs retracted as her predator tension relaxed and dissipated. Without the direct sight of the blood, the spell was broken. Columbine tottered two paces backwards and dropped into a convenient couch in what looked to be a partial swoon. It took Marieko's presence of mind to assume control and use the interruption to restore both the contemporary and the ordinary. She found, somewhat miraculously, she could instantly adopt a normal tone of casual domestic authority. Perhaps her training went deeper than even she imagined. "A chauffeur?"

"He has Mr. Renquist's luggage."

"Thank you, Bolingbroke. You may take the bags to the room that was prepared for Mr. Renquist."

As Bolingbroke made his characteristic groveling exit, Destry actually laughed. Her powers of recovery were equally formidable. Marieko may have restored a sense of civilization, but it took Destry to break the impasse. "So what do we do now? All smoke cigarettes and avoid each others' eyes?"

"I fear I may have gone a little far."

"The word that springs to mind is *overkill*."

"Possibly."

"Possibly, you say? First you stalk us, then you give us an Armageddon mindfuck of a psychic firework display, and finally you greet us in Latin. Is this your normal modus operandi, or did you have something to prove?"

"Perhaps a measure of both, coupled with a need to restore drama to a monochrome world."

Destry laughed, but Marieko remained politely accusatory. "Or maybe you thought you would catch us off guard, and we'd reveal some terrible secret or malign design?"

Renquist nodded. "That also crossed my mind."

If Renquist hadn't felt so relaxed and comfortable, he might never had admitted such a thing, but as he sat back in the leather armchair beside the fire, with an IV feed of whole blood flowing into his left arm and a balloon glass of superior cognac in his right hand, he felt at his most expansive since he'd left California. The ghost energy of the transfusion tingled softly through his now-weary metabolism, and the situation was further eased by Columbine deciding to sequester herself in another part of the house, declaring that she'd had quite enough of Victor Renquist for one evening. Renquist was now well aware the centuries had done little to mellow Columbine, and she was still a dangerous—even deadly—child he had now antagonized all over again, and he was relieved to have her at least temporarily at a distance. She had departed with a warning exit line delivered for full effect from the doorway. "Be careful of him. He'll try to win you over with his charm and cheap tricks. He's millennium slick."

After the fortuitous interruption by the thrall, the Oriental woman, Marieko, the one in the futuristic attire and with one breast exposed, took charge of the amenities and conventions of hospitality. Once Columbine had flounced from the room, she had approached Renquist and bowed. *"Fratri in sanguinem,* I am Marieko Matsunaga. We spoke on the telephone."

Renquist also bowed, but carefully so as not to bend

quite so low as Marieko had. "*Konnichiha*, Marieko-san."

With the formalities properly observed, Marieko turned to the matter of Renquist's welfare. "Does your hand require attention?"

Renquist shook his head. "No. It's already almost healed."

Now the other one joined her, the tall female with the chestnut hair, who wore a man's black tuxedo with satin lapels and high, scarlet heels. "But you've lost blood."

Renquist couldn't deny this, or that he was feeling a certain weakness. "That's true."

"It should be replaced."

Renquist was at something of a loss to locate the woman's accent. English was her first language, but the vowels were either Australian, or from one of the former British possessions in southern Africa. Perhaps Kenya or Rhodesia, but much modified by considerable travel. "Won't that put you to some considerable trouble?"

She had a hard and direct practicality, as if she had spent at lot of time moving among military men, perhaps mercenaries or guerrillas. "We can't offer you live prey tonight, but if a blood pack from County General would suffice, that's easily done."

"A blood pack would be perfect."

The tall woman paused at the door before going about her errand. "The name's Destry Maitland, by the way, and yes. I've been all over. Not for as long as you, but I've seen my share."

Renquist made a mental note to maintain caution around Destry Maitland. Admittedly he was tired, but she had just scanned his mind without him knowing, and that was no meager trick. She returned in a matter of minutes with a plastic pack of thawed blood, the needle, the tubes, and the rest of the modern paraphernalia. Apparently the Ravenkeep troika's survival system was nearly identical to the one maintained by the colony in Los Angeles. By some probably criminal maneuver, they obtained packs of frozen blood from a local hospital, but also regularly hunted live prey, to head off the perilously psychotic, killing-hunger that triggered the uncontrollable phenomenon known as Feasting. As Marieko rigged the transfusion, Destry went to what could only be a conventional liquor cabinet. "Can I pour you a brandy, Victor? You don't mind if I call you Victor, do you?"

"Not in the least."

"So?"

"Yes, I'd like a brandy."

"You drink alcohol regularly, or are you just being polite?"

"Quite regularly. I enjoy the sensation."

"Good on you, Victor. I like a man who drinks."

Renquist found Destry Maitland highly refreshing after the hothouse, self-indulgent theatrics of Columbine. "If it's not an inappropriate question, when you do take live prey—"

"Where do we go for it?"

Destry smiled, swirled the brandy in her glass, and inhaled the bouquet. "Well, of course, Mistress Columbine has her playthings, her gilded young men. Which I suppose can be a hazardous flirtation, but she manages to get away with it."

Marieko's face was impassive. "Columbine has an almost supernatural propensity for getting away with it."

Destry continued. "Marieko and I, on the other hand, usually head north in the night."

"North?"

Marieko explained. "A number of depressed industrial towns within easy enough reach for hunting."

"We cull the unhappy of the herd. The unemployed and Maggie's Girls."

"Maggie's Girls?" Renquist had never heard the expression.

"It's a colloquial legacy of the eighties. Bottom-rung street prostitutes. Maggie's Girls from northern towns so decimated by the late Lady Thatcher's economic policies they never recovered."

"And how do you dispose of the dead?"

Marieko's expression and aura were unreadable. "We had a full crematorium furnace installed in one of the cellars a number of years ago."

"Indeed." Renquist was impressed. It would make a lot of sense to have something similar at the Residence in California.

"We are reasonably well organized."

Renquist looked around the room and then sipped his cognac. "So it would seem."

"But like all nosferatu, we collect things."

"You should see my library."

Marieko inclined her head deferentially. "I would very much like to see your library if ever that was possible."

Destry again inhaled her brandy, as if she enjoyed breathing the spirit rather than actually drinking it. "Marieko is our resident academic."

"I have already admired her calligraphy."

Marieko covered her face in a gesture of modesty. "I am but an amateur."

Renquist gestured to Marieko's extensive tattoo of waves and sea demons that ran from her right wrist, over her shoulder, and down to her tiny breast. "You're tattoos are very beautiful. They remind me of the work of the great Yoshiwara."

Marieko laughed a trifle nervously. "That is possibly because they were drawn by his grandson."

Renquist realized the laugh contained what might be a warning. Even if it was only Yoshiwara's grandson who had created the body art, she would still have survived those chaotic times of brutal Japan civil-strife of the seventeenth and eighteenth centuries in which he himself had once been briefly but bloodily embroiled. He knew nothing of this female's background, not even her age, but it was possible they had been with different warring factions. It seemed, this early in their acquaintance, probably a good idea to avoid the subject of their individual histories in the long and troubled time that followed the Onin War. He decided it was time to change the subject, not only as an exercise in mannered delicacy, but also because the time had come to raise the subject of why he was there in the first place. "On the subject of calligraphy, you said in your third letter that these human archaeologists, the ones conducting the excavation at Morton Downs, had discovered a fragment of mica?"

"That is correct."

"And it bore a single character of the flame script?"

Marieko and Destry looked at each other, both hesitating before Marieko answered. "A single *nya*."

Renquist pretended he hadn't noticed the hesitation. "Any writing on mica has, by definition, to be very old indeed. Possibly from the lost ages of the Nephilim and the Original Beings. A full fifteen thousand years."

The two females again seemed reluctant to reply, and Renquist looked at them questioningly. "Would you be more comfortable talking about this if and when Columbine finally rejoins us?"

Destry and Marieko stared at each other. He could tell from their auras a silent debate was taking place, but good manners dictated he neither probe nor scan. Finally Destry voiced what was obviously a mutual decision. "Columbine is responsible for her own behavior. We can at least fill you in on the details. It seems only fair after you've come all this way."

Marieko glanced briefly at the beamed ceiling, as though she knew Columbine was almost certainly somewhere upstairs eavesdropping on every word. "The mica fragment was clearly a shard of a much larger piece. Its triangular shape suggested it was a corner fragment from a larger rectangular sheet."

"Do you have the fragment?"

Marieko shook her head. "I had the chance to remove it, but to do so seemed unwise. The humans have no idea what it is, but they are well aware it's an anomaly, an object that definitely doesn't belong in any Bronze Age burial site. To steal it would have been too obvious, and the police would almost certainly have become involved."

Renquist allowed his aura to indicate that he agreed Marieko had made the most sensible decision, but he still regretted that such a relic should be in the hands of humans. "And no other fragments have been found?"

"Not as yet, but the humans still have not penetrated that far into the mound."

"So there may be more?"

"I would expect so."

Renquist thought about this. The more he learned, the more he felt a definite sense of urgency. "I presume it's too late to go to this place tonight."

Destry didn't have to consult a clock to know the night was hardly young. "We would never make it there and back before the dawn."

"Tomorrow?"

"Definitely tomorrow."

"Then perhaps, in the meantime, you could describe how you first came to learn of this fragment."

The situation was clearly one in which words were simply too cumbersome and time consuming. She simply opened her mind and let Renquist view her full recall of the discovery. It had been the fourth of her nocturnal visits to the excavation, and the first time she had arrived to find a human still at the dig. Her usual schedule was to leave Ravenkeep in the Range Rover a little after midnight. By that hour, Dr. Campion and his student excavators had departed for wherever they spent the night, but this time was different. Fortunately she had seen the light before she'd detected any other clue to a lingering human. She had quickly parked the Range Rover far enough away so that whoever might be working late would not be alerted by the sound of the engine.

Leaving the truck, she had sped over the springy down-land turf, only slowing down when she was near to the tent, where a single figure was working alone by an electric light that was powered by a small portable generator. Gently manipulating his mind so he would not become aware of her presence, she probed his thoughts from a distance, and the first thing she discovered was that this human was none other than Dr. Campion himself, and, right at that moment, he was a worried man.

William Campion, Ph.D., was a man of modest ambition. He was of middle age, in his early forties, and his sandy hair was thinning as fast as his youthful dreams of glory. Where once he had made brave protestations, at least to himself, that he would one day make a major contribution to the sum total of human knowledge, he was now bleakly satisfied with his secure tenure at Wessex University, the prospect of a small body of published work, and a comfortable retirement. Initially, the excavation at Morton Downs had been mundanely routine. Dr. Campion had embarked on the project as little more than an exercise for his graduate students and a chance for him to oversee the work, looking authoritative in his faded blue jeans and corduroy shirt, and maybe catch the attention of one of the more attractive young female volunteers. The dig had remained as mundane as expected until, in one of the early trenches, the mica fragment had come to light. Since neither the material nor the sophistication of the processing seemed to have any relation to the Bronze Age, and the single written character burned into the thing appeared to be of a language he had never encountered before, it worried him. Such an object shouldn't have been there, and Campion had reached the age and disposition to distrust anything that turned up where it shouldn't logically be.

What seemed to worry the man most was how he might explain such an anomalous discovery to a set of skeptical and potentially hostile colleagues. The piece of mica had been unearthed in a layer of subsoil that totally precluded it having come to the site at a later time, and yet, to believe that such an object might be contemporary with or, worse still, even older than the burial mound could start the kind of furor in the fundamentally conservative world of archeology that constituted Campion's worst scholastic nightmare. Public revelation of things that didn't ought to be could consign one to the intellectual hell reserved for those who claimed the Great Pyramid was built by aliens or that Atlantis had existed off the coast of Bimini. Such controversy could also destroy reputations, threaten tenure, and generally reduce one to the status of laughingstock. Of course, Marieko was well aware of how the Great Pyramid had been constructed; she knew exactly what had been off Bimini, and she held the benighted human ideas of history in nothing less than complete contempt—but she was not about to enlighten Campion. His problems were none of her concern. Marieko's first instinct was simply to take the mica fragment, by force if necessary, and make an end to the matter. Fortunately, she had the foresight to be aware that rudimentary theft would not be the end of the matter, and she also quickly discovered, by a deeper scan of Campion's mind, that the fragment was no longer at the dig. In his fear of the unexplained, he had sent it back to his lab at the university while he pondered his subsequent moves. Campion was apprehensive of what he might find next, and until a solution presented itself, his best idea was to tighten operations at the dig to prevent any premature disclosure and to face whatever might come next when it presented itself.

The student Campion had made responsible for taking the object back to the lab at the university was a twenty-year-old Jamaican studying for his master's. He was called Winston "Youth" Shakespeare, and sported red, green, and black tie-dye, a full head of dreadlocks, and a near genius IQ concealed beneath Rastafarian ganja patois. Marieko had already abandoned the idea of stealing the fragment—totally impractical—but she definitely wanted to examine it herself and not just rely on Campion's imprecise impression. The easiest and most direct course would be to intercept this Shakespeare and either get him to bring the fragment to her or take her to the fragment. As it turned out, the latter option proved the most practical. Interception was easy. Wessex University was hardly crowded with full-dress Rastas, and Youth Shakespeare required little luring away from his studies when the lurer was a hot if enigmatic Japanese. In a country pub just outside of Casterbridge, and afterwards in the boy's rattletrap Ford Fiesta, she had first seduced him and then blanked out his mind. Under her full control, he had led her to Campion's lab.

One look confirmed what she'd already seen in Campion's mind. The character on the mica was the *nya* of the nosferatu flame script. While the young Jamaican stood blank-eyed, she had stared at the object with a reverential awe. So reverential, in fact, her control on him momentarily slipped. He'd stirred briefly, and she had to swiftly clamp him down before turning back to the tiny, postage-stamp-size link with an impossible past. No doubt, the piece of mica was as old as the nosferatu themselves. A fabulous remnant of the days when the great starships of the Nephilim had hung in orbit and the shuttlecraft had risen and descended on the vast spaceport of Baalbek. It dated back to those colonial days when the Great Ones from the stars had conducted their genetic experiments on the native hominids, creating the Original Beings—the failed biotech warriors who'd been the forebears of all modern nosferatu, current *Homo sapiens,* and much more besides. The obvious implication was that, in some way Marieko couldn't even guess, long-vanished nosferatu, or at least some kind of unknown but close kin, had once used the burial mound either as a refuge or, at least, as a cache for their valuables.

The temptation to take the tiny piece of mica and disappear into the night was almost overwhelming, but

Marieko had resisted, loath as she was to leave such a treasure in the possession of a human. For the time being, secrecy was more important than ownership even of such a unique object. She also resisted the secondary temptation to feed from the student. Since she had become engrossed in archeology, her feeding had been, at best, perfunctory—but she let the boy be. Aside from the commotion his disappearance would cause, she was firm on the maxim that it never paid to mix business and necessity. Planting a small bookmark in his mind so she could locate him if she needed him, she had left him sufficiently immobilized that he remained standing, stiff and uncomprehending, for a couple of more hours and then came to with a headache and a false, guilt-ridden memory of how he had drunk too much while on an important errand for Dr. Campion.

"I hope you agree I handled the circumstance correctly."

"You appear to have handled it perfectly."

Marieko inclined her head and shoulders in what amounted to a seated bow in acknowledgment of Renquist's praise. "You are very kind."

"I am merely stating the truth. You assessed the situation and acted accordingly. I could have done no better myself."

Destry frowned. "I don't like the idea of such an article being in humans' hands."

Renquist agreed. "I don't like it either, but it doesn't, in itself, present any real threat. From what Marieko has observed, this Campion, despite his education, is an intellectual coward with a second-rate mind. The most exceptional of humans would be hard-pressed to glean any information from a single character. Even de Richleau, whom Columbine knew well, was never able to decipher the flame script, and he had an entire book to work from. Our real problem is not the single fragment—it's whatever else may lie under that mound."

Marieko attempted to keep her aura absolutely blank,

but the slightest flicker betrayed her. Renquist's face hardened. "You know something?"

She avoided his eyes. "I sensed something."

"Something alive?"

"I'm not sure."

"How can you expect me to work with you if you withhold what might be crucial information?"

Destry quickly intervened on Marieko's behalf. "Hold up, there, Victor. You can't expect us to tip off our entire hand in one go."

Renquist made no secret of his nascent anger. "I came to this place at considerable risk and expense. It wasn't to play a game of bluff and counterbluff."

Destry stood her ground. "So what was your big entrance all about?"

Renquist could not help but smile. "Yes, I suppose you have me there."

"So?"

"So we call it even and lay all our cards on the table." Renquist turned his attention to Marieko. "You believe something is inside that mound, but you're not sure if it's alive?"

Marieko looked down at the rug on the floor that still showed the dark drop stains of Renquist's blood. "The first time I went to Morton Downs, I sensed something; a power."

"A power?"

"Not human and not of our kind, but . . ."

"But?"

"But perhaps related to our kind."

Renquist considered this. "I think I should look at this place as soon as possible. Is that all you have to tell me?"

This time the flicker of aura betrayed both the females. "Well?"

"Columbine had been having these dreams."

"Dreams?" Even before he asked, he knew neither Marieko nor Destry was going to elaborate.

"Columbine will have to tell you about her dreams."

Marieko nodded. "It would not be appropriate for us to do such a thing."

Victor Renquist suddenly felt exceedingly tired. "I understand."

All three of them seemed to share the fatigue. Destry went once more to the liquor cabinet. "Can I pour you another brandy before the dawn."

Renquist nodded. "I'd be grateful."

"And then Marieko can show you to your room."

Marieko rose and bowed. "I'd be honored."

CHAPTER THREE

When Renquist awoke, he found Marieko gone. All that remained was a small origami dragon placed on the pillow, two curls of paper representing the smoke and fire of its breath. He was mildly surprised. It could only be maybe fifteen or twenty minutes after the moment of sunset. The transcontinental flight had slightly distorted his time sense, but not to such an extent that he would drastically oversleep while the household, in which he was a somewhat undefined guest, was up and about its business. He sat up and found that he was still in total and somewhat airless darkness. After a moment of disorientation, he realized the heavy tapestry curtains enclosing the massive Elizabethan four-poster canopy bed were still closed. They rattled on their antique wooden rings as he drew them back, and, swinging his legs over the side of the bed, he looked around the room. He'd had little chance to observe his accommodations in the prelude to the previous dawn. Marieko had led him to the upstairs room by the light of a guttering candle and then, slipping out of her already sufficiently revealing clothing, made it clear that she intended to stay and share the huge bed with him. He'd found both the act and the assumption he'd welcome her diurnal company a little surprising, but if such was her desire, and also the custom of the house and the troika, he had decided he'd be a churl to object. As she'd eased off her metallic leather jeans, he discovered she bore a second, smaller piece of body art on her left thigh. Although the crossed axe pattern enclosed in a perfect double circle looked more like a functional brand of ownership or fealty than decoration, it also warned him that, sometime in the past, she had been the creature of the Yarabachi clan, and, technically, the two of them had been natural enemies in the days of the shogunates.

He'd also discovered the servants had laid out his traveling things; the fur rug was spread like a cover on the four poster, and Marieko, once undressed, had crawled over it, fondling the fur with a childlike delight. "This is very old, I think?"

"Indeed it is."

"And you travel with it always?"

"Correct."

"You are a male who enjoys a single sense of continuity wherever he may rest?"

"You could have read my mind."

"I assure you I didn't."

Renquist, having divested himself of his own clothing, joined Marieko on the fur. She drew shut the curtains of the formidable piece of furniture, adding an extra density of darkness and enclosing them in what was almost another small private chamber of their own. She then turned and embraced him, arms immediately encircling him, pressing her body close to his. Time was long, extremely long, since Renquist had engaged in even an approximation of human sex, unless one counted the telepathic sleight of erotic hand he regularly practiced on potential prey or others he wished to bring under his control. If Marieko was not aware of this already, he made it no secret, and he let the fact be clearly reflected in his aura to avoid any later misunderstandings. Her instant response, however, indicated that such a confusion was not a possibility. "Do not worry, Victor-san. Just look on this as a physical welcome to our Residence. What might be considered a tradition of the Priory."

Renquist wasn't sure if he believed her, and when he woke, in the wake of the vivid and highly perverse dreams that seemed to have occupied his entire day's sleep, he was even less certain. As far as he could tell, the dreams had begun immediately, commencing by caressing him, stroking his mind to a more than mortal ecstasy immediately as his consciousness had withdrawn, and then, by way of extreme contrast, plunging him into a welter of unfocused and mindless violence. The first dream—or if the whole day was to be considered as a single epic vision, the first phase of the dream—was a deceptive sanctuary of calm tranquillity. He made his entry to the dreamstate in a walled garden, and, although he had no solid information to substantiate it, he knew he was sometime in the past, in Japan, and, as far as he could tell, somewhere inside Edo Castle, the stronghold of the great Shogun Tokugawa Ieyasu, in what was now Tokyo. This indicated he was most probably in the early seventeenth century, at approximately the same time as, in the real world, he had arrived there in the hold of a Portuguese merchantman, after a series of events he still found close to unfathomable.

The garden was a place of quiet delicacy, despite the monumental stone blocks and heavy balks of timber that were the basic form of its surrounding military construction. A cherry tree in bloom stood beside a fast-flowing, man-made stream that created a high melodic splashing while, beneath the surface, very old and lazy carp took their leisure. The stream was spanned by a miniature bridge, which he knew he was supposed to cross. In the dream he was dressed in a simple black kimono, and in the sash at his waist he carried the self-same Bushido sword that was among his luggage back at the Savoy, the one given him by Hideo Matsutani, the legendary undead swordsman of Kyoto. He suspected the back of his kimono bore the red trefoil of the Kenzu Clan, to whom Hideo had owed his fealty. Renquist knew much of the content of the dream was being fed to him directly from the mind of Marieko, who, in the physical world, held him tightly to her. It could have been a purely random occurrence, but the segment of Renquist's consciousness that knew he was dreaming, and remained fully analytical, doubted this. The dream experience was too aptly contrived, and, if that was the case, Marieko Matsunaga was an extreme rarity among the undead. She was a vision-shifter, a dreamwright, an manipulatrix of unconscious fantasy, and, as such, a dangerously powerful individual. Perhaps it was a gift, or maybe an acquired discipline. Either way, he should, in the future, treat her with the most extreme circumspection.

As if to confirm his speculation, a dream-Marieko sat formally cross-legged beneath the cherry tree, as if waiting for him. Her hands were concealed in the sleeves of a white kimono that seemed to glow with its own internal light. Her eyes were cast down, and her breathing was so slow and shallow that he wondered if she were in a trance. She looked up, however, as he crossed the bridge, and smiled. "So you have finally come, Victor-san. Even though you are bound to the Kenzu, and I am of the Yarabachi."

So Marieko knew that they had been on opposing sides centuries earlier. Was she about to weave this strand of truth into some Romeo-and-Juliet fantasy of doomed lovers—and, if so, how doomed? Renquist answered carefully. Even in dreams, caution was advisable, and in a dream like this, it should be multiplied by many additional factors. "I am here, but whether I came or was brought is something I have yet to conclude."

Marieko continued to smile. "In the end, does it really matter?"

"I suppose not. Although it might say much about my freedom of will."

Marieko's face was expressionless under its geisha makeup. "Does your freedom of will concern you?"

"I try to shape my own destiny."

"Is your will sufficiently free to release control and follow mine?"

"To where?"

"What is an adventure if it doesn't commence with a secret?"

Marieko held out a hand, and Renquist, without thought or hesitation, grasped it. Instantly he was elsewhere. The second phase was a place of shadows where he was soon to be a principal participant in a highly inhuman coupling. Alone and naked, he lay bound, strapped down with leather thongs at his wrists and ankles, bound to a bed of swords, identical blades, razor edges upward, racked precisely at four-inch intervals on a rectangular frame of black wood lacquered to a mirror finish. To avoid fatally slicing himself into strips of flesh, he was forced to extend the discipline of the fakir to a quantum degree, a torture of focus and an energy drain of near levitation.

"Do not move, Victor-san. Do not move at all, my love from the Kenzu, or the swords will cut your flesh clear to your naked spine."

At first he couldn't see her. He again knew instinctively they were still in Edo Castle, although he wasn't sure if it was the same time-space. Now he was deep in the bowels of the great fortress, in a dungeon so deep maybe only demons and the undead frequented it. Somewhere to his left, flames licked and leapt from the coals of an iron brazier, bathing everything, including his own nosferatu corpse-body, in an infernal red-orange light. It was as though the Shogun Tokugawa had comissioned the building of his very own hell.

"What am I doing here?"

"You are doing absolutely nothing, my love. As I just said, do not even move."

Her voice came from somewhere in the red-dark, beyond even his peripheral vision. He didn't dare turn his head and seek her presence. Even at perfect rest, the edges of the swords threatened to split his skin. "Would you care to explain?"

"It is a devised experience, my love. I hoped it would prove a challenge even for you who has done so much and known so many."

Now she was in his sight. Her body was oiled, and the tattoos gleamed in the firelight. Her hair was tied up into a samurai topknot. To say she was clothed was something of an overstatement. Protected was a better word. Her hands and forearms, knees and calves were sheathed in light steel mail over leather, a broad belt of similar material cinched her waist, and the armored ensemble was completed by a wide collar covering her throat. She was also masked. A blank expression wrought in what looked to be highly polished silver replaced her face. As she walked determinedly toward him, she adopted a stride in complete contrast to the usual short subservient steps of Japanese courtesans. Renquist realized, with a degree of horror, her intention was to straddle his body on the bed of swords and consummate a form of carnal interaction during which the slightest movement on his part, voluntary or involuntary, could result in, if not his actual destruction, at least some decidedly horrible wounds. To admit an unaccustomed level of fear was more than Renquist cared to do. Enough of his mind remained detached to remind him all was just a dream—at worse a test, at best a game. He would endure, and, since he appeared to have little choice in the matter, he might as well quite literally lie back and do his best to derive what satisfaction he could from Marieko's "devised experience."

Her body was not only oiled, but also perfumed, and

the sweet musky scent overwhelmed him as she carefully
mounted the bench, balancing deftly on the edges of the
swords with her armored knees and the palms of her
hands. With the physical precision of a highly trained
gymnast, she swung one leg over his body and lowered
herself so she was seated across his hips. Her naked
thighs grasped him with an unexpected firmness and authority for so slight a figure. She leaned forward so she
was lying along the length of his torso, although not
bringing the whole of her weight to bear. Her tiny
breasts touched his chest, her undead nipples hard and
her concealed face close to his. Her breathing was audible and rasped slightly as though amplified by the
mask. Fire reflected in the distorting curves of its mir-
rored surface. He noticed a tiny silver teardrop, crafted
by the unknown silversmith who had made the thing, as
though it had just welled from the inner corner of the
dark, right-hand eye-slit—a cliché, maybe, but he found
it fitting.

To remain absolutely motionless or suffer the razor-
sharp blades was being made far from easy by Marieko.
She moved on top of him, and he began to feel a long-
forgotten sensual stirring, decidedly more human than
nosferatu. She was actually taking him to at least a ghost
memory of long-lost human passion. He was definitely
not in control of this dream, but, almost to his chagrin,
he was beginning to enjoy not only the risky tactile experience, but also the actual passivity. To Renquist's
complete surprise, he actually heard himself moan softly.
Marieko responded with a sigh. "So how does vulnerability feel, Victor-san?"

He wished he could see her face behind the mask.
"Why are you doing this?"

"Does it not please you?"

"It pleases me, but . . ."

"But a part of your mind still wonders?"

He would not admit it, but of course it did. A questing
and rational part of his brain wanted answers. Was this

strange and customized dream-scenario an allegorical
warning he had yet fully to grasp, or a cover as the
deeper areas of his mind were probed for his plans and
intentions? And, indeed, was all this purely the work of
Marieko on her own, or a concerted triple threat in con-
cert with Columbine and Destry? After the way Columbine had behaved in the real world—all the business
of attempting to run him through with the saber, and
then her furious exit—he could hardly believe she was
in any frame of mind to contribute to this dreamstate
imagination. This did not exclude, however, the strong
possibility of Marieko being the actual dreamweaver, but
charged to report back all she learned to the full troika.
Also not precluded was the chance Destry might be lurking unseen somewhere in the fantasy, probing his mind
as deeply as she was able to delve without being detected. One, two, or three, if they truly believed a mere
shadow play of half-forgotten sexuality would unlock his
secrets, his only response was "Think again, my dears."
More than a sleeping illusion of weird erotica was
needed to pry loose the private schemes of Victor Renquist.

Marieko must have sensed either his questioning detachment or instinctive resistance because her hips thrust
down upon him harder and with more determined intensity than before, as though she now rode his body with
a corrective authority, to impose such discipline on his
mind as she thought fitting. With an unconscious recalci-
trance, he met this motion of command with a counter-
thrust of his own. He had no sooner moved, though, when
he felt a blade bite into his back, breaking a three-inch
section of skin and causing blood to flow. He was so
instantly aware of his overreaching error, he didn't need
Marieko's whispered reminder. "I warned you, my love,
even the slightest movement exacts its penalty."

Fresh flesh wounds very quickly became Renquist's
only way of measuring the passage of time in the dreamstate. How long the experience was set to last defied

even the most approximate guesswork. Marieko seemed
to have precipitated him into an eternity of slow and
painfully voluptuous teasing that, each time he was provoked to a response, carved another slice into his bleeding body. Although he couldn't see them, puddles of
blood were already forming on the flagstones beneath
the bed of swords, spreading, soon to become a single
pool. Perhaps the slow but languorous weakening might
have gone on until he was actually consumed by the
dream, and Marieko would have revealed a true dominion over the arts of the succubus, if the situation had not
abruptly and radically changed.

The fanged group of ninja came out of nowhere. He
heard a snarl from behind the silver mask, which indicated they were absolutely not of Marieko's conjuring.
The creatures were more easily distinguished by their
smoke trails of visibly destructive vibrations than by
their actual forms. Their glowing red eyes served as the
finite centers of their shadowy, exterminating-demon
presence. An agony of immobility was suddenly transformed into a violent and whirling vortex of motion. The
ninja came with a full variety of weapons to cut, impale,
or stab: pikes and lances, axes, swords and daggers of
all lengths and shapes. Somewhere above and beyond
the confines of the dungeon and the walls of the fortress,
Renquist could hear the dull crump of what had to be
large siege guns, as though the castle itself was under
attack. It was the wrong technology for the wrong culture in the wrong era, but Renquist didn't expect total
authenticity in any dreamstate, and the sound of the guns
definitely added to the sense of menace and impending
doom. The undead ninja themselves might be elusive
figures, hooded and robed, but the surgical finish on the
cutting edges of their deadly steel glittered in the dancing flames of the brazier. Renquist reminded himself that
all was but a dream, and yet the purpose of the ninja
seemed too deliberate. If cut down in what was so
clearly an outside attack, he and Marieko might not re-

turn to the waking world with their minds and bodies totally intact. A dream—but he was convinced the danger should be taken seriously.

Marieko obviously felt the same way. She rose from the bed as though by a form of speed levitation, but not without badly gashing her thigh on the exposed edge of one of the swords. She didn't, however, appear to notice the injury, and dropped to her feet in a defensive posture, fully ready to face the undead ninja alone if need be. Blood streamed down her leg, but twin-bladed butterfly knives appeared in both her hands. Renquist didn't know if the weapons had been somehow sheathed in the armor on her forearms or if she had simply dream-invoked them in response to the emergency. Right then, though, he didn't especially care. He was free of her weight but still bound at the wrists and ankles, and functionally helpless. In any normal setting, he should have easily been able to rip himself free from any restraint of wood and leather, but the dream environment appeared to have been adjusted to render him unnaturally helpless. Fortunately, though, the environment itself was under attack. As he watched, the smoke-trail vibrations of the ninja had a direct and corrosive effect on the dream's reality. As blades clashed, striking electric sparks in the gloom, and Marieko, plainly a consummate martial artist, faced two and even three ninja at a time, previously indestructible stone pillars were being eaten away like soft chalk by the enemy backwash. A swirl of dark foulness wafted across the bed frame that was holding him fast. He felt the stubborn bonds weaken, and he wrenched at them with all his might. It was time to exert his own dream control.

The strap holding his right wrist snapped first, and after it, the others were disposed of in less than a second. Now he, too, was on his feet, first ripping two swords loose from his bed frame of love and torture, and then swinging round to face the enemy, spraying blood as he turned. He moved close to Marieko, covering her back with his whirling blades. For a while, their almost balletic, high-speed moves kept the ninja at bay. Jeté, pirouette, and slash with the backhand stroke, but—although they coordinated perfectly and cut down the attackers by the dozens, blades describing bright afterimage arcs in the air around them—the enemy kept coming as though part of an inexhaustible supply, and they found themselves being pressed back, constantly on the defensive.

Renquist also began to feel he was at a distinct disadvantage. Even with a weapon in each hand, a naked man in a sword fight is uncomfortably akin to the long-tailed cat in the old American adage that finds itself in a roomful of rocking chairs. Marieko's scanty armor left her almost as exposed, but he saw no chivalrous reason why he should remain that way. In dreams, no matter who designed the original configuration, many more things were possible than in harsh reality. In the real world, nosferatu shape-shifting had been a lost art for millennia. In a dream, who knew? Renquist concentrated and willed himself to assume the form of one of the Original Beings, the ancestors of all contemporary nosferatu, the genetically engineered warrior subspecies of Nephilim experiments fifteen thousand years in the past. The Original Beings had proved a disaster for their alien creators, but in this context, their remnants in Renquist's DNA might prove to be his dreamstate salvation. He fixed on all that he could detect of the ancient ones inside himself and willed it to rise.

Initially all he experienced was indescribable pain as his entire skeleton ground and groaned, the long bones in his legs and arms, and individual vertebrae extending so his height increased by a full ten inches. The shape of his skull altered, and fangs projected down into his mouth. His skin thickened to an armored hide; his fingers became talons. Finally his mind clouded with a subliterate, hostile fury, and he knew nothing but an inbred rage. This thing he had become in no way thought the way Renquist did. Indeed, it hardly thought at all in the accepted sense. Its sole motivation was to damage and destroy its enemies and to protect and assist Marieko, whom it saw as a partner and confederate. His swords fell from claws unable to properly wield them, and he advanced on the ninja with a grunt and a snarl, ready to do battle with nothing more than his natural assets. Although Renquist was beyond perceiving it, his transformation had an immediate and unexpected effect on the attacking ninja. They actually fell back, as if his dream-state shape-shifting had given pause to whoever or whatever was creating the invasion.

He seized the nearest one and simply ripped its head from its body. The Original Beings had been supremely powerful but highly lacking in precise refinement. Indeed, their implacable brutality had made them totally uncontrollable and prompted the Nephilim to declare their creation a failure, attempting to exterminate it with deathrays and sunbombs. Mercifully for the continuing survival of nosferatu-kind, the mutant cleansing was less than a total success, and the genetic foundation of the few survivors had remained intact—if diluted—clear down to the contemporary undead.

The thing Renquist had become seemed satisfied with its first kill and repeated the decapitation process, this time with two of the enemy, simply grabbing a head in each clawed hand and twisting. Its intense and relentless ferocity relegated Marieko, despite her exquisite handling of the butterfly knives, to a secondary role of protecting the Being from ninja attempting to work their way behind him. Most of the time she succeeded, but one ninja, although she had managed to disarm him, leapt onto Renquist's back, sinking its long yellow fangs into his armored hide and hanging on like a pit bull.

At first, the beast Renquist had become failed to notice the tenacious attacker, but finally pain and the insistent weight made itself known through the singular will to slaughter. The Original Being let out a bellow of rage and sought to dislodge the attacker by the simple but effective maneuver of spinning rapidly round. Executing a tyrannosaur windmill, both arms extended like rotating hammers, the beast not only whirled loose its immediate opponent but also felled two more with its huge fists. On a superficial level, Marieko and Renquist's beast were holding their own, if not actually prevailing against the seemingly endless inhuman waves of attackers, but unfortunately, the fight itself was severely damaging the very vision-fabric of the dream. Its reality had become increasingly tenuous, shimmering and undulating like the air over a heated highway. Structure was misshaped and twisted into the outlandish and angular distortion of a German Expressionist movie. Had Renquist been himself, he would have known instantly the dreamstate was fragmenting into nightmare and recalled how being caught in a fragment of nightmare could be a shortcut to madness. Shifted as he was, though, into the Original Being, he was insensible to everything but the enemy at hand. He hardly heard Marieko, even when she started screaming at him.

"Victor-san! You must shift back."

The sound of his name caused a dull recognition, but it only hung and twisted in the void his intelligence had vacated when he'd changed form.

"Change back now, Victor-san. We have to leave this place. We remain at our peril."

Fortunately, as the dreamstate spoiled, so did Renquist's faux ability to shape-shift. He started to revert to his normal, quasi-human form. Now he suffered the pain of return.

"Victor, we have to get out of here."

"I . . ."

For immeasurable moments, the blind agony was too great for him to move or speak. The dark and indistinct ninja closed in a circle around them but waited, as though savoring the moment, anticipating, before they moved to end it all with the final kill. At the same time, the siege guns fell silent.

"Victor-san, help me. I don't know if I can find a means of escape."

Renquist looked at the vaporous ring of black swordsmen. His head still hurt where the fangs had protruded and his skull had changed its form, and he saw no reason to be charming or even polite to Marieko. "There ought to be some kind of penalty—"

"What?"

"—exacted of those who interfere in the dreaming of others and then fail to provide an adequate exit."

Still the deadly encirclement held and waited. Marieko looked round helplessly. "I stand humiliated, Victor-san."

"And so you should. You were taught well, but not well enough."

Renquist stared intently at a single spot on the floor. A corner where four of the dungeon flagstones met. "Let go of any control you may still have over this."

"But Victor-san—"

"Just do it. Now!"

Marieko closed her eyes. Renquist concentrated for a few more moments and then snapped at Marieko. "Open your eyes and look."

A whirlpool of matter had opened at their feet. Marieko was unable to prevent a sharp gasp of shock as she began to fall. Renquist actually laughed. "In every dream, there's a way out—no matter how crude. Remember that."

"But where are we falling to?"

"To simple oblivion. Which is where I intend to remain all the way to sunset."

And, indeed, he did remain in simple oblivion until after sunset, when he woke to find the origami dragon and Marieko departed. Perhaps it was just as well she'd left. To face each other in reality, after such dreamstate intensity, would require a degree of effort beyond him so early in the night, and following the Jungian day they had just experienced.

"I left him sleeping. What else was I supposed to do?" Marieko strongly resented the other two putting her on the defensive. "Something invaded the creation. Something external, deliberate, and overtly hostile."

"But not overly skilled at dreamweaving?"

"The ninja were crudely crafted, like something out of a bad Hong Kong movie."

"More force than finesse?"

"The illusion relied on speed and motion, a smoke mirage of indistinct fury. Beyond that, it was pure cliché. Their eyes even glowed red."

Columbine came close to a sneer. "But, of course, your vision of Edo Castle was perfect in every detail."

Marieko turned the near-insult back on her. "Naturally. What else would you expect? I had a job to do, and I did it."

"But you succeeded in learning nothing."

"I learned that no single one of us should attempt to challenge Victor Renquist. Much the same lesson as you learned last night when you tried to run him through with a saber."

Destry glared at Columbine and Marieko. "Will you two knock it off?"

The troika had gathered in Columbine's bedroom. She had insisted. Marieko would have preferred to meet in the kitchen, as she and Destry had always done in the first important hour after sunset. It was a time when stock was taken, missions considered, plans and lists made, and plots hatched. Columbine had always lacked the early rising, practical determination of her two companions. All too often she would be content to loiter in slow and sprawling serpentine dalliance with her live-in victim of the moment until well after the stars were out. Since the young boys had been banished for the duration, she had instituted the idea that the trio should

gather in her boudoir while she conducted what she liked
to call her *toilette,* which mainly consisted of fussing
and fretting with a tray of perfume bottles. Columbine
constantly proved herself incapable of abandoning these
irritating throwbacks to the eighteenth century. Seemingly Marie Antoinette had held similar audiences in
what had probably been an equally vast expanse of cushions and coverlets.

As often as possible, Destry and Marieko made excuses and ducked these scented, candlelit, boudoir over-
tures to the night. A regular first item on the agenda was
an inevitable and lengthy complaint by Columbine on
the hideousness of the nightmare from which she had
just wakened. On this particular evening, Marieko
wanted to hear nothing about anyone else's dreams and
would gladly have ignored Columbine when she'd sent
Grendl to summon to her. The invitation was couched,
however, in terms that made it clear Columbine would
throw such a merciless tantrum, followed by such protracted sulking and recrimination, that Marieko's and
Destry's existences would be made miserable for the entire span of the night and maybe longer. It was Columbine's method of reassertion after she had steered them
so close to the metaphoric rocks of disaster the previous
night. Thus Marieko sat cross-legged in a Louis XV
chair while Destry—in her now almost-perpetual riding
habit, and with a riding crop hanging from her right
wrist—paced impatiently and treated them like a pair of
bickering schoolgirls.

"I've about had it up to here with this nonsense. To
a greater or lesser degree, you've both botched either
bringing Victor Renquist under our control or finding out
if he arrived here with any hidden agenda of his own."

Marieko hardly regarded this as fair and said so. The
only reason Destry could accuse anyone of failure was
because she had yet to go one-on-one with the male. "I
had everything set for the maximum possible chance of
his inadvertently revealing himself."

Columbine fluffed a pillow. "But you were so busy having fun with him, you let some unknown third party introduce a horde of badly drawn assassins to the mix who almost did away with the both of you."

"That was not the way it happened, and you know it."

"Oh, yes? I suppose you hated every moment on the bed of swords?"

"I wouldn't claim that. I admit some parts were highly pleasurable. I didn't have to play the whore."

"Perhaps you should have done so. Maybe we would have gleaned more than that he can shape-shift in dreams."

"And I suppose lunging at him with a sword was a highly reasoned ploy to put him off his guard?"

Destry turned in her pacing and glared, flexing the crop between gloved hands. "I've already told you both to knock it off. I'm not joking."

Destry so plainly wasn't joking, Marieko and Columbine fell silent. Marieko became even more still and formal in her lotus pose while Columbine agitatedly removed and replaced the stoppers of her perfume bottles. Destry and Marieko had often discussed whether Columbine derived some kind of stimulant or narcotic effect from combinations of the various aromas. Once, while Columbine had been in London, snaring one of her boy victims, they had tried a selection for themselves, but experienced no discernible results. Some discreet research by Destry had revealed that the sole source of Columbine's perfumes was a small shop in the city of York, run by an elderly Hasidic Jew. The family-owned business was so old and long established that it claimed the title of "perfumer and apothecary," but when she had attempted to delve further into what exactly was being supplied to Columbine, Destry had been countered with a wall of silence under the guise of customer confidentiality. The only thing the old human with skullcap and beard had let slip was that a majority of the products he supplied to Columbine by regular registered mail were compounds blended according the client's own specific formulas.

Columbine applied a little of one of the fragrances to the side of her throat with a small glass wand incorporated into the stopper of the bottle. "So now, whatever has been invading my dreams took it upon itself to infect the dream scenario devised for Renquist."

Marieko lowered her eyes and, at the same time, shook her head. "I don't think so."

"What do you mean, you don't think so?"

"Of course, you can accuse me of presuming. I know I haven't experienced your dreams firsthand, but from all you've told and shown us, they would seem to be the product of another's complete and vivid memories. This infection, as you put it, this intrusion, was nothing more than a crude assault. A deliberate disruption of the plan as I devised it. I even heard the sound of artillery outside the castle walls. It was so out of place, it would have been laughable, had it not been so aggressively mounted and so deliberately designed to do damage."

"You have another of your theories?"

"I believe this intrusion was by another nosferatu."

"Perhaps Victor himself, looking to beat you at your own game?"

"No."

"No? It would seem the obvious answer. A perfect example of his usual perfidious trickery. You saw how he tried to confuse us last night by sneaking in the way he did and staging that ridiculous display."

Marieko was tempted to point out that Renquist's display, far from being ridiculous, had set Columbine completely off balance, but she knew Destry wouldn't tolerate any resumption of verbal sparring. "When he took control at the end, the change was so profound, I'm certain he was not the author of the earlier interruption. I would have noticed something, I'm sure."

"He's a master of deception."

"But I'm not stupid."

Columbine seemed poised to make some disparaging remark but was quelled with a look from Destry. "So who, if not Victor?"

Destry dropped into a chair as though she felt she was no longer needed to keep the peace between her hissing sisters. She casually hooked one leg over the arm of the chair and, employing one of her more masculine mannerisms, swung a thoughtful, boot-shod foot. "Fenrior or one of his clan would seem the most likely candidate."

The idea took Columbine by surprise. "Fenrior? How, pray, could that noisome brute be part of the picture? He hasn't paid us any attention in years."

"We have Renquist here."

"He doesn't know that."

"Sure he does."

Columbine considered this. "I suppose it's possible that Renquist's arrival was detected. That unspeakable pair, Theda and Cyrce, can be very perceptive when they want to be. And that horrible Gallowglass who—"

Destry tapped her boot with the whip. "It's not a possibility. It's a near certainty. Fenrior may ape the barbarian, but he's brutally shrewd and wholly dedicated to the protection of his clan."

"But they're all the way up in the wilds of the Highlands."

"You think he doesn't have spies in London? Loners, solitaries, even humans with the sight? London may have no indigenous clans or colonies, but it has its population. Renquist checking into the Savoy probably didn't go unnoticed. And last night's fireworks display could have been detected for miles around, if anyone was paying attention. There's probably more than one of our kind wondering what Victor Renquist is doing here, but I still believe Fenrior is the prime suspect, simply because he's the closest."

As Destry made each point of her argument, she continued to tap the toe of her boot with the crop until Columbine raised a pale and protesting hand. "Would

you stop doing that? There are no men here to be excited
by it."

"It disturbs you?"

Columbine toyed nervously with her perfume bottles.
"Everything disturbs me this evening. I need to feed. I
need blood even if it has to come from a damned pack.
Where's Grendl?"

Destry looked around. "Where *is* Grendl?"

Marieko supplied the answer. "She's taking water to
Victor."

"Water?"

"Everyone knows Victor Renquist wakes with an unnatural thirst."

"He never needed water when I knew him."

"That was a long time ago, my dear."

What was it with England's dreaming? Obviously Renquist dreamed in other places, but since he had arrived
in the antique island, the dreamstate had been as much
the center of drama as the so-called real world. It could
even be said Columbine's dreams brought him there in
the first place. He wondered if the colorful fervor of all
this dreaming could be related to the complex and
energy-intense convergence of the Nephilim ley-line ma-
trix that still pulsed under southern England. Such a
subject was certainly worthy of further research, but research was a thing of the future. He needed to put consideration of dreams firmly to one side. Above and
beyond anything else, he was thirsty.

If he had planned ahead before retiring, he would have
requested a jug of cold water. Marieko would have been
more than happy to command one of the servants to
bring it, but Marieko had proved such a distraction, even
before the dreaming, the idea had completely slipped his
mind. Now that she was gone, he wasn't quite certain
what to do. The undead visited so little, the etiquette for
houseguests was far from defined. Should he attempt to
summon a servant? He, of course, knew exactly where

to find the kitchen, water, and ice, but that would involve prowling the halls of Ravenkeep Priory without having been categorically invited to make himself at home. Of course, after having bedded and dreamed with one of the primary residents, such freedom to wander might have been tacitly assumed, but Renquist was old-fashioned in his punctilious observance of the minutiae of good manners, and he also knew one could never be too careful around female nosferatu on their home territory, especially when one of those female nosferatu had attempted to destroy him less than twelve hours earlier.

Very gently, he cast around for the auras of his hostess troika and discovered all three of them gathered in another of the bedrooms. That Columbine was the one still in bed tended to indicate the bedroom was hers, and that she was conducting some form of retro-toilette. Would it be egocentric of him to assume he was the subject under discussion? It might be, but it was also very likely to be the truth. They could, of course, be making domestic arrangements or just small talk, but he doubted it after all that had transpired. He couldn't read the details of their conversation without making his eavesdropping obvious, but he guessed one topic had to be the origin of the determined outside assault on his and Marieko's shared dream. It was something he needed to think about very carefully himself before he blundered in any deeper, but again, his paramount consideration was water, and only after he'd rehydrated himself would he be able to commence that level of analytical thinking. Life would have been so much simpler if he had just thought ahead, and a cool, clear jug was standing on the night table.

As he would have expected, the huge Elizabethan four-poster—still covered with his rumpled and disorganized fur rug—generally dictated the style of the dark, wood-paneled bedroom. Two narrow lancet windows, rendered eyeless against the day by solid oak fitted shutters, were an approximation of the period, as was the somewhat grim tapestry of a hanged man with an apparently amused crow looking down on him from the horizontal gallows beam. The same conformity, though, could not be found in the large triptych of Victorian lithograph prints depicting various groups of Christians being unpleasantly martyred in the ancient Roman arena in the days of Nero or maybe Caligula. The unfortunates, mainly attractive young women with rounded flesh and plaintive, soulful eyes, were being flogged, burned, and crucified, and one was about to be torn apart by a team of four garlanded oxen. The work was a typical and hypocritical Victorian trick of presenting overtly sadomasochist imagery under the pretense of religion, but maybe also indicative of the prevailing Ravenkeep attitude? The danger of crosses and other holy relics might be a human, Hollywood, and Hammer Films myth, but few nosferatu could tolerate a Christian.

Whatever the protocols, Renquist was not going to allow himself to be tortured beyond endurance by a waking thirst. He may not have formally been given the run of the house, but he was going to look for water. In the bedroom closet he found his robe. He slipped it on, but as he approached the door, a rapping came from the other side, taking him completely by surprise.

"Who is it?" As he spoke, he could perceive only a faint and listless aura of a human who seemed scarcely alive.

"It's Grendl, sir."

The thrall was endowed with all the humanity and animation of sculpted lard. It would appear Columbine and her two companions psychically, and perhaps physically, drained their servants to the point of near mindlessness. In principle, Renquist strongly disapproved of such behavior. He certainly didn't treat Lamar, his chauffeur in Los Angeles, like that, or any of the other human servants he'd had under his power down the years, but it was hardly his place to comment on how other nosferatu conducted their business—and in any

case, the woman was holding a tray with a clean glass
and a large pitcher of ice water. She made a clumsy
curtsy and addressed him in a slow monotone, as if re-
citing memorized lines. "Mistress Marieko said I should
bring this for you, sir."

Renquist, ignoring both gentility and the glass, took
the jug itself and drained a long lupine draft; then he let
out a protracted sigh. Grendl the thrall stood looking at
him blankly, and he dismissed her with a motion of the
pitcher. "Thank you. You can go now. I'm sure your
mistresses have other tasks for you."

The human continued to look blankly at him for a
further few seconds before dropping a second ungainly
curtsy and shuffling away. One of the reasons Renquist
never reduced his own servants to such shambling in-
capacity was a matter of practicality rather than any
moral altruism. They were simply of so little use in that
condition. If a human servant was allowed to retain at
least a modicum of character and dignity, he or she was
invariably more efficient. Another reason was aesthetic.
Servants needed a certain snap to their attention. He
didn't want to be surrounded by torpid, bipedal slugs.
Servant loyalty didn't need to be maintained by full-burn
mind control. The combination of nosferatu charisma
and the hinted promise of eventual immortality was more
than enough to create a willing thrall able to think for
him- or herself and act with intelligence and initiative.

He carried the jug of water back into the bedroom,
took another long drink, and as he began to rehydrate,
he noticed, for the first time, the drop of only recently
dried blood on the exposed sheet where the fur was
turned back. Was the blood his or Marieko's, and if it
was, how had the injuries they'd both sustained in the
dreamstate carried through into the waking world? He
certainly had no marks on him that he could see or feel.
He tentatively sniffed at the bed, but the general odor of
both their bodies was too strong for him to isolate the

source of the blood, and he was none the wiser. The mysteries were piling up with an uncomfortable rapidity.

Columbine was aware she'd been rather making a fool of herself. The presence of Victor Renquist under her roof had plunged her into the most enduringly foul of moods, but by the same token, she knew she had to pull herself together before Destry and Marieko completely lost patience with her and the integrity, and even the continuation, of the highly useful troika became fatally jeopardized. Mercifully, Destry had finally stopped tapping the damned riding crop on her boot, but Marieko continued to sit as rigid and unbendingly exquisite as a jade figurine, her mouth growing smaller and tighter by the moment, a clear indication that she was very close to being unforgivingly offended. Another display of pettishness by Columbine might well push one or both of them over an emotional edge from which they might possibly not return—and yet she still felt an almost overwhelming need to pout and drum her heels.

Columbine was the first to recognize her problem, although she would also be the last to admit it. If she wasn't extremely careful, the mask of thoughtless hedonism that had protected her for so long would turn into a threat, and her cultivated duality might actually prove her undoing. She had grown to womanhood and made the Change to the undead in a time when men were near-essential protectors and the most effective weapon in the arsenal of the adventuress was a facade of infantile—if sexually charged—helplessness, and she was loath to admit the games of the time she'd learned from contemporaries like Caroline Lamb, Emma Hamilton, and Harriette Wilson had become less and less applicable as the years passed. In the current situation, she knew absolutely nothing positive could be achieved by acting like a spoiled brat, and indeed, the results could, in a worst-case scenario, wreak disastrously negative havoc. The call was for cunning, but she still clung to the need for petulance, out of nothing more than a sense of comfort and habit.

The matter of Renquist was a case in point. The child in her wished they had never invited him to Ravenkeep. The mature and seasonedly sensible undead part of her knew she had to rationally accept that he was needed to solve the problem of the dreams that threatened to drive her to madness and the unidentified strangeness that apparently lurked inside the prehistoric mound at Morton Downs. The spoiled brat had used Renquist as the symbolic great betrayer, inflating his importance until he had become her own internal legend. Reason dictated she had to put aside this romantic and largely illusionary creation and work with him as an eminent and respected nosferatu. Yet, when he had appeared the previous night in his egomaniac display of psychic quasi-majesty, she'd immediately bought completely into his power play and tried to run him through with one of her favorite sabers. The act had been stupidly impulsive, and instead of humbling him, she had been humiliated herself. Bending him to her will in the way she desired would now be even harder.

To complicate circumstances further, her dreamlife was deteriorating faster than she was either prepared or able to accept. Although she didn't truly believe it was anything but coincidental, she had earlier woken from what appeared to be yet another phase in the transmitted dreaming. This belief in the coincidental, however, didn't prevent her from blaming him. Victor arrived at Ravenkeep, and her dreams sank deeper into the cesspool of emotional disturbance. In the new phase, in the sleep from which she had so recently arisen, she had found herself blind and entombed. The blindness was pure horror. A night-seeing nosferatu was never blind. As her eyes probed for anything at all, her own breathing rasped loud and dry in her ears, and the tiny sounds of body functions were amplified to near deafening. She was absolutely certain, in the total and sightless dark, she could even detect the small booming reverberations in the Earth itself, as the planet moved and groaned along with tectonic plates on their infinite and implacable onward momentum. Her body was swathed in some sticky and all-enveloping, slightly elastic material with just a slight give, permitting her only the most minimal movement. Her hands were immobilized, crossed across her chest, but by pressing hard against the cling of the sticky stuff, she found that, in a small way, she could explore the inexplicable space she occupied. The mucuslike swaddling appeared to be only an inner layer. Feeling with shoulders and elbows, she could detect an outer shell of solid construct, apparently form-tailored to the contours of her body—a womb or a tomb, presenting a choice of dying or being born. She was in a container or sarcophagus, a casket, or one of those suspended-animation tanks from the realm of science fiction, but without any real clue as to which.

Sealed in with nothing but herself, she had more than ample time for theorizing. Accepting Marieko's supposition that, while dreaming, she was somehow coming under the slumbering influence of the powerful entity allegedly buried in the mound at Morton Downs, she had been shifted in time. The idylls and then the subsequent devastation of the sixth century, the entity's overspilling dreams, were long in the past. The new darkness was present time. The entity was drawing near to waking, and she was sharing the experience. If she was correct, what would happen if this thing of conjecture should actually come alive? Would she be drawn to it, or cast aside? One very unpleasant idea had crossed her mind and then, despite how hard her revulsion might try, refused to be dismissed. The state in which she found herself was much like the way certain arachnids incapacitated their live prey in order to eat them later. If that were the case, was she doomed to be consumed? Was she condemned to be a metaphoric spider's breakfast? Perhaps their real investigation should be to find a way to destroy the thing before it ever emerged.

The worst part of all this dream-induced consternation and lurking fear was that, with Renquist in the house, she felt obliged to keep it all to herself. Had it just been Destry and Marieko in residence, she would have shamelessly created a living hell for those around her, ranting and sobbing that her dreams were in full decay and she was clearly finished. Her aversion wasn't only to diminishing herself further by throwing another tantrum in front of Victor. She still didn't trust him. She wanted him to go to Morton Downs and see what he could discern with as little foreknowledge as possible. Marieko provided a further source of humiliation. By greeting the new night so full of herself after her own dreamstate adventures with Victor, she had the edge with her swashbuckling ninja, and was the dream-star of the evening. It went further, though, than Marieko stealing her thunder. She felt she now needed to be a good deal more guarded around the other two females. Ruminating in the black hole of her dream, she decided Victor being in the house was a catalyst for competition, subterfuge, and challenge, and she must expect snapping, snarling, and two-faced backstabbing. Where they normally went about their business without too much resort to the balance of the natural pecking order, the male, if he became an object of the desire to bond, could wreck all that and return them to the violence of the pack. In the pack, the acknowledged alpha female must never show weakness. If she did, her rivals would inevitably drag her down—not out of conscious spite, but just in obedience to the natural law. From now on, she decided, she would play her cards, no matter how distressing the hand, very close to her bosom.

"I have to get to grips with my duality."

Destry and Marieko both nodded. "We're glad you've finally acknowledged that."

Now that she was thinking rationally again, an unpleasant and obvious thought struck her. "Oh, shit."

"What?"

"Did it occur to either of you he could be listening to us right now?"

Neither Marieko nor Destry seemed to share her concern. "I think we would have noticed. Besides, does it matter? We're hardly exchanging state secrets."

"We should get him out of the house. Even if it's only for an hour or so."

"Why?"

"Because I need to gather my thoughts. We need to talk, and I won't feel comfortable if he's just a couple of rooms away."

Marieko glanced at Destry. "He'll be expecting me to take him to the excavation."

"We have to talk first."

"What should I tell him?"

"Tell him that we need to wait, that this Campion and his students may still be there."

Destry looked skeptical. "Okay, so we tell him that. He'll probably buy it, but what do we do then? Suggest he take a walk around the grounds so we can talk about him behind his back?"

"Offer him the use of your horse."

Destry's jaw slowly dropped, as though she couldn't believe what she was hearing. "Are you joking? Let Renquist ride Dormandu? That horse will only be ridden by me."

Columbine was secretly pleased and amused by Destry's reaction. She might tap her riding crop disdainfully on her boot at the weaknesses of others, but the moment it was suggested she sacrifice one of her own preciously held and exclusive vanities, she treated it as a violation. "Victor prides himself as an equestrian. The horse would be the perfect temptation."

"Damn you, Columbine. How long have you been setting me up for this?"

"I'm not setting you up, Destry, dear. I'm just suggesting you let Renquist ride your horse."

"But I've bonded with the animal."

"It would hardly damage that bonding if Victor were to ride the brute for an hour or more."

"It sticks in my craw. I went to a lot of trouble to acquire Dormandu, and I don't like the idea of his being ridden like some hack by all and sundry."

Now Marieko was with Columbine. "Victor Renquist is hardly all and sundry, and it is the ideal way of getting him out of the house for a while. I agree with Columbine. We do need to talk without being overheard."

For a few moments, Destry stared stubbornly at the floor. Finally she looked up and met the eyes of the other two. "Okay, okay, the point's been made. I'm being petty. I'll offer Dormandu to Renquist if that's what's needed." She rose from the chair. "I'll do it, but I don't have to like it."

"Good evening, Victor."

"Good evening, Ms. Maitland."

"Please, not so formal. You have to call me Destry. I told you that last night."

"Good evening, Destry."

Renquist had broken the impasse of the neglected country house-guest by dressing and then leaving his room to explore the Priory on his own. He had chosen an ensemble of a casual tuxedo-cut leather jacket over narrow pants and a silk shirt, and feeling suitably attired, he commenced to wander the house until one of its three mistresses came to find him. Although, to all outward appearances, his movements were aimless and idle, Renquist had never been blessed with any talent for idling, and he made his seemingly random wandering a cover for filling in as much background as possible on the three females with whom he now found himself involved.

As Renquist moved silently from room to room, he gleaned only the most obvious basics from the possessions, decor, and furniture. He found the Priory completely typical of most nosferatu Residences. It contained the disorganized clutter of centuries; the use of the interior space was not well planned, and in some parts, not planned at all. Domestic cleanliness was of such a habitually low priority the least-used rooms had closed atmospheres of dust, must, and creeping decay. The interests and personalities of the troika were, on the other hand, very well represented. Columbine's fixation on her Georgian and Regency roots took a definite precedence, since she had been there the longest, but there were also souvenirs and artifacts of Marieko's long history in the Far East, and Destry's career seemed to be that of a warrior maid-of-fortune around the colonial flash points of the twentieth century.

Renquist had yet to learn the exact history of Destry Maitland and how long she had been one of the undead, but the array of mementos that were undoubtedly hers could be read as indicating she had followed the camps of both revolutionaries and counterinsurgents, primarily in Central Africa and South and Central America. A collection of personally inscribed photos—Fidel Castro; Patrice Lumumba; Augusto Pinochet; Leon Trotsky, in Mexico City toward the end of his life; Eva Perón; and the notorious cocaine baron Pablo Escobar—seemed to confirm that her intimates had been players of the highest order. On a high shelf, Renquist noted a number of blue document binders that carried the circular eagle-and-shield logo of the Central Intelligence Agency, but curious as he might be, he did not think this preliminary reconnoiter was the time to take them down for closer examination. For all he knew, the binders might hold truly devastating material and sources of limitless blackmail, but for such things to be gathering dust on a shelf was not in any way unusual. Nosferatu were notoriously careless with all kinds of treasures.

A hand-cranked power unit for a military-style field telephone, battered and worn, with chipped olive drab paint came with two electric cables attached to it that ended in alligator clip electrodes, suggesting a grimly

mute story. Was this Destry's keepsake of some un-
wholesome past adventure or even an avowed calling?
If such were the case, it would not be the first time a
nosferatu had hired out to humans as a torturer. The
Inquisition itself had maintained its uneasy contacts with
the subworld of nosferatu, and Lupo, Renquist's strong
right arm back in the Los Angeles colony, whose history
went back to the Italian city-states of the Renaissance,
had extracted many a confession under duress in his
time, despite his regular profession of hired assassin.

Renquist was most surprised by what he didn't find
on this first unsupervised excursion through the modern
Priory. As far as he could tell, no armadillos had made
their home in the great rambling pile. With its extensions
and additions, its dozens of rooms, and assorted styles
and periods of architecture, Ravenkeep should have provided the perfect habitat. According to nosferatu superstition, the absence of armadillos did not bode well for
either a location or its inhabitants. Ever since the small,
ancient animals had been brought to Europe from the
Americans and displayed their inexplicable propensity
for seeking out the undead and taking up abode with
them, their presence had been judged a sign of security
and good fortune by his kind. The excuse could, of
course, be made that armadillos were hardly indigenous
to the countryside of southern England, but it was hardly
an argument that held up for Renquist. Neither the island
of Manhattan nor the Los Angles basin had a natural
armadillo population, but the little creatures peered from
the corners and wainscots of his Residences in both lo-
cations and provided a powerful comfort. He had even
known nosferatu households that, when the armadillos
failed to find them, had actually imported pairs of the
species. The most charitably optimistic explanation was
that Columbine and her companions were too self-
absorbed to observe such irrational niceties of tradition,
but Renquist knew he would be a fool not to take into

consideration that maybe the armadillos sensed something about the Priory that he didn't.

In one of the corridors that served the building like
an organic circulatory system, he stopped by a partially
open door. The medium-size room that lay beyond was
so austere and harmonious it could only be Marieko's
private retreat. He was tempted to step inside, but that
seemed well beyond the bounds of good manners. He
knew he would hate such an invasion of privacy to be
inflicted on him. When in doubt, he always used his own
feelings to gauge what might be appropriate behavior,
his own customized version of "Do unto others as you'd
have them do unto you." He didn't, however, feel the
need to forgo peering in from outside. Craning slightly,
he saw screens, backlit walls, a lacquered table, a koto,
a decoratively raked sandbox, a large aquarium, which
was home to an emerald frog, and a rush mat of the kind
used for *sinshu*. All this conformed to the opinions Renquist had formed already, but then his eye fell on an
object on the lacquered table. It was a silver mask, identical to the one Marieko had just been wearing in the
dream. He was too far away to see if the teardrop was
sculpted beneath the mask's right eye, but he would have
wagered it was. The mask raised a number of questions:
Had Marieko simply used the object as a piece of top
dressing on her creation, or did the thing have a greater
significance? Was it perhaps a talisman, an object of
power bridging the gap between fantasy and reality?

Renquist was pondering this when Destry appeared.
"Good evening, Victor."

"Good evening, Ms. Maitland."

"Please, not so formal. You have to call me Destry. I
told you that last night."

"Good evening, Destry."

Destry's greeting was as cordial as one might expect
from hostess to guest, and good manners dictated she
make no scan of his thoughts, but he didn't doubt she

was wondering what he might have learned in the parts of the house he'd briefly inspected.

"We enter Marieko's private domain somewhat at our peril."

"I would never think of entering."

"But a look through the open door was different?"

"I surrendered to the temptation."

Destry laughed. "If one has to surrender to anything, it might as well be temptation."

"I won't argue with that."

Destry treated Renquist to a questioning, sidelong stare. "I understand you did some rather spectacular dreaming with Marieko through the day that's just gone. She tells us you were something of a hero."

So they all knew about it. No secrets between sisters? Not on this level, apparently. He made blandly self-depreciating gestures. "It's easy to be a hero in the dreamstate." He hesitated. "Actually, I was wondering where Marieko was now. I was under the impression we were to visit this excavation."

Renquist was being somewhat disingenuous by asking the question. He was well aware Marieko was still with Columbine in her boudoir, and Destry must have known that he would have located their auras as soon as he'd emerged from his room, if not before. It was a simple, silly deception hardly intended to deceive. More a matter of nosferatu gentility and the pretense that their world was not a shadow place of whispered secrets, intrigue, and counterplot—when it almost always was.

Destry's aura became deliberately vague. "I think she's otherwise occupied right now. I never really know what Marieko gets up to with all her studies, meditations, and disciplines. She's by far the most active of the three of us, no question about that."

"I thought it was a matter of some urgency that I take a preliminary look at whatever's at Morton Downs."

"All business, Victor?"

"I believe that's why I'm here."

"Marieko seems to think that it would be best not to go to the dig until later. Maybe around midnight. That way we minimize running into Dr. Campion and any of his people who might be working late."

"I see."

"Now you're wondering what you're going to do in the meantime."

"I'm sure I can find some way to occupy myself."

"Why don't you come and ride with me?"

"Ride?"

"As in horse."

The suggestion took Renquist completely by surprise. Destry watched his confusion with an amused smile. "I thought you were a horseman, Victor?"

"I haven't been on a horse in many years, but there was, of course, a time—"

"This is what I heard. How you led your own regiment of night cavalry."

"It was only a troop of boyars."

"So? I can promise you a horse worthy of your experience."

Renquist held his aura firmly in check. He didn't want Destry to be aware of either his disbelief or excitement. A horse worthy of his experience? Did she really intend to let him ride the huge, black brute he had seen in the stables the night before? He slowly nodded. "Yes, why not? I'd be delighted to ride with you."

As they walked to the stables, Renquist reflected on his being passed around among the three females in succession. First he bedded and dreamed with Marieko; now he was going riding with Destry. Would he next be handed over to Columbine? And what would she want to do with him? Or maybe the truth was that she'd taken her turn already. Had it been her turn last night in the drawing room, when her desire had been to gut him like a hog in the slaughterhouse? He was also aware that the potential for a very dangerous game was contained in this arrangement, and he refused to believe the three females didn't appreciate the risks they were running. Among the nosferatu, three females and a lone male had always been an incendiary recipe. It was the combination Bram Stoker had accidentally imagined in the Carpathian castle in his unfortunate novel: three females serving a single lord, a deadly mixture of jealously, inequality, and gender oppression that invariably spelled trouble. The history of Renquist's kind was littered with spectacularly abusive masters on one hand, and on the other, troikas who had risen up and slain their lords. Some had also suffered hideous penalties for their efforts, and in the twentieth century, it had generally come to be accepted as an arrangement to be avoided. Many, though, were yet still drawn to it, and Renquist couldn't believe that at least some shadow of history and perverse temptation would fail to fall over this enterprise.

As they approached the stables, Destry shouted commandingly for the thrall Bolingbroke, and the human swiftly appeared as if he'd already been waiting for her in the darkness.

"Saddle Dormandu and the gelding."

Bolingbroke grovelled. "Yes, mistress."

As he straightened up, Destry flicked the thrall with her crop. "And hurry, damn you."

Only a sharp intake of breath and a brief, back-curled cringe indicated how painful even a touch of the whip might be when delivered with undead strength. As the man shuffled off, Renquist used the cover of Destry's irritation fleetingly to probe the man's mind. As he expected, he found nothing of any significance. In fact, the man's mind contained very little at all except a turgidly hopeless morass the color of stagnant pond water. Destry glanced at Renquist as though expecting to see a kindred spirit for whom human retainers represented tiresome burden. "Thralls can be such a pain. After you've had them for a while, they become so damned slow, and everything but the simplest routine task has to be explained in the most painstaking detail. After a while, even beating them doesn't do much to sharpen them up."

Renquist nodded, at the same time hoping they treated their horses better than they treated their humans. "I tend to let mine retain a good deal of their native intelligence."

"But then they're always mooning around wondering when you're going to make them immortal."

"The occasional crumb of hope can go a long way."

"I suppose it's true what they say about humans."

"It depends which particular saying you had in mind."

Destry laughed. "Can't live with them but can't live without them."

Destry's observations on the shortcomings of humanity were interrupted by Bolingbroke's return. He led two horses, a pretty, high-stepping grey of obvious Arabian heritage and the great black stallion from the Uzbek bloodline. Renquist quickly remembered Destry didn't know he'd inspected the horse the previous night, and he made his aura register a combination of surprise and delight, along with a touch of awe. Such fakery really didn't require too much effort and, indeed, hardly qualified as fakery at all. As Dormandu stood in the moonlight, with his red-rimmed eyes, arrogant bearing, and detailed musculature clearly defined beneath his gleaming black coat, the steed was as much an object of wonderment on this second encounter as he had been on the first.

Renquist kept his voice hushed. "Magnificent."

Destry glowed as if she herself were being paid the compliment. "He's a beautiful creature."

"He could have walked out of the stables of Pathan Gash."

"Dormandu is only one-quarter of the Uzbek blood, unfortunately."

"He would appear to have inherited most of the genes. I'd heard that a few of the bloodline had survived, but this is the first one I've seen since the Great Slaughter."

"The cossacks of the Red Army preserved some spec-

imens. A few others went to Argentina where they ran
near wild on the pampas. Dormandu came from a clandestine stable near Budapest that had remained a secret
all the time the Communists were in power."

"You are very fortunate."

Destry nodded. "I tell myself that each time I ride
him."

"I envy you such a mount."

"Perhaps . . . you'd like to try him."

The offer didn't come out with much conviction or
authenticity, as though the very last thing she wanted
was anyone else harnessing the power of the horse. Renquist quickly shook his head. "No. He's yours. You must
ride him. It hardly seems appropriate. The two of you
must have bonded."

"I'm being spontaneously generous, Victor. Magnan-
imous, even. Take me up on the offer before I change
my mind. Can you really turn down the chance to mount
a descendant of the great Uzbekians?"

She moved to the horse, patted its head, and stroked
its muzzle. "Come here, Victor. Make the acquaintance
of Dormandu."

Renquist stood beside Destry and also petted the
beast. He could almost hear the air humming as she
locked down her aura not to reveal her true feelings. She
hated the idea of Renquist even being near the horse, so
why was she making the offer when it caused her such
obvious anguish? He glanced at her one last time
"You're sure you don't mind?"

"Go ahead."

Renquist put a foot into the stirrup and swung easily
into the English saddle.

The horse reared slightly, and as Renquist calmed him,
Destry had to bite back a flash of jealous rage. Since
Dormandu had come to Ravenkeep, no one had ridden
him but Destry, and she profoundly wished the horse
would instantly buck Victor Renquist out of the saddle

and pitch him humiliatingly to the ground, but she knew, as he mounted, he was far too good a horseman for that. He might not have ridden in years, but he had no trouble recalling the absolutely correct touch and feel. Dormandu was skittish at having a stranger in the saddle, but Renquist knew exactly the right measure of composed, unruffled authority that, within a matter of seconds, would have the huge creature trusting him and ready to do his bidding. Destry could see why Columbine made such an issue of Victor. He really was too completely assured of his own perfection. After a thousand years, could he not have the good grace to fuck up now and again? Still secretly seething, she mounted the gelding, dismissed Bolingbroke with a snarl she kept from Victor, and the two of them walked their mounts away from the stables.

The plan was to appear to be riding with Victor but then to tell him to give Dormandu his head and really let the stallion stretch out. The slightly built gelding could never keep up with the huge demon charger, and Destry would quickly fall behind. Once Renquist was out of sight, she could turn and go quickly back to the house, where the troika would formulate their strategies without the risk of being overheard, while he, meanwhile, galloped on, they hoped, completely absorbed in the novel and powerful sensation of riding such an exceptional mount. This part proved another wrench for Destry. That Renquist was riding her pride and joy was bad enough, but to allow him to disappear into the darkness with him would take all her willpower and self-control.

She waited until they were out on the open downland before she steeled herself for this next stage in the devious game. "Why don't you let him run?"

"Suppose I lose you?"

Destry was glad Renquist was slightly ahead, and that he only turned once to glance back at her. It took all her skill and energy to contain her violent reluctance. "I'm sure . . . you and Dormandu will find your way back. Besides, a horse like him needs to exercise at full gallop."

"If you don't mind."

"No, give him his head, goddamn it."

Renquist only had to put his heels to the big black's flanks, and he was off. Within seconds, even their twin auras were out of her sight. Destry slowly turned the gelding and headed back to the Priory with a distinct sense she'd lost something very important to her. Dormandu would never again be her exclusive property. She sincerely hoped it would all turn out to be worth the sacrifice.

The great horse ran, and Renquist exulted. He forgot about the troika and their strange machinations. He forgot about Destry's ambivalence about his riding the Uzbekian. He was transported back across the centuries to the days when the horse under him had virtually been an extension of himself. He carried no lance or saber, and no boyars galloped at his heels, but he could almost imagine the thunder of their following hooves. The broad black body rose and plunged beneath him as he gripped with his knees, hardly using the reins, letting Dormandu run a free straight course, at full steeplechase pelt, but still using a subtle pressure to remind the beast he was master. The downland over which they passed seemed to roll like the sea, and the hillside moonlight and the mist in the vales and hollows whipped his face and exposed hands in the slipstream of their passing. The leather jacket billowed, and he half wished he had worn a full-flowing cape as in the days of old.

The entire experience brought back many memories and also the wistful realization that nosferatu were never truly designed to inhabit the cities of modern times. His kind should not find themselves the shifty nocturnal kindred of rats and limping urban pigeons. Their true heritage was to roam like the wolf, wild and free, and yet, just as the wild wolves had been decimated by trappers and the cattlemen's bounty hunters, the nosferatu had been forced to adapt to the restraints and limitations of so-called civilization. The days were gone when the blood of peasants chilled at the first hard-rhythmic drumming of night-riders' hooves and the lordly undead could descend at whim on croft, hut, or cottage—and extinguish sorry mortal lives for their survival and satisfaction in a howling feast of lunar abandon. The wild freedom of the ride invoked a wealth of thoughts of what had been and what might have been, a nostalgia for all the proud savagery exchanged for the security of the invisible profile. The unfortunate truth was that contemporary nosferatu skulked. They were furtive. They might skulk as Renquist and his peers did, under the opulent cloak of material luxury, but they skulked all the same. Human-style wealth provided a small sop to their pride. For a being who didn't die, it was small challenge to amass a fortune in the capitalist nations and equally easy to rise to dangerous power and lethal political influence in any totalitarian regime. Renquist knew, however, deep inside, it was only a sophisticated and glossy substitute for a wholly abandoned, but still mourned, feral and untamed life of the ranging predator.

In the far distance, he could see the lights of a farm, or, in these days, possibly the country home of an investment banker or media entrepreneur. The temptation was strong to throw temptation literally to the winds and ride furiously down on the habitation, drag all he found from their television sets and their gin and tonics, and make them victim to his personal orgy of bloody destruction. He reined in Dormandu, and the horse halted, his breathing scarcely labored, despite a gallop of two or more miles. Renquist merely sat in the darkness, in the saddle of the Uzbek, and stared. Such a violent atrocity was appealing, but so foolhardy, Renquist knew it had to be strictly relegated to the realm of fantasy and what-if. He wasn't prepared to accept responsibility for the hue and cry that would follow the slaughter of an English family in their home.

He was about to turn the horse, when he saw the second set of lights, and these lights were moving, apparently coming in his direction, a pair of headlights, the yellow of cats' eyes. He first thought they were those of the Priory Range Rover. Marieko was coming to find him, perhaps following his and the horse's auras, to take him to Morton Downs and the mysterious excavation? Then he heard the sound of the vehicle's engine. Fine-tuned but elderly, it was no Range Rover, and oddly, it seemed to be moving within its own cloud of mist. In almost the same second, he perceived the auras of those inside. The car's passengers, if indeed it was a car, appeared to consist of a nosferatu and two almost comatose humans. The humans could have been Bolingbroke and Grendl, but they weren't, and the nosferatu was definitely not one of the Ravenkeep females. He was male, old, perhaps as old as Lupo, and making no attempt at concealment. Even employing a totally unreasonable degree of modesty, Renquist had to assume this was no bizarre coincidence, and he was the ultimate target of this unknown nosferatu inexplicably motoring through the countryside. The choice confronting him was simple and binary: he could investigate or flee.

Had the vehicle merely contained humans, he would simply have melted away into the darkness, but a strange nosferatu making such an out-of-the-midnight-blue appearance dictated Renquist stand his ground, come what may. Admittedly, he was unarmed, but he felt the odds were in his favor, and he could best any lone undead who might come against him. He remained in the saddle, though, waiting for the vehicle to draw closer. The precaution was reasonable. He was fairly certain Dormandu could outrun any ambush or assault, and even if it didn't come to that, the mounted rider had the psychological advantage over the individual on foot.

Once Renquist had decided to remain, the headlights

seemed to come toward him with excruciating slowness. Also, the car continued to be surrounded by its own grey-white cloud, thick to the point of miasma and coloring the headlights their unique tint of yellow. Renquist was aware mist-movers still existed among the undead, but he knew they were few and far between and usually centuries old. He had experimented with it on a number of occasions but found himself unable to master the technique. Weather just wasn't his forte.

Apparently, this mist-mover was so habitual, he carried his cloud with him even when riding in an automobile. As the surreal vehicle came closer, its antiquity was obvious. A Rolls-Royce 2025, Renquist thought, the 1933 model, but he would be the first to admit his knowledge of cars was far from precise. As it finally approached him, it vanished for a few seconds into a shallow fold in the downs and then reappeared again, close to where he waited on the bare hillside. The Rolls halted some fifty feet from him. Dormandu tensed and stepped a couple of paces sideways. As Renquist quieted the stallion, it snorted loudly and tossed its head once; then it showed no more signs of agitation, even when the driver's door opened and a figure stepped out.

"My Lord Renquist?"

The nosferatu looked quite as old as Renquist had anticipated. A skeletal stick figure, dressed in Victorian undertaker's weeds with a venerable rust on them, and with a weathered, near-mummified face little more than skin stretched over a high-cheekboned skull and a prominent, hawklike nose. He rolled the *r*s in both the words *Lord* and *Renquist*. "My Lorrrrd Rrrrenquisssst." He had the same combination of burr and lisp on which the actor Sean Connery had built his entire vocal style.

Renquist didn't move. He and Dormandu remained motionless. Let this strange nosferatu come to him. "I'm a master, not a lord."

"Aye, well, Master Renquist, I bring ye greetings an' a gift."

Renquist maintained his caution. "A gift?"

"From m' lord th' Fenrior of Fenrior."

"Your Lord Fenrior?"

"Tha's right."

"And who might you be?"

"Th' name's Gallowglass, Master Renquist, an' I serve m' lord i' all things."

"Do you, indeed?"

The angular figure advanced on Renquist, trailing tatters of mist marking his progress from the car. "M' Lord Fenrior also requests an' requires ye visit wi' him when ye've finished tarryin' wi' yon vampire lassies."

"Requests and requires?"

"Tha's how he put i'. Tha's how he usually puts things."

"Your Lord Fenrior is a plain speaker?"

"He prides himself on i'."

"Where I come from, we do not use *vampire*."

Gallowglass nodded with the air of one who learns something new every day—and very little of it meets his approval. "Aye. I did hear tell o' such airs an' graces. On Fenrior land we call things by th' plain words rather than the pretty."

"So it would seem."

"So I can tell m' lord he can be expectin' ye presently?"

"I will certainly visit with him, but it could be I'll be 'tarrying wi' the lassies' for a while. I have business with them that may prove important."

Gallowglass halted ten feet from Renquist. "M' lord understands th' wee Chinagirl ha' been leading ye merry dreamin' already."

The nosferatu didn't appear to be armed, but Renquist was still watchful. Also, he was less than happy with Gallowglass's attitude. He might be the loyal vassal to his lord, but he was assuming too readily that Fenrior was Renquist's natural superior. Renquist decided he needed to be chided back into his place. He sat stiffly in the saddle, showing plainly he was on the verge of mild offense. "Marieko Matsunaga is Japanese, not Chinese, and, above all, she is nosferatu."

Gallowglass, however, was unrepentant. "All're heathens o' th' Orient t' m' Lord Fenrior."

"That would seem a narrow view."

"Tha' wouldna' be f' me t' comment upon, Master Renquist. But, if ye'd not find i' out o' place, I'd offer a word o' advice."

"Only a fool doesn't take advice."

"The Fenrior o' Fenrior doesna' take kindly t' bein' kept waitin'."

"I'll remember that."

"Aye."

"You mentioned something about a gift?"

"Aye, tha' I did."

They seemed to have struck an impasse. Neither spoke, and then Gallowglass turned and started walking back to the Rolls. "Ye'll ha' t' step down fra' tha' great beast o' yorn."

Renquist hesitated. Was this the start of the ambush he feared? The concern must have shown in his aura because Gallowglass laughed. "Din'a fret y'self, Master Renquist. No skulduggery lays i' wait. If m' lord wanted ye' gone, ye'd be gone by now."

Renquist swung down from the saddle. "You think so?"

Gallowglass glanced back. "I ken ye have a mighty reputation, Master Renquist, but i' this land ye are only one, an' the Fenrior ha' many at his beck an' call, an' even more i' his debt."

Renquist followed Gallowglass to the Rolls, leading the horse. "So I wouldn't have a chance?"

"No chance at all."

Gallowglass now leaned into the car, beckoned, and then stepped back. In response to the gesture, two young women, humans, scarcely more that teenagers, crawled from the car with difficulty and stood unsteadily. Gallowglass had the pair so tightly controlled, they were effectively brain-dead. "Lord Fenrior doubted th' lassies were feedin' ye anything more substantial than plastic blood fra' th' infirmary, so he instructed me t' bring you these."

The girls were cheaply and vapidly pretty. Short dresses, high heels, sequins, and temptation lipstick. One had long black hair worn with a fringe that covered her forehead and all but hid her now vacant eyes. The other had short blond hair slicked down with mousse. They were not prostitutes, more likely good-time nightclub girls from some provincial city. "O' course, they're no up t' th' ones we breed ourselves, but those ones din'a travel well, y'ken?"

Fenrior bred his own humans? Renquist stored this piece of information for future use. "I have no complaints. In fact, I appreciate Lord Fenrior's thoughtfulness. Please tell him that."

Gallowglass nodded and then indicated that Renquist should select his first victim with the air of a messenger who has a long way to go before dawn. "I'll willin'ly hold y' horse for ye."

"He's strong."

"He'll be no trouble."

Renquist handed Gallowglass the reins. "His name's Dormandu."

"Come, Dormandu. Walk wi' me."

The black horse whickered softly but then went willingly with the emaciated Gallowglass. Nosferatu and horse moved off to a discreet distance, and by way of extra privacy, Renquist found himself and the two zombie girls surrounded by a screen of glittering mist. If this was the way he served his lord, Gallowglass had to be a valuable asset. Renquist pointed at the dark-haired girl, ordering her to come to him. While the blonde remained blank and motionless, the dark one swayed very slowly toward him, as though in the grip of an immensely powerful but far from unpleasant narcotic. A fine smoke trail, all that was left of her consciousness, curled from magenta to deep blue, frightened but also lethargically excited. Lost from reality and completely unable to translate what was happening to her, she was vacuously happy something was bringing her the shadowy and mysterious drama so completely lacking in drab real life. Gallowglass was very good. She would embrace every one of her last moments with a previously unpracticed passion. She stood in front of him, stiff and unseeing, but then one level of control seemed to give way, and she sagged into Renquist with a confused sigh. "I don't understand."

Renquist caught her easily with his left arm, as though they were about to dance. His right hand slipped into the pocket of his leather jacket, closing around the smooth silver tube. "You never will."

"I don't mind."

The tube was out of his pocket, and he thumbed the button. The sharp steel spike snicked out. "I know."

As the steel pierced her throat, she emitted a soft gasp, and she gave up her fantasies to drift like insubstantial gossamer balloons, regrets for what had never been and was never to be. A dreamland of purple romance, handsome men, expensive cars, and impossible idyllic and uncomplicated sexual gratification, shopgirl clichés of satin sheets, champagne, and silk lingerie. Renquist put his lips to the flow of blood from her throat and gradually reduced the images to pure pleasurable abstraction. Despite nostril and navel rings, her life had been deadeningly circumscribed, and she let it go like a Technicolor movie fading to black, or the sunset dying into night. Her body went limp, and he lowered it to the ground. She was gone, as though she had never been. Too many humans for every one of them to achieve even small significance. No wonder they killed themselves in such numbers. He turned and spoke into the mist. "Gallowglass?"

"Aye."

Renquist glanced at the blonde. She was completely unaware of all that had transpired. To also feed on her would be excessive. Not that Renquist was averse to excess in its rightful place, but this was far from being the rightful place. One human would energize him and make him far more able to deal with the tag-team tactics of Columbine, Destry, and Marieko. Two would simply be gorging. It would show in his eyes and the color of skin. "I think the one will be enough."

"Th' Lord Fenrior specifically instructed two human lassies be supplied f' ye."

"I don't need to prove my manhood with gluttony."

"I din'a think tha' was m' lord's intention."

"Could I offer the remaining one to you?"

Gallowglass stepped from the fog he'd created, leading the black horse. He looked down at the dead girl at Renquist's feet and then at the still-standing blonde. "I neither think tha's what m' lord had i' mind."

"Would you be insulted if we were to consider her a gratuity from me to you?"

Gallowglass all but smiled. "I'm never insulted by a gratuity, Master Renquist."

He handed Dormandu's reins to Renquist, and now it was his turn to move off to a discreet distance.

After a long silence, Gallowglass spoke. "Ride back t' th' lassies, Master Renquist. I will dispose o' th' leavin's."

He picked up both the corpses and tossed them effortlessly into the back of the car. Gallowglass was not only a mist-shifter, but immensely strong. Renquist stroked Dormandu's muzzle and climbed back into the saddle. "Gallowglass . . ."

Gallowglass was in the act of getting into the Rolls himself. "Aye, Master Renquist?"

"Thank you for the mist. It was a nice touch."

"There aren't many o' us left i' these modern times."

"You sound as though you don't favor modern times?"

"D' ye, Master Renquist?"

Without waiting for a reply, Gallowglass released the brake and let the car roll forward until it gathered some speed. He then must have let out the clutch, because the engine suddenly came to life. Dormandu arched his neck as though taken by surprise. Renquist petted the horse and turned him in the direction of Ravenkeep. "I don't think I care to explain the last half hour to your mistress and her companions."

Columbine knew in an instant. Renquist had fed. The signs were blatantly evident: the faint flush and the sheen of excitement on his skin, the slight veining in the whites of his eyes. They all told the story. Maybe Destry and Marieko wouldn't have noticed, but Columbine had fed with Renquist in the old times. Although—to her initial chagrin and later fury—they had never bonded, she had seen him more than once immediately after a kill. It may have been a very long time ago, even in nosferatu terms, but it was something one didn't forget. Her first reaction was one of proprietary outrage. Victor had gone off on Destry's huge black horse and then, so full of himself he'd thrown all caution to the winds, actually stopped to feed on some human from the surrounding countryside. As she was starting to entertain visions of a massive police investigation, roadblocks, and a countywide manhunt, she abruptly realized, no matter how much she might resent or dislike him, she could not reasonably accuse Victor of being either stupid or careless. Quite the reverse. He was dauntingly bright, ultra-wary, and painstakingly judicious in everything he did. He would no more slaughter random humans so close to even a temporary home than he would attempt to fly in the air. If that was the case, though, on whose blood had he been so obviously feasting?

Once again, Victor had interrupted the three of them in the large drawing room. Destry had straightaway left to check on Dormandu, to see that the horse had suffered

no ill effects from being ridden by Renquist. As Destry
made her exit, Renquist had stepped more fully into the
light, and Columbine had known. Coolly deciding that
a planned but seemingly hysterical confrontation was
probably the only way to elicit the truth, she flung out
a theatrically accusing arm worthy of Sarah Bernhardt
in her prime. She could only just resist placing a
clenched fist to her forehead. "You have killed tonight,
Victor."

Renquist's response was glacial rather than guilty. "I
really don't think that's any of your concern."

Columbine was momentarily fazed, but she quickly
recovered. "You're a guest in my damned house, Victor.
It's very much my concern if you intend on galloping
around in the night, slaughtering the locals like the head-
less horseman."

"You know very well, my dear, I would do nothing
of the sort."

"But you've fed. You don't deny that, do you?"

Columbine had half expected Marieko to be reacting
with embarrassment to what could be looked on as a
second angry encounter between her and Victor in
twenty-four hours, but she was gratified to find her also
staring intently at him, also wondering where he might
have found a victim while on horseback on the open
downs.

"How and where I might feed is simply none of your
business, Columbine. Assure yourself I'm both tidy and
circumspect, and that's all you need to know." Before
Columbine could formulate a reply, he turned to Marieko. "I realize tempting me with the Uzbekian was a
ploy to get me away from the house so the three of you
could talk in private, but I really think it's time you took
me to see this supposed artifact. I've come a long way.
My entire interest is to discover the nature of this alleged
power source, and I certainly don't intend to stand here
and be subjected to some overwrought interrogation. So

shall we go, or do I hire a car to take me back to London?"

Columbine wasn't exactly sure what she intended to do. Renquist may have played all his cards, but he also seemed to have won. Afterwards, all she could recall was an overwhelming red rage. Fortunately, Destry came through the door before she could act, just in time to catch the end of the conversation. "I wouldn't call the cab quite yet, Victor."

Renquist at least had the decency to look a little disconcerted. "No?"

"Not until you explain why Fenrior's closest henchman should be bringing you a brace of warm victims as a gift."

Columbine let out a slow hiss. She could hardly believe what she was hearing. She expected Renquist to be arrogant and overbearing, but not to openly betray them. "He met with—"

"He met with Gallowglass."

"Gallowglass? Fenrior's creeping shadow?"

"That's the only Gallowglass I know."

Columbine slowly turned and faced Renquist. Destry moved up beside her. At the same time, Marieko got to her feet. Columbine couldn't believe the sudden and radical change of course. Without the slightest effort on her part, Victor had seemingly done the impossible. He had united the entire troika against him.

Renquist found himself again facing three dangerously angry females. An undivided and savagely united force, they dared him to talk his way out of this predicament. Columbine hissed a second time, threatening and reptilian, and reality receded as a perilous anger turned the room scarlet and purple. The air cracked with furious energy, and rationality was lost in the movement to physical conflict. Renquist knew, if the three attacked him with equal determination, the odds were definitely in their favor. Should he manage to emerge without having suffered complete destruction, he would still be badly mauled. Fangs were already extending and hands tensed into damaging claws. Without looking, he judged the distance to the crossed sabers on the wall. He wondered, if worst came to worst, could he leap for one or both of the blades before the troika dragged him down? Perhaps with a weapon in each hand, he could fight his way out. If he could decapitate one very quickly, ideally Columbine, he might just make it out of Ravenkeep intact.

At that point, Renquist caught himself. He realized his own, mindless, undead gorge was rising, and very shortly, no one in the room would be thinking clearly if they were thinking at all. He had to make one last attempt to restore sanity before all was a heedless ripping hell of steel, flesh, and bone.

"Wait!"

But Columbine's rage had driven her past judgment or language. She sprang at him with a sound between a hiss and a howl. Renquist deftly sidestepped, at the same time throwing all his energy into the voice of command. "I SAID WAIT, DAMN YOU!"

Columbine actually recoiled, but she instantly recovered and came back at Renquist. The only positive factor was that her response was at least verbal. She retained the tone of an angry cobra, but did form words. "Wait? Why? So we can listen to more of your deceits?"

"How do you know I met with Gallowglass?"

All previous empathy had gone from Destry Maitland, but even when psyched to kill, she retained an essential colonial cool. "The horse gave you away, Victor. Dormandu has a memory, and he lets me read it. That's part of the bond."

Marieko felt a need to amplify. "The horse is like a recording machine. Destry went to the stables and she saw. She saw Gallowglass arrive in the Rolls. She saw the victims. She saw him create the mist."

Renquist played his ace. "And does Dormandu speak English?"

The females looked at each other. Destry raised an eyebrow. "What do you mean?"

"You saw what happened, but did you hear what was said?"

"It seemed fairly obvious. Gallowglass came from Fenrior and provided you with prey."

"And you think that was at my request?"

The fire in the air receded as thought took over. Auras became slightly less intense, but Renquist knew his position was still fraught. Perhaps, though, he now he had a chance.

"How could it be otherwise?"

Marieko had asked the question, and with her it was possible to argue logic. "You ask how could it be otherwise, and I can only respond 'How could it be?' I arrived in England a little more than forty-eight hours ago, but you seem to think I've had time both to travel down here and consummate a conspiracy with a clan in the remote Highlands of Scotland, and then have one of their retainers drive all that distance, picking up a pair of human nightclub trash on the way, to meet me and feed me on a random hillside, when I just happened to be out riding because you three had felt the need to get me out of the house so you could talk about me in private. Wouldn't that seem something of a challenge even to my supposed diabolic powers of duplicity?"

Marieko was clearly impressed by the cleanliness of Renquist's reasoning. She glanced at Columbine. "He makes a persuasive case."

Columbine merely hissed. "I still think he's lying."

"It could well be Fenrior was aware of Victor's arrival in this country and sent Gallowglass to intercept him."

"He's the very worst kind of liar. He uses the very hollowness of his lies to give them the ring of truth."

"Fenrior would be naturally curious why Victor Renquist should be visiting us."

Renquist said nothing. He could let Marieko make his case for him, even if it cut no ice with Columbine. He preferred it when they were one against another rather than all bearing down on him.

Columbine was shaking her head, keeping reason at bay. "I still believe he's in cahoots with Fenrior."

Renquist knew he must not in any way react. He had divided the troika, and they hadn't noticed. If he let slip even the faintest twitch of triumph, they might be back to reckless tooth and nail in an instant. Now he pressed to put the females on the defensive. "Words like *betrayal, conspiracy,* and *cahoots* would tend to indicate a state of hostilities. I wasn't aware Ravenkeep was at war with Fenrior, and such a thing was definitely not mentioned in any of your letters. Is there some disharmony with the Highland clan? Don't you think I should have been warned if such was the case? I might have thought twice about walking into a war."

Marieko and Destry looked at Columbine as though it was her place to explain. When she remained silent, Marieko attempted to be diplomatic. "It's not so much we and Fenrior are at war—"

Columbine rudely interrupted. "Fenrior is a barbarian. Do you expect us to bond with grotesques, savages, and brigands?"

Both Destry and Marieko looked hard at Columbine. "We think, Columbine, you need to explain the situation a little more fully to Victor."

"I need to explain nothing to Victor."

Renquist made his voice very soft. The violence had passed, but the potential remained. Columbine was delicately poised. "If there are things I have to know, one of you had better tell me now."

"Or?"

"Or I cannot continue. I must leave here and return to London. I will visit with Fenrior, and then arrange to fly back to California."

Destry's voice was as soft as Renquist's. "We need

him here, Columbine. If only to find the source of your dreams."

Columbine, for her part, actually seemed to be making an effort at control, something Renquist definitely welcomed. She was silent for a moment and then bought more time by walking to the side table and opening the art deco cigarette box. She took out a cigarette, placed it between her lips, and picked up the matching table lighter. At that point, she stopped and glanced at Destry. "Did Bolingbroke fill the lighters?"

Destry shrugged. "I hope so, for his sake."

Columbine flicked, and a flame appeared. Again Renquist was grateful. The distraction of Columbine going into a snit over an unfilled table lighter was exactly what he didn't need right then. She inhaled and blew a perfect smoke ring. Renquist was impressed but also prompted to a greater wariness. In the course of the modest piece of theater, her personality had undergone a radical transformation from the infantile hysteric to the cold and calculating. Even among European nosferatu, universally noted for their complex volatility, Renquist had to judge Columbine as exceptional in her capacity to shift moods, seemingly at will. She was a temperamental roller-coaster ride, and he could easily be unseated if he didn't pay constant attention.

Renquist said nothing through the entire show, waiting to hear how the new Columbine was going to open this phase of the game. Her tone became brittle and defensive. "Very well. I do admit that I was perhaps a little overzealous, when, a few years ago, I thought a closer alliance between the House of Fenrior and the Ravenkeep Troika might be mutually advantageous. Since that time, relations have been strained."

"Not to say strange." Destry's short but cynical postscript confirmed what Renquist could easily imagine. Columbine's idea of an alliance almost certainly wouldn't have been one of equitable partnership. As he read it, she had probably made a failed play to become

the Lady of Fenrior, and grudges were being nursed
in the protracted and festering way that is only available
to the functionally immoral. This introduced the Fenrior
clan to the picture in a way he'd not anticipated, but
before he could think through what this might mean to
him—apart from regretting he'd ever come here in the
first place—Columbine continued. Her act of contrition
was over, and she turned back on Renquist. "So, Victor,
you can perhaps see why anyone holding clandestine
meetings with the Lord Fenrior's henchman has to be
suspect in this house?"

"I've already told you the encounter was random. I
don't intend to repeat myself all night. Either you accept
that, or I'm about my business."

Destry and Marieko both stared at Columbine as
though willing her to accept reality. Renquist decided he
would give her a little help. "If I were in your position,
I'd get my input on this burial mound as quickly as
possible. We've seen how my arrival has attracted Fenrior's attention, and how he is making his own tentative
moves. Speed would appear to be of the essence."

Destry and Marieko were all but nodding agreement.
Columbine surrendered to Marieko. "Very well. Take
him there. See if he can be of any use to us."

Destry quickly intervened. "I think maybe I should go
with them."

Columbine seemed torn. "I'd be left here on my own,
but, on the other hand, it might be a good idea if you
were there to keep an eye on Victor."

Renquist noticed it was accepted, under no circumstances, would Columbine be going to Morton Downs.
She assumed the leadership in most other things, and yet
she appeared to be unable or unwilling to visit the
mound. Could it be she was afraid of whatever they
thought was there? He knew something was affecting
Columbine's dreaming, and he supposed the troika had
decided it was somehow connected to the mound. This
was another piece of speculation he filed away for future

thought. Right now he wanted to move. He wanted to get out of Ravenkeep and into the fresh air and the moonlight. He'd also come a long way to investigate this strangeness at the burial mound, and he was tired of waiting on the machinations of these females. "Could we do this now? I think we've argued long enough. It's time for inquiry and action."

Columbine looked at Destry. "You'd better go with them. I don't trust Victor alone with Marieko."

Marieko raised a perfectly drawn eyebrow. "Do you trust me alone with him?"

Before Columbine could reply, Renquist stepped in. "Before we start arguing who trusts who with whom, there's one thing I should make clear."

"And what might that be?"

"If indeed, by some chance, an confrontation should occur with the Clan Fenrior, I cannot take sides. I am a master of my own colony. I have to observe the traditional protocols."

Columbine seemed about to dispute this, but Destry quickly closed the door on any further wrangling. "We understand, Victor. Everything will be done strictly according to tradition."

Columbine glared at Destry but then prepared to make her exit. "I suppose, if I'm no longer needed—"

Renquist decided on a spur-of-the-moment test. "Why don't you come with us?"

Columbine shook her head. "No."

That seemed to be all she intended to say, but in the doorway she turned, in the classic manner, to deliver an exit line. "I love my condition, Victor, and I serve it always."

The concepts of sanity and madness were highly relative among the nosferatu, verging on meaningless in terms applicable to humans, but Renquist couldn't help concluding that, after two hundred years, Columbine might be redefining the definitions. Had she been human, she would have been declared, if not a psychopath, at least dangerously neurotic, and even by the more lax nosferatu standards, she was decidedly rare.

Columbine was gone, and before Renquist could say anything, Marieko announced she, too, was going—in her case to dress for the outside world. Since Renquist and Destry were already fully attired from their ride, there was nothing to do but wait. The moment they were alone, Destry smiled knowingly at Renquist. "Don't think I didn't see what you just did."

Renquist raised an amused eyebrow. "I just assisted a logical calm to prevail. Columbine doesn't like reality coming at her unannounced, does she? I know she has no objection to creating mayhem on her own terms, but when it's beyond her control, she can become highly vexed. Of course, that's only my observation."

"You're pretty slick, Victor. Pretty damned slick, but don't think divide and rule will work on us girls all the time. Charm only goes so far, sweetheart. Sisterhood has depths you might not appreciate."

Marieko had turned the Range Rover off the road, and it was now bumping down a rutted track, lights out, running in complete darkness. Although Renquist very rarely drove a car, he was aware headlights really served only to impede nosferatu night vision. A deep silence settled on Destry and Renquist as the truck bounced up a low rise, and, cresting it, treated them to their first glimpse of the burial mound. From a distance, and to the normal vision, it was hardly impressive. Just an elongated hemisphere stretched to an elongated half ovoid, with barely enough symmetry to distinguish it from a natural formation. To the deep vision, however, it was a unique phenomenon. The tinted safety glass of the Range Rover's windshield made the nosferatu deep vision foggy and less than precise, but the psychic radiation that drifted in approximate circles, like a miniature lazy nebula of microstars orbiting the earthworks, was irrefutable proof that some great dormant power lay beneath the small man-made hill.

Destry let out a soft gasp. "Holy shit. Will you look at that?"

Renquist glanced sharply at Marieko. "Was it like this the other times you came here?"

Marieko shook her head. "Never so intense. The aura's been growing, but this is quantum."

Destry was still awed. "I've never seen anything like it."

Renquist also stared at the energy flow. "None of us have."

Marieko brought the Range Rover to a halt, but all three nosferatu seemed reluctant to be first to open a door and exit the vehicle. Renquist was glad he had, right before leaving, ordered Bolingbroke to fetch his cane. He felt better advancing into the extreme unknown with weapon firmly grasped in his hand, even a symbolic one. Marieko was leaning forward, peering through the windshield. "Campion and his people have been busy."

She pointed to a fairly deep trench dug into one end of the mound. The chosen spot was an educated guess, even for humans, as to where they might reasonably expect to find an entrance. Two small gushers of energy rose from each wall of the trench, shaped by its contours. "They've dug deep enough that it's leaking power."

Destry, who was sitting in the back, leaned between Renquist and Marieko. "Do you think they have any clue what they're doing?"

Marieko shook her head. "None."

"So? Shall we get out and take a closer look?"

Destry nodded. "That's what we came here for."

The moment Renquist opened the door, it was tumultuously apparent how sheltered they had been inside the Range Rover. The slow waltz of energy challenged the night-shine of the sky, and the very air shivered with a measureless potential. At the same time, an audio background boomed with a stately rhythm, well below the lower extremes of human hearing. A sound like the deep somnolent breath of a huge and deeply slumbering reptile washed over Renquist. He knew this flow of power would not have diminished by day, and he failed to understand how mortal men and women could excavate in this place without sensing anything at all, even if the power they delved into manifested itself as nothing more than a seemingly groundless sense of fear. Maybe humans were becoming desensitized by their culture of horror, or maybe it was just that modern archaeologists had grown more stern in their calling. Less than a hundred years ago, such power flow would have been the foundation of tales of curses, maledictions, and enchantments.

With a firm grip on his silver-topped cane, Renquist advanced across the grass of Morton Downs toward the mound. The energy flowed around him like the mist created by Gallowglass, only less dense and substantial. He could feel a tapestry of images woven into the flow, but he brought under the tightest control the part of his mind that might give them form and fully realize them as conscious visions. The sound, imagery, and color didn't seem to be either directed or even deliberately threatening, but he knew he must resist becoming a temporary part of it despite the inquiring temptation. *Temporary* could prove highly relative, and he might find it hard to disengage—and the chance of sunrise discovering him still wandering transfixed, oblivious to his imminent destruction was too great a risk.

He glanced behind. Destry and Marieko were following a few yards back, letting Renquist take the point and be the first to draw any fire, physical or metaphysical. Both had the effortless floating walk of the undead that once caused peasants to bar windows, flee for their lives, or clutch worthless crosses and equally worthless garlic flowers, as though their meager lives depended on one or the other for spurious protection. Destry and Marieko had instinctively adopted the formation of an advancing patrol, and both were very definitely arrayed as implacable and unconventional warrior women of the undead, on a mission even more vital and challenging than the blood hunt. Still in her riding habit and still carrying her whip, Destry appeared ready for anything, and when Marieko had dressed for the expedition, she had done so with a vengeance. The laced-up Doc Martens left no prints in the turf, but the vinyl catsuit did make small plastic creaks as she moved, and her long leather duster flapped behind her, also audible. Formidable, maybe, but Renquist did notice, how, every so often, one of them would glance round as though startled. They, too, were encountering the apparitions of the energy stream. Should he warn them to exclude the visions entirely, or let them use their judgment? The latter seemed appropriate. He was on point, the offered target; that was more than enough of a contribution to the mutual good.

He wished Lupo were with him from the colony—not only because the broad, bullnecked nosferatu was a squat pillar of strength and could be counted on to make exactly the right move at exactly the right time, but also because his age gave him insights into the most outlandish and singular of situations. Ever since Renquist had become master of his colony, Lupo had been there, at his back. All he had at his back now, in this completely unpredictable situation, was a pair of unknown quantities. Marieko had proved herself capable when a dreamstate of her own devising was compromised from outside, but he had no idea how she might respond in the real world. Destry appeared to be able to handle herself, but appearances could be deceptive.

The three of them were now nearing the humans' excavated trench. Renquist halted and indicated the females should do the same. He wanted to make a careful scrutiny of what had been unearthed before he went plunging in. Campion and his volunteers had already uncovered stonework; a heavy lintel of a pale limestone, supported by two granite uprights. Set back between the uprights was a third block that acted as what Renquist could only interpret as a door. Sometime in the past, one of the uprights appeared to have slipped slightly, and the door was no longer of a fully flush fit. Through the gaps left by this movement of the ground, all the energy was leaking. It flowed out from the imperfections around the door frame, and then immediately rose straight up, following the sides of the trench, to dissipate in the circular movement in the air above the mound.

Renquist stepped closer, and Marieko followed. Destry, meanwhile, stood and watched, acting as rear guard for the exploration. The door troubled him. From a distance, it didn't appear to match with the surrounding stone either in period or composition, and he was at a loss to know from what material it was made. He needed to get down into the trench and look more closely, but that would involve him in passing through one of the energy streams, an action about which he had distinct misgivings. Power abounded even at a distance, and to physically touch one of the denser streams could be courting disaster. Renquist was torn. To stop here would not only be an intolerable frustration, but also a considerable loss of face in front of the females. To press on, though, was an advance into the concealed and totally unpredictable. In the end, a combination of curiosity and vanity overrode his qualms, and he decided to play the hero. He jumped lightly down into the trench, but, for the moment, he still avoided contact with the direct flows of energy. Marieko made to follow him, but he waved her back.

"Don't come down here."

Destry was beside her. "Don't try to claim some male monopoly by taking all the risks."

"If something happens, I may need you two to drag me out."

Renquist might, to a degree, have been showing off, but he also knew that if he was to learn anything, he had to brave the glowing escape of shining psychic energy.

He extended a wary hand toward the nearest roiling ten-
dril of light, but Marieko spoke before he could actually
touch it. "I don't think you should do that, Victor."

"I don't see any other way."

"Then take it very slowly, and pull back if you feel
any ill effects."

"That's exactly what I intend."

"I still don't like it."

"Can you think of a better solution?"

Marieko shook her head. "No."

"Then let's see what happens."

Very gently, a half inch at a time, he extended his
finger until his whole hand was in the energy flow. To
his surprise, he initially experienced little sensation at
all. The silver band of his onyx ring seemed to shine,
and the metal felt cold on his finger, but that was about
the sum total. If he been looking for thunderbolts of
static discharge, or a sudden upheaval of his entire nervous system, he was mercifully disappointed.

"Are you okay?" Marieko's voice was concerned.

Renquist removed his hand from the power flow. "So
it would seem. Let me try it again."

He put his hand back into the stream of energy. The
silver of his ring again glowed, but very little else happened. "Remarkable."

Then, even as he spoke, things changed. He had expected fireworks, but instead, gradually at first but with
increasing force, he found himself inundated by images.
It seemed to be a haphazard and totally disjointed assault
of jumbled visions and data coming at him in the form
of abstract hallucinations. He must have shown some
outward sign of what was happening to him because, as
though from a great distance, he heard Destry calling to
him. "Victor. Are you all right?"

He diverted the hallucinations as best he could in the
direction of his already distorted subconscious and tried
to confine the frontal areas of his mind to analytical
thought. "I . . . think so."

"Should we pull you out of there?"

"No. I can handle it."

"Handle what?"

"I can't explain. It seems to want something."

A central theme in the strange data—and the only one with a real urgency—was something wanting him to look at the left-hand upright. Renquist allowed himself to be swayed. He moved closer to what he accepted without question as a door. This involved him in moving bodily through three of the primary source energy streams. The strange force howled around him like sound made visible. The hallucinations became totally incomprehensible. One idea kept drumming in his head. The left upright. The left upright. Scarcely able to see with all that was battering on his mind, he pulled himself out of the direct path of the power flow. He leaned against the door; his first impression had been right. The door didn't fit with the otherwise Bronze Age structure. It was metal, but no metal he recognized. After being buried for hundreds, maybe thousands of years, it was blemished only by the faintest dulling patina of corrosion. He had no time to ponder, though. The left upright. The left upright. He turned his head and looked at it. The print of a human hand suddenly appeared, glowing on the surface of the rock, as if etched there in light. He knew instinctively that this was the access mechanism to whatever was inside. He was being told what to do. He needed only to place his hand over the glowing handprint. He was also being informed he had no choice in the matter. He would do it whether he wanted to or not. Somewhere he could hear Marieko and Destry, but he couldn't answer them.

"Victor!"

"Victor! What's happening?"

He placed his hand over the glowing rock and felt something like a mild electrical shock, but at first, that was all. Then dust began to cascade down from the joints where the uprights supported the lintel. The door was starting to move, but because of the misalignment of the uprights, it was sticking. Then it seemingly freed itself and grated slowly open, moving back and to the side. As the aperture widened, an all-consuming brilliance streamed out. A floodgate had been opened. Renquist had a chance to utter a single cry of warning to Marieko and Destry before the blazing force swamped him. "Protect yourselves any way you can!"

CHAPTER FOUR

Renquist's mind had become a whirling kaleidoscope, his undead brain fragmenting as every neuron independently saved its own life. Sound was a multiple scream, spiking way above and deep below the limits of even his undead hearing. Vision was nothing more than a blinding arc speckled with a spider-net of nervous blood vessels. As the full discharge of energy engulfed him in the previously sealed entrance of the burial mound, the only comparison was being exposed to the full and deadly glare of the sun. More than once in his long existence, Renquist had come dangerously close to being caught in the sun. The most recent near-miss had been back in New York City when he'd found himself engaged, with extreme prejudice, in struggle for dominance with the young upstart Kurt Carfax. After barely a second of full daylight (and with as much protection as his street clothes could afford him), his skin had singed and smoked, and he'd been deprived of all sight for a number of hours. He knew the mind protected itself by never remembering the full intensity of physical pain, but he truly believed the agony and confusion now dragging at him like a cosmic riptide was worse than that Manhattan exposure.

Renquist had all but resigned himself to the end and was attempting to hold off his fury, albeit unsuccessfully, at eternity being snatched from him by a stupid mistake on an English hillside. Fatalism might claim a life span of a thousand years constituted a reasonable run, but he wasn't about to buy that. As he prepared not to go quietly into the poet's dark night, the chaos began to mitigate, and the anguish diminished. The blazing arc was split into strobes and afterimages, and a certain awareness of his surroundings returned. Although he hurt, the possibility presented itself he might survive the ordeal. His stomach spasmed, and cramps locked his muscles like a DC electric current was being channeled through them, but his actual integrity of being was gradually reasserting itself. As the power flow visibly ebbed, enough of his mind once again functioned for him to realize that what he'd first believed was a continuous force was only a limited surge, a flash flood of pent-up energy being released from a long confinement.

Still deprived of a sense of time, Renquist did not— and would never—know how long it took the accumulated force to discharge itself and for Morton Downs to grow quiet again, with only small glitters of aftermath crackle-dancing in the air. When he was finally released from the tumult's furious vise, he found himself lying on his side, fetally curled in the damp bottom of the trench, mud all over his pants and leather jacket. Even the effort of straightening his legs was a reprise of pain, and he waited awhile before he attempted to stand. As his normal sight returned, he discovered the silver-topped sword cane just a few inches from his right hand, but when he used it to assist him to his feet, his entire body protested. His nosferatu control and resilience left him unaccustomed to purely physical suffering, and he refused to accept it with fortitude. Renquist didn't like to hurt to this degree, and only a major effort of will stopped him howling out his anger and frustration.

He was also unaccustomed to lying in the bottom of a trench. The last time he had been obliged to do such a thing was during the Great Slaughter of 1919, when he had been forced to hide not only in abandoned World War I trenches, but also in ditches, cellars, and broken shell-shocked ruins, to save himself from the axes, fires, and sharpened stakes of the howling and highly mobilized followers of Bishop Rausch, the last great vampire hunter of the Catholic Church. When the Slaughter finally passed, Renquist had sworn he would never be forced into such skulking again, yet here he was, maybe not skulking, but muddy, sick, and with his head spinning. He felt a growing fury at the thing, whatever it was, that evidently lurked in the burial place, generating such careless levels of psychic radiation.

"Victor? Marieko?"

The voice was Destry's, and it sounded lost and confused. Up to that moment, Victor had been so completely absorbed by his own pain and outrage, he hadn't given a thought to whether the two females from Ravenkeep had survived the psychic onslaught, or in what condition it might have left them. He regretted the lapse as, if nothing else, extremely ungentlemanly, and he was about to speak when the equally weak voice of Marieko preempted him.

"Destry?"

"Marieko? Where are you? I still can't see properly. I think I've been blinded."

Marieko's voice was soothing. "Don't be frightened. It'll pass. I'm over here. The same thing happened to me, but I'm starting to recover."

"What the hell was all that?"

"I don't know. The last thing I remember was looking down at Victor in the trench, and then it was like a door opened and the terrible light escaped."

Renquist, as he leaned on his cane, trying to clear his senses, could hear Marieko and Destry moving. After a few moments they appeared to find each other. Marieko sounded as though she was caring for Destry. "Are you starting to see again?"

"A little."

"Can you stand?"

"I think so."

"Here. Let me help you."

"Do you know what happened to Victor?"

Marieko's tone was bleak. "I don't know. One minute he was there, and the next he was completely swallowed up by the light."

"What will become of us if the world thinks we destroyed Victor Renquist?"

Renquist was grimly amused that Destry's first thoughts were of the possible repercussions of his destruction, and he felt less guilty about his own self-absorption. He raised his voice and called from the trench. "Don't worry. I'm still here. The discharge didn't kill me, although I'm not sure it made me any stronger."

Two faces appeared over the edge of the trench. "Victor!"

"The very same."

"You're all right?"

"That might be a slight exaggeration, but I have survived."

"What was that?"

"I think we've confirmed that something is alive inside this mausoleum."

"But all that energy."

"Perhaps generated by its changing metabolism. I think you were right, Marieko. Whatever it is, it's slowly waking from a very long sleep."

A bright confetti of charged particles wafted from the door. Destry flinched. "Will it happen again?"

"I don't think so. What we just saw was most likely

a discharge of buildup. Now the tomb is unsealed, it shouldn't occur again."

She didn't seem too convinced. "How do you know that?"

"I was the one that opened the door, wasn't I?"

Renquist had now recovered almost all his strength. He gathered himself and leapt from the trench. To be holding a conversation between the top and bottom of the excavation was absurd. He landed lightly between Marieko and Destry, who looked hollow-eyed and shocked but otherwise undamaged. They were also considerably cleaner than he, having only been thrown to the turf and not the mud of the trench. Marieko looked him up and down, sufficiently recovered to be amused by his condition. "When confronted by a mysterious door, do you always open it?"

Renquist exhaled and leaned on his cane, but he was able to return her smile. "It's the fastest way to learn what's on the other side."

"Maybe you should go a little slower next time."

Destry was showing distinct signs of returning to her former self. "Yeah, Victor. Next time think twice, okay? I mean, those visions . . ."

Marieko and Renquist looked sharply at her. "Visions? You had visions?"

"It was like I was getting the entire history of the world, except in random, out-of-sync cutups. I saw it all. I saw hominid apes fleeing from the advancing ice sheets. I saw the great ships of the Nephilim descending from the sky. I saw the lifting rays and the pyramids under construction. I saw the Original Beings and the other creatures of Marduk Ra's experiments. I saw them being hunted by the skycraft, the deathrays burning them down and the sunbombs detonating—"

A weirding seemed to be gathering force inside Destry, an amped-up, poststress hysteria. Marieko quickly put a hand on her arm. "Easy, my dear."

Renquist made his voice as gentle as possible. "We

have all dreamed dreams of the ancient times. The memories are bonded into our DNA, but I will admit they usually surface in the dreamstate and not some insane energy field."

Marieko had recovered sufficiently to nitpick. "Who's to say what might happen in an insane energy field. Isn't such a thing, by definition, unpredictable?"

Renquist conceded. "You have a point."

Destry shook her head. "No, you don't understand. I've never had those dreams before."

Renquist was surprised. "You've never had DNA dreams?"

"Never. I'd started to assume something was wrong with me."

"They take time. For some, it can be truly hard. I had a number of teachers who helped me awaken them."

Destry avoided Renquist's eyes. "I never had a teacher."

The statement was so forlorn, so out of character, Renquist knew a story was buried there. This was not, however, the time for speculation over Destry's history. "The real question is, do we go on?"

"What?" Destry pointed to the dark entrance of the barrow. "You want to go back in there after all that's happened?"

"I think it's a chance worth taking. Also we can't afford to waste any time. After such a massive psychic explosion, this place is no longer a secret."

"Are the humans aware of it? Could they see any of that?"

"I would have thought they felt something. Although, these days, when the majority are so heavily drugged on one thing or another, maybe not. Right now, though, humans are not my primary concern. They'll rationalize anything they might have seen or felt as unidentified flying objects, or angels, or another of their pet paranormal fixations. I'm thinking more of the others of our kind. For them, that discharge blazed to the high heavens

like a comet. It must have been visible halfway across
Europe."

Marieko spoke softly. "Fenrior must have seen it."

Renquist gave her a sidelong look. "His people could
hardly have missed it. In fact, if I were him, I'd already
be on my way."

"Gallowglass is already here."

"All the more reason that we should go inside right
now."

"You used the word *we*."

"I did, didn't I?"

"Does that mean you've united with us in this endeavor?"

Renquist was not so easily hooked. "It means I would
like to be the first to look at this thing that all but finished me. I think I've earned the right."

"I think we all have." Destry seemed to have recovered enough to assert herself.

Renquist made a slight bow. "I wouldn't argue about
that. My only concern is how much time we have left.
My timesense was scrambled back there."

Marieko frowned, as though making the same discovery. "Mine, too."

Destry looked up at the sky. "We have a few hours
before dawn."

Renquist was surprised. "You can tell time from the
stars?"

"It's something I taught myself. I'm better near the
equator. That's where I had the most practice."

Again Renquist was curious about Destry's background. Now she talked almost as though she were some
nosferatu jungle girl raised by undead primates. Sooner
or later, he would find out for sure. In the meantime, he
wanted to see inside the mound despite all that had happened. "Shall we go?"

Marieko hesitated. "Are you sure that was just a discharge of buildup?"

Renquist jumped down into the trench and looked

back up at her. "I believe so. I could, of course, be
wrong. I was, after all, the one stupid enough to open
the door in the first place."

Columbine could only watch in awe as the sky exploded
and soft, dreamlike shock waves tingled through her
body and mind. At a distance, it was spectacular and
pleasurable, as though her very cells were being energized, but she could imagine it would be a burning
trauma to anyone near ground zero, and she knew
ground zero could only be Morton Downs. No line of
sight existed between Ravenkeep and Morton Downs.
Two or maybe three hills were in the way, and she
hadn't climbed to one of the high turret rooms in the
oldest part of the building specifically to see if Marieko,
Destry, and Renquist's visit might produce any visible
reaction. Nothing had occurred during any of Marieko's
visits, although it did appear that, where Renquist went,
drama and exhibition tended to follow. Climbing to the
ruined turrets had long been a solitary habit for Columbine. High above the pile of brick and stone, above
everything save the highest flying birds, she felt a connection to reality she found in few other places. Leaning
on her elbows, hands cupped under her chin, she could
become part of that perfect conjunction of past, present,
future that is the unique joy to those for whom death is
not a certainty.

When totally alone, Columbine harbored few illusions
about herself. She knew she lacked standing among the
serious nosferatu of Europe. Many thought she wasted
her time and talent on hedonism and gratuitous evil. In
illusion she could adopt the scales and posture of the
reptile, but never its implacable patience and singleness
of purpose. She played the scatterbrain with flounces,
airs, and perfumes because, in most respects, she really
was a scatterbrain. Her attention span was short. She was
driven by emotion rather than reason. When she made
plans, they were often marred by a lack of attention to

detail, as had happened during the Fenrior debacle. She didn't study and could in no way equal the erudition of Renquist. Even Fenrior had more education. She lacked both Destry's fast practicality and Marieko's creativity. Raw power was really her only hope. If she couldn't command the skills, her only alternative was to grasp and hold the power. Even in that, though, she had let a certain indolence get the better of her. If she was to be absolutely honest, she'd all too often been criminally lazy, content to lord it over mere humans, content to impose her will on thralls, slaves, serfs, darklost, and craving obsessives. Easy worship and effortless adulation had ever been too much of a temptation.

Columbine could feel herself sinking. One of the problems of coming to the high turrets was that her time there usually started with hopes and grand aspirations, but contemplating their accomplishment easily turned her to introspection. In turn, introspection led to an increasingly negative self-analysis, and ultimately plunged her into the deep end of self-pity. Self-pity would of course, in turn, harden into a need to punish someone other than herself for her discomfort. Subordinates would suffer, and as she contemplated that relief, she reminded herself how few could outstrip her at creative cruelty when she put her mind to it.

She would never know whether it was accident or unconscious design that positioned her at the window looking exactly in the direction of Morton Downs and placed her in the perfect spot to observe what transpired. The first apparition was a soft sparkle, like a slow whirling dance of iridescent snowflakes. At first she was annoyed that this bizarre phenomenon, these diamonds in the sky, was interrupting her well-worn circle of fluctuating self-esteem, but then she realized how damned stupid that was, and in the same instant, the diamonds fused into the red aerial glow of a distant fire. Her absorption in herself dropped away, and she watched with increasing disbelief, as the red glow brightened, turned to violet, and finally to a searing white heat. Thick fire ropes of energy streamed vertically into the sky, like the psychic equivalent of a Hiroshima burst, and Columbine unconsciously took a step back.

"What the hell have you three done?"

If Renquist, Destry, and Marieko were at the source of all that power, what chance of survival did they have? Was it the destruction of whatever was in the burial ground? Were her awful dreams at an end? Then an ugly thought presented itself: If the three who had gone to Morton Downs had been destroyed, she was alone. What the hell was she going to do? She didn't care about Renquist, or at least, she would pretend not to care about Renquist for as long as she could, but without the other two in the troika, how was she going to organize her survival? She couldn't run this whole estate with just two thralls and some day laborers.

Away in the distance, the fireball had contracted into a single blazing beam, a narrow lance of light stabbing to infinity, exactly vertical, all the way to the upper stratosphere. As the background radiation passed through her, Columbine could hear voices whispering in the air, a soft and inexplicable Babel of a hundred tongues. Most she didn't recognize, but they sounded ancient or archaic to her admittedly untrained ear. She thought she detected Latin and, disturbingly, languages from her recent and recurring dreams. Strangest of all, she definitely heard words from the Old Speech, the deep and secret, original language of the nosferatu.

Columbine was both fascinated and repelled. The mystery was deepening, but the more it deepened, the less she liked it—if, indeed, she had ever liked it at all. Columbine preferred the kind of mystery where she dictated the game and knew all the answers. In this adventure, she knew none of the answers. It was Renquist's kind of game, where deduction and informed guesswork prevailed rather than spite, guile, and manipulation. The column of light glowed brighter, extending all the way into space. The radiation was harder on her body, not painful, but definitely more aggressive, with a touch that generated a certain veiled excitement. But what was happening, she again asked herself, to Victor and her two companions? Columbine's only consolation was feeling none of the signs that always accompanied the departure of one of the undead from this realm of existence.

Columbine knew exactly what happened when a nosferatu was suddenly and violently lost to this world. She had observed the process, up close and firsthand, on that terrible blazing morning she had hidden undetected in the dark cellar of the ruined Persian mosque, outside of the stinking little town of Kashan, while, above her, Dr. Feisal and his Bedouin cutthroats had conducted the screaming ritual impalement of Sir Francis Varney. Poor, idiotic Varney's destruction had been like a ballooning vacuum, appearing in the very air itself and then vanishing in a silent clap of implosion. In this case, Columbine sensed no such unquiet disappearance, and it allowed her at least some reason to hope. To be left on her own at a time like this was completely unthinkable. This was not to say, however, the minds of the three might not be wiped clean by the psychic detonation. They might return as functionless zombies—if they returned at all, and she didn't have to go out herself and find them.

A sudden burst of radiation caused concentric shock waves to race horizontally across the contours of the hills, but they were the power surge's final encore. The spear of light collapsed like a fountain with the pressure shut off, and all was once more normal night. At first Columbine could only stand and stare, marveling at what had just come to pass. Finally (and to her extreme distaste) she realized she might actually have to take some kind of action. Columbine preferred to issue instructions rather than carry them out, but she found herself without anyone to follow her orders, save for the human thralls, and they were too slow and dimwitted to be of any use

in a situation like this. The question was also what action
should she take? Obviously a long-distance scan, an attempt see if she could detect anything, was a place to
start. If only she had taken the time to exercise and extend her powers as Marieko did. She could perceive
nothing except a distant and generalized afterglow. Marieko, Destry, and Victor appeared to have vanished without trace, as though the landscape had swallowed them
up or the energy onslaught had stripped them of their
auras.

"Damn it to hell!"

She would have to go there herself, and she would
have to ride on horseback. The others had the Range
Rover, and it was the only Ravenkeep vehicle, aside
from the rarely used Bentley, totally without the kind of
all-terrain capability she would need. Like Renquist,
Columbine preferred to be chauffeured than to drive, and
up until this spectacular emergency, it had worked out
fine, since Marieko and Destry shared the Range Rover
and Columbine had Bolingbroke call the car service.
Now, she was forced to improvise. It wasn't that she
minded riding; she had, in fact, prior to ascending the
turret room, toyed with the idea of, if not actually hunting, at least reconnoitering a pair of possible prey. A
strange woman who had apparently once been something
vaguely important in punk rock had purchased a cottage
some seven or eight miles away, where she and a highly
androgynous companion had taken up alcoholic residence and appeared to be building a recording studio.
They were exactly the kind who might disappear under
mysterious circumstances without the Wessex Constab-
ulary raising much more than a token hue and cry. Those
plans would now have to be postponed. Psychic energy
explosions could be a damned inconvenience. With a
flash of anger, she used the voice of authority to bellow
for Bolingbroke.

"Get to the stables! I need a horse saddled."

But which horse? Her first instinct was to take the

infinitely manageable and practical gelding she would
have ridden on her hunting sortie, but the great black
Dormandu was by far the more stylistically suitable for
Morton Downs. Of course, Destry would be furious, but
wasn't Columbine coming to her blasted rescue?

"Saddle Dormandu for me!"

Before descending to prepare for her one-woman cavalry charge, she made a final attempt to locate any trace
of Marieko, Destry, or Renquist. Again she saw nothing
except empty night. Then she happened to glance down
at the grounds of the estate, especially the area immediately beneath her high vantage point. A mist had
formed over the lake and was advancing up the incline
of the lawn. Under other circumstances, she might have
been intrigued by the seemingly determined movement
of this localized fog, but her entire attention was focused
on her now avowed mission, and no space remained for
comparative meteorology. Thus she dismissed the odd
fog without thinking and started down the rubble-strewn
stone stairs to the lower, occupied levels.

A further ten minutes found Columbine on her way
to the stables, in black-and-red riding habit, maybe more
tightly form-fitting than function might have dictated,
but in some areas, she allowed no room for compromise.
Her sense of style included no limits to absurdity.
Against her leg she lightly tapped a leather crop with an
ivory head, carved in the shape of a coiled cobra. Destry
wasn't the only one who could handle a whip as an
accessory. She entered the stables, fully expecting Bolingbroke to have the black stallion saddled and ready.
Instead, she discovered him, held fast, apparently the
prisoner of two huge red-bearded male nosferatu, who,
if not brothers, were at least close cousins. Their filthy
ginger hair hung well past their shoulders and was partially braided and decorated with beads, pheasant feathers, and small bones, either human or animal. They wore
the ragged, never-laundered plaid of wild Highlanders
over body armor of studded leather, while basket-hilt

claymores hung at their hips in heavy scabbards. Yellow fangs extended in canine grins, and even in a stable, their rank smell was offensive: smoke, whisky, old blood, vomit, and other repulsiveness she didn't care to recognize. Dormandu snorted uneasily in his stall. Columbine didn't know whether to run or curse them with all her power, but while she was making the choice, a heavy hand fell on her arm.

"Oh, no, ye don't, Mistresss Dasssshwood, ye'll no be ridin' oot any place this night."

Marieko paused and sniffed the air. The passageway beyond the door Victor had so precipitously opened, that presumably led to the main chamber of the burial mound, had a rich earthy smell, dark loam, brown soil, dust, rust, and long-composted vegetation, part decay and part regeneration. Up ahead, Renquist ducked and scrabbled. The ceiling of the passageway was low, scarcely more than four feet at its highest, and where rock had crumbled and shifted, and dirt and debris had fallen through, they had to struggle to keep their footing. Fortunately, they could see perfectly in the total blackness, and were unburdened and unencumbered by lanterns or flashlights as humans might have been. Renquist, noticing that Marieko had stopped, glanced back. "Are you okay?"

Marieko quickly found her voice. "Yes, yes, keep going."

Despite her assurances, Renquist continued to peer at her in the dark. Did he sense she was having certain difficulties? "Surprisingly, I have met a number of nosferatu who have mixed feelings about enclosed spaces under the earth."

In Marieko's case, mixed feelings was an understatement. Was Victor being kind? The entry to the interior of the burial mound, the smell, and the enclosed darkness caused unpleasant memories to surface from the time when, a hundred years earlier, she had been forcibly

entombed while held hostage by the Clan of Kenzu during the final grinding conflict of the late nineteenth century between the Kenzu and her own Yarabachi Clan
that had all but destroyed both their ancient houses.
Taken during her daytime weakness by ninja thralls of
the Kenzu, transported to the enemy stronghold in an
iron-bound, carved wood casket that at least protected
her from the lethal ravages of the sun, she had then been
buried in the same box with a full twelve feet of earth
packed above her. At the time—and since none of her
abductors had felt the need to inform her otherwise—
she had believed she had been selected at random for a
cruel and lingering destruction. Only later, she discovered she and twelve more of the most favored Yarabachi
females, the concubines and bonded hunting partners of
the clan's undead lords, had been taken as hostages. The
Kenzu threat had been to destroy them slowly if the
Yarabachi Clan didn't concede to the Kenzu's territorial
and authoritarian demands. In fact, had she known this,
it would have done nothing to mitigate her anger or fear.
Even the numerically significant sacrifice of thirteen favored females was hardly sufficient to sway the will of
the ever implacable Yarabachi.

For eighteen days, she had retained her composure.
She tuned back her senses and dominated all of the negative thought process that would lead inevitably to panic
and horror. She managed to convince herself she no
longer cared, and lived in temporal moment-by-moment
illusion in which destruction held no terror, and, in the
greater picture of herself and the universe, her passing
was of no significance and certainly no tragedy. Once
she had mastered the desperation and adrenal hysteria
inherent in the drive to self-preservation, she had found
an almost blissful passivity, a nothing-to-lose capacity
to relish the tightly narrowed band of her senses. The
pressure of the earth around her, the illusions that her
vision created in all absence of light, the sounds of the
disturbed ground settling, and the burrowing of worms,

voles, and other subterranean creatures became a micro-universe of infinite possibilities.

After these eighteen days, however, her resolve inexorably cracked. She had screamed. One scream to experiment, to see how it would feel, a second to confirm how it felt, and then a third that was infinitely protracted, near mindless and deafening in a place of subterranean loam where only she could hear it. She had gone to the brink of madness, sank helplessly, but finally surfaced again, by an effort of will she still couldn't quite believe. As far as she knew, she had screamed for five days. In the end, the preserving miracle had come in the form of Katoh. Katoh was her very huge human thrall, the size of a sumo wrestler, whose near-adoring loyalty had been bestowed on her as an indication of her elevation among the Yarabachi females. After she'd been missing for more than three weeks, he'd managed to locate her deep burial plot, and in one frenzied night with a pick and a shovel, and a body count of four dead Kenzu sword-thralls, he had been transformed from slave to liberator.

The two of them had embarked on a nightmare escape in the hellish hold of a freighter bound for Sumatra, a rusting, wheezing hulk from the depths of a Joseph Conrad story. Unfortunately, toward the end of the voyage, she had become so weak and depleted, rather than take the risk of preying on the already highly superstitious and suspicious lascar crew, she had been forced to feed on Katoh, so repeatedly it had resulted in his death. Katoh dying that she might survive had been a definitive nosferatu paradox, in that, for the first part of the transaction, she had been too weak to bestow immortality upon the man, and for the second half, he was too weak to receive it.

Even though the deranged Katoh had been willing, even happy to sacrifice himself so she might survive, she still felt an unaccustomed guilt about abandoning him as a corpse. The ordeal of enforced burial, the sacrifice of a devoted servant, and the loss of the highly idiosyncratic and all-embracing culture of the Japanese clans had been a turning point and trauma in her existence that would stay with her through all of her undead eternity, and the current reek of grave earth brought it all too vividly back. The idea of following Renquist into this hole in the ground had so horrified her she had taken it as a challenge, to confront her fear and not to lose face by backing away from the ordeal.

Marieko moved forward again. To pause for long was impossible, Destry was bringing up the rear, and none of them wanted to be contorted in the cramped passage for longer than was necessary. The urge to flee, to get away from the confines of the place was powerful, but not so overwhelming that she would fail to steel her courage and continue. First the passage ran straight, but then it descended steeply, making progress even more awkward. Mercifully, the slope eventually ended and after maybe another dozen horizontal yards, it finally opened out into what could only be the main chamber, and the main chamber was sufficiently impressive to cause Renquist to straighten up and stare, and make Marieko forget her cold burden of old fear and bad memories.

Destry, always in touch with the basics, let out a low whistle. "Holy shit."

Renquist exactly shared her sentiments. "This wasn't built by any Bronze Age culture."

The inner chamber was cavernous in comparison to the cramped crawl space of the access passage. Spacious and rectilinear, the blocks of stone from which it was constructed formed an interlocking mosaic, irregular in shape, but cut with such precision a single sheet of paper could not have been slid between any of the mortarless joints. The construction would have been impressive had the blocks been only a foot or so across, but these finished stones were huge, the largest weighing several tons. Not content with a masterpiece of the stonemason's art, the walls themselves were covered with giant frescoes. Towering and unrecognizable, the depicted creatures were able to dwarf even the trio of nosferatu with their graphic menace. Monumentally misshapen bodies held contorted poses; writhing tentacles were stilled for all time while floating eyes on dislocated stalks stared mutely at the intruders. The passage of time and chemical interaction had turned most of the murals' red pigments a uniform rust, but the greens and blues remained clear and pure, which gave the immense paintings a decidedly submarine aspect.

Marieko remained silent, waiting for Renquist to say something, but it was Destry who finally spoke. "These things don't look like they're even from this planet."

"Some of them aren't."

The floor was a deep dish of granite chips, which made for perfect drainage, and in the very center of the chamber was a single flat stone, rough-hewn around the edges but perfectly flat and polished on the top, as though a large boulder had been sliced smoothly in half by some thought-cutter or particle beam device yet to be invented. The slab was approximately ten feet long and four feet wide, but with nothing like the geometry of the rest of the chamber. Clearly it had been designed as the resting place of a king, if not a more elevated being. This was confirmed by a pile of armor, weapons, jewelry, and human bones scattered on the floor, as though the previous tenant or tenants had been unceremoniously swept aside when the current occupant had taken possession of the massive stone bier. A gold crown lay among this jetsam if anyone doubted the monarchic status of those who'd been displaced.

The rank of the present occupant hardly mattered. Its outlandish form transcended all mundanely relative nobility. It was a thing of pure strangeness, and Marieko reflected how strangeness seemed to come in degrees, ranging from the merely untoward to objects so alien they brought their own fearful aura with them. This was definitely one of the latter. It lay on its granite plinth like a giant cocoon or chrysalis. Seven feet long, a ribbed and misshapen, elongated hard shell, dark reddish brown, that might possibly have contained the mummified body of a human or being of similar form. Daggerlike spines extended from it as what could only be a defense against carrion scavengers. Marieko was unable even to hazard a guess from what material the shell might be made. It looked as though layers of a viscous liquid had somehow been extruded, allowed to harden, and then recoated over and over again. How the spikes formed was a secondary mystery all of its own.

While Marieko and Destry looked on, Renquist walked slowly toward the object on the slab. "I didn't believe any still existed. I never even dared hope."

Marieko looked at him with awe. "You know what this thing is?"

"I think I do. It would seem impossible it's here, but I think I do."

Columbine found herself staring up into the death mask that was the face of Gallowglass. Anemic parchment skin was stretched over the contours of his skull like a distorted drumhead, and his nose projected in a vulture beak. One cold, scrawny hand, with thick, ropelike veins, was locked around her wrist like a manacle; his black undertaker's coat smelled of recent feeding, and the veins in his eyes told the same story. Almost speechless with outrage, she struggled against him to free herself. "Unhand me, damn you!"

Gallowglass smiled, showing stained yellow fangs turning brown toward the roots. "I canna' do tha', lassie."

"Don't call me lassie! I am not a sheepdog."

"Would 'Mistress Dashwood' be more t' y'r likin'?"

"What are you doing in my stable? How did you get here?"

"When ye were up i' th' turret surveyin' th' landscape, ye should ha' maybe looked a wee bit closer t' home.

Th' Children o' th' Mist come veiled. We walked through y' lake an' ye never saw us."

"How dare you invade my Residence in this way?"

"They do say 'who dares wins.' "

Angry that this creature should bandy words on the assumption that she was wholly helpless, she pivoted on one foot and kicked a riding boot hard into the back of Gallowglass's knee. Taken by surprise, he stumbled one pace forward, and she took the instant to wrench her hand free of his. In the process, she ripped the skirt of her riding habit. The outer seam tore so it was slit almost to her waist. Gallowglass came after her, but instead of attempting to flee, she slashed him hard across the face with her whip. "Keep your damned hands off me!"

Gallowglass halted and ruefully rubbed his cheek. The crop had left a red welt. He glanced at the two Highlanders holding Bolingbroke. "She ha' a powerful lot of spirit, this wee one."

"This is intolerable."

Gallowglass sighed. "Just be a good young lady an' din'a cause th' lads an' I any more trouble."

Five figures stepped out of the shadows. Some massive and some small but virulent. All vassals, henchmen, and bonded companions of the Fenrior Clan, and all with the same, hard, penetrating, undead eyes. They were what Fenrior called his Children of the Mists. All wore the same plaid in various varieties of dash and decay. All carried claymores, save for two. One was a massive brute with a shaved Mohican scalp lock, who packed a long, double-handed broadsword in a sheath on his back, its hilt protruding over his left shoulder. The other was the smallest of the gang, a tensely compact, ferret of a man with a tattooed face and gold hoop earrings, who wielded what looked uncomfortably like a headsman's axe—almost too big for his small frame if nosferatu strength wasn't taken into account. Fenrior must be taking something very seriously to dispatch Gallowglass and a total of seven undead cutthroats to invade the peace of Ravenkeep. About the only mercy Columbine could see was that even these savages shared the universal nosferatu distaste for firearms. The day that taboo was lifted, the world of the undead would wholly change.

The two red-haired brothers released their hold on Bolingbroke, pushing the thrall roughly to the ground, where he remained on all fours, alternately coughing and whimpering. While Gallowglass stood apart as the commander of the action, the seven males moved to form a circle around Columbine. The move was carried out with the easy skill of a practiced fighting unit, and for the first time, she saw something beyond just hard barbarism in their eyes. They had a unity, a discipline, a berserker commonality of purpose that made them at one and the same time, formidable night raiders, but also throwbacks to times long past and supposedly outmoded. In the current situation, however, Columbine found these savages anything but outmoded. They certainly had the edge over her. She made a tentative dart to slip between two of them and break for her freedom, perhaps hoping to lose their pursuit in the labyrinth of Ravenkeep's interior, but they smoothly closed ranks to intercept her, hands going meaningfully to the hilts of their swords. She made a second attempt in a different direction, but was again thwarted by the same maneuver. Unable to break out of the circle of Highlanders, she turned to face Gallowglass. "I don't know what you want, but do you realize the wrath that would come down on you and your bloody lord if you were to destroy me, here and now, without cause or justification?"

"If it's harm we do ye, ye will ha' brought i' on ye self."

"You know the penalties exacted for the wanton destruction of another of your own kind?"

"Aye, we ken, but we also ken we want wha' we want, an' we'll no be leaving wi'oot i', wha'ever th' cost."

"So you're threatening me?"

"Aye, tha' I am, mistress."

"I don't threaten easily."

"Maybe I should start by breakin' yon thrall t' wee pieces o' flesh."

"You think that would particularly bother me?"

Gallowglass sighed at how, to the English, self-interest seemed to be everything. "Perhaps no."

"What else do you have to offer, then?"

Gallowglass took his time reflecting on this. The mark of Columbine's whip was still scarlet across his face. "The boys could make quite a mess o' ye wi'oot actually doin' away wi' ye, if they took a mind t' i'."

"You really think so?"

"Ye don't?"

Without Gallowglass making so much as a sign of instruction, the Highlanders moved as one, closing the circle. Columbine refused to be intimidated. "I've faced far worse than you—and conditioned myself to enjoy the experience."

Gallowglass made an amused gesture to the Highlanders. "Ye see lads. Powerful spirited."

"And will not be threatened."

Gallowglass sighed as though he'd been hoping to avoid what he now had to say. "There may be one thing. . . ."

"Yes?"

"W' could maybe set a torch t' this fine house an', come th' dawn, ye'd find ye self between a fire an' th' sun. That way w'd no be actually doin' th' destroyin', so t' speak, but . . ."

Columbine blanched. He had her. Only pride prevented weakness and shock from overtaking her. "You wouldn't?"

"Oh, aye, miss, tha' w' would."

"Yes. I believe you." Columbine knew her only remaining hope was negotiation. "But what do you want with me?"

"It's not ye w' want, Miss Dashwood. 'Tis Master Victor Renquist wi' whom w' ha' our business."

*   *   *

"With the correct rhythms, we might awaken it. It might only require a simple Helmholtz Resonance. A base of around two beats a second with building multiples should do it."

Destry shook her head warningly. "Don't you dare, Victor."

"I was only theorizing."

Marieko added her weight to Destry's warning. "Please, Victor, let it remain theory for the moment."

Renquist moved away from the object on the slab and turned his attention to the inlaid copper strips that formed a complex pattern, along with the ancient and unearthly murals on the walls of the burial chamber. "These are like huge pieces of circuitry."

The metallic strips, heavily coated with a green layer of verdigris, were approximately as wide as one of Renquist's hands. "I would even hazard a guess they once tapped directly into the power of the Nephilim ley lines."

Destry looked at Renquist, her aura flashing impatiently. "You're having a serious attack of pedantry."

"I'm sorry. This is something of a revelation. It has to be from the ancient days."

Marieko moved closer to the thing on the slab, but he stopped a few feet from it, as though reluctant to go any closer. "No Bronze Age tomb?"

Renquist shook his head. "The Bronze Age exterior was added much later, probably to disguise the true nature of the place. In here is pure Zep Tepi."

Marieko looked puzzled. "Zep Tepi."

"The era of the Nephilim. The attempt at alien colonization of Earth. The ancient Egyptians called it Zep Tepi, the First Time, the Perfect Time. When the gods, the ones they called the Neteru, lived on Earth and mated with the children of men."

Destry frowned. "Mated with the children of men?"

"That's how it's described in human legend."

"A primitive description of the Nephilim genetic experiments?"

Renquist nodded. He liked the way Marieko kept up with him. "The very same, as seen through a fifteen-thousand-year filter of ignorance and misunderstanding."

"The ancient Egyptians seem to have had a far more benign view of history than our own kind."

"For humanity, it must have seemed like a golden age, the true Garden of Eden. When the Nephilim enhanced human DNA, they were benefactors, divine beings who had elevated the species from the animal state. In the aftermath of a terrible Ice Age, they raised them to enlightenment. They gave them knowledge, intellect, and the capacity to write, reason, invent, and construct. Humanity has no real cause to curse the Nephilim. For them, Marduk Ra, the Nephilim overlord, was deserving of deification. We, of course, take a very different perspective. No sooner had we been created than we were all but destroyed."

"But this cocoon thing is neither human nor nosferatu?"

"It's Urshu."

Marieko frowned. "Urshu?"

"Humanity and the nosferatu were by no means the sum total of Nephilim creative efforts. Until his domain proved unmanageable, Marduk Ra had big plans for this planet."

Renquist approached the thing on the slab. Destry couldn't help herself and blurted a warning. "Don't touch it, Victor, anything could happen."

"I think it's safe."

"We only just recovered from your opening the damned door to this place. Let's not rely too much on guesswork. I don't think I could go through something like that again."

Renquist stopped, hand poised above the huge chrysalis. "Perhaps you're right."

Marieko brought his attention back on track. "You were explaining the Urshu."

Renquist nodded. He wanted to further investigate the thing on the slab, but he knew Marieko and Destry wouldn't be content until he had offered them as much of an explanation as he could. "You might know the Urshu better as the Watchers."

Marieko put the pieces quickly together. "The Watchers that occur all through human folklore?"

"In many respects the Urshu—the 'Watchers'—were the most successful product of the entire Nephilim colonization. They were as effectively immortal as we are. They had no problems with sunlight, and as far as I can tell, they were of superior intelligence. The Original Beings thoroughly detested them and called them *courtiers*, but that was perfectly understandable. Taking the Original Beings' bellicose mind-set into account, they and the Urshu could only have been arch rivals. Our ancestors were designed for combat. The Urshu were administrators and negotiators specifically, in the context of Earth, designed to act as mediators between humanity and the Nephilim, whom the humans presumed to be gods."

Destry interjected. "You sound like you're giving a damned lecture."

Renquist blinked. Already he'd been accused of pedantry. "I'm sorry."

Destry waved away the apology. "No, no, go on. It's good to have the details filled in for a change. I don't have DNA dreams and all that stuff. I'm one of the ignorant undead, and I don't mind admitting it."

Yet again, Renquist wondered where Destry might have come from and how she had made the Change to nosferatu. So much of her defied easy explanation. In some areas, as in the case of the horse Dormandu, she seemed close to an expert, and yet great gaps seemed to exist in her knowledge of the origins and history of their kind. History, however, was the topic at hand, so Renquist continued. "Like all the Nephilim creations, the Ur-shu were unfortunately less than perfect. From the very start, they were few in number, compared to the regiments of Original Being, or the vast tribes of humans who were selectively bred for release into the wild. They also had a reproductive problem."

Destry chuckled. "They had trouble with sex?"

Renquist even permitted himself a dry smile. "According to everything I read, they were all created hermaphrodite, but with external characteristics that were predominately male."

"That caused them a problem?"

"Although they were capable of sexual gratification, and some appeared to relish it, they were unable to reproduce, either in the distasteful mode of the humans or in our own more ritualized fashion."

"So how did the Nephilim react to having created a race of mules?"

"Seemingly they tolerated it. The Urshu performed their function and found favor with the Nephilim on a practical level. We really know so little about them because by far the majority left with Marduk Ra when colonial Earth was abandoned, and the ones who stayed were skilled in disguise and illusion."

"How many of them remained?"

Renquist shook his head. "There's no record I've ever seen, but it would seem to be no more than a handful, because most of them are known to either history or legend."

"We know them?"

Renquist shrugged. "Humanity has either known their names or given them their names. They may not have know what they were, but they knew them. They were the bringers of light, and of fire, the teachers of astronomy and agriculture. They attempted to maintain what remnants of Nephilim colonial civilization they could." He arched an eyebrow and regarded Destry and Marieko. "They also, according to some accounts, attempted to eradicate cannibalism, human sacrifice, and the drinking of blood."

Getting no immediate response to this tidbit, he went on. "Quetzalcoatl would seem to have been an Urshu who intervened in South and Central America, in other areas there was Osiris, Ahura Mazda, the Sumerian Uan, Loki, Gilgamesh, Viracocha in the high Andes; the Greeks had Deucalion and Prometheus. Some even say Confucius was a Watcher, others Pericles, some Jesus Christ—"

At the final name, Destry hissed. Nosferatu prejudice could be deep and intractable. Renquist spread his hands. "I'm not making a case for the Urshu. I'm just giving you the standard list of semi-divine teachers that may have been Nephilim hybrids."

"What other weaknesses did they have, aside from not being able to reproduce?"

"The greatest peculiarity would emerge only after the colony was abandoned and most of the Urshu had gone with the Nephilim."

"And what was that?"

"They developed a need to hibernate."

All three pairs of undead eyes turned to the great red-brown cocoon on the slab.

"They would enjoy a lifespan of three, four, maybe even five hundred years, and then suddenly they'd vanish, only to reemerge hundreds of years later. It would seem, just as humans must sleep by night, and we by day, the Urshu had to retreat into a kind of suspended animation for long periods of time. I wasn't aware though, that they actually cocooned themselves like this."

For a few moments, the three nosferatu were silent. Renquist's revelations required a measure of digestion. Marieko moved nearer to the cocoon and peered closely at it, still careful not to touch the thing. "It seems to be covered in these hairline cracks, as though it was starting to fragment."

"I believe it's preparing to wake."

"All that energy that escaped when the door was opened?"

"Overspill from an ongoing process of energization."

Destry took a deep breath, as though the deluge of new concepts was taking its toll. "Victor, how sure are you of any of this?"

"Much of it is only historical speculation, but it's speculation that would seem to fit with what we've found. I'm certain he's going to wake."

"He?"

Renquist realized that, in his chill, undead excitement, he may have said more than he had intended. "They were all ostensibly male."

Destry and Marieko both stared hard at Renquist. "Don't bullshit us, Victor."

"You said *he*."

"You have an actual idea of the identity of what's in that cocoon, don't you?"

They had him. He might as well go ahead and tell them the rest of what had been passing through his mind as he'd answered their questions, but he attempted to present it as casually as possible, even though the ramifications might prove incalculable. "I would have thought it was obvious from the location."

"What's the location got to do with it?"

"There's a great deal of evidence pointing to the conclusion Taliesin may very well have been an Urshu. He would appear to have come here during the Roman occupation, but remained here after the Imperial withdrawal, attempting to unite the local tribes under the Pendragon banner in the face of Saxon invasion and, at the same time, doing all he could to slow the inroads of Christianity and its miserable priests."

Marieko was shaking her head. "I fear you have the better of me. I may sound lamentably ignorant, but I have never heard of Taliesin."

"Taliesin? Taliesin the Great Merlin?"

"Merlin? You mean Merlin? As in King Arthur?"

Renquist had metaphorically turned over his entire hand. "The very same. Do you see now why I came all this way?"

"You knew all along."

Renquist shook his head. "At first it was only a working hypothesis, but it seems to have paid off."

In the same metaphor, Destry had seen the cards but didn't quite believe them. "But Merlin's just storybook stuff, myth, movies, Malory and Tennyson."

Renquist smiled. "And to many, my dear Destry, so are we. Myth, magic, and Christopher Lee."

Marieko had been thinking. "Arthur Pendragon was reputed to have died between A.D. 539 and 541. Around the same time, Merlin is supposed to have disappeared."

"Is that significant?"

"Columbine claimed the first phases of her dreams came from the sixth century."

"Someone is going to have to tell me about Columbine's dreams."

"They might be a print-through? Caused by this thing's memory starting to surface?"

Destry suddenly interjected. "Damn!"

Both Renquist and Marieko turned and stared at her. "What?"

"The damned locals call this place Merlin's Rest. I only just remembered."

Marieko looked blank. "I never heard that."

Destry scored a point. "You don't have as much contact with the yokels as I do."

Marieko's lip acquired the slightest curl. "I suppose not. I don't ride horses."

Renquist cloaked himself in the mantle of superiority. Sooner or later Marieko might prove a challenge. "Sometimes it pays to take the natives seriously."

The Highlanders formed up around Columbine, to conduct her from the stables to another part of the house, where they would presumably wait for the return of Renquist, Destry, and Marieko. She felt as though under close military escort, like royalty perhaps, although possibly a condemned queen going to her own execution. She was a little unkempt, however, for such a stately occasion and, with her skirt torn, showing rather more of her thighs than she deemed appropriate in present company. Gallowglass took the out-of-doors route, and she found herself crunching across the gravel of the driveway, next to the small ferretlike male with the blue spiral tattoos on his face, the gold earrings, and the headsman's axe. The weapon in itself contributed considerably to the execution motif. She glanced at him as they walked. "Do you have any idea what you're doing here?"

The male looked at her with a benign resignation. "None wha'ever, miss."

"And that doesn't bother you."

"No."

"You just come here and invade my home and don't even wonder why?"

"'M' lord commands, an' I obey.' Like i' says i' th' song, 'over th' hills an' far away.' "

"You have a name?"

"Aye."

"You want to tell me what it is?"

"They call me Prestwick, miss."

"So, Prestwick, should I recommend you to your lord, appraise him of what an unquestioning vassal he has in you?"

Prestwick's expression or aura didn't so much as flicker. "M' lord kens well wha' he ha' i' me, miss. Din'a he raise me fra' the dyin' on th' field after Culloden?"

Clearly no wiles could be practiced on these coarse barbarians, and Columbine was wasting her time if she thought she could smile and seduce her way out of the current problem. Renquist would probably have been in-

trigued by the fact that Fenrior had once raised his retainers by bringing the wounded on the battlefield
through the Change, and all but back from the dead, but
such insights were not Columbine's way, and even if
they had been, she was left with no time to mull or
consider. They had reached the front door of the house,
and Gallowglass wanted something. "Miss Dashwood,
do we ha' y' permission t' cross th' threshold o' y' Residence?"

So, despite the absurdity of the situation, Gallowglass
still wished to observe the time-honored niceties. "It
would be pointless to refuse, I suspect."

"Aye, mistress, quite pointless, but why ignore th' formalities? They cost us nothin'."

Columbine's expression was as blankly venomous as
a reptile. "Welcome to Ravenkeep, Cousin Gallowglass.
You and your companions may enter now by your own
free will."

Blue fire briefly encircled each Highlander as he
stepped through the door. Columbine was surprised. She
and her companions were never so highly charged. Did
these brutes enjoy a surfeit of power in their primitive
isolation? Was that one of the fringe benefits of cold
nights and the simple life? As the Highlanders filed into
the drawing room, Columbine realized perhaps it was
her wits rather than her allure that might extricate her
from this dangerous intrusion. Her first realization was
that they were not too comfortable in the house. Even
the troika's clutter of furniture and bric-a-brac was too
much civilization for these tribal yahoos. They could
only really be at home in stone halls with straw and
wolfhounds on the floor, with the social finesse of the
barn and the stench of a sty. Once inside, they stood
uncomfortably. A few awkwardly removed their plaid
bonnets, unsure of how to act away from the bonhomie
of fighting and farting. Even the small Prestwick seemed
too large, too stained and battle-scarred, too heavily
armed for the room.

Her second realization was that her destruction was not a part of their designated task. She didn't doubt Fenrior had instructed Gallowglass to dispose of her without hesitation if she presented any kind of obstacle, but these were not her own specific assassins. If they had meant to finish her, they would have done it by now. Renquist was their target, and that's why they were standing in her drawing room, all stink and broad shoulders, waiting for him like gormless oafs. The knowledge was a gift of instant power. She took the moment to light a cigarette and then turned and faced the invaders. "Should I offer you all a drink or something?"

The Highlanders looked for direction to Gallowglass, but he shook his head. "We're fine as we are, Mistress Dashwood."

"Then perhaps I could suggest a more practical offer?"

"I'm one who favors practicality."

"How would you respond, Gallowglass, if I were to offer you Renquist?"

"Master Renquist is hardly yorn t' offer, mistress."

"He could be taken with far greater ease if you had my cooperation."

"And wha' might ye be wantin' in return, lassie?"

"I asked you not to call me lassie."

"But y'r th' one who's trying t' save her head."

"All I want is my companions and me left in peace."

Gallowglass thought about this, taking his time; he had no reason to hurry. "It's certainly a practical solution, but wi'out much honor."

"The superior combatant is the one who regards honor as dictated by circumstance."

"Did th' wee Chinagirl teach ye that?"

"She did, as a matter of fact."

Destry was the first to think of it. "Does anyone have a sense of time?"

Renquist had been so absorbed, first with the momentous discovery, and then explaining just how momentous it was to Marieko and Destry, that he had lost touch with whole idea of time passing. The dousing in the flood of psychic energy had thrown a number of his unconscious abilities out of harmony. "I have to admit I don't have a clue."

Marieko also shook her head, apparently shocked at her lapse. "I, too, am at a loss."

Destry took the initiative. "I had better go back up the passageway and take a look at the sky."

The last thing Renquist wanted was to leave the place. "Even if the sun was to rise, we'd be safe here."

Marieko shuddered. "I don't believe I'd want to stay the day here."

"And there's Campion's people."

Renquist sighed. They were right. "Campion's people? Yes, to dispose of them would be inconvenient, messy, and very noticeable."

Destry had no time for wishing or debate. She was a female of action. "You two stay where you are. I'll be right back."

She ducked into the dark mouth of the entry passage. Renquist and Marieko heard her riding boots retreating down its rubble-strewn length.

"Did you ever see one of the Urshu?" Marieko tried to make the question as offhand as possible, but Renquist knew she was attempting to visualize what was inside the cocoon. She was as excited as he was about the discovery, but also a little afraid.

"Never one I recognized as such, although, like I said, they're reputed to have the power of absolute disguise."

"And in dreams? You can't tell me your DNA dreams don't go back to the Original Beings. I know better than that, now, don't I?"

For a long time, the furthest Renquist had been able to venture back in a DNA dream had been to the time know as the Flight. He opened his memory to Marieko, showing how he had occupied bodies of those Original Beings who had survived the Nephilim eradication.

Through their eyes he showed her the refugees attempting to escape after the sunbomb attack on Baalbeck. He let her enter their primitive minds as they struggled across white burning sand, already subject to the weakening effect of direct sunlight. She went to ground with them as the Nephilim saucers silently passed overhead, raking the desert with their hunter-seeker deathrays, and she felt their hate-filled fury and black desperation at their Nephilim masters who had created them only to then decide to wipe them out as defective. He also showed her how, much later, they had been accepted as gods by the clusters of humans in the upper valleys of the Indus, who had paid them tribute in blood.

"For a long time, even with the help of Dietrich, my old mentor, I found myself unable to penetrate any further into our collective past. I was starting to believe some kind of barrier existed, preventing me from reaching any vision of how it was when the Nephilim walked the Earth. It was only recently that I ever found myself in a DNA vision of the time before the uprising, and that came only when I badly needed it."

"When you confronted Cthulhu?"

Renquist laughed. Marieko's eagerness to experience the past had a seductive charm all of its own. "I didn't confront Cthulhu. No one confronts Cthulhu, not even a nosferatu. I merely discouraged a very small part of him from entering this dimension, and even that wasn't totally successful. A darklost called Philipa De Reske is somewhere in this world with a tiny piece of the living Cthulhu preserved in the disembodied head of her ex-husband's mistress. I fear I have not seen the last of her."

"You live a complicated life, Victor-san."

"Let me show you."

Again he opened his mind, this time giving a first panorama of Great Nephilim Spaceport of Baalbeck in all its glory. He showed her the obelisks and trilithons, the central Baalbeck landing ziggurat. The relentless sun beat down on the massive, precision-hewn granite power-stones that were the primary construction material, reflecting from their marble, titanium, and gold facings. Flags and banners, with strange devices and unreadable designs, streamed and fluttered in the breeze, while imposing gushers of brightly colored vapor jetted up from vents in the lower levels of the ziggurat, and huge iron wind chimes clashed and clanged. Overhead, the perfect blue sky was alive with a formidable air show that began with a flight of five white disks maintaining a perfect V. As they approached the airspace over the landing ziggurat, they finally broke formation and spread out, positioning themselves like the five points of an extended stylized star. Once the disks were in position, flotillas of vimanas rose from the ground and clustered around them like schools of lesser aerial fish. Other aircraft, flying too high to be seen in detail, inscribed white cross-hatchings of contrails. At the climax of the display, a disturbance started in the sky itself. Spiral clouds began to form where no clouds had been before, with flashes of shuddering, violet and white static electricity at their epicenter. As the ancient air show reached this meteorological climax, the humans fully prostrated themselves, knees bent, arms spread, fearful faces pressed to the ground. The moment for which they had all been assembled was close at hand. What could only be a space vehicle appeared in the center of the whirling celestial vortex.

"That was Baalbeck?" Marieko's voice was strained, as though a form of ecstasy had been contained in the vision.

"That was Baalbeck."

"And you were contained in the mind of an Original Being?"

"He was very different to the ones in the Flight—arrogant, warrior proud, self-assured, and contemptuous of his creators—but he followed a distinct if unregimented structure. I could also feel the restless resentment that would eventually erupt in that doomed uprising."

In the dream, Renquist's host had stood, eyes heavily hooded against the glare, awaiting the arrival of the God King Marduk Ra from the Great Orbiting Mothership. He'd watched the craft bearing Marduk Ra in the final stages of its descent. It had dropped slowly and ponderously on a cushion of energy only visible as a violent shimmer in the air. It required no burning jets or flaming, smoking retro rockets either to impress or to slow its drop down the gravity well. The humans were already on their knees in worshipful abasement. In addition to the Original Beings and the humans, other things were also present in the highly stratified and segregated throng. Small grey bio-entities, humanoid but hardly human, scarcely more than three feet tall, with overlarge infantile heads and huge black eyes, milled around in another section of the landing area, chattering in high-pitched voices, beyond the range of human hearing but fully audible to the Original Beings. On a raised platform, beneath the largest of the trilithons, the Urshu were gathered—the courtiers—and the primary target of the Original Beings' resentment. The Urshu were much closer to human in form, but as tall as the Original Beings and dazzling in the magnificence of their shining robes and tall gold headpieces. They seemed to be an exquisite and wholly complete summation of how the groveling men and women might have imagined a tribe of glorious demigods, something that had made Renquist reluctant to accept them completely for what they appeared to be.

"The problem with this kind of dream perception is seeing everything through the eyes and, indirectly, the subjective prejudices and misconceptions of the host."

"So you think the Urshu can be anything they want to be?"

"That would seem to be the indication of both dream and history."

"And if the cocoon splits, what will emerge?"

"I'd be hard-pressed to imagine."

Destry crawled from the tunnel. "First, you'd better imagine this. We've lingered longer than was healthy."

"What?"

"If we get out of here right now, we might just make it back to the Priory before the dawn fries us."

"It's that late?"

"It's that late."

Renquist looked around helplessly. So much remained to examine and admire. He knew how the humans Howard Carter and Lord Carnarvon must have felt when they entered the tomb of Tutankhamen in the Valley of the Kings, except, in their case, they didn't have the added excitement of knowing Tut might very well wake and start walking around before very long. "I hate to leave it all for Campion. He shouldn't so much as know about this. No human should."

"You don't have a choice."

"If it wasn't for the sun—"

"How many of our kind have said that?"

"I'm wondering"—he gestured to the cocoon—"if we should take it with us. The weight would be no problem."

"But maneuvering it down that low passage would take about twice as much time as we have. Not to mention the problems those damned spikes could cause."

"You're right."

Marieko also agreed with Destry. "I shudder to think what might happen if we cracked it."

"Or stabbed ourselves with one of the spines."

Renquist was hard-pressed to control the frustration that threatened to overwhelm him. "The first thing Campion will do is crack it open."

Marieko shook her head. "He won't do that."

"You don't think so?"

"I know he won't. I've been inside his mind. He's afraid of this place already. The mica fragment set him off balance. All this, as they used to say, will blow his mind. I guarantee he'll be extremely circumspect. He'll want to keep it secret while he searches vainly for an acceptable theory."

Renquist was adamant. "We must return at sunset and take the cocoon out of here."

Destry was now more nervous than impatient. "If we agree to that, can we get out of here?"

"Yes, we have to. We can't fight the sun."

Had Gallowglass's character made him prone to pacing, he would have paced. It didn't, however. He was the kind to remain motionless except when actually doing something. He was also the kind who asked questions and expected them to be answered. Thus, he glared balefully at Columbine. "Ha' ye been deceiving me, woman?"

"Don't be a fool, I've too much to lose."

The skeletal Highlander's stress was compounded by having the men under him look on as he waited, so far fruitlessly, for other denizens of Ravenkeep to return. "So where are Master Renquist an' y' two pretty cohabitants?"

Columbine shifted constantly between fear and fury. "You think I'm not wondering that myself?"

"They couldna' ha' gone t' some other place?"

The pointless interrogation didn't help. "They'd have no reason to."

"Maybe ye warned them?"

"You know I haven't done that. You've been watching me like a hawk."

"Aye, tha' I have."

"So?"

"So if they din'a come rollin' up th' drive i' a matter o' minutes, they're fried i' th' sun. No mistake about tha'."

Columbine could think of nothing to say that wouldn't be stating the obvious, so she simply kept quiet. Gallowglass, on the other hand, needed to talk. Hadn't he heard the Scots were supposed to be taciturn? "M' lord no ordered me t' bring back Master Renquist's ashes. He wanted him up an' walkin'.'"

"I expect Master Renquist would also prefer to be up and walking."

Marieko drove fast, foot hard down on the gas pedal, and talked with a clipped rapidity. The Range Rover bounced over open hillside, the sky at the eastern horizon showed a faint paling, and the three nosferatu were gripped by an all-pervading urgency, not to say anxiety. "Are you certain we need to remove the cocoon?"

Renquist nodded grimly. "I believe we have to take possession of it by any means necessary. It has to be moved to a place of safety."

"Do you have any idea what will happen when Taliesin wakes?"

"Not even a theory, but we have to work on the assumption it'll be spectacular. I'd like to find out more for myself, before the humans open the cocoon live on CNN."

Marieko bumped the Range Rover out of the fields and onto a narrow country road. "Or MI6 or the NSA spirit it away to some mysterious Hangar Eighteen, and it vanishes in the alphabet soup of secret intrigue."

Destry's expression was as grim as Renquist's. "Let me remind you, Victor—before we start talking 'any means necessary'—Marieko, Columbine, and I have to live around here."

"Eventually every Residence has to be abandoned. Too many of them have fallen victim to the curse of the castle and lingered fatally long in familiar surroundings."

"It's that serious?"

"All I know is a demigod will wake here in the twenty-first century after being asleep for fifteen hundred years. I don't think human civilization is in any way equipped to deal with him or the power that he may well have at his disposal. I also doubt that he'll be at all sympathetic to what human civilization has become."

"And we are?"

"I believe so."

"Don't you feel that's taking on one hell of a responsibility?"

"No."

"No?"

Renquist was terse. Dawn was too close, and he was tired of answering questions. "Shall we ignore for the moment our innate superiority over humans as it's defined by our relative positions in the food chain?"

Destry seemed equally weary. "Okay."

"Then we, as nosfertatu, at least know something of Taliesin's true history."

"That's true."

"In all likelihood, he will go into fairly substantial culture shock when he first sees his surroundings."

Marieko flicked on the headlights, not to help her see, but to warn other cars of their presence, and also to comply with the law. The last thing they needed was to be stopped for a rural traffic ticket. As usual she was able to project a number of possible scenarios at the same time. "And that shock could be disastrous if he should wake in a secret sub-basement of some CIA mental hospital, or in a Pay Per View TV studio."

"From television to nuclear weapons, he will see many things he hasn't known for not just fifteen hundred years, but fifteen thousand."

Marieko glanced at Destry. "He went to sleep in the aftermath of the Roman Empire."

Destry shook her head as if the facts were still hard to grasp. Renquist pressed home the point. He wanted them to be ready to get the cocoon at sunset. He knew it was dangerous, but was convinced to do otherwise would court far worse disaster. "I span nearly two-thirds of the time he's been separated from the world."

Destry still wasn't sure. "We have to talk to Columbine about this."

Renquist shook his head. "The time for Columbine's games is long past."

A new argument seemed about to commence over Columbine's role in things as Marieko swung the Range Rover through the open gates of the Priory. Atop their granite columns, the le Corbeau ravens maintained their cast-iron silence.

"Wait."

"Wha'?"

"There they are."

A Range Rover was coming fast up the driveway, and the dawn was only short minutes away. Gallowglass dropped the shutter into place over the last drawing room window open to the light, and the room was in instant, daytime darkness.

"T' y' places lads."

Now they had something to do, the Highlanders moved with prompt efficiency. They left the drawing room to take up assigned positions at as many of the obvious entrances to the Priory as could be covered by the seven. Gallowglass himself headed for the front door, and Columbine followed.

As they entered the hallway, the handle of the heavy wooden door turned as though one of the three was already trying to get inside, not knowing the door was already barred and bolted, and even a nosferatu couldn't break it down in the time that was left. Without thinking, Columbine protested. "You can't go through with this. You can't leave them out there to burn."

"It's no up t' me, lassie. Th' choice is Master Renquist's."

"You said if I helped you, you would harm neither me nor my companions."

"Perhaps they should be more careful o' th' company they keep."

"I thought you were a creature of honor."

"What was i' ye said a while ago? 'Honor is dictated by circumstance'?"

Marieko brought the Range Rover to a lurching halt. She didn't even have to tell Destry and Victor to go straight to the house. Beams of sunlight would soon be shafting through the trees to the east of Ravenkeep. They could only leave the vehicle in the driveway and bolt for safety. As Marieko slammed the driver's door closed, she saw Destry had reached the front door, and Renquist wasn't far behind her, but then something seemed to be wrong. Destry was tugging at the handle as if the door was refusing to open. Renquist caught up with her, and he, too, tried with the same lack of avail. He quickly shouted to Marieko.

"Get back in the car!"

Renquist was right. The Range Rover, with its tinted windows, would provide at least temporary protection from the fast-coming sun, but no sooner had Marieko turned to retrace her steps than a missile flew from a second-floor window, as if by prearranged signal. Hurled with nosferatu strength, it described a soaring arc and then dropped with unpleasant accuracy on the Range Rover's windshield, completely shattering it. The car was no use as a refuge. At the same time, Marieko could hear Destry screaming furiously for Columbine.

"What the fuck you think you're doing, you demented psycho? Let us in this instant!"

Columbine's voice came from inside the door. "It's not me that's doing this. It's—"

A second voice interrupted her. "It's Gallowglass, Master Renquist. Whether this door opens or no is entirely up t' you."

Destry continued to rave. "What the fuck are you talking about? We're going to burn out here in a matter of seconds."

"Th' choice is Master Renquist's."

Renquist pushed Destry and Marieko into the corner

of the doorway that would be touched last by the sunlight. "I don't understand. What choice?"

"Ye either give ye self up t' the Lord Fenrior, or ye stay where y'are an' perish."

"Are you telling me to surrender to you or burn?"

"Aye. Tha's th' long an' short o' it."

Destry and Marieko cowered in the corner of the doorway.

"Answer him, Victor. I really don't want to carbonize out here like a damned fool."

Renquist took a deep breath. "Very well. You have my word. I surrender to Fenrior. Now open the damned door."

The sound of locks being turned and bolts being drawn back was followed by the door swinging inward. Renquist stepped back as Marieko and Destry fell inside; then he entered, and the door was slammed behind him. He was no sooner inside and out of the danger of the sun than a new threat made itself known. He found himself facing six undead Highlanders with five claymores and a broadsword pointed unerringly at his throat, while a seventh hefted an axe and measured the distance to his neck. Renquist eyed the points of the swords and then looked past them to Gallowglass. "Is this essential? I gave my word of surrender."

"My instructions are t' take no chances."

"So what changed, Gallowglass? Just now you were bringing me prey and extending your laird's cordial invitation to visit."

Gallowglass showed no expression. "Since then, th' situation ha' changed an' m' lord's invitation ha' become more imperative."

"What situation?"

"Th' Lord Fenrior well kens ye burrowin' i' th' hillside." He looked round at the three females. "Aye, an' wha' ye found there, an' all th' rest o' i'."

Chapter Five

A light rain was falling as the two Hummers roared up the Ravenkeep driveway. Matte black and without markings or number plates, lights blazing in the overcast dusk, they approached the house like a paranoid fantasy on wheels, a conspiracy vision of New World Order covert operations. They came to a fast stop in front of the house, and Highlanders tumbled out of them, ready for anything. Plaid and old leather, dirks and claymores, one even carried a small circular shield—it was as though these modern vehicles had transported a crowd of passengers from another era. The Highlanders made no attempt to hide the high spirits of wild nosferatu who have just collectively fed, and Renquist looked askance at all that was wrong with the picture. Was Fenrior insane or did he feel so distant and invulnerable in his Scottish stronghold, he had no compunction about letting his men run bloody and unchecked in heavily populated southern England?

While Renquist speculated where and on whom these

new arrivals might have fed, Gallowglass hurried to hear a report from their apparent leader. "Duncanon?"

A young nosferatu with a swagger that should have been a warning to all who encountered him stepped from the self-congratulatory group. "Aye?"

"Did all go well, boy?"

"I' aw went like clockwork."

The object of Gallowglass's questions was by no means the biggest of the new arrivals, but he had an instantly recognizable and untamed authority. He was the kind others would follow, even into situations their better judgment would normally cause them to avoid. If Fenrior had to guard himself against aspirants to his leadership—invariably the case in any nosferatu community—this young one certainly merited watching. Although still in the unruly sword-vassal mode, Duncanon was considerably more stylish and conscious of his appearance that his comrades. Cleaner and clean shaved, with his long and currently wet hair hanging almost to his waist, he sported rings and heavy bracelets of finely crafted silver. His sword was slung from the wide silver-studded belt at a high strutting angle, and he habitually kept one hand on the basketwork hilt. Renquist knew the pose well. He had adopted it himself in his younger days.

The relationship between the young Duncanon and the venerable Gallowglass was easy to read. The young one acted insolent and cocky with every movement of his body, striving for superiority, but was ultimately forced to defer to Gallowglass's superior rank, age, and status. The meeting also told Renquist this operation had two simultaneous objectives, and with both accomplished, the two halves of the combined task force had just been reunited. Obviously the goal of the one led by Gallowglass had been to take Renquist alive and presumably bring him north to Fenrior. What the other party, the one apparently captained by Duncanon, had been assigned to do was yet to be seen, but the presence of the two Hummers and the large number of armed undead retainers made it very clear the lord was taking something very seriously. Renquist could only assume that something was the phenomenon at Morton Downs. This operation was not, however, a mission undertaken on the spur of the moment or mounted in the space of a single day. Despite all Columbine's cries of betrayal and treachery, Ravenkeep must have had been leaking information well before he had ever arrived in England.

The numbers of the Highlanders alone also came as a surprise to Renquist. He'd known Fenrior's clan was large, but he'd never imagined it to be this large. Gallowglass had seven at his back, while Duncanon commanded another eight. Fifteen plus the two captains made a raiding party of seventeen. Projecting these figures—and even if Fenrior had sent every sword under his command on this strange raid—a certain number of females and noncombatants must have remained at the castle, which led Renquist to believe the entire clan numbered thirty or forty. If he was correct, Fenrior lorded over the largest community of the undead since the Theatre Raoul Privache in Paris had been quietly but forcibly dispersed by a confederation of nosferatu luminaries and a cabal of human secret societies. Over the centuries, Renquist had observed how, when a conclave of the undead grew too large, it sooner or later embarked on a self-destructive course that inevitably led to a violent and high-profile bloodbath that thoroughly unnerved the human bystanders. The seeds of trouble were usually sown when the leader or leadership of the overlarge clan or colony became too confident of the power he, she, or they believed was at their command. Perhaps it was an illusion of perceived power that had caused the laird to send what amounted to an armed expedition so far out of his accepted hunting grounds.

Being told everything went like clockwork hardly seemed to satisfy Gallowglass. "So wha' happened at yon place? I wan' t' hear every detail, boy."

Renquist was standing in the shelter of the main door of Ravenkeep, looking out into the rain. Two Highlanders stood behind him with drawn swords, but they appeared to have accepted that he had given his word of surrender and intended to stand by it. He could just about hear the conversation by Gallowglass and Duncanon, but the rain was growing heavier, and he feared he might miss crucial words. He casually stepped out of the door, doing his best to look as though he were simply stretching his legs after a cramped day of hardly sleeping. Instead of stopping him, his pair of Highlanders merely followed. Attempting to show no specific interest in anything but the general scene and the two black Hummers—the state-of-the-art American military vehicles had to be something of a rarity in England—Renquist ambled until he was in effective earshot. Duncanon was giving Gallowglass a report of his troops' endeavors.

"We did i' just as m' lord ordered. By th' time Renquist an' th' lassies left th' tomb i' were too close t' dawn, so we retired t' our body bags t' wait out th' day."

This was an innovation Renquist had never come across before. To use rubber, military-style body bags as a means of protection from the sun was a wholly novel idea, but he supposed it must work.

"Come sunset w' took th' mound."

"Humans?"

"Campion ha' brought i' a couple o' security guards, but they were no trouble. And there was this Rastafarian."

"Rastafarian?"

"Aye, but he ran off an' we let him go. He was kinda likeable an' wi'out too much credibility goin' f' him anyway. Who's gonna believe a ganja-smokin' dread when he tells them he was chased off an ancient archeological site by blood-drinkin' Scotsmen?"

Renquist knew this had to be Winston Shakespeare, the young man who had led Marieko to the mica fragment. She had let him live in return, and Renquist imagined she'd be happy he'd escaped with his life a second time. Gallowglass continued to quiz Duncanon. "So wha' happened next, after ye'd dealt wi' th' humans."

"We went inside an' brought oot th' Merlin's sarcophagus an' th' rest o' th' stuff. I' was a bastard gettin' i' all down tha' tunnel. Th' fuckin' thing turned oot t' be covered i' spikes like a bloody cactus, so we had t' hack 'em off a'fore we moved i'."

"Ye didna damage i', did ye?"

"I' seemed all right."

"So where is it now?"

Duncanon gestured to the second of the Hummers. "Yon."

"So we're ready t' move out?"

"No reason not. We're gonna ha' t' motor t' be back t' home a'fore dawn."

Gallowglass looked round for Renquist. "Master Renquist, would ye come over here?"

Renquist walked to where Gallowglass and Duncanon were standing. "You seem to have brought an entire army down here."

"Th' Lord Fenrior believes i' safety i' numbers."

"It's unfortunate the Lord Fenrior doesn't believe in the very basic nosferatu protocols."

"Jus' followin' ma orders, Master Renquist. Th' niceties ye'll have t' bring up wi' th' laird himself."

Duncanon's smooth face curled into a sneer of contempt. "Th' only thing he'll be doin' when he meets th' laird will be grovelin' f' his head."

Renquist's eyes and aura became as hard and brittle as cold iron. "That's what you believe, is it, young man?"

Duncanon seemed about to reply in kind, but Gallowglass cut him off, stepping between the fresh Highlander and Renquist. "Don't show ye self up as more o' a fool than ye really are, lad. This is Victor Renquist fra th' Americas, an' you'll no see him grovelin' t' anyone."

"He's our prisoner, isn't he?"

"Get about ye business, boy. Get ye lads on th' truck an' ready t' travel."

With a final sneer of postponed hostilities for Renquist, Duncanon swaggered off—and Gallowglass shook his head. "Full o' piss an' vinegar an' more trouble than he's worth."

Renquist nodded, happy to play the seasoned veteran and give Gallowglass and himself a certain common ground. "I had one like him myself a few years ago. He went by the name of Carfax, and I had to push him out into the sun before he learned any manners."

Gallowglass smiled wanly. "Sometimes yon's th' only remedy. Unfortunately tha' one's favored by m' lord, so he'd be missed."

"Did you say you have the cocoon in one of those trucks?"

It was the crucial question, but Renquist let it drop almost casually. Gallowglass looked at Renquist, disappointed at the ploy. "If tha's wha' ye heard, tha's wha' I said. It's goin' back t' Fenrior where it belongs."

"You know what it is?"

"Aye."

"Are you sure?"

"Ye know as well as I, Master Renquist, it's th' old Merlin, fast asleep. M' lord wants t' be there when he wakes, as I believe d' ye."

"You knew all that?"

"Aye. An' if y'r worried, it's bein' well protected, so if ye don't ha' any more questions, we need t' get goin'. Are ye ready?"

"I just need my traveling bags."

Gallowglass gestured toward the house."

"Tha's th' lassies' thrall bringin' them now, I think."

Marieko was stunned beyond any hope of fast recovery. Events had turned on them so quickly she was hard-pressed to accept she could go from elation to near destruction in all but the blink of an eye, and then survive only to find herself a prisoner in her own Residence. She was equally amazed Victor should take the turnaround so calmly. Had Columbine sold her out to save her own miserable skin the way she had sold out Renquist to the Highlanders, she would have thrown herself on her and torn her apart. Victor, on the other hand, took the base betrayal in his stride and was talking with all cordiality to Gallowglass. The only positive aspect of the situation was that the Highlanders, after committing something perilously close to an act of war, were apparently pulling out. They were, however, taking not only Victor, but also the chrysalis of Taliesin the Merlin with them.

The worst part was her sense of impotency. Marieko could do nothing about what was happening around her. She might battle ninja in her dreams, but to take on fifteen armed Highlanders in the pouring rain of a real evening, even with Destry beside her, would be nothing short of suicidal. She could only watch the Scotsmen make their preparations to leave, glare at them, and suppress the need to snap, snarl, and hurt. She even reserved the right to make Columbine suffer for her perfidy at some later time. Columbine had wisely made herself scarce after the front door had opened, and they'd staggered in from the moment of dawn, and Renquist had, of course, found himself facing the half circle of sword points. Destry was also mute, glaring at the Highlanders. Since the moment they knew they were not going to be destroyed, she hadn't uttered a word. The experience of coming close to losing all in the sunrise had a profound effect on any nosferatu, young or old.

Marieko stood in the hall of Ravenkeep, watching Victor and the males of Fenrior through the open door. She had thought all the action was outside and was thus surprised to hear a clumsy noise from behind her. She turned to find Bolingbroke, dried blood still on his face from where the Highlanders had mishandled him, laden down with Victor's traveling bags and the fur rug on which she and Victor had spent their memorable day. "Where do you think you're going with those?"

"I am taking them to . . . Mr. Renquist. Mistress Columbine said . . . that I should—"

Marieko cut him off. She had no time for his slurred and halting explanation. "Yes, yes, just get along, and don't take forever."

It seemed Columbine wasn't so upset it impaired her from giving orders to speed Victor's departure. Marieko's anger blazed afresh. She couldn't see how the troika could continue under the present circumstances, and even if it did, the dynamics would have to be completely different. Destry came up behind her and grasped her hand. "We should say good-bye to Victor. We have no idea if and when we'll see him again."

Marieko collected herself. "Yes, it's the least we can do."

"For now."

"For now?"

Destry nodded. "For now. You think this is at an end of it?"

Destry glanced around. A few of the Highlanders were paying a passing male-female attention, but most were ignoring them. Gallowglass seemed to have issued orders that the females were strictly off-limits to his wild men. This had come as welcome news. When Marieko and Destry had fallen through the door, skin already scoured by the coming sun, the sight of six Highlanders containing Victor in a ring of sharp steel had produced the logical projection that they might well be next, and instead of spending just a watchful, sleepless day waiting for nightfall and the return of Duncanon and his males, they might have been the principal entertainment of a roaring and bloody Clan Fenrior orgy of unnatural physical abuse.

"We'll talk about what's to be done later."

Marieko nodded. Her face was like stone. "And later we'll also talk to Columbine."

Destry gestured to the Highlanders. "When our Scottish visitors have departed. In the meantime, we'll just bid Victor farewell."

For a moment Marieko seemed reluctant to move, but then, hand in hand, she and Destry followed Bolingbroke to where Renquist was standing with Gallowglass.

The two Hummers purred smoothly up the Motorway, headlights cutting through what was now a downpour, wide heavy-duty tires singing on the wet road surface, traveling in excess of a hundred miles an hour—and a full thirty over the United Kingdom speed limit. To facilitate this flagrant breach of the traffic laws, a pair of red lights flashed on each vehicle's roof, creating a second set of haloes in the downpour. When Gallowglass talked about "motorin'," he tolerated no half measures. The trucks were being driven flat out. Renquist had voiced his surprise that traveling in such a manner didn't immediately cause them to fall foul of the police. At this, the sticklike nosferatu had smiled knowingly. "There's th' canny part o' i'. The coppers all think we're some exceptional big deal. Some big-arse special unit goin' about its secret dirty work, y' ken? Tha's th' trouble wi' th' English. They don't like t' ask about wha' they don't know. We even have sirens if we need t' really impress."

"What will your lord come up with next, Gallowglass? A black helicopter?"

"Gi' him time, Master Renquist. Gi' him time."

Although it transpired the Clan Fenrior kept concealed bolt-holes up and down the British Isles, and it would be possible to pass the day in any one of half a dozen of them along the approximate route, Gallowglass wanted to make the long journey to Castle Fenrior in a single night. The lord had demanded the cocoon of Merlin under his roof as soon as possible it seemed, and thus the need for the headlong rush and the rotating warning lights. Renquist did suspect, without even the goading of their laird, the Highlanders would have driven that

way in any case. Reckless speed and splitting the night
with sound and fury seemed absolutely in keeping with
their character.

That the raiding party of Highlanders should be divided into two groups was dictated by their having to
travel in two vehicles. Renquist, Gallowglass, and some
nine others were crowded into the lead Hummer, packed
tight and smelling of damp plaid, while Duncanon and
a further six, along with the Merlin cocoon, brought up
the rear. Renquist noticed that he had been kept separate
from the cocoon, and he assumed this was deliberate.
Either Gallowglass or Fenrior or both must have decided
Renquist riding in the same truck as the cocoon ran the
risk of his accidentally learning some fresh secret in
transit. He found it an encouraging sign; at least a partial
indication he was not being transported all the way to
the north of Scotland simply to be exterminated. Renquist was operating on the optimistic assumption Fenrior
had ordered him seized for his mind, rather than his destruction. Renquist could picture a flash of lordly nosferatu impatience. Renquist had procrastinated over the
more civil "request and require" invitation, so Fenrior
decided to have him brought by force. It suggested to
Renquist the Highland lord had reached that advanced
state of hubris in which he believed he could get away
with just about anything.

Although Gallowglass had wanted the Highlanders
moved out of Ravenkeep as fast as possible, there had
been a certain degree of inevitable lingering and delay,
and Duncanon had taken the time to speculate aloud
about the number of hideous fates and methods of agonizing destruction for which Renquist should prepare
himself when he finally came before Fenrior. Even this
had not served to dent Renquist's hopeful mood. He decided the insolent young troop leader was simply mouth-
ing off, and if Fenrior had wanted him destroyed, he
would have simply been left to burn in the sun, and
Gallowglass would neither have asked for his word of

surrender nor opened the door to him when he gave it.

Renquist thought he heard the sound of singing voices from the second Hummer, but he couldn't be sure over the drumming of the rain, the slapping of the windshield wipers, and the occasional *whoosh* as the truck hit standing water and threw up curved waves of spray. He found it reasonably plausible, however, and could imagine Duncanon and his crew, Fenrior's Children of the Mist, crouched around the Merlin cocoon, bawling out some muscular ballad about laughing in the face of death, just as they had hundreds of years previously around any campfire in the lee of a rocky outcrop, amid gorse and purple heather. Every so often the two vehicles would pass what the British called a "service area," harsh islands of blue-white neon where travelers could find gas, maps, souvenir trinkets, and food. Inside the lighted, aquarium-like restaurants, humans fueled up on rubber eggs, mysterious pork products, and greasy chips and killed their boredom on pinball machines and arcade games, while, just a few yards away, out on the six-lane highway, two truckloads of inhuman nightmare and the more than mortal remains of a historical legend raced past at breakneck speed.

"They're goin' t' make th' whole world like this a'fore too long."

"The whole world does look like this."

"We keep our part o' i' th' way i' should be."

"How long do you think that will last?"

"Many ha' come t' tek i' from us, an' none ha' managed i' so far."

Both Renquist and Gallowglass were silent for a long time, contemplating the world through the windshield. Finally Gallowglass was moved to comment. "Are y' thinking o' th' lassies?"

"I'm thinking they may have problems."

"Problems?"

"It depends on how many bodies your Highlanders left behind."

Gallowglass shrugged noncommittally. "Duncanon an' his lads know how t' live off th' land."

Renquist nodded. "Then the ladies may have problems."

Destry stormed into Columbine's boudoir. "What the fuck do you think you're doing?"

"I would have thought it was obvious. I'm packing."

Columbine, still in her torn riding habit, hair falling and unkempt, and a dangerously wild look in her eyes, was haphazardly throwing things into an assortment of leather bags.

"I have to get away from here."

Destry planted her hands on her hips. "Not suffering remorse at your advanced age?"

"I didn't suffer remorse at any age."

"Throwing Victor to the Highlanders was cold even by your standards."

"I only did it to save the three of us, but you're determined not to believe me."

"We might if you tried to explain what happened."

"I made a deal with Gallowglass that we wouldn't be harmed if I helped him take Victor. That's all you need to know."

"That's not all we need to know. Maybe you had to do what you had to do. We can't tell. What we do know is that you can't just go running off into the night. You can't escape what's happened."

Columbine let out a brittle laugh. "Don't flatter yourself. I'm not running from you, or any supposed betrayal of Victor, or even the bodycount with which the Highlands have undoubtedly strewn the local landscape."

"So what are you running away from?"

"I have to get away from him."

"Him?"

"Your Taliesin, the Great Merlin."

Marieko entered the room. She had stopped to lock doors and generally secure the house in the wake of the

Highlanders depature. "What new madness is this, Columbine? I think I speak for both myself and Destry when I say we're at the limits of our patience."

"When they moved him, I felt something. I could feel him leaving the tomb. He's waking, and for some reason he wants me to come to him."

"That's absurd, Columbine, and you know it."

"I swear. I can feel this pull."

"So you're running to follow the Merlin to Fenrior?"

Columbine looked at Destry as though she was the crazy one. "I'm not that insane. I'm running away from him."

"Now you're making no sense at all."

"I don't want any part of this. It's too weird, and worse than that, it's too damned monumental. I don't want to be part of history. All I really want is to enjoy myself, to have fun. I don't want to have to know about the damned Nephilim, or the Original Beings, or even the bloody Merlin. I want to get away from the whole fucking mess!"

"And how do you intend to do that?"

"I'm going to London, and I'm going to kill. I'm going to kill, and kill, and inflict pain on the helpless, and feed until I'm glutted. I am going to preside over a bloody reign of terror that will live in infamy, to quote FDR, and if the humans get too close to me, I'll move on to Paris and start all over again. And then Rome, and then maybe Budapest for old times' sake. I don't really care about the geography. I'm going. I intend completely to exist in the moment. Perhaps I'll start a salon and save beautiful young poets from the horrors of growing old."

"Is there anything in any of those perfume bottles that might calm you down? Because this is mania, my darling. You may soon pass the point of no return."

"What do you care?"

"We were . . . are . . . a troika. The theory is that we look out for each other."

"We don't even believe each other."

Marieko, who had stood apart from the confrontation between Columbine and Destry suddenly interrupted. "I believe you."

Columbine looked at her in amazement. "You do what?"

"I believe you."

Columbine's eyes narrowed. Had she been a reptile, her tongue would have flicked out. "What's the trick, my Oriental darling?"

"There's no trick."

"I don't understand."

"The dreams were the first phase of his waking. We've pretty much agreed on that."

"Okay, go on."

"Unconsciously he was putting out feelers. Reaching for a kindred or receptive mind."

"Why should this Urshu do that?"

Marieko shook her head. "I don't know why, but the theory fits."

"You sound like Victor."

"That's the way he approached a problem." She added a pointed qualification: "When he was a free man, that is."

Columbine ignored the taunt. Marieko and Destry might be buzzing with hostility, but at least she was the center of attention again. "So you think there is now some kind of link between me and this Merlin thing?"

"I'm practically certain of it."

"A kindred mind, I think you said?"

"I actually said a kindred or receptive mind."

"Are you implying I'm merely receptive?"

"Draw your own conclusions."

Columbine apparently didn't care to do so. "And what happens to this alleged link when he wakes?"

Marieko spread her hands. "I think that's what you're soon going to find out."

"What I don't understand is why me?"

"Again. I can't tell you. Maybe it was purely random."

"Maybe he sensed something about me. He had a female partner, didn't he?"

Marieko nodded. "Morgana or Morgan le Fey."

"So I'll be his Morgan le Fey, and wreak even further havoc."

Marieko looked wanly at Columbine. "I don't think so."

"What do you mean you don't think so?"

Marieko had taken quite enough of Columbine and she saw no reason to sugarcoat the pill. "Because you are just receptive. You're no kin of this thing. All you could ever be for an entity like Taliesin would be a plaything, similar, in fact, to one of those boys you like to have around the place until you've drained the life out of them."

Columbine's aura turned a dangerous thunder-at-sunset magenta. "Are you telling me it's beyond my capabilities to control an Urshu that's just woken from a fifteen-hundred-year sleep?"

"Totally. That's exactly what I'm telling you. You wouldn't have a chance in hell. You may be nosferatu, but you're so damned vain and lazy, you're adept at next to nothing."

For a moment, Columbine didn't react. Her aura became neutral and unreadable, but then her fangs began to extended, and when she spoke, her tone was pure spite. "You misbegotten Oriental cunt!"

In the second before she sprang, Destry made her move, knocking Columbine off balance, so instead of leaping at Marieko, ready to rip and tear, she went sprawling on the boudoir carpet. Destry stood over her. "Stay down, Columbine, or I swear I'll hurt you."

Marieko stepped forward. "No, no, let her up. This has to be taken to its logical conclusion." She looked down at Columbine. "Shall we just do it? Is that the tactile and emotional experience you're finally craving, the destroyer or the destroyed? Swords in the twilight, my dear? Because if it is, Marieko Matsunaga is at your service." She turned. "Since we lack seconds, Destry, will you take control of the dueling staff and oversee the combat?"

The Motorway went on and on, the view through the windshield and from the side windows was one of mobile monotony, and Renquist wished he could just doze like a human. Every now and again, the sameness of the drive might be relieved by the lights of a town or a large industrial plant, but even at the speeds the two Hummers were able to maintain, the miles could grow long and the journey—which was, after all, from one end of the British Isles to the other—grew tedious in the extreme. About the only diversion was in bouts of conversation with Gallowglass. To Renquist's surprise, as long as they'd kept away from matters immediately at hand and what possible fate might await him when the small convoy arrived at Fenrior Castle, the tall thin nosferatu appeared happy enough to talk away the time.

"Aye, awhile, Master Renquist, I've been wi' th' Lord Fenrior quite awhile. Like many o' us, he brought me fra th' battlefield when all hope seemed lost an' gave me th' gift o' th' Change. I' my case, i' was i' th' churchyard at Dunkeld."

The only problem with Gallowglass's stories was that he seemed to assume Renquist knew much more about the convoluted and bloodsoaked history of the Highlands of Scotland than he actually did. "Dunkeld?"

"I' was where we made our final stand after Bonnie Dundee went down. We had fallen on th' English under Mackay i' th' gorge o' Killiecrankie. All th' great ones were there, all th' Highland Jacobites, th' Macleans, th' MacDonalds, th' Stewarts of Appin an' th' Grants o' Glenmorrison, th' MacLeods, MacNeils, Robertsons an' Farquharsons—" Gallowglass recited the names of the clans as though he were repeating a holy, or maybe unholy, litany—"an' a thousand Camerons led by Sir

Ewen Cameron o' Lochiel, then i' his sixties, th' same Lochiel who bit an English officer's throat out wi' his bare teeth, an' him only a human at th' time."

"You sound as though you should have claimed the victory."

"Aye, an' we almost did. It was a terrible slaughter, an' th' English took th' worst o' it, an' then, cursed by luck no deserved by a dog, at th' moment th' English should ha' run aw th' way home, Dundee was struck down."

Aside from the contortions of religion, politics, vendetta, fighting the English, conspiring with the French, and the straightforward rape, adultery, and cattle rustling that seemed to have plagued the Scottish Highlands since at least the eighth century, the principal protagonists had more titles, nicknames, and pseudonyms than the characters in a nineteenth-century Russian novel, and this caused Renquist even more confusion.

"Dundee?"

"Aye, Master Renquist, Bonnie Dundee, th' Dundee, John Graham o' Claverhouse, Viscount Dundee, also known as Bloody Claverse, after th' way he brought i' t' th' Covenanters w' fire an' sword. Fair o' face wi' tha' smile an' his long black hair t' his shoulders, an' his deep brown eyes, we aw loved him an' would ha' followed him t' th' gates o' Hell, an' aw but did. So when he fell, th' Highlanders were dumbstruck, an' Mackay was able t' rally an' drive us back aw th' way t' th' Dunkeld churchyard, where th' killing started i' earnest right between th' headstones an' crosses."

Renquist's third problem in keeping up with Gallowglass's tales of havoc in the glens was that he talked as though everything was so recent, as though it had all happened just a matter of months ago, although Renquist knew they were dealing in centuries.

"So this would have been 1745?"

Gallowglass laughed at Renquist's temporal foolishness. "Och no, man, I'm no talkin' about th' forty-five, tha' was Culloden an' Bonnie Prince Charlie. Th' year o' 1689 is th' time t' which I refer. July i' was. Ye have get ye uprisings straight, ye ken."

"I'm doing my best. There seem to have been rather many of them."

"Aye. You could say tha'. I blame i' mainly on th' English always coming up t' interfere, although I ha' t' admit, between themselves, th' clans were masters o' holding grudges an' exactin' revenge. Like when MacFarlane o' Arrochar learned tha' his wife ha' been seduced by his neighbor t' th' south, Colquhoun o' Luss, he burned down th' Colquhoun castle at Rossdhu wi' its owner inside i' an' then served his unfaithful spouse her lover's charred an' blackened privates on a platter f' dinner, remarking 'This is your share. You'll understand ye self what i' is.' "

After this less than savory tidbit, Renquist attempted to steer the conversation back to a more generalized history. "Were you the only one rescued from among the wounded?"

"Fra' th' gory bed, as they say? I was th' only one fra' Killiecrankie an' Dunkeld. Who knows? Maybe th' laird would ha' brought Dundee himself home if he hadna' died so fast."

"Strange to raise your vassals from among the dying."

"Strange, Master Renquist?"

"Perhaps just strange that I never considered it."

"Aye, but aren't most changes shaped by some measure o' night politics, though? M' lord is no only a vampire but th' immortal leader o' a human clan, ye understand. He needs th' loyalty o' his swords an' th' minds a' his back, ye ken?"

Renquist nodded. He was learning a lot fast. These Highlanders might not be fastidious, but that was no reason to consider them stupid. They were as sharp as their ever-present swords and, in many respects, lived far deeper in the nosferatu world than he did, always teetering the edges commanded by the foibles of humans and their world of machines, figures, and manipulations. In their comparative isolation, these Highlanders were able to demonstrate with some strutting that they were the top of the food chain, and they owned the night in their own glens, and on their own mountainsides.

With very much that attitude, Gallowglass continued. "A man who's been brought t' immortality from thinking aw he had left t' him was t' cough oot his life i' th' ruin o' th' killing field has more than just a passin' loyalty t' th' one who raised him up." Gallowglass permitted himself a wry smile. "An undyin' loyalty, ye might say."

He gestured to the small Highlander with the headsman's axe. "Take Prestwick here. M' lord brought him home fra' Culloden, tha' sorry wreck o' all tha' was fine an' good. Pulled out fra' right under th' nose o' Butcher Cumberland an' th' grapeshot an' bayonets o' his damned Hessians."

Renquist nodded to Prestwick, who returned the nod with no flicker of expression. He realized Fenrior was living much closer to the way he himself had existed when he had his boyars at his back and the nature of the predator needed far less veneer.

"M lord ha' brought lads home fra' most o' th' great battles. Some are wi' us an' some have gone. We still ha' th' venerable Shaggy Lachlan who fought at Flodden Field."

If Renquist's recollection was correct, the Battle of Flodden, which resulted in the death of Scotland's king James IV, had taken place in 1513. Thus Fenrior must be at least five hundred years old. Renquist was assembling a picture of this lord to whom he'd surrendered that was, to say the least, interesting. He was imagining a bloody and devious autocrat, with both advisors and veteran warriors from whom he demanded and received absolute devotion. Then he remembered something from the first meeting with Gallowglass. He had let slip how, at Fenrior, they bred their own humans. If nothing else, the Lord Fenrior should prove a challenge, and Renquist missed Lupo more than ever.

The rain had stopped, and a white moon had broken through unraveling clouds. They had chosen the lake as their arena. Columbine seemed to favor the idea of fighting Marieko against the background of Ravenkeep's moonlit lake, demonstrating that, as always, she saw what was happening as a romantic drama rather than a life-and-death crisis very much of her own making. The three walked from the house, a small tense procession, Columbine and Marieko side by side but keeping a good and hostile distance between them. Destry walked slightly behind, carrying the long staff in her right hand, the staff with the uncut emerald in the silver setting at the head that was her symbol of authority in this damned silly but nonetheless highly formal nosferatu confrontation. A pair of matched sabers, wrapped in a black sheepskin, were under her left arm. They were not the ones from the wall in the drawing room but a more recent and virgin pair Columbine had deemed more suitable for the duel since neither had drawn blood since their forging. As the party to receive the challenge, Columbine had made the choice of weapons, and sabers gave her a distinct advantage. For a human of Columbine's size and sex, the saber was too heavy and unwieldy a weapon, but with her undead strength behind the blade, it could be both accurate and deadly. Of course, the same applied to Marieko, but she simply wasn't as skilled with that style of weapon. She might be an expert with ninja butterfly knives and the lighter sword of the samurai, but Marieko was largely unfamiliar with the heavy European saber.

Destry had decided, for the moment, attempting to stop the pair was pointless. She would play her role as mistress and overseer of the combat and, along the way, find a way to intervene: to end the duel before one killed the other. Destry knew Columbine well enough to be aware, after she'd worked off some of her guilt and anger over Renquist being taken by the Highlanders, she might view at least her own destruction as a less than desirable idea. If Destry presented a good enough reason to cease the combat and allowed Columbine the space to save face, she would back off. Marieko, though, was a wholly different matter. Although Columbine had totally provoked her, she'd been the one who'd issued the challenge. Harder, more determined, and with a more implacably developed sense of tradition, Marieko might actually be far more difficult to stop once started. Destry hoped, however, Marieko's fundamental common sense would prevail. In the meantime, her only option was to continue the charade and wish for no early tragedy.

Destry positioned herself with her back to the lake, facing the lights that still burned in the house. She folded back the sheepskin, exposing the steel-and-lizardskin hilts of the two sabers, and beckoned to the antagonists. Columbine made the first choice of blade. She drew it carefully from the sheepskin and swung it experimentally, feeling the weight and balance. Marieko took the second weapon with much less show and flourish. Marieko's hands were sufficiently small for both to fit inside the guard on the hilt, and she was able to grasp it in the two-handed Japanese manner. Columbine had taken her time dressing for the occasion. In tights, Robin Hood boots, and a floppy Errol Flynn pirate shirt, she looked to Destry like a combination of Peter Pan and Hamlet. In direct competition, and refusing to be psyched by any enforced waiting, Marieko had used the time to do the same, and appeared in a flame-scarlet kimono with the crossed axes of the Yarabachi Clan on the back in hand-painted gold. She also wore a scarlet silk band around her head with the same insignia. Both had put their hair up, Marieko in the same traditional warrior topknot that—although neither Destry or Columbine knew it—she had assumed for the violent dream she had shared with Renquist. Columbine had adopted a looser, Gibson

Girl roll of the kind popular in the 1900s. It might have been more dashing, but to Destry, it appeared a great deal less practical. Already stray strands were starting to fall loose.

With considerable reluctance, Destry tapped the end of her staff twice on the ground to bring the inevitable to order. "Ladies, commend upon your weapons."

Each female adopted her individual stance, and in so doing, they couldn't have been more at odds. Columbine favored the high-wristed, blade-angled-down posture of a mounted dragoon. Marieko, in complete contrast, held her sword high, hilt at shoulder-level and with the blade perfectly vertical. Destry noted the grass was still wet from the rain, and Columbine's stylish boots could well start slipping and sliding, giving Marieko, who was fighting barefoot, a distinct advantage.

For what seemed like an eternity, neither combatant moved. Both stood rigid, stone-faced, gazes locked one on the other, watchful and patient as panthers, concentration rapt, motionless players in a game where the first to blink took on a massive psychological disadvantage. As Destry fully expected, it was Columbine who finally lost her composure and, swinging her saber, took a long-booted step, following the momentum of a blade that would have gutted Marieko—had she not skillfully twisted away on ballerina pointes. After the wild cut, Columbine was slightly off balance. Marieko came at her with a two-three combination of a downward slash, a thrust, and a fast upward slice that ripped the flowing sleeve of Columbine's shirt and pinked her upper arm so spots of crimson showed on the white fabric. Destry quickly extended her cane ordering the adversaries to disengage.

"Blood has been drawn. The contest may, at this time, be concluded without loss of honor."

Columbine didn't bother so much as to acknowledge the chance to withdraw. She swung at Marieko, who parried quickly. Their steel shot sparks, and darts of fire-like hostility snarled between them. With their nosferatu speed, a human would never have been able to follow the moves in the sudden flurry of action that followed, and even Destry had to step swiftly aside to avoid lunging blades and pivoting bodies. Marieko sustained a cut on the shoulder, and the sleeve of her kimono was ripped to a trailing rag, but she had managed to strike Columbine no less than three times, and seemed, so far, to be getting the best of the encounter. Columbine was bleeding copiously, and her shirt was shredded. Both of them backed off and circled. Marieko ran a nervous tongue over dry lips, and her eyes glinted as she stared at the bleeding wounds on Columbine's upper body. This was what Destry had feared. The sight of blood would enflame their senses, and now the duel would be impossible to stop, short of its complete and definitive outcome.

Columbine and Marieko continued to circle, using the opportunity to collect their strength for the next exchange. They were not out of breath the way two human swordsmen might have been, but the fighting was taking a toll on even their undead energy. Each grimly looked for an opening, and this time Marieko went on the offensive. This second clashing steel duel was of shorter duration than the first, and the two quickly moved back to a safer distance and resumed their circling. Both were now losing blood, and Destry herself felt a dangerous stirring at the sight. Marieko's scarlet silk hardly showed the extent of her wounds, but what had been Columbine's crisp white buccaneer shirt was now nothing more than a crimson rag. Destry tightened her grip on her staff. It wouldn't do for the adjudicator to succumb to crude bloodlust.

Marieko finally spoke. The first time either of them had made a sound except soft cries, gasps, and intakes of breath. "Do you yield, Columbine?"

"It's only blood, you bitch. I can still best you."

"You believe that?"

"I know that."

Now Columbine also gripped her saber double handed, as though her arms were tiring. She aimed a diagonal slash at Marieko, but suddenly Marieko wasn't where she was supposed to be. Removing one hand from the hilt of her sword, she came at Columbine, her point describing circles in the air, and suddenly Columbine was disarmed. The move was so fast and accomplished Destry hardly saw it, and would have been hard-pressed to describe it later. Columbine stood bemused and swaying slightly, her breasts and torso slick with her own blood. Her saber was stuck at an angle in the lawn, some twelve feet away. Marieko was poised to finish her, but Destry raised her staff.

"Hold!"

Marieko's face was streaked with both Columbine's blood and her own and she could only stare at Destry with a sullen, semi-comprehension. "Hold? Why should I hold? She's mine now. She wanted this, and now it's hers."

"I said hold!"

Marieko, caught up in the fury of the fight, now raised her sword to Destry. "I will not hold!"

Destry pointed at her with the staff. "You will obey!"

Marieko, reason gone, prepared to swing at Destry, who stood very still and quickly used the voice of authority at almost its most and full commanding power. "Strike me at your peril, madame!"

The voice was enough to cause Marieko to hesitate, and as she faltered, Destry struck her hard across the wrist with the heavy emerald-and-silver head of the ceremonial staff. All in one, Marieko dropped her saber, clutched her wrist, and cursed. "Fuck you, Destry. I think the bone's broken."

"You'll mend. The fight stops here."

Columbine glanced in the direction of her own sword, but Destry picked up Marieko's dropped saber and gestured warningly. "Don't even think about it, my dear."

Both Marieko and Columbine stared at Destry. The two of them were bloody, breathing through flared nostrils, but not speaking. Destry retrieved the sheepskin and walked to where Columbine's sword was stuck in the ground. She jerked it from the earth, spread out the fur, laid the stained blades on it, and carefully rewrapped them. "Ready to resume reality, ladies?"

Marieko began to protest. "You have no authority to stop the proceedings like this."

"No? How about we try to recall this is the twenty-first century, and we do not fight duels to the true death because one of us supposedly insulted the other in the heat of argument?"

Again she was met with silence.

"While you two were dressing for your bloody pas de deux, a thought occurred to me. We have never factored Renquist's people into this equation." With so much visible blood, it was hard for Destry to sound as calm and logical as she might have wished, but somehow she managed it. She knew her only hope of avoiding disaster was to get their minds rather than their emotions working again before they once more went at it like two hell-cats. If they completely lost it, she'd be powerless to stop them. The staff was only a symbol, and useless if they turned feral. In that state, they wouldn't bother with the sabers. They'd rend each other tooth and claw like creatures of the primeval wild. "I would imagine if word was to reach California that Victor had been taken captive, it would cause a good deal of consternation among the other members of his colony. We might even find ourselves with some long-distance allies."

Marieko winced as she forcibly set the bone in her wrist. Columbine stripped off the rag that was her blood-soaked shirt and was naked to the waist. Destry was through to their cognitive minds.

"Why didn't you tell us before we fell into all this?"

Marieko also seemed to somehow blame Destry. "That's right. Why didn't you stop us?"

Destry snorted with derision. "Me stop you two? Give me a break. You were too damned determined for that. Too much psychic poison was flowing."

Columbine seemed about to say something, but Destry cut her off. "Don't say a word. Not a word. Just consider how ridiculous you look standing there with your tits bare to the night and bleeding like a stuck pig."

Marieko pulled her slashed kimono tighter around her body. "I—"

"And you. Don't you say a word, either. I don't want to hear any more of this. The episode is closed. Go and get cleaned up. After that, we'll discuss other options beyond simply turning on each other."

"So how old would that make the Lord Fenrior?"

Gallowglass looked sideways at Renquist. They had just left the town of Carlisle behind them and were out of England and into Scotland. "D' ye take me f' fool, Master Renquist?"

"Certainly not."

"Oh, aye, old Gallowglass will ramble on wi' his tales o' gore an' glory, an' th' daring deeds o' yesteryear, an' no doubt ye've been thinkin' I've let slip a muckle mess about th' background o' Fenrior an' Fenrior, but truth is ye've learned little except some proud history o' this grand land. Ye don't know th' half o' i', an' wi'oot th' half o' it, ye really know nothin'. Do I make m'self plain?"

Renquist smiled at his own presumption. "Eminently plain, my friend."

"The vampire is like a good malt. He improves with age. But I was forgetting ye din'a like yon word, do ye?"

"I don't use it myself. Not after 1919."

"Oh, aye, I ken your sensibilities. Mercifully we kept oot o' aw tha'."

"You were lucky."

Gallowglass shook his head. "We were careful. We

stayed i' our own realm an' avoided foreign entanglements."

"So what, between us, do we actually know about the others in Renquist's colony?" At Destry's businesslike question, Marieko and Columbine both looked at each other, not quite making eye contact. Neither wanted to speak first. Destry was uncompromising. "Still in shock, are we, dears? A little weak from our cuts and exertions, and loss of precious bodily fluids? Well, that's going to be just too bad, because right now we have to focus. An act of war has been committed against Ravenkeep, and we must act accordingly, if only for the sake of appearances. We cannot have this troika seen as vulnerable to any gang of undead ruffians who walks in here smelling of sweat and with naked swords. Very soon, we'll have the reputation of being three helpless females and find ourselves overrun by opportunists, adventurers, and the worst class of nosferatu carpetbagger. I don't intend to wait around for that. We'll consider the incident of the duel to be closed, filed under catharsis, because as of now, ladies, we are at war. If anyone doubts it, let her speak out right away, otherwise it can be our only priority. If nothing else, we have to be seen to exact payback from Fenrior to prevent our autonomy being compromised."

Marieko and Columbine again remained mute, but their auras showed Destry a greater sense of purpose. Destry nodded. "Good. Okay. Now I'll repeat the question: What do we collectively know about the Renquist colony?"

Marieko was the first to volunteer information. "There's one named Lupo who Victor actually misses. I've gleaned that he's essentially Victor's strong right arm. He is from the Italian Renaissance, and the story goes that he never came through the Change, but was actually created by Craft."

Columbine sniffed. "Many claim to be created by

Craft, but I never met one who could prove or authenticate it."

Marieko glanced at Columbine. Their eyes met for the first time since the duel. For an instant, it seemed as though competition might be rekindled, but Marieko shrugged. "If there ever was an authentic one, it would be Lupo. I understand he refers to Victor as his don. This Lupo is also supposedly a legendary figure in the human underworld, among crime families in both the United States and Europe. He is spoken of as the perfect assassin."

Recognition dawned on Destry. "Joey Nightshade."

Columbine was mystified. "Who or what is Joey Nightshade?"

Destry pushed back her chestnut hair. "It was a long time ago in Marseilles. I had some brief connection with men who worked for the Guerini brothers, the Corsicans who ran the heroin trade, what they later called the French connection. They knew stories about this almost mythic character Joey Nightshade, who was reputed to be the absolutely unstoppable hitman. Seemingly, once he'd taken a contract, no target could be made safe from him. The other part of the myth was that he always killed by night. When I first heard that, I wondered if he might be nosferatu."

"You believe this Nightshade character and Lupo are one and the same?"

"I think it's infinitely possible."

"And if this Lupo heard his don was in danger?"

"I think he'd move heaven and earth to be with him."

"Okay, so that's Lupo. What about the others?"

Destry stared at Columbine, who bridled slightly, saying, "What would I know about Victor's extended family?"

Destry's eyes flashed dangerously. "Get off it, darling. You've followed his career like a bloody fan. This is no time to be coy."

Columbine huffed impatiently. "All right, all right.

The most I know is that after the destruction of Renquist's darling Cynara, there was trouble. The colony was forced to flee from New York, and by that point, their numbers were down to just seven."

"Just seven?"

Columbine nodded. "Seven. That's all. The Residence in New York had succumbed to a bad outbreak of Feasting, and some of the young ones attempted a coup. I heard Victor had to cull the young males."

Marieko frowned. "Seven is a very small colony. Hardly viable."

Columbine continued. "There were rumors they'd brought others through the Change, in Los Angeles, around the time of the Cthulhu incident, but I have no idea how many or what they might be like. Of the original seven, three can be excluded immediately, as far as we're concerned."

"Excluded?"

"The weird sisters Dahlia and Imogene would never travel across the Atlantic."

"Why not?"

"They're peculiar."

"How peculiar?"

"Too peculiar to go among humans. One maintains the outward physical appearance of a ten-year-old, and the other is simply too bizarre even by nosferatu standards."

"And the third?"

"A traffic-stopping grotesque called Segal."

"So who does that leave apart from Lupo?"

"A female nonentity called, I think, Sada and, of course—" Columbine hesitated. "—Julia Aschenbach."

Destry raised an eyebrow. "Julia Aschenbach? I've heard that name. There was a Julia Aschenbach working in the NKVD's paranormal division. And then I heard about the same Julia surfacing in the very darkest end of CIA counterinsurgency. She was doing stuff at which even I drew the line."

Columbine nodded. "That's Julia. She's had many to-talitarian adventures. Even before her Change, she had been a budding starlet in the Nazi film industry and re-putedly one of Joseph Goebbels's countless mistresses. Also there's a neatly incestuous factor in Julia's case."

Marieko looked interested. "Incestuous?"

"The story is that Victor created Julia and then aban-doned her. He'd assumed she was nothing more than a stunningly vacant beauty, but as a nosferatu, she turned out to be a viciously consummate survivor."

Marieko was expressionless. "You sound as though you don't like her."

"She's dangerous and, by all accounts, a headstrong wild card, totally a nosferatu of the twentieth century. Stories have circulated how it was really her that fo-mented the trouble in New York, but then, at the last minute, she sold out the young males and sided with Victor. Her ambition has always been to bond with Vic-tor and become his full consort, but he's held her off with an equal determination."

Marieko almost smiled. "That should at least please you."

Columbine frowned. "The problem is she'd be ideal for our purpose. To have Julia and Lupo with us would be a positive asset. Indeed, it might be all we'd need."

"So what's the problem except she has eyes for Vic-tor?"

"The mixture could be just too volatile and backfire on us."

Marieko held up a hand. "Wait a moment. Aren't we moving a little ahead of ourselves? We are deciding which of Renquist's people might be of use to us, and we haven't even been in contact with them."

Columbine waved a dismissive hand. "That will be no problem. We simply call this Lupo and tell him his don is being held prisoner. All else should follow from that without any effort on our part."

Destry looked skeptical. "You think it's that easy?"

Columbine nodded, as if she entertained not a single doubt. "If what you've both said about him is true, his loyalty will be all the driving force we need. After he hears what has happened, he will be honor-bound to destroy Fenrior, and that awful Gallowglass, too."

Destry shook her head. "But, no matter how powerful, he's just one. How could he go up against Fenrior and all his swords?"

Marieko smiled. "You think Lupo doesn't have his contacts?"

The two Hummers were now in the true wild Highlands. That, at least was how it appeared to Renquist, staring out through the windshield. And, as yet, no sign of dawn was showing. The old nosferatu maxim would seem to be correct in this case, the undead indeed traveled fast. The road along which they now rolled, still maintaining their preposterous speeds, was a simple two-lane blacktop that conformed to the contours of the countryside rather than a Motorway arbitrarily slicing through hills and bridging valleys. At one point they roared past a herd of Highland cattle. The shaggy creatures, with their curved horns and long matted hair, opened bleary eyes, but the vehicles had come and gone before their slow bovine brains could react. Only the road told Renquist he was anywhere in the twenty-first century. Apart from the narrow strip of macadam, the scene could have been the same any time in the past twenty thousand years. In the foreground, bleak and sere hills supported little more than short coarse grass, gorse, and heather, while further in the distance, blue and purple mountains were silhouetted against the night sky. Now that he was actually here, he could see how easy it would be, in such surroundings, to detach from all modern reality and live according to time-honored but not overly practical tradition.

"It'll no be long th' noo."

"We're almost there?"

"Aye, very soon ye should ha' y' first sight o' Fenrior."

In just over fifteen minutes, Gallowglass was proved as good as his word. The trucks crested a high ridge, and suddenly Renquist could see for himself. He had experienced a great many castles in his near-millennium. Some he recalled fondly, and others he remembered with dread. In terms of magnificence, Fenrior hardly ranked with the military extravaganzas the Crusaders had erected in the Holy Land, the Moorish edifices in Spain, or the excesses of the more elaborate gingerbread French chateaux. Outwardly, it looked to be a cluster of vertical, almost windowless towers that had merged one with the other, growing together, but still rising to an irregular apex of steeply peaked roofs and conical turrets. A flat-topped, square-sided redoubt was joined to the rest of the structure by a formidable curtain wall like a man-made cliff. Its plain and Scottishly practical design, however, was offset by its impressive natural setting. Actually built on its own small and rocky island, it stood a few hundred yards out into the waters of a loch surrounded by high wooded crags. It was joined to the mainland, first by a causeway and then by a bridge over the last stretch of open water. The bridge was buttressed by four squat, towerlike supports, and Renquist's experienced eye told him that, as a fortress, it was well planned and highly defensible, both by land and lake. Even a modern army couldn't take the Castle Fenrior without resorting to air support and structural devastation.

Renquist's major surprise was not the castle, which, within its own idiosyncratic parameters was pretty much what he'd expected. His puzzlement was on the mainland at the other end of the causeway, where he could see the warm lights of what looked like a small village centered round a single main street and a small dock on the lakeshore. He glanced inquiringly at Gallowglass.

"What are those lights? They look like a human habitation."

"Aye, tha's exactly wha' they are."

"A village of humans?"

"Why th' no?"

"It's hardly usual."

"Is i'? There's many a nosferatu lord i' eastern Europe tha' has his boyars, his serfs, his gypsies livin' right by him an' no trouble. Did ye think Fenrior was some isolated pile on th' side o' a bare mountain like th' vampire castles i' th' movin' pictures?"

"No, but—"

"So?"

"But how can all this be maintained?"

Gallowglass tapped the side of his beaklike nose. "I' th' Highlands, th' old ties go deep. Clan loyalty makes no distinction between th' living an' th' undead, th' warm an' th' cold. The Lord Fenrior is clan chief o' both nosferatu an' human, demanding fealty fra' all."

"And the humans don't question this?"

Gallowglass treated the question as little short of retarded. "He's no just some feudal leader. He's regarded as th' very embodiment o' th' common ancestors way down th' years, an', i' these parts, tha' makes m' Lord Fenrior powerfully close to a god. Why d' ye think his name an' th' name of th' place are one an' th' same? All serve their laird i' their own way, an' if, for th' humans, i' means giving o' their blood or even o' their lives, so be i'. Th' life o' the individual ha' always been secondary t' th' survival o' th' clan. Such ha' always been expected i' time o' war. In Fenrior i' also applies i' peace, an' i'll never be questioned."

Seeing Renquist was still perplexed, Gallowglass smiled dourly. "Never forget this is a hard country, peopled by hard men an' hard women. Even as humans we were capable o' so much more i' th' Highlands. On th' run fra' th' damned redcoats, we drank th' blood o' living cattle. No French velvet homoerotic theatricals i' these mountains." He glanced back at the Highlanders packed into the back of the Hummer. "Is tha' no th' truth, lads?"

The Highlanders laughed.

Very shortly, Renquist was able to see this unique human community able to exist cheek by jowl with the largest clan of nosferatu Renquist had encountered in at least 150 years. To all outward appearances, it was a wholly normal Scottish village with a village store and post office, a fish-and-chips shop, a telephone box, and a public house with a sign declaring it to be called THE RED HAND. Only a certain lack of advertising signs and the general antiquity of most of the parked cars provided a subtle hint all might not be as normal as it seemed. In the small hours of the morning, only a black-and-white terrier was moving on the streets, and the dog seemed little concerned when the Hummers roared through. The streetlights burned, though, and a few lights showed from behind curtained windows. Then they were on the causeway, the village was behind them, and Renquist had no more chance to observe. The two trucks crossed the bridge and slowed as they approached the high arched main gates of the castle itself. As they entered, blue flashes flared in concentric circles around each Hummer in turn, like a protective energy screen created from the low-level radiation of the living rock.

The two vehicles came to a stop in a courtyard with high granite-block walls rising on all four sides. The Highlanders with whom Renquist had made the journey dismounted with the stiff limbs and slightly bemused air of those who have traveled long and hard. Others of their kind waited for them, plaids and swords, hard faces and unkempt hair in the darkness; some carried burning torches, casting a flame-red light and creating flickering shadows that provided a primitive contrast to the extreme functional modernity of the two black trucks. Laughter, questions, some hand shaking, backslapping, and Gaelic ribaldry greeted the returning raiders and was reciprocated in kind. Renquist also found himself the target of appraising undead eyes—eyes that looked him up and down, assessing his potential as an adversary. He didn't doubt his reputation had preceded him, or that the Highlanders were curious about the infamous foreigner and wondered whether he truly measured up to the tales told about him and his exploits. He had half expected Fenrior himself would be there to greet him and personally welcome him to his domain, but apparently the lord had more important things to occupy his time, or he was making it plain who wielded the power by allowing his prisoner/guest to wait on his pleasure.

The cocoon of Merlin was being unloaded from the second of the trucks. Renquist badly wanted to go over and take a look at it, to see if it had been damaged in transit or undergone any changes since he had last seen it inside the burial mound, but he found his way blocked, not only by Gallowglass, but a big darklost sword-thrall with massive shoulders and a humorless demeanor. Gallowglass gestured to the man. "This is Droon, Master Renquist. He'll be lookin' out for ye while y're here."

The decision had finally been made; Marieko should place the actual call. To instantly convince whoever might answer the telephone in Los Angeles of their bonafides, the caller was going to talk in the nosferatu Old Speech, and since Marieko was by far the most fluent, she had been elected to make the first approach. Both Destry and Columbine had the Old Speech burned into their genetics, but Marieko, as always, had studied and practiced, so her fluency and pronunciation were far superior. Some confusion had ensued over the correct time to call, but finally, after some arithmetical wrangling, Destry and Marieko had come up with a short window in time when the sun shone on neither England nor on the Pacific Coast of the USA.

While arguing the pros and cons of their course of action, and then finalizing the details, Marieko had felt calm and analytical, but when it came to the moment to pick up the drawing room telephone and start dialing the international code, an anxiety close to weakness came over her. She could only describe it as stage fright, although she had never engaged in drama as a means of entertainment. For a brief instant she found herself unable to continue with the call. The full import of what she was about to do had suddenly dropped on her like a tangible and physical weight. If her course of action were taken to its logical conclusion, it could mean open warfare between nosferatu. She realized she might actually be creating history. She had played her part in undead history before. She had no illusions about that. Never before, though, had she been cast in such a crucially instigative role. She put down the phone and stood very straight, concentrating hard to stop her trembling. Columbine and Destry were watching her like a pair of unblinking hawks. "What's wrong?"

"Nothing. I misdialed."

They both knew she was lying, but they said nothing. They easily read her weighty realization. She again picked up the receiver and dialed once more. The phone rang four times in the single tone of the North American telephone system. Finally a female voice answered, chilly and neutral. "Yes."

Marieko took a deep breath and began. *"Alai ku nushi ilani mushiti itti kunu."*

Whoever was on the other end of the line was masterly in the way she contained her surprise and responded in the Old Speech. *"Alsi au ushitum kallatum?"*

Marieko launched into a carefully worded explanation of the situation. *"Alai ku itti kunu-a* Marieko Matsunaga *eli qabitla. Upu alsi b-ia dinm dina* Columbine Dashwood *nubu-u* Destry Maitland. *Amru-sana amru-usanku alakti ku epishia* Victor Renquist. *Sha limnutikla kla limda sumj rabuti iqer kal ubbiraanni amastus-ha* Clan Fenrior *vah naepiv haa."*

"One moment please."

For maybe thirty seconds all Marieko could hear were voices muffled by what had to be a hand over the mouthpiece of the phone. Then the first voice returned. "Just to be absolutely certain, would you mind repeating what you just said in English?"

"I said that I am Marieko Matsunaga, and I am calling from Ravenkeep Priory, where Victor Renquist has just been taken captive by a raiding party of the Clan Fenrior. I assure you this is not a mistake, a ruse, or a hoax. Victor was our guest when the attack occurred."

Droon led Renquist along the echoing passageway, the burning torch held high so its flames reflected from the wet algae slime on the stone walls. In the Castle Fenrior, electricity was used extremely sparingly.

"So I'm a prisoner?"

"I wouldn'a ken."

The phrase "I wouldn'a ken" seemed to be Droon's answer to everything. When Gallowglass had announced in the courtyard that Droon would be "lookin' out" for Renquist, he hadn't been exactly sure what this was supposed to mean, but it very quickly became clear the hulking human was a combination of guard, guide, spy, escort, and servant. Marks on his neck were a clear indication blood was taken from him on a regular basis. That Renquist had been assigned a human as his escort made plain no attempt on his part to escape was anticipated. He could, of course, easily have overpowered Droon—physically or mentally, it made little difference. The man could have been his in an instant, but what would be the point? Supposing Renquist sneaked or fought his way out of the castle, what options did he have then? A trek across the wild Highlands leading nowhere but to a final sunrise? Maybe he could have stolen a vehicle, but that would have hardly put him in any stronger position. He had only the most vague and general idea of where he was, and most likely he could spend the time until daybreak trying vainly to connect with the local geography. Besides, the idea of over-powering Droon was really nothing more than a fantasy. Beyond a shadow of a doubt, the man's mind was being monitored, and as such, he was nothing more than a living surveillance camera. If Renquist so much as attempted to either attack or elude him, an instant alarm would certainly be triggered.

The air in the passage was chill, and this struck Renquist as both less than comfortable and decidedly insulting. If he was going to be incarcerated, he saw no reason why the incarceration should be in some dank dungeon with water dripping to pools on a stone floor. If nothing else, his status alone demanded he be lodged with more ease and dignity. On the other hand, two house thralls were bringing up the rear with his bags and the fur rug. He was being led to durance vile, but his creature comforts were coming with him. Odd. "It feels as though we're actually under the loch."

"I wouldn'a ken."

This was one time too many for Renquist. He stopped in his tracks ready to make a stand. "I think I need to speak to the Lord Fenrior about the accommodation. I'll not be quartered at the bottom of a damned lake."

Droon came as close as was possible to smiling. "Din'a fret, Master Renquist. Ye'll be snug, dry, an' warm. Ye ha' m' lord's word on tha'."

And indeed he did. Very shortly Droon made a right turn, and Renquist and the thralls followed him up two flights of stone steps. By the time they'd reached the top of the second flight, the feeling of damp and gloom was left beneath them. They moved down a corridor until Droon stopped outside a very old wooden door with heavy iron bolts and hinges. He opened it and then stepped back, allowing Renquist to enter. The room was much closer to Renquist's expectations. Stone walls did a prison make, but at least the room they enclosed was fairly spacious, even though it lacked any kind of window and therefore tended to resemble a cave. It was a

suitable abode for the imprisoned aristocrat who had
found himself on the losing side in a political intrigue
and now awaited either a compromised release or execution, and the cell had probably been used quite regularly
as such in times past. A smoky peat fire burned in a small
grate, and the furniture, which must have been at least
four hundred years old, was solidly and simply made.

While the thralls brought in his bag, Renquist looked
around at what he hoped was his strictly temporary new
home. The single attempt at decoration was a watercolor
of Highland cattle, maybe ancestors of the ones he'd
seen on the way there. He did notice, however, that a
large Jacobean jug, filled to the brim with clear water,
had been placed on the top of a stout dresser. Attention
had been paid to detail, and someone in Fenrior had a
detailed knowledge of his needs. Also a young woman,
with the seemingly inevitable red hair and white freckled
skin, lay on the room's narrow bed covered only in a
thin sheet, watching him with an anxious-to-please expression. He smiled at her and nodded. "And who might
you be?"

"I'm Annie Munro, Master Renquist."

"You know my name?"

Annie Munro laughed. "Bless ye, sir. There's been
talk o' nothing else a' night through th' halls an' kitch-
ens."

"And what's your part in all this?"

"I'm t' feed ye an' provide wha' other comfort I
may."

The house thralls had left the room, and Droon interrupted with a final word. "I'll be goin' th' noo', Master
Renquist."

"Thank you, Droon."

"Aye."

Droon made his exit, closing the door behind him. The
sound of bolts being shot home and a key being turned
in the lock were a clearly audible indication he might
have Annie Munro to keep him company and provide

him with sustenance, but he was very definitely a prisoner. Renquist sat down on the bed next to Annie Munro. It had to be well past dawn outside, and he felt tired and depleted. "So you're my welcoming gift, are you, Annie Munro?"

"Ye're no t' drain an' kill me. Tha's th' laird's only order."

Prey that answered back. Renquist was amused. "Is it, now?"

"I'm darklost, an' when th' time comes, I'll live forever."

"And until then?"

"I hope an' I serve."

"You hope?"

"No' all are Changed, Master Renquist. Many are called, but few are chosen. Thus we all try t' be o' service." She treated him to the best depraved smile she could muster. "But wi' one like ye th' service willna' be a chore."

The greatest irony was that everything she said she believed to be true. The darklost could be single-minded. Those humans who had been brought partway into the nosferatu world but had yet to pass through the Change and achieve true, undead immortality, lived for nothing but the moment when they, too, became more than mortal. Annie Munro sincerely believed eternal life could be achieved by merit for ceaseless effort to please those she so admired and envied. Her mind was as naked as her body. A child without ego. She happily lusted after Renquist with frank and dirty innocence—quite unlike any other darklost he had encountered. She seemed well aware of the possibility Renquist might become carried away with his feeding, forget Fenrior's directive, and drain and kill her, but she lived so entirely in the moment this scarcely seemed to bother her. He noted also how her living in the moment also protected her from the loitering yearning of most other darklost who had ever attached themselves to him. If anything, she reminded

Renquist of the San Francisco Manson girls of the late sixties, whom he and the late lamented Cynara had briefly encountered in Haight Ashbury in the so-called Summer of Love.

He didn't, however, fall into the very obvious trap of believing Annie Munro's presence in his cell was as innocent and functional as her personality. She was Fenrior's new watchdog now that Droon was gone, and as integral a part of his genteel incarceration as the stone walls or the bolted door. Annie was now the means of surveillance, although, insomuch as she would be keeping him amused, diverted, and nourished, she was infinitely preferable to an eye at a spyhole or any electronic device. Even in such diversions as they might engage, he would be providing his undead captor with at least minimally valuable information. His guard would be down, and unless he totally shunned Annie Munro, he'd be revealing himself with every move he had. A nosferatu can betray volumes about his personal depths if observed while feeding. In turn, though, Annie Munro's mind would be showing him a great deal, especially about the Castle Fenrior, its social structure, its population, and the power dynamics of their lord's control. Even his first glance into Annie Munro left him amazed and impressed by the brute sophistication and simple logic with which Fenrior's realm of coexisting humans and nosferatu was made to function.

When Gallowglass had told him Fenrior was close to being regarded as a god, Renquist had assumed the statement contained a degree of exaggeration, or at least metaphor. Annie's mind told him, in fact, it had been pretty much the unvarnished truth. Although she viewed the world with a certain servant cynicism, the girl believed that her lord was the very source of all life, both transitory and eternal. He also caused the rain to fall, the wind to blow, and the mist to roll in off the loch. The humans in both the castle and the village lived and died at his command, but by the same token, he could also, on a whim, bring them to immortality. The thinking may have been simplistic, but it made as much primitive sense as any human religion, and as an added bonus for the few who were blessed, the immortality was absolutely genuine.

Annie Munro may have been savvy and irreverent, but she, and seemingly all the other inhabitants of Fenrior, never questioned the basics. To their way of thinking, their god delivered. The laird gave and the laird took away on both the most basic and most elevated level. That was how it was, world without end. While the sun continued to come up in the morning, no sparks of revolution were ever kindled in the domain of the Lord Fenrior. Renquist had, of course, seen similar unquestioning devotion to a nosferatu lord, but not for at least two centuries, and never one so keyed into the complexity of the modern world—unless one counted Joseph Stalin, who was not strictly nosferatu, but a complete aberration unto himself. He also didn't doubt Fenrior's influence dug deep into the cutthroat politics of Scotland ancient and modern, and human puppets in both Edinburgh and Westminster danced to his orchestrated strings and enabled him to maintain so much in such secrecy.

Already, though, Renquist was reasonably convinced Fenrior had his weaknesses and insecurities, no matter how godlike he might appear. It was obvious Annie had been presented to him as a gift in his cell not only to monitor and feed him, but also to impress—and, indeed, Renquist was duly impressed. It was a fine point of hospitality. In addition, he was intrigued. That Fenrior would have a need to impress him told him a lot, but it also posed many questions. In addition, it provided some solid encouragement. A leader dazzled with his skill and cunning only those with whom he or she wanted to negotiate or maybe hoped to manipulate, definitely not with an individual slated for destuction. The kind of megalomaniac who needed to explain his master plan for world domination before cutting James Bond in half with a laser was strictly a product of the need for exposition in romantic fiction. In reality, enemies were reduced to carrion without benefit of any self-congratulatory denouement.

Renquist would have liked to delve deeper into the organizational structure of Fenrior's domain. He was already fascinated by roles played by darklost like Droon and Annie, and how the laird seemed to maintain them as a servant class, manipulating their desire for the Changing to use them as a buffer against the rank and file humans of the village. To really explore the nuts and bolts, however, he would have to put Annie Munro out completely before he could seriously hunt around in her memory and subconscious, and his innate sense of nosferatu manners told him this would be extremely bad form. The girl had not been given to him to immediately be rendered unconscious and mind-stripped. To do so would also be incredibly stupid, and it would be bound to trigger some kind of investigation. At worst, the result could be a change of venue for his confinement. Thoughts returned of dripping dungeons and the damp in the corridors below. He looked around at the relative creature comfort of the cell. He had best hang on to what he'd already got, relax as best he could with the warm and spluttering fire and the equally warm young woman, and count himself lucky until the next revelation.

"Y' must be famished after such a journey. They say you came all th' way from th' bottom o' England." Annie Munro was looking at him with a calculated flirtatiousness, and it was enough to divert his attention from her mind. Renquist might have become a pedantic and investigative adventurer over the centuries, but he was also predator flesh, and those needs must still be served. "You give of yourself freely?"

Annie Munro smiled. "It's my pleasure."

She knelt up on the bed and raised a bare arm. Renquist took her hand and saw previous bite marks. Poor ravaged Annie. Would she ever achieve the immortality she so craved? He looked her directly in the eyes. Although it was not a thing he would have done himself, he was quite convinced the Lord Fenrior would be watching him feed through those selfsame eyes. Was he expected to provide the lord with a telling dance of near-death? Renquist half smiled. So damn you, Fenrior. Observe this, you undead autocratic Peeping Tom.

Marieko slowly hung up the phone.

Destry and Columbine both moved on her. "Well?"

"They will call us back."

"What?"

"It turned out I was talking with Dahlia, the one who looks like a child. She used a great deal of profanity. She said she or one of the others would call us back."

Columbine seemed to blame Marieko for the lack of an immediate resolution to the problem. "Did she say when?"

"When they've discussed the situation among themselves and contacted other informed sources."

"Informed sources?"

"They're checking us out. Probably as we speak."

"Checking us out?"

Destry looked wearily at Columbine. Sleep seemed to be becoming a premium luxury. "Get real, will you? Their master comes to visit us, and then, after two or three days, we call up and tell them we've lost him. What would you do?"

Columbine looked away. "I'd check us out."

"Exactly."

"So we continue to wait?"

Neither Destry nor Marieko seemed to feel the question merited an answer.

The game Annie Munro was playing became immediately clear. That Renquist would take her blood was a given. The scenario, though, could play out in one of two ways. He could take it from unthinking necessity, with no more than a physical contact with the prey—or while he fed, he could, at the same time, conjure raging and contorting ecstasies for her as a hallucinatory diversion from the essentially clinical procedure. Aside from wanting to serve her lord and win supposed points toward her eventual immortality, Annie Munro also craved such ecstasies with the passion of a true addict, and Renquist saw no reason why she shouldn't have her enjoyment at the same time as he had his. At the very least, it seemed only fair. The fact also remained that Fenrior or some of his people might be watching. Why not let them see him as courteous and debonair, a gentleman vampire willing to permit the victim to have her fun? Better that than to be viewed as a greedy and selfish boor with consideration for nothing beyond his own wallowing gratification.

Although he was resigned to being observed, the idea still didn't sit particularly well with Renquist. Since the time humanity had developed the motion picture, and then the video camera, he had, on a number of occasions, found himself being secretly filmed or recorded. Fortunately Renquist had always been able to fog photographic film and distort the images on magnetic tape, thwarting any possible visual chronicle of his most exclusive gratifications. Of course, those who'd tried had absolutely no idea just how exclusive Renquist's gratifications really were. They were expecting sex, and believed themselves deprived of sex when the film returned from processing as nothing more than an abstract grey swirl pattern. Had the images survived, however, they would have found themselves with documentation far beyond petty pornography. Some, like the late but hardly lamented J. Edgar Hoover (not to deny the FBI director's capacity for masturbatory voyeurism) commissioned this kind of sexual keyhole work primarily to extend their power base of triumph-through-blackmail. Others did it for their own unabashed amusement.

Renquist recalled Eva and Juan Perón had been in the

forefront of those who had made both an art and a fetish out of such bedchamber spying. In the guest rooms of the presidential palace, the charismatic but megalomaniac couple had secretly filmed the intimately private moments of their more prominent guests with ex-Gestapo espionage hardware, the most highly advanced equipment for the time. Renquist had found himself briefly in Buenos Aires, in the chaos immediately following World War II, when the SS and their gold—and some extremely outlandish tastes in recreation—were sailing into town in their U-boats and unknowingly turning the city into a nosferatu paradise. When, through his connections, he'd merited an overnight invitation to the palace, they had attempted to film him with a dark-eyed nightclub singer. The expectation was that he'd kill her, as he in fact did, and the Peróns would have their very own snuff movie. Evita had provided the woman, believing that Renquist was just one more totalitarian ghoul who'd acquired the taste for death between the sheets, and she felt she probably needed to make him simultaneously happy and vulnerable. Renquist had exacted payback by stealing some of the Peróns' high-society pornography and letting it fall into the hands of determined Nazi hunters from the Stern Gang.

The reverie of reminiscing was quite deliberate. At the same time as fulfilling the cravings of Annie Munro, Renquist did nothing to hide the fantasies he was unreeling for her, or his opinions on optical surveillance as a quasi-sexual preference. Let Fenrior know Renquist had walked the planet among the high and the mighty for a very long time, and had not spent centuries holed up in his remote bloody castle, breeding his own humans and pretending William Wallace was still running amok. As the tiny Dahlia might have bluntly put it, he was going to make it clear Victor Renquist was not a being with whom to fuck.

Annie had balked slightly when he'd snapped open the steel spike. She'd never seen anything like it before, and Renquist had to explain how, in other parts of the world, it was fashionable for the undead to have their fangs surgically removed, information she received with total disbelief. "Ge' along wi' ye. Why should they do a foolish thing like tha'?"

"The way of the Castle Fenrior isn't the only way things are done."

"I wouldna' ken about tha'."

"No, you wouldn't."

Her hand trembled slightly—the first sign the girl wasn't totally blasé about the entire procedure. "Will i' hurt?"

As he slid the spike into her wrist, he also consigned her mind to the undulations of a plastic roller-coaster ride of abstract erotica. "Does that hurt?"

The girl let out a long and satisfied sigh. "Oh, no, Master Renquist, tha' din'a hurt one wee bit."

As he put his lips to her wrist, Renquist realized that this was far from the first time Annie had taken a ride of this kind. She cleaved to his projections with the practiced alacrity of a desperate spirit coming home to the only place she felt safe, wanted, and emotionally wonderful. He increased the intensity of the erotica that was steaming through her mind and directly caressed the pleasure centers. Annie groaned. "Oh, Master Renquist, wha' ye' doin' t' me? What ye doin' t' me."

"You know very well what I'm doing to you."

Annie Munro's naked and freckled limbs writhed and wriggled with an uninhibited and unashamed display of pure pleasure. She made kitten noises, and with her free hand, she clutched at Renquist's shirt, and he feared for a moment the girl's involuntarily clawed, grasping hand might rip the fabric.

"Ye can think wha' ye like o' me, but please keep doin' i', please keep doin' i'."

And for a while he did, but then her color changed ominously, and Renquist removed his mouth from her wrist, before he took so much blood from her he'd cause her to expire. She lay limply on her back and made a sound deep in her throat, of simultaneous satisfaction and disappointment. "Aaaaah. Ye stopped."

"Any more and you would have died."

"Aye, but I'd happily die if tha' was t' be th' end of i'. Some say th' moment o' death goes on forever."

Renquist saw no reason to be excessively kind to the darklost, poor confused thing that she might be. "And you may yet die exactly like that."

Weak as she was, her eyes and aura both turned knowing. "I'd no die at all if ye were t' Change me, right here tonight, Master Victor."

Cunning little vixen. And insolent, too. Calling him "Master Victor," indeed. She scarcely had enough blood left in her body to remain conscious, and she was resolutely hustling him. "I should put you through the Change? For what earthly reason should I want to do that?"

"Ye're all alone here, an' ye might need all th' friends ye can get."

For a split second Renquist was tempted. It would be an audacious gesture of defiance, but he already knew the inevitable outcome. "Your lord would destroy me on the spot if I tried such a damned fool move."

Annie Munro tried to sit up and look beseeching, but she couldn't manage to raise herself. "Would he ha' t' know?"

"Oh, he'd know. He'd know in an instant."

"Oh."

Damn but Fenrior bred his humans hardy.

"You don't really know what the Ceremony of Changing entails, do you?"

She weakly shook her head. "No, Master, tha's th' Great Secret."

"Then believe me when I tell you I couldn't do it here, now, and on my own even if I wanted to. It's very much more complicated than that."

Annie Munro smiled ruefully. "Aye, well. I could but ask. Y' canna' blame a girl f' tryin'."

Her voice trailed off, and then she was unconscious. Finally Renquist could sleep.

"Lupo is coming."

"That's all?"

"It could only have been Lupo himself. He said three words and hung up. 'Lupo is coming.'"

For two long hours Marieko, Destry, and Columbine had watched the phone. Marieko, seemingly the designated speaker, had answered, but hung up after just a matter of seconds. Destry and Columbine's first assumption was that their unspoken plea for help had been rejected out of hand, and Victor's colony had decided to leave its Master to his fate. Then Marieko, in a decidedly unbelieving tone, had repeated the three words said to her.

"Lupo is coming."

Destry was angry. "What the fuck is that supposed to mean? He's coming to England. He's coming here? He's coming to us?"

Surprisingly, Columbine had the answer. "I doubt we even signify in his plans."

"Are you saying he thinks he doesn't need us?"

"I'm saying exactly that. He doesn't need us. Lupo isn't thinking of us at all. He will go where Victor is being held captive, and he will rescue his don or perish trying. In Lupo's terms it's as simple as that."

"Could he do it?"

Columbine shrugged. She held an unlit cigarette between her fingers. She'd been intending to light it when the phone had rung. "It's possible. I've never had cause to meet Lupo, but I have met others from a similar background. The word *implacable* was coined for ones like them."

"Fenrior has a lot of swords at his back."

"I doubt Lupo intends any kind of frontal attack. He's

probably quite able to slip through an entire regiment of Fenrior's Highlanders completely undetected. He might go directly to the top and kill Fenrior. It's been said those old-time Renaissance killers could walk through walls, could make themselves functionally invisible."

"Joey Nightshade."

"Precisely. Once a nosferatu like Lupo had been set in motion, stopping him is all but impossible."

They all arrived at the same question at the same moment, but Marieko voiced it. "If Lupo doesn't intend to so much as meet up with us, what do we do?"

Before any attempt could be made to answer the question, Columbine twitched, and the phone rang again. Marieko looked at Columbine and Destry. They both nodded, and she picked it up. "Ravenkeep."

After a short pause, she nodded. "Yes, this is Marieko Matsunaga."

The next pause seemed to run to the eternal before she snapped her fingers and made a writing motion. Destry handed her a pad and pen. She quickly wrote down a sequence of figures. "Yes, I have it."

Another long silence ensued, and then Marieko nodded once more. "I absolutely understand. There is no problem. We will be at the rendezvous."

After the seemingly interminable and tantalizingly one-sided phone call, Destry and Columbine were all but beside themselves. Marieko let them suffer a little. "I was speaking to Julia Aschenbach."

"And?"

"She had a lot to say for herself. To cut a long conversation short, she wants us to meet her at a private airstrip in the Midlands. At two A.M. tomorrow."

"Tomorrow?"

"There will be a jet."

Destry frowned. "Her and Lupo?

Marieko shook her head. "Just her."

"Just her? They're not traveling together?"

Marieko tore the page with the numbers written on it

and carefully folded it in half. "My impression was that Julia and Lupo are acting totally independent of each other."

"That makes no sense."

Columbine pointed to the folded page from the pad. "What's that?"

"The map coordinates of the airstrip."

Destry leaned back in her chair. "Does anyone mind if I briefly recap?"

Columbine finally lit her cigarette. "Recap away, my dear."

"We have called California, and the sum total result is that Lupo and Julia will be coming here. Lupo declines to even so much as contact us, and Julia will be showing up in a private jet. Did she suggest any course of action when she got here?"

Marieko tucked the map coordinates into her pocket. "No."

"We are not exactly creating a grand alliance with which to confront Fenrior and his claymore-wielding cohorts."

Columbine smiled resignedly. Her voice was brightly cynical. "Well, my dears, I think we can agree this has all the absurdity of any nosferatu effort at coordinated action. Once again, we are reminded why we are the top of the food chain but we don't rule the world."

The door swung back, and the cell was filled with the sound of boots on stone. Renquist was plunged into a world of cold and noise, initially not knowing where he was. It seemed, in his befuddled condition, that he had hardly made it to the dreamstate, and he couldn't have slept for more than a few minutes. Realization was slow to return of how he was prisoner in an anonymous cell in the Castle Fenrior, and Gallowglass was bending over the bed shaking him. "Wake up, Master Renquist. Time t' g' up an' go."

"Damn. I feel like shit."

"You'll get over i'."

Annie Munro had wrapped herself in a sheet and was making a rapid exit, doing her best to remain beneath the radar of the nosferatu. Two sturdy Highlanders flanked the door to the cell: Prestwick, the small one who carried the axe and the big brute with the broadsword and scalplock. They took no notice of Annie, however, as she slipped between them. Their eyes were riveted on Renquist, who, right at that moment, didn't feel like having even friendly eyes riveted on him. He sat up with a groan and gestured to Gallowglass. "Would you be good enough to pass me the water."

Gallowglass reached for the Jacobean glass jug and handed it to Renquist, who took a long drink. As he rehydrated, he began to feel sufficiently improved to at least put a bold face on this unwanted arousal. "So, for what occasion do you come to drag me from my bed, good Gallowglass? Is it to be my beheading, or just some preliminary torture?"

Gallowglass laughed. "Why neither one nor th' other, Master Renquist. The Clan is gathering i' th' Great Hall, an' m' lord would ha' you attend on him."

Chapter Six

The Master of Ceremonies roared like a stentor over the hubbub of voices.

"Master Victor Renquist of California!"

A hush fell over the Great Hall of the Castle Fenrior. It was the largest gathering of the undead he'd seen under one roof in almost a century. His prediction that the Fenrior community would number sixty or more had turned out to be highly accurate, and, at the announcement of the honored guest and celebrity prisoner, every one of them looked up at him. The smoky kaleidoscope of auras turned to a uniform orange-gold curiosity. So this was Victor Renquist, about whom many had heard, but a nosferatu few had ever seen. He had entered the Great Hall by an upper gallery, and now he stood at the top of a flight of stone steps that led down into the body of the hall with its high, smoke-blackened, gothic-arched ceiling. These were stairs by which one made a formal entrance—stairs to be walked down at the dead center, head held aloof, back stiffened with exterior pride, doing one's best to look casual but invincible, while the whole Clan Fenrior watched and evaluated. Renquist was determined, at least in his public behavior, that he would not be found wanting.

He was pleased he'd had the foresight to pack a tuxedo for the trip to Ravenkeep. In fact, it wasn't a tuxedo, it was evening dress. He'd been living in the United States for far too long. The long frock jacket came to just above his knee, and it boasted black on black embroidery on the facings and a row of close, almost ecclesiastical Victorian buttons. A last-minute instinct had told him not to underestimate his surroundings. The Great Hall of Fenrior might not be the brawling midden described in thirdhand tales. Among nosferatu it was folly to expect anything to be predictable. The unexpected was the rule. In addition, by all the precepts and protocols, colony to colony, he came to Fenrior with something close to ambassadorial status, and he wasn't about to relinquish rank simply because he'd been brought here by force. He would dress with the maximum style the contents of his traveling bags would allow.

With no model to work from, Renquist had pictured Fenrior as some nosferatu approximation of the court of Catherine the Great, where unwashed cossacks held orgies in a palace of gilt and marble, but as he stood leaning lightly on his silver-topped cane, waiting for the prearranged signal to descend the stairs, he knew in the first instant he had underestimated quite drastically. Despite all his efforts, he had seriously misjudged the degree of decadence possible in a place that had been so isolated and such a law unto itself for so many centuries. Forget about Catherine, her cossacks, and their horses— Fenrior was even stranger that Renquist had anticipated. The Great Hall was a seemingly impossible mixture of the barbaric and the sophisticatedly bizarre.

At least the basic layout was as medieval as could be expected. The high table, on the raised platform, at the

end of the vaulted space was straight out of any baronial
hall, as were the other two longer lower tables, at right
angles to it, seating the rank and file. The blazing logs
in the massive carved fireplace also made no connection
with modern times. The lounging, sprawling Highlanders with their beards, dirty plaid, fearsome tattoos,
unkempt hair, and the weapons that they wore even to
the feast also contributed in no small part to the atmosphere of wild ages long gone. Much the same could be
said for the scantily clad but heavily bejeweled young
humans, most darklost, kin of Annie Munro, who had
been provided for the Highlanders' amusement. Although, in their wisps of silk, gold collars, headpieces,
and the bangles at their wrists and ankles, they resembled more the denizens of some Turk's seraglio than
anything from the Middle Ages.

At this point, though, the strict resemblance to the
fourteenth and fifteenth century ended, taking a turn in
the direction of pure nosferatu caprice. The furniture in
the hall of any medieval baron or earl would, even allowing for an element of decoration, have been solid,
foursquare carpentry. In the Great Hall of Fenrior, the
creators of the furniture seemed to have studied under
no less than Dalí, Henry Moore, or both. The long tables
and the chairs and benches had been carved from living
wood into sweeping curves following the form of the
grain. Polished and finished, and then distressed by long
years of hard use and abuse, the forms were as wild and
organic in their invention as the Highlanders who sat at
them. Instead of straight lines, they undulated like the
distortions of a hallucination, with strange insets, lique-
fying faces and torsos, inlays, patterns of jewels and mo-
saics, gold and silver inlaid coins, and the irregular heads
of huge, individually designed iron nails. Made for de-
cadent function, though, the angry, storm-tossed kinetics
of the designs were softened by expanses of velvet cushions, pillows, leather upholstery, tapestry, and exotic
rugs. The central seat at the high table was little short

of a throne, and obviously where Fenrior himself must
sit. The two lesser seats flanking him were actual
sculpted forms, more distorted human figures, but in this
case huge, with angular arms and blind staring eyes,
racked and misshapen into contortions to conform to and
enhance the seated figure of the lord.

The walls were equally surreal in their decorations.
Vast expanses of stone, in some cases stretching from
floor to ceiling, had been carved into complex and apocalyptic bas-reliefs depicting some end-time horror of
monsters, seemingly from some nightmare location beyond space and time, carrying out the flesh-rending destruction of a hapless humanity. Renquist had to believe
the carnage was the vision of the stone carver. If the
scenes were based in any earthly mythology, it was one
quite unknown to him, although he suspected some of
the figures might be representation of the Old Ones, the
dire and fearsome contemporaries of Cthulhu. Where the
walls had escaped the carvers' grim art, they were hung
with a profusion of paintings. An art collection worthy
of the most exacting human multimillionaire looked
down on the assembled clan and its bacchanal. Some
were what might be found in any Scottish stately
home. Armed aristocrats in kilt and plaid posed against
impressive mountain backgrounds with dogs at their feet,
or lurking behind them, or in the more exotic examples,
a falcon perched on a gauntlet. In addition, though, violent abstracts by an artist Renquist didn't recognize
shared vertical space with at least one Francis Bacon, a
William Blake lithograph, two of Turner's more spectacular sea battles, some of Goya's more unpleasant horrors of war, a scattering of German decadents, and one
of the best-known death-row paintings of a notorious
serial killer. Sculpture also played a part. A special al-
cove had been constructed to house the almost perfect,
twice-lifesize stone idol of an Assyrian bull god, while
other niches contained smaller pieces, both ancient and
modern. Fenrior's taste, taken as whole, seemed to favor

art created near the brink of the abyss. At the foot of the stairs, the rearing form of Madigan's notorious *The Balrog* (which humanity believed stolen from a New York gallery in the 1950s and lost to the world) seemed to guard the approaches. The mind that had conceived the Great Hall was unusual, even by Renquist's standards, which accepted many outer extremes as still near to the norm.

No matter how outlandish the decor, it was no match for the sinister diversity of the assembled crowd. Although the rough nosferatu Highlanders made up the majority, they were by no means the only guests at this feast of the undead. A representative selection of archetypes ensured it was no simple gathering of kilts and fangs. Some present could never have ventured out of the castle, while others obviously traveled regularly to London and Edinburgh and, for all Renquist knew, Paris, New York, and Singapore, where, after dark, they made profitable sport with merchant bankers and the political elite. Renquist spotted an exquisite in a powdered wig apparently left over from the court of Versailles, unable to move on in either fashion or manners. Nearby, a hairless and massively obese grotesque in a blue-and-gold kaftan stroked the naked legs of a darklost plaything and drooled unappetizingly in anticipation of some gross gratification on which Renquist didn't care to dwell.

A dour group of five in ceremonial black robes and cowls stood apart from the festivities. Renquist suspected they might be a pentacle coven of the Craftworkers, who many claimed were now nothing more than a part of history. He recognized a young male in white tie and tails with hair like Fred Astaire: Henri Brazil, a Euro-trash nosferatu whom Renquist recalled as being an incredible and vapid nuisance in la dolce vita of the 1950s. A flamboyant and voluptuous undead female with purple hair and proud curves contained in a form-fitting leather sheath barked orders at a younger companion harnessed as a pony and wearing platform

heels of an absurdist altitude. The orders were reinforced
with cuts from a flexible switch, and Highlanders
watched the interaction with leering appreciation. They
similarly stared at another female, who was fully naked
apart from shoes and a full head owl mask, but paid no
attention to a thing enclosed in a rubber garment akin to
a diving suit, its face covered with circular goggles and
a snoutlike air filter, as though the very atmosphere acted
on it as a toxin, sitting by itself and looking from side
to side with slow rhythmic turns of its head.

Liveried thralls moved among the crowd, fetching and
carrying, and even removing the human playthings rendered unconscious or dead by the depredations of the
guests. Renquist might have been surprised at the thralls
serving many of the guests, particularly the Highlanders,
with whisky by the bottle, had Gallowglass not warned
him in advance how it was a practice of the Clan to
become intoxicated by a microfungi introduced into the
raw spirit by a process of filtering through peat. Gallowglass had also, somewhat primly, warned that, before
Renquist "went tryin' i'," he should remember it was a
long-acquired taste. He could observe how groups of
armed Highlanders were already showing a noticeable
boisterousness. The group around Duncanon was acting
particularly frisky, and all but butting heads in cock-of-
the-walk male competition, and Renquist couldn't see
how the night could fail to end with swordplay and
drunken fury, unless Fenrior was a genius at keeping his
wild ones in check.

A quintet of musicians was grouped in a corner close
to the high table. The ensemble consisted of two
nosferatu (one on keyboards and the other on tenor
saxophone), a darklost on percussion, and a human
bass player, who was there with a guarantee of non-
molestation from Fenrior simply because he enjoyed the
music. They played a syncopated form Renquist could
only assume was of their own creating. To his ear it
sounded like overcast bebop with decidedly sinister Af-

rican polyrhythms, but also traces of a keening hunger from the mountains of eastern Europe. At one and the same time, it was both savage and mournful, and couched, as Renquist walked, in a very loose instrumental reading of Bob Dylan's "The Gates of Eden." The musicians stopped, however, when a female at the high table rose to her feet from the semi-throne on the Lord Fenrior's right hand and made a discreet signal. The lady was willow-slender, clad in white, gold, and silver, ethereal in a diaphanous dress and a coronet of large, faceted diamonds. Renquist could tell, even at a distance, that if the court had its high alpha-female, she was it. As the quintet fell silent, six other females detached themselves from the crowd and started to make their way to the foot of the stairs where Renquist waited.

Gallowglass had told Renquist to stay where he was until the leading ladies of Fenrior, known through the Castle as Fenrior's Seven Stars, made their formal approach and bade him enter the festivities—and now that formality seemed to be under way. The voluptuous one with the leather and the purple hair, who wielded the switch on her companion, was one. Whether the pony girl who followed behind her with an extraordinary high-stepping gait was a second or just an accessory remained to be seen. The lady from the high table was also making her way toward the stairs, drifting rather than walking, as though her feet hardly needed to touch the ground. She was joined by a Victorian study in scarlet and a rail-thin, long-legged, sixties vision in a Mylar mini-dress. Two more females fell in behind her, completing the seven. One was a distaff version of the untamed Highlanders, a sword-maiden through-and-through, with the same plaid and the same red hair. Renquist was starting to wonder if the proliferation of red hair was a sign of too much past inbreeding that maybe still continued among the humans of the village. The seventh of the Seven Stars was one of the figures in black robes, an apparent Craft-worker. This surprised Renquist. In other parts of the world, the undead discussed whether the Craft was practiced at all. Here a supposed adept occupied a position of power, and Renquist was starting to suspect the Castle Fenrior might prove the grave of many popular illusions. The robed female seemed to complete the set, and since no other joined the group moving toward him, Renquist could only assume the pony girl was actually one of the exalted seven despite her costume of submission.

The Seven Stars reached the foot of the stairs and waited for the lady from the high table to join them. When she reached them, she didn't hesitate. At the first step, she seemed to simply rise. The leather and the purple hair followed with pony girl close behind, separated only by the length of her reins. Purple hair undulated, sensual and self-aware. The pony girl teetered. Behind her, the Victorian in scarlet imposed a sense of melodrama, the go-go dream all but danced, the sword maiden strode resolutely with her claymore in a shoulder sheath, and the cloaked figure brought up the rear with anonymous determination. They came toward him in single file, close to the left-hand balustrade. Renquist thought they would come all the way to where he was standing, but instead, the lady from the high table stopped at exactly the halfway point. The others halted behind her, each standing two steps below the female in front, against the balustrade almost like a ceremonial receiving line.

"Welcome, Master Victor Renquist of California. Welcome to Fenrior and all it has to offer. Come down and meet the Seven Stars."

A slight salute with his cane, and Renquist started down, halting one step above where the lady from the high table was standing. He bowed low, taking a proffered hand in a white kid glove and kissing it. "Madame, I fear you have the better of me."

The lady smiled. He noticed she wore a ring over the glove, with a diamond worth a not particularly modest fortune. "No need to fear, Master Renquist. I am the Lady Gethsemany."

The only word for her was radiant. Her face was both timeless and ageless, knowing and wise, but strangely neutral in that it was neither cruel nor compassionate, simply and wholly confident in her unquestioned authority and power of total command. She seemed like something unique among nosferatu: one who was always courteous because she never needed to be otherwise. Renquist imagined she could send men and women to their deaths without so much as raising her voice. Up close the dress she wore was revealed to be of the finest silk, translucent in that it hinted at but didn't quite reveal the slender white body beneath. It was enhanced by a wide silver collar engraved with both runes and flame script from which hung shining pendant diamonds almost as large as the one on her hand. On her head was a silver crown set with more diamondlike spikes of ice crystal.

The crown and the way all appeared to bend to her will suggested that Gethsemany could only be Fenrior's first consort, but Renquist had no idea how the Lord Fenrior conducted his relationships. Were the Seven Stars his brides, his consorts, his hunting partners, his concubines, or was their multiple association more distinctively original in its patterns and complexities? Renquist had no easy way of finding out, but he imagined, if he kept his senses alert, he would discover at least some of the answers in the fullness of the night. From Gethsemany he moved on to the female with the purple hair, and like Gethsemany, she, too, extended her hand to be kissed. As Victor leaned forward, he couldn't help but note the intricate fastening on her leather dress and the way it accentuated her ample cleavage. "Welcome, Victor. I'm Theda."

"I'm charmed."

Where Gethsemany was ethereal, Theda was fully of the flesh, sensual and, Renquist suspected, greedy and infantile when the mood took her. But he didn't doubt that she could also be a ready and probably extreme source of risky amusement should the occasion arise. Theda indicated the pony girl who was next in the line. "This is Cyrce. She can't speak for herself, she has a bit between her teeth."

"I'm enchanted to meet you, Cyrce."

Cyrce snorted and nodded her head, carrying the equine pantomime to its logical conclusion, but Renquist saw a calculation in her eyes. She was no oppressed victim, and her current costume and restraint—and even the stinging cuts she received from Theda's switch—had to be part of a long and continuing game in which she was a more than willing and totally equal participant. He would not even attempt to divine what went on between Theda and Cyrce. Back at the colony, he had Dahlia and Imogene, whose behavior frequently challenged even the most distorted concepts of reality. He had never truly worked them out, and he wasn't about to delve for instant explanations of another pair of equally bizarre females.

"*Fratri in sanguinem,* Master Renquist, I am Lithbet."

Lithbet, in the scarlet ball gown, had no fangs, but instead wore what could only be described as an extended thimble on the little finger of her right hand. Wrought from what looked to be steel set in a spiral basketwork of gold, it ended in a small but undoubtedly efficient blade, which he could only suppose she used on her prey. As Renquist kissed her hand, she folded the device back against her palm to avoid stabbing him in the cheek.

"I met Cynara once, a very long time ago. I can only offer my condolences."

"Thank you. I still greatly miss her."

Lithbet's voice was soft and with the trace of an accent, perhaps from Georgia or Tennessee. He wasn't sure, and he wondered how she had managed to make her way to the north of Scotland. He would have thought the climate too cold and the manners too rough to suit a Dixie peach. Cynara had been in the South during the War Between the States, and since Lithbet's costume came from approximately the same period, he wondered if they might have encountered each other in Confederate Richmond or Atlanta. He didn't have time to ask, though. He was now being moved down the line quite quickly, and Gethsemany, Theda, and Cyrce were descending the stairs behind him creating the ingredients of a small procession.

"I'm Starr."

Starr could easily have been a dancer on the television show *Shindig*. A young Goldie Hawn with makeup so heavily and uniformly applied it masked all behind a blank cartoon of sexuality. White lips, white stockings, a short, bleached, Vidal Sassoon haircut—even her eyes were hidden behind small circular opalescent psychedelic glasses. Starr was giving absolutely nothing away.

"I'm pleased to make your acquaintance."

The blank mask hardly smiled. "Groovy."

Groovy? How long was it since he'd heard that word used with any seriousness?

The warrior-maid was tough as nails, and, although protocol decreed she greet Renquist cordially, her look told him she regarded his presence at the castle as little more than an unwanted intrusion. She plainly didn't require her hand kissed. "Goneril."

"Right."

That just left the figure in the cowl. Even standing right in front of her, the hood was pulled so far forward, her face was still invisible to Renquist. The only clue to the mood or nature of the supposed Craft-worker was the voice, and it was cold, neutral, and not even speaking English. *"Ei kur azkak, fratri in sanguinem."*

Presented with both the Old Speech and Latin, Renquist could only bow low and respond in kind. *"Ei kur azkak kia ante malada, sorori in sanguinem."*

With a whole new menu of puzzling questions nagging at his mind, Renquist allowed himself to be ushered on down the stone steps. Gethsemany walked beside him, and the rest of the Seven Stars closed behind them like an honor guard. Every eye in the Great Hall was on him, but he found it hard to read the humor of the assembled nosferatu. He had hardly anticipated being greeted with riotous applause, and he'd expected the prevailing atmosphere to be one of curiosity tinged with suspicion. Such would have been the way of it even in a small enclave of the undead. At this unprecedentedly large gathering, everything had to be on a greatly enhanced level. Yet Renquist sensed something else. The interest the crowd in the hall showed in him was somehow related to something larger. He knew his having been lifted by Gallowglass was connected with the waking of Taliesin, but was the whole gathering a part of the Merlin's return? If that was the case, then Fenrior had known the secret of the burial mount at Morton Downs for much longer than Columbine and her friends, and Renquist should regret having allowed himself to brought into this situation by anyone as shallow, vain, and uninformed as Columbine Dashwood. On the other hand, if Columbine hadn't contacted him, he would never have known about any of this, and no matter what the ultimate outcome, he would not have wished to miss the awakening of Merlin and the spectacle of an Urshu walking the Earth—under any circumstances.

In addition to the speculation and curiosity his arrival seemed to have triggered, Renquist could also sense a strong element of hostility. Most of this seemed to come from Fenrior's Highland bully boys. It was really only to be expected. Violent and tightly knit communities were instinctively wary of outsiders, and wariness could all too readily turn into furious, claymore-swinging hatred given the required but easy provocation. When a sudden eruption of laughter came from a section of one of the lower tables occupied by Duncanon and his cronies, Renquist knew it had been triggered by some de-

rogatory remark about him. Before he had time to react,
though, further mirth was quelled with a look from Gethsemany, which, if nothing else, indicated the extent of
her authority. Gallowglass had been unable to command
such instant obedience from Duncanon with nothing
more than a look.

The Lady Gethsemany took Renquist by the arm.
"You're being seated at the high table."

"I'm honored, my lady."

Gethsemany looked amused. It was the first time Renquist had seen her express a real and spontaneous emotion, and for a brief moment, she ceased to be ethereal
and looked almost down-to-earth. "Don't be too honored. You are quite near the end of the high table, I'm
afraid. Next to Shaggy Lachlan, who occupies his place
primarily because he's the oldest of the swordbearers in
the clan. There was some dispute about you being at the
high table at all, you being—to put it delicately—hardly
here of your own accord."

"I'm sure Shaggy Lachlan will be entertaining company."

Gethsemany laughed. "No, he won't. First he'll get
your measure by trying to scare you, and then he'll fall
asleep." She hesitated and then delivered a warning.
"Don't overdo the courtly diplomacy, Victor. This place
has its rough and dangerous side."

"Don't worry, ma'am. I've already seen some of that."

Gethsemany nodded. "Yes, I suppose you have. Did
anyone warn you about the whisky?"

"Gallowglass."

"Yes, he would. He has his puritan streak."

Gethsemany returned to her place on the left of Fenrior's empty seat, and Renquist took his debated seat
next to venerable Shaggy, who had fought at Flodden.
He had expected all of the Seven Stars to have places
at the high table, but this didn't seem to be the case.
Goneril returned to her whisky-swilling Highlanders.
Theda and Cyrce went back to mingling with the more

socially flamboyant. Starr did take a place at the opposite end of the high table from Renquist and Lachlan, and then immediately proceeded to look bored. The one move that took him completely by surprise was that of the hooded Craft-worker who had not given her name. After his formal entrance, she had moved to where the four of her coven were still keeping their own company, but only stayed with them for what seemed to be a fast and whispered discussion. When that was concluded, she hurried to the high table, and, to Renquist's amazement, seated herself to the right of Fenrior's throne. The indication was that she had equal power to that of the Lady Gethsemany, and Fenrior had what in human terms would constitute a witch occupying a crucial place in his inner circle.

Before Renquist could consider what this latest development might mean and how it might affect him, Shaggy Lachlan grunted. "So ye be Renquist, aye?"

"I'm Renquist."

Shaggy Lachlan's face was completely covered with tattoos, abstract Celtic swirls and spirals. About the only skin that didn't carry the blue and magenta ink was the long grey scar that ran from his hairline, past his left eye, down his cheek, then continued down his throat, and was finally hidden by the greasy leather tunic under his plaid. Renquist could only imagine Lachlan must have been close to cleaved in half when Fenrior had saved him. The combination of the scar and that he looked at least sixty years old led Renquist to suppose no time had been available for cosmetic adjustment when bringing the dying and bleeding man through the Change.

"Strangers don't find too warm a welcome round these parts."

Renquist responded without expression. "Everyone has been very courteous so far."

"Tha's because ye bin moonin' wi' th' woman."

Apparently no one had told Shaggy how Renquist had

come to be there. "Ye're fra' th' south, I ken?"

"I'm from the United States. California to be precise, but before that—"

Shaggy didn't seem overly interested in before that. "Th' Americas, hey? Well, tha'll no save ye."

"Save me from what?"

"Like as no one o' th' lads'll call ye oot a'fore th' death o' th' night."

Before either could say more, a young serving thrall in garlands crushed by the embraces of Highlanders high on microfungi placed bottles of whisky in front of both Shaggy and Renquist. As the newcomer, Renquist also received a pewter mug. Shaggy pulled the cork from the bottle with his teeth. " 'Tis a dark bottle so i' din'a look ugly when i's half empty."

He splashed the scotch into his own pot until it was at least half full, guzzled a quantity, and then nodded to Renquist. "Ye better get some o' yon down you, lad. It'll stiffen ye when they come t' take ye head."

Renquist realized he was being subjected to peer pressure, but when the peer pressure comes from a five-hundred-year-old, bad-tempered, broadsword-killer Scotsman, it can be very persuasive. He knew, when both Gallowglass and Gethsemany had warned him about the whisky, sooner or later, he would sample it, if for no other reason than, with nearly a millennium behind him, new and novel experiences were not so common or easy to come by. "Microfungi?"

"Tha's wha' they say."

The intoxication took a minute or so to reach his brain, but when it did, it hit hard. "Damn me!"

"This is y' first time?"

Renquist gasped out the single word. "Yes."

"An' ye're feelin' i'?"

"Oh, yes, I'm feeling it, all right."

"And how do you find our Uisge Beatha?"

"It's certainly novel."

"I suppose tha's one way o' puttin' i' f' a southern jasmine limp-wrist."

The customs and practices of the court of Fenrior probably required Renquist to take exception to being called a "southern jasmine limp-wrist," but right at that moment he was swimming in a sea of tranquillity, and it had been many ages since he had found himself so immersed. At various times and in various places—and almost nonstop through the latter half of the twentieth century—Renquist had absorbed a comprehensive pharmacopoeia from the blood of his victims, but no intoxicant had even come close to the microfungi in the whisky. How was it no other nosferatu knew about this? The undead metabolism made the nosferatu immune to so many of the chemical diversions enjoyed by humans and other lower animals. It seemed hardly right Clan Fenrior kept such a thing to themselves. Renquist was totally unused to stimulation, except the jolting energy rage of the blood feast. Initially he found himself filled with a golden glow of affection. All things were bright and beautiful—even Shaggy Lachlan, whom Renquist only just managed not to embrace. Lachlan must have read it all in Renquist's aura because he winked knowingly. "I'll bet ye're loving everyone reet noo. Din'a worry lad, i' willna' last. Next y'll be wantin' t' laugh, an' then y'll be feelin' no fear an' want t' fight everyone i' th' room single-handed."

The experience was so intense that Renquist knew he was at very great risk of losing control, and this was neither the time nor the place to let that happen. And yet he couldn't seem to be overly concerned. It was all so futile. All his care and conspiracy and plotting for eternal survival: loaded on the microfungi, he could only find it all laughable. He noticed an influx of new guests in the hall that he suspected only he could see. He also noticed Lachlan staring at him and blurted, "It's all so ironic."

"Ye probably feel like laughin' helplessly right now."

Renquist could scarcely suppress a guffaw. "I do."

"Well din'a, because ye're at th' high table, an' y'll look like a bloody fool."

For an instant, Renquist's mood tilted, and he wanted to punch Lachlan hard in the face, but then his feelings shifted once more, and all seemed hilarious again. "It's hard to resist. I mean, we're all bloody fools."

"Some bigger an' some smaller, an' some who ken when i's time t' shut th' fuck up because th' laird's a-comin'."

Renquist looked up at the stairs but saw nothing. Were his senses so impaired? It seemed Shaggy wasn't the only one who sensed the coming of Fenrior. The quintet fell silent. The standing crowd between the lower tables began either to take their seats or melt back toward the walls. It was only then that Renquist heard the mournful skirl of a single piper. Lachlan whispered in his ear. "That's Angus Crimmon, the laird's own piper."

Renquist was swaying slightly. "Is that so?"

"Aye. He's playin' 'The Black Swan.' After a while ye get t' ken th' laird's mood accordin' t' th' tune he orders."

"And what does 'The Black Swan' mean?"

But before Lachlan could answer, the laird had appeared. Preceded by an angry undead dwarf who restrained two huge wolfhounds that tugged at their leashes, and with Gallowglass, Crimmon the Piper, and a huge bodyguard Highlander, the Lord Fenrior stood at the top of the stairs, exactly where Renquist had paused a short while earlier.

Columbine stared through the Range Rover's brand-new windshield, only replaced earlier that day. By a near miracle, Bolingbroke had managed to organize the repair while the troika slept. Almost immediately she started to protest. "You must have misread the bloody map. It's nothing but an empty field with mist and an old barn."

"It's only an old barn until one sees the antennas."

Columbine sighed. "Antennas on barns. I'm not ready for this modern world. I've always hated science fiction."

"You'd better get ready for it, because science fiction is coming right at you, and at a considerable rate of knots."

Columbine's problem was that she simply hadn't kept up. The last time she had learned anything new was during the wartime occupation of Ravenkeep by de Richleau and his madmen. As that generation of humans finally died out, Columbine had increasingly ceased to identify with the new times. The Goddess Cult had been easy. They'd made that up as they went along, but after it was abandoned, she'd contented herself with her perfumes, her foibles, her undead neuroses, and her boys. Marieko and Destry always seemed to know, and usually made the right decisions, so she'd amused herself and let them take care of the day-to-day business. Day to day, however, had turned into year to year, and decade to decade, and really, without noticing, she had lost track of the passage of time. Fad, fashion, and technology came and went without Columbine being anything more than peripherally aware of them. Every season brought new haircuts, gadgets, and pop music, but all proved infinitely replaceable. But then the dreams had started, and the rest of the mess had coagulated around her, and she was completely unprepared. Now she found herself in a field waiting for a mysterious aircraft bringing a woman who, for Columbine, was about as welcome as anthrax.

"Wait," Marieko warned.

"What?"

"Men are coming."

Two human figures had detached themselves from the dark mass of the barn—large men in combat coats, blue jeans, and knit caps. They carried compact machine pistols down by their sides. Destry would have recognized them as Czech AKs, but Columbine was far from au courant with such things. The pair moved toward the Range Rover with a casual caution that spoke of expert military training. They could well have previously served in some elite unit like the Special Air Service.

One stood back while the other walked to the driver's side. Destry rolled down the window. "We're here to meet the plane."

"Do you have identification?"

Destry looked at them as though, armed as they might be, they were total idiots. "Of course we don't. You think we're crazy?"

This seemed to be exactly the right answer. The man nodded and signaled to his partner to relax. "Just wait where you are. It'd be best if you didn't get out of the vehicle until the plane's down and secured, okay?"

Destry nodded. "No problem. Is the plane going to be on time?"

The possible ex-SAS man shook his head. "They don't tell us. You'll know when the field lights come on."

In fact, it took twenty minutes for the field lights to come on. And in that time, three more cars drew up to wait for the plane. Each was stopped and was inspected as the Range Rover had been, and each hinted at a story. An antique James Bond Aston Martin DB3, an embassy-loaded Mercedes town car (obviously bulletproof and with a great many options), and a lavender Rolls-Royce Silver Cloud made exotic companions for the Ravenkeep Range Rover. Even these diversions, though, did little to cushion Columbine's impatience. "What is this? A scheduled service?"

Destry seemed fascinated and possibly quite excited. "It's a Black Plane."

"A what?"

"I'd heard about them but I'd never seen one. It's a private and highly secret network for people who want to move around under the radar and have the price of a very costly ticket. They commute regularly between

New York, London, Moscow, all over. Governments use them when they need a whole shitload of deniability." She paused and listened. "I think I hear something."

Marieko nodded. "It's a small jet."

What seemed like a flat meadow suddenly blossomed with parallel rows of landing lights that extended far enough into the distance to provide the needed runway length for a small private jet to land and taxi to a halt. Columbine looked at Destry and Marieko in amazement. "Well, I'll be damned. It's like a bloody spy movie or a meeting with the aliens."

Marieko nodded. "Or a very big cocaine deal."

Destry was now really excited. She seemed to thrive on this human shadow-world stuff. "Possibly all three. That's what the Black Plane's all about."

Columbine pretended to be unimpressed by the sudden appearance of an airfield out of nowhere. "Who does this woman think she is?"

Destry shrugged. "She's Julia Aschenbach. Who's to judge? She used to be a player. Old habits die hard." Destry faltered. "Holy shit, that's some plane."

It had been difficult to see beyond the lights, and the plane only became visible at the very last moment. The Black Plane was a drama unto itself, without even taking into account the location and supporting cast, and now not even Columbine could remain blasé. It had probably started its life as a small twin-engined executive jet but had then been so extensively customized, all the way to extra, stealth-style airfoils and fuselage panels, and strange lancelike probes extending from its nose, until it had become the matte black Chevy Stingray of the skies. Destry nodded in admiration. "It sure beats an Air America DC-3."

"It's the Batplane." Marieko was positively delighted, in a way Columbine found close to unseemly. She was Japanese and harbored what Columbine considered an unhealthy liking for all that was new, modern, and outrageous. "Elvis couldn't have lived without one."

Columbine was bored with all this aircraft worship. "Elvis didn't live."

"Exactly."

Columbine changed the subject. "Did Victor fly like this?"

Destry shook her head. "No, Victor still likes to fly the old-fashioned way, as high-maintenance freight."

The Black Plane's wheels had touched, and though it had come out of stealth darkness, its lights were blazing as it braked on the runway, rolled to a near stop, described a half turn, and then halted completely. The doors quickly opened and two heavy-set security men, again with machine pistols, jumped down and assumed defensive postures. The original guards from the barn approached them, words were exchanged, and the area appeared to be declared safe for the passengers to disembark. Just four passengers came down the short ladder: a suave middle-aged man with no luggage, who made straight for the Aston Martin; a short worried man, with an uncanny resemblance to Peter Lorre, hurried to the bulletproof Mercedes; and a tall black man in an ankle-length fur, wide-brimmed hat, and dark glasses strolled casually to the Rolls as if it were all no big thing. Even if being the only female hadn't given it away, Julia would have been immediately recognizable. Tall, model-thin, and blonde, she seemed to have taken the idea of flying on the Black Plane rather too much to heart, and dressed in the style of a 1930s aviatrix. This stopped Columbine, who was right in the act of getting out of the Range Rover. "Good grief, she's dressed up like Hannah Reich."

Julia's butter-leather flying suit was midnight blue with contrasting lapels and piping, and although loosely cut, it clung crucially to various parts of her body as she moved. The ensemble was completed by a matching leather flying helmet with pushed-back purple goggles.

"The Third Reich via Rodeo Drive. Either way, it's a Nazi whore on wings."

"Stop it, Columbine. She's our best ally so far."

The man in the hat and sunglasses gave Julia an appraising look and the slightest of waves, which Julia returned, before he ducked into the Silver Cloud. Columbine was even more determined not to like Julia Aschenbach. "Will we be expected to feed her?"

"I expect so. She is our guest. Now shut up or she'll hear you."

Destry and Marieko stepped forward to greet Julia, but Columbine lagged behind. Julia pointed to each of the three in turn, proving she'd done her homework. "Destry? Marieko? And this must be Columbine?"

Columbine's forced smile took on the sweetness of acid. "Did you have a good flight?"

Julia waved it away as if she did it all the time. "It was uneventful. One of the humans was amusing, but the other two were exceedingly tedious."

They walked quickly to the Range Rover, and Marieko slipped behind the wheel. Columbine pointedly sat in the front passenger seat, leaving Destry and Julia to climb into the back. Already the Black Plane was being refueled and restocked, and three figures were coming out of the barn, apparently a new roster of passengers. Marieko put the Rover in gear, and Julia glanced at Destry. "Where are we going?"

"To Ravenkeep. To our Residence. Do you have any plans?"

"If no one has a better idea, I intend to present myself at Fenrior Castle and demand to see my master. As a right, not as a privilege."

Columbine turned back to face Julia. She should perhaps be aware with what she would be dealing. "Fenrior has an entire tribe of undead savages behind him."

Julia didn't seem too concerned. "To deny me access to Victor would be nothing short of an outrage. It would be to turn all Europe against him. Not only our own kind, but the humans in power who know."

Destry and Columbine exchanged glances. Hadn't Julia considered how Fenrior didn't seem too worried about committing outrage, or the opinion of the world community of the undead and of the human cognoscenti? That would have to be dealt with later, however. Marieko voiced the question foremost in all their minds. "And Lupo?"

"If Lupo has a plan, he isn't going to reveal it to us. Not even to me. Lupo will free Victor and exact any revenge he deems suitable. I imagine he'll destroy Fenrior. In this context, I am the diplomat and Lupo is the executioner."

Columbine was skeptical. "Lupo thinks he can do all that on his own?"

"You think Lupo doesn't have contacts? Or resources he can call on?"

Marieko looked briefly back at Julia. "That's exactly what I told her."

Columbine didn't like it at all that Marieko had used Julia to score a point against her, and she began to wonder about the possibility of a German-Japanese axis. It had, after all, happened before.

The Lady Gethsemany rose to her feet, and all those who weren't already standing followed suit. Their laird was among them, and as one, the clan paid their tribute and made salute. Renquist's manners hadn't completely deserted him, although the microfungi were still at work in his head, and he rose with the rest despite his obvious anger at Fenrior and the uncertainty of his status in the Great Hall and in the Castle Fenrior as a whole. He had been anticipating a massive, woolly, untamed bear of a man who could subdue his rowdy followers by force of sheer size and intimidation. To describe the figure who paused briefly at the top of the stairs and then descended to the tune of "The Black Swan" played on the pipes as the exact opposite was a slight exaggeration, but Renquist's expectations were so far off the mark the statement came close to the truth. Fenrior was tall, slim,

almost boyish, and charismatically handsome, although
Renquist found it hard to tell in which century he believed himself to be residing.

The side-paneled dark glasses that hid his eyes were
the perfect example—they could equally have been ul-
tramodern, futuristic Victorian, or simply copied from
the actor Vincent Price in the motion picture made from
Edgar Allan Poe's "Ligeia." Much the same could be
said of the long, decorative leather waistcoat. It might
have been eighteenth century, but Renquist had seen
similar garments worn by gentleman rock musicians in
the 1960s and seventies—except gentleman rock musicians didn't also wear the kind of straight dress sword
that hung at Fenrior's side. As Lord of Fenrior, he was
obliged to wear that plaid, but he had it nonchalantly
draped over one shoulder, secured by a large rose-and-
dagger pin. He'd also forgone the kilt, instead wearing
high, above-the-knee boots with rows of silver buckles,
very akin to ones often worn by successful Mexican ban-
ditos of the nineteenth century, over contemporary plain
black jeans. The paradox was continued by the sheaths
for two long dirks that were built into the top fold of
each boot.

A second surprise for Renquist was that Fenrior didn't
have red hair. Seemingly he hadn't contributed anything
to the gene pool's prevailing pigmentation. His hair was
jet black, dead straight, long, limp, hanging almost to
his waist, and contained a single white streak that ran
from the center parting. A secondary function of the dark
glasses might well have been to keep the fall of this
relaxed mane out of his eyes. He made his way to the
high table, exchanging jokes and brief pleasantries with
individuals along the way, proving himself very much
the Lord of the People, although Renquist noted the continuing skirl of the pipes enabled Fenrior to play the
Ronald Reagan trick of pretending to be deaf to those
he didn't wish to hear. He mounted the high table dais
at the opposite side from Renquist and moved quickly

to his throne, where he stood and slowly surveyed the assembly. "The Black Swan" ended, but Fenrior, with definite theatrical timing, waited for the pipes' wheezing deflation to finish before he spoke.

"Please be seated, my friends. Let's not stand on ceremony. We are to feast on the indulgence of vices before our adventures to come."

Renquist didn't know to what adventures Fenrior specifically referred, but he was sure they included both him and the cocoon of Merlin. Fenrior's voice was precise and educated, perhaps deceptively languid, as if the laird fancied he suffered from the ennui of power. It had none of the burr, swallowed vowels, and bizarre syntax favored by Gallowglass, Shaggy Lachlan, and the rest of the Fenrior wild bunch. Fenrior was the undead version of those paradoxical Scots aristocracy who, throughout history, had toured Europe, been educated at the Sorbonne, but, back in their native banks and braes, could adopt an attitude of murderous and demented savagery with no apparent effort. Renquist could imagine Fenrior had fed on whole families—but probably with an unsurpassed gentility of manners.

"I have an entertainment planned for you later—"

At this, the Highlanders roared their approval, and some even drew their swords and beat the flat of their blades upon the table. To make noise seemed to be a popular social pastime in Fenrior. As the hammering subsided, the lord held up his hand for quiet.

"As is tradition, however, before we have our fun, I have to ask if any present might have a question, demand, or petition to address to me. As a preliminary to the feast, the lord must hear and know all that may be undone or amiss."

The Highlanders scanned one another's faces, but their auras showed it was only a matter of form. No one was expected to speak up or complain. Everything in Fenrior was supposedly as it should be. In confirmation, Duncanon got to his feet and declared, with what Renquist considered an excessive degree of ass-kissing mock bravado, "Nothin' undone or amiss here m' lord."

It all seemed to be part of a regular routine, and the Highlanders cheered, applauded, and engaged in more sword-banging. Renquist wasn't sure if he'd have done what he did if he hadn't ingested the microfungi. He'd like to think he'd be prepared to face down entire Clan Fenrior and its lord, alone, unarmed and cold sober, but he had to admit the intoxication helped. Hadn't Shaggy Lachlan said there would be a phase of him wanting "t' fight everyone i' th' room"? Renquist may have been putting his own unique spin on the prediction as he rose to his feet and faced Fenrior. "I have a question, my lord."

The Great Hall fell silent as Fenrior looked along the high table at Renquist. "A question?"

"Perhaps even a demand."

"Do I know you, sir?"

"You should know me, my lord, since I believe it was you who ordered my abduction."

Renquist's open accusation produced shocked expressions throughout the hall. Clearly no one in a long time had taken such a tone with the Lord Fenrior. The only exception was Lady Gethsemany, who smiled with open amusement.

Fenrior turned. "Ah . . . Master Renquist, I presume."

"The same, my lord."

"And your question, Master Renquist?"

Renquist sensed the way the confrontation was going to be played out. Fenrior seemed to favor an archaically mannered wordplay. Of course, that was no hard thing when one enjoyed absolute power, but Renquist would play along. By this point, he really had no choice—or means to back down without a maybe fatal loss of face. Incorporated in Fenrior's maintenance of power was a need to remain popular. It was a weakness with potential for exploitation. Wasn't it the will to popularity that had, in the late twentieth century, destroyed the human concept of democracy in all but name? It could do the same in an absolute monarchy if the monarch wasn't careful. "I am a trifle confused, my lord. I sit at your high table as a supposed guest, and yet you have deprived me of both my liberty and my sword."

"Your sword?"

"My sword is at the Savoy, sir.

"Your sword is at the Savoy, sir?"

"So I believe. I carry it with me when I travel to wear on formal occasions such as this, when swords are apparently worn. Now I come to your hall as a nosferatu master deprived of his sword and therefore deprived of his status. Deprived of my sword, I can only consider myself a prisoner and leave this feast forthwith, since a prisoner has no business here."

An angry muttering had begun among the Highlanders, but Fenrior seemed to savor Renquist's juggling of protocols. "This is a sword of some significance?"

"It was given to me some centuries ago by Hideo Matsutani, the great swordsman of Kyoto."

"So how does it come to be at the Savoy, Master Renquist?"

"I had no time to collect it, my lord, when I was seized by Gallowglass and his companions. It remains in London, in my suite at the Savoy, with the rest of my luggage."

The muttering of the Highlanders grew in vehemence. The common view being Renquist was indeed a "southern jasmine limp-wrist," giving insolent lip to their lord. Fenrior turned and quieted them with a gesture that also seemed to indicate the best had yet to come. "You are mistaken about that, sir."

"Mistaken about what, my lord?"

"That your sword is at the Savoy."

"Indeed, sir?"

"Your sword is not at the Savoy. Your sword is here, sir."

As if on cue Droon appeared bearing the Bushido

blade in its ivory sheath. The Highlanders exploded with laughter as the joke seemed to be on Renquist, but then the laughter abruptly died and hands went to hilts as Renquist slid the sword from its scabbard. He turned it slightly, so the light was reflected from the old and exquisitely fashioned steel. In the body of the hall, claymores were being slowly drawn, but Fenrior himself simply watched with the detached interest of one who truly believes nothing can happen to him.

Renquist knew he had to judge the mood of the Highlanders with great accuracy, which wasn't made easy by the microfungi. At the very moment they seemed ready to rise and rush him, he stiffened slowly and brought the blade up to formally salute Fenrior, then dashingly cut it away, sheathed it in a single motion, and smiled. "Thank you for the return of my blade, my lord. You can count on its service while I remain your guest."

The Highlanders were silent for all but a half minute; then Gallowglass and a number of the older retainers broke into an appreciative round of applause. The Lady Gethsemany joined in, and then the rest of the hall followed suit. The only ones whose hands remained firmly on their swords were the young ones around Duncanon, and Renquist was well aware they wouldn't like anything he did. Boys would always be boys. He and Fenrior bowed low to each other like two actors who have just completed a scene. On the unspoken levels of undead diplomacy, much more than a scene had been concluded. Fenrior had flexed his muscles, but he had also made a concession to Renquist, and a message had been sent. The matter of Renquist's abduction would be shelved for the moment, but his status as an honored and untouchable guest had been clearly established in front of the entire clan.

Fenrior turned away and faced the hall. "And now, friends, the entertainment."

*   *   *

Marieko observed from a distance as Julia and Destry walked the horse and noted how many mannerisms Julia had consciously or unconsciously copied from Victor. She wondered what this newcomer really thought about Renquist. He was her creator, and that alone was a source of tension without any further or added complications. Gossip claimed that Julia wanted to become Renquist's consort, and gossip also maintained that, if she hadn't actually connived the destruction of Cynara, his previous longtime companion and hunting partner, she had at least been instrumental in manufacturing the chaos that had made such a thing possible. Marieko somehow doubted Julia was quite so obsessively infatuated with Victor as international undead chatter seemed to assume, except insofar as Julia saw Victor as the next step on her personal stairway to power. Although, might she be judging Julia a little too harshly? How many relationships weren't, in one way or another, based on one or both partners' self-interest? On the other hand, she wasn't convinced. An ever-present hue in Julia's chill aura told that she might pose a very special kind of threat. She would do exactly what suited her at the time, and only a fool would act on the assumption that Julia would behave according to the rational dictates of the common good. In Julia, Marieko observed a most unique of beings, a cold and calculating tactile hedonist. She would have to be studied.

Julia and Destry were, for the moment at least, the fastest to achieve the superficial bonding of the newly acquainted. They were both young, both twentieth century, and their kindred cloak-and-dagger backgrounds provided an extra commonality. On first arriving at Ravenkeep, Julia had sensed the horse and, on finding out Destry was its mistress, had begged to be allowed to see the incredibly rare Uzbek. While Julia continued to praise and flatter the horse and, indirectly, his owner, Destry positively glowed—and if things continued in the same vein, they would soon be hunting together. Unless of course, Julia decided to prevail on Destry to let her ride Dormandu. Whether she asked and, if she did ask, whether she pressed the point would prove a strong augury of how matters might continue.

Seemingly Julia had not made the request, because Destry turned and handed Dormandu's halter to Bolingbroke so the thrall could return the stallion to his loose box. She then called out to Marieko. "You look like you're spying on us, lurking over there like that."

"I was being discreet while you two equestrians went about your business."

"Just breaking the ice."

"And you were doing it so well, I thought I'd stay out of it."

Julia's aura remained carefully furled, but for an instant she looked curiously at Marieko, as though considering a possible rival. She looked more openly at Destry. Apparently Julia didn't feel threatened by Destry. "Is she always like this?"

Destry nodded. "Inscrutability is her profession."

Marieko gave a polite social laugh. "That's a stereotype, sister dear, and you know it."

Julia looked from one to the other. "I've never been part of a troika."

Destry smiled. "You should try it sometime. It's not all it appears."

Marieko glanced up. "Sometimes it's less than it appears."

Above them, on the second floor of Ravenkeep, a curtain moved and an aura flickered. Columbine, having pleaded she needed to rest after the journey to meet the plane, had left the three of them to inspect Dormandu. Instead of resting, however, Columbine now seemed to be spying on the other three, doubtlessly eavesdropping on their conversation to hear if they were talking about her. Julia frowned. "Will she be okay?"

"When you ask will she be okay, I take it the intention is we all go to Scotland together?"

Julia looked surprised. "What else?"

Marieko nodded. "Then she will be okay." Even Columbine needed an occasional encouragement.

Having been at least partially reassured about Columbine, an idea seemed to come to Julia. "We should take Dormandu with us."

The suggestion hit Destry like a small bomb. "What?"

Marieko saw the point. "It is an idea. Mobility in the wild."

Julia smiled sweetly at Destry. "Think about it. That great horse in the Highlands putting the fear into those barbarians."

Julia had obviously conjured an epic Valkyrie vision in Destry's mind. "Could we do it? I mean practically?"

"I'm sure it can be worked out. All it takes is money."

Renquist failed to notice when a cover was discreetly placed over the Bechtstein. That the piano needed protection should have warned him of the carnage to come, but unfortunately, he didn't make the connection until the entertainment was well in progress. Unprepared as he was, the start of the proceedings gave him a moment's pause. He had expected advanced degeneracy, and instead, he was presented with a moment of innocence. Two fiddlers and an accordion augmented the quintet, and the eight musicians launched into sprightly traditional dance music. Renquist knew virtually nothing about Scottish folk-dancing so he could not identify the tune, and even if he had, he probably would have been too distracted by the troop of twelve human dancers, six teenage girls and six teenage boys, presumably all from the village, who came running down the stairs, positioned themselves in formation in the open space between the two lower tables, and commenced to dance.

They looked so neat, so innocently practiced and enthusiastic, virginal, and maybe strangest of all, they looked so alike they could have had common parentage. Only one lacked the standard red hair. Spines ramrod straight, knees high, feet flying, but with united precision, they danced their hearts out for their laird. The boys and girls were dressed identically—kilts to just above the knee and crisp white blouses over juvenile breasts or hairless chests—but with grave faces, beyond all youth, indicating a subconscious knowledge this night was a fulfillment, and therefore an ending, an ending to a life that had been nothing but a single long rehearsal for this moment of diversion for their lord. Renquist knew it wasn't *Riverdance,* but to his untrained eye, unable to tell a jig from a reel, it seemed a close approximation. Renquist realized the ultimate outcome long before it was even partially revealed; the only real question was how long Fenrior would drag it out. Once again, he seemed to be leading his people with what really amounted to a lordly sense of showmanship. As soon as the Highlanders began to grow restless with the display, the atmosphere in the hall went through a slow but theatrical change. Candles guttered, the flames in the fireplace leaped higher, as if competing with the dancers, and the lights in Fenrior's Great Hall grew progressively more dim. The dancers' firelit shadows grew long and sinister, as did those of the Highlanders who watched them intently. The eyes of the massed nosferatu all but glowed in the gloom, but Renquist had to concede the dancers had been superbly trained. Even as the tension built, their expressions of concentration hardly flickered, except for one of the girls, whose eyes were tightly shut. There was, however, no mistaking the bright fear in their auras and the smell of their dread as they anticipated their feudal doom.

To say who made the first move was hard. The bubble of peace and innocence seemed to burst violently and almost all at once. A Highlander on one side of the hall let out something between a bark and a howl, and one on the other side responded with the same sound. Maybe half a dozen rose from their seats and scrambled over tables, closing on the dancers. In an instant, everyone in the hall seemed to become part of a single snarling pack. Guests even jumped down from the high table. Dancers were screaming. Shaggy Lachlan was gone like a venerable flash. One of the boy dancers tried to flee up the stairs but was brought down by Theda, whose leather dress was already stained with gore. Renquist saw Duncanon rise from the crimson scrimmage for an instant, his mouth, chin, and throat red with blood. Of course, twelve teenagers among sixty or seventy nosferatu was little more than a token; a communion seemed an apt metaphor to Renquist. As an offering to the clan, they were more symbolic that substantial sustenance, and first one, and then another of the serving thralls were dragged to the killing floor, along with the darklost who had been there all along for the clan's amusement.

It wasn't that Renquist felt himself above a blood orgy of this kind or that he didn't feel his own primitive stirrings. Indeed, when he decided to sit out this phase of the feast, he was glad he had very recently been able to feed on Annie Munro. He had no hunger in him, and thus found it easier to resist what a cockney vampire had once called "wallowing in the claret." His main reason for abstaining was that he felt it was far too early to get that intimate with the rank and file of the Fenrior Clan. To be in that splattered maelstrom of heaving, ripping, grunting, live and undead flesh, fangs and claws, the cries and moans of the still living and momentarily dying, was hardly the place for a less-than-trusted stranger. The clan's collective blood was quite literally up, and that, coupled with the effects of the microfungi in the whisky, made them highly volatile and unpredictable. Here and there fights were already breaking out between Highlanders disputing the ownership of prey, and Renquist knew, if he were down there, it would be all too simple for Duncanon or one of his crony boys, to use the cover of the bloodletting to thrust an unseen dirk into his heart.

As the Great Hall grew even darker and the blood

flowed over the flagstones, Renquist turned away and noticed he was not the only one sitting out the entertainment. The musicians had backed off into a corner, protecting their instruments from the spray. The human bass player had vanished altogether. Both Fenrior and Gethsemany had also remained in their thrones, but the Craft-maker was either down in the bloody mosh or had wafted away with her coven early in the festivities. Fenrior and Gethsemany watched the happening with an indulgent and almost parental amusement, but when Fenrior saw Renquist looking at him, he rose from the throne and walked along the dais toward him.

"A little barbaric for your taste?"

Renquist gently brushed a drop of blood from his jacket. "I have a limited wardrobe. I didn't want to ruin this suit."

"The lads need their fun. It keeps them in line."

"I can well believe that. You appear to take good care of them."

Fenrior shrugged. "I bring them into this world. I am responsible for their management."

"The burden of leadership."

"You understand?"

"Of course I do. I have a colony of my own. Smaller in number, of course, but I know what's required at times."

"There are some European nosferatu who consider us uncivilized."

"Rest assured, my lord. I am not one of them. I have never been all that enamored of civilization. Too human a concept."

"If they think its uncivilized now, they should have seen us in the old days."

"I can imagine."

Fenrior nodded. "Aye, you probably can. You have the age on you."

"I saw the Thirty Years' War. After that I could believe anything."

"Some of the old lads had to be weaned of eating the flesh."

"The Native Americans call them wendigo."

"I called it bloody uncouth, and had it stopped on pain of sunlight. I also put a stop to the spread-eagle."

"The spread-eagle?"

"Opening the chest and prying the ribs apart like the wings of a bird to drink directly from the heart."

"It sounds messy."

Below Renquist and Fenrior, the supply of humans had apparently run out. Some Highlanders were performing their own shuffling dance, while others beat time on the table with the hilts of their swords. A high keening started from throats just slaked with blood, and Renquist wondered what dementia might follow. Fenrior seemed to sense this and gestured to an exit from the hall behind the high table. "Walk with me, Master Renquist. Walk with me a little. The aftermath is never pretty."

The Range Rover swung into the parking lot of an international chain motel with perhaps forty-five minutes to spare before dawn. They were somewhere south of Newcastle, according to the road atlas. They pulled up in front of the main entrance, and Julia indicated she would get out and check them all in. "There's no point in the desk clerks getting a good look at all of us. It'll be far easier to fog their minds if it's just me. Also I have platinum credit cards in a variety of untraceable names."

Destry, Marieko, and Columbine waited in the vehicle while Julia went inside. She had changed out of her leather flying suit, replacing it with jeans, a T-shirt dedicated to the rock band Metallica, a flowing canvas duster coat, and a beat-up straw cowboy hat pulled down over her eyes. The original plan, as Julia and Destry had laid it out was to start promptly at sunset and attempt to make it to Scotland by dawn. Julia and Destry had taken over the planning stage of the journey to Castle Fenrior, while Marieko said little but reserved her doubts, and Columbine complained and made difficulties. Columbine seemed to be increasingly getting on Julia's nerves. So far, the new arrival had yet to flash her anger, but Marieko could easily read how an eventual confrontation was building, as the difficulties multiplied and the departure time grew later and later. Getting through to Grendl and Bolingbroke and making it clear to the confused thralls that they were expected to maintain and run the house while their mistresses were away, had proved comparatively easy. A company that specialized in the transportation of valuable horses had been recruited to move Dormandu, but outside problems delayed the arrival of the horse box that was to take the stallion to Scotland and eventually to meet the four of them at a prearranged point near to Fenrior. Columbine had also contributed her share of holdups, and indeed, Columbine appeared to be growing quickly and progressively less stable. Her newest drama was a lengthy procrastination about leaving Ravenkeep. "Leave Ravenkeep indefinitely? How can I leave Ravenkeep indefinitely?"

Finally Destry had to snap at her. "Stop being Scarlett O'Hara, and pack the minimum you think you'll need."

Another unplanned pause had occurred when a report of the killing of security guards at Morton Downs appeared on the local TV news. A student, Winston Shakespeare, was missing, but it was unclear if the authorities were treating him as a suspect or a mislaid potential victim. Nothing in the story indicated any connection to Ravenkeep or the troika, and no witnesses came forward claiming the perpetrators were a gang of wild vampire Scotsmen. It still seemed a good time, though, to be away from home. Let the thralls confuse any county CID detectives who might happen by to ask questions.

After Julia had been inside the hotel for a full five minutes, Columbine took it as her cue to start complaining. "What's taking her so long?"

"You know how long it can take to check in anywhere

these days. Computers are inevitably down."

"And why's she doing it, anyway?"

"She has the documentation."

Columbine was being gratuitously petulant, but she was on a roll and seemingly didn't feel it safe to stop. "We have our own documentation."

Marieko knew it was pointless to argue with her when a mood of this kind had hold of her, but she argued anyway. "Why use our documentation when she's willing to use hers? It gives us three an extra degree of separation."

"I don't know. She seems to be taking over. I don't recall putting her in charge."

Destry had heard enough. "Columbine, get off it. Stop pissing and moaning, or I swear I'll damage you."

Marieko continued to appeal to reason. "Victor is, after all, the master of her colony. It's only natural she should take a proprietary interest. And besides, she's German."

"She doesn't give a tinker's cuss about Victor, except as a means to an end."

"Is that what's really bothering you? It still starts and ends with Victor?"

"No, but—"

Now Marieko reached her limit. "Shut up, Columbine. I swear, if you don't stop whining, I'll let it slip to Julia how you sold out Victor to Gallowglass."

"You wouldn't?"

"Keep up the negativity and find out."

Destry gestured for them both to stop. Julia was coming back. She opened the door and showed Marieko where to park the Range Rover. "They claimed they were short of rooms because they had some kind of convention booked in. I had to use my high beams on them."

"So there's no problem?"

"Not now there isn't."

Julia had booked four rooms, two that connected. The interior of each motel room was globally unremarkable:

easy-clean furniture, a muted color scheme, the obligatory bad landscape on the wall above the king-size bed, a black TV set, a beige phone, and individually wrapped soap. They really could have been anywhere on the planet. Before separating to sleep, they gathered in one of the two connected rooms to unwind and generally review their situation. Destry switched the black television to CNN to see if anything more was emerging about the killings at Morton Downs, but the story didn't seem to have penetrated that far north. Julia removed her hat, and Destry quickly turned from the TV. "Just one thing, please. Don't throw your hat on the bed."

"It spooks you?"

"We all have our foibles."

She dropped her hat on top of her overnight bag and faced the troika. "I think there's something I need to say before we go any further."

"What's that?"

"I'm getting the impression you all feel too much reliance is being placed on the invincibility of Lupo."

Marieko was defensive. "None of us have said that."

"But you've thought it?"

Marieko nodded. "I certainly have. The Lord Fenrior commands his own army."

Destry added emphasis. "That's really no exaggeration. There must be dozens of those undead Highlanders. All armed to the teeth."

Marieko continued. "I do think we'd feel more confident if we had something even slightly similar behind us."

"You believe we need an army?"

"Not an army, but I don't know what the four of us can really achieve."

"I could make some calls if you sincerely feel that way about reinforcements."

"It's pointless hiring humans."

"There are some of our kind I could contact."

Marieko liked that idea. "It might be worth at least

seeing how the land lay in terms of possible support."

Julia shrugged. "There's no time like the present, and since it's not quite dawn here in Europe, most won't have retired yet."

She fished in her bag, produced a cell phone, dialed a thirteen-digit number, and spoke in rapid Italian. After some minutes of both talking and listening, she snapped the phone closed. "That was not good."

"How not good?"

"You might say double plus ungood. It seems most of the Euro-clans would agree Victor being snatched by Fenrior was quite beyond the boundaries of good manners, but no one wants to get involved. They'd all prefer to see the show. It's an event. They feel it could be the first great confrontation of the new century, and they all want to sit on the sidelines and watch it play out."

Columbine snorted. "Selfish bastards."

"That's the undead for you. Spectacle before justice. We don't get enough thrills in our lives these days."

"I still think they're selfish bastards."

"Wouldn't you do the same?"

"Of course, but that's not the point."

Destry shook her head. "There's no sense in starting yet another bloody discussion. We have no backup, and that's that. We're right where we started. We can only confront Fenrior, and if he doesn't decide to do the right thing and release Victor, we can only hope Lupo will pull our chestnuts out of the fire."

Julia removed her duster and inspected the bed. "I was offered one piece of advice."

"What was that?"

"As four females, we should make our demands of the Lady Gethsemany, and not Fenrior. If she refuses, any of us are quite within our rights to call her out in single combat."

Destry nodded slowly. "I think I could take her."

Marieko sighed. "I would have no problem facing her."

Julia sat down on the bed and started pulling off her boots. "We can talk about that after we've slept."

Columbine picked up her overnight things as a prelude to finding her room. "You should probably know Gethsemany hates me."

Julia looked up at her with one boot on her foot and the other in her hand. "Now, I wonder why that might be."

Fenrior and Renquist walked down a corridor lit by hundreds upon hundreds of candles. The place smelled of small flames, melting wax, and an elusive perfume. "It was Gethsemany's idea. Pleasant, don't you think?"

An armadillo scuttled under a low wax-crusted table as the two nosferatu approached. One thing in Fenrior was as it should be. Renquist nodded politely. "Very pleasant."

"You recognize the perfume?"

"No."

"It's one of her own design. She has it made up by an old human in York. Still calls himself an apothecary."

Renquist noticed, even in this soft gothic gloom, Fenrior didn't remove his dark glasses. Could it be something was wrong with the lord's eyes? Had they accidentally or deliberately been damaged at some time in the past, or were they perhaps strange and unsightly to look upon? Obviously it was something one didn't inquire about, but he couldn't help wonder.

"The Lady Gethsemany is constantly redesigning and making changes to the interior rooms of the castle. It passes the nights for her, but I must confess, there are times even I don't know where I am."

Fenrior's joking admission confirmed something Renquist had already begun to realize. The Castle Fenrior was an absolute labyrinth of rooms, corridors, and, from what he'd seen earlier, a warren of subterranean tunnels. It was impossible to guess how far the structure might extend underground or stretch beneath the lake. Fenrior had been able to work on the enlargement of his edifice for centuries, and Renquist couldn't imagine he hadn't put the time to good use. The idea of escaping became even more remote. Far from finding his way out of the Scottish Highlands before he was caught by the sun, he realized he'd actually be lucky to find his way out of the castle. Thought of escape moved very logically to thoughts on what Lupo might be doing. Lupo could go to ground for a month in place like this, suddenly appearing, destroying Highlanders when they were least expecting it, and then disappearing again.

"Now that we're alone, there is something I need to ask you."

Fenrior looked at Renquist a little warily. "That sounds ominous."

"Why did you have Gallowglass take me the way he did? I had every intention of coming here."

"I suppose you could say I grew impatient. I was no longer able to wait. And anyway, I had to know if I could trust you. I knew your reputation, but I had to check. You could have been as big a liar as that fool Saint Germaine."

"But you trust me now?"

"I watched you feed, didn't I?"

"I rather resented that."

"That's what I saw."

Renquist waited a few moments before playing his last, what he hoped would be his trump card. "You are aware that Lupo, if he's heard what's happened, may well come and take your head?"

Fenrior nodded slowly like a man being apprised of something he'd overlooked. "Ah, Lupo. I suppose I should take that seriously."

"If he arrived here, I would obviously dissuade him, but he might decide to finish you before he looked for me."

"Or my lads might finish him."

Renquist smiled coldly. "I very much doubt that."

"Could you contact him?"

"I don't know. If he's left already, I can't. Even I don't know how Lupo travels. And if I could, what could I say to him? I don't know what I'm doing here, or how long I'm going to be doing it."

"I thought we had your status fully established."

"That was for the clan. For Lupo, I would have to know the reality."

Fenrior drew himself up to his full height. "I'm a vampire lord, Master Renquist, and you are pressing me hard."

Fenrior was a little taller than Renquist, but Renquist refused to be intimidated. "And I am a thousand years old, my lord. I suspect time is pressing the both of us."

"I wanted you here for when Taliesin wakes. And the Merlin is waking faster than I expected."

"I didn't have to be brought here for that. I would have come in an instant."

"I may also need your help to destroy it."

Renquist's shock robbed him of caution. "What?"

"I said destroy it. My present intention for the Urshu is welcome it, study it, and having won its trust, kill it."

"Kill it? Are you insane?"

"It takes a lot of courage to ask an absolute ruler if he's insane."

"The question stands."

Fenrior laughed once, a soft, ironic bark. "You really are a thousand years old, aren't you?"

Renquist nodded. "And not getting any younger. You talked earlier about your impatience to get me here. I have my own impatience."

As Fenrior spoke, all Renquist could see was the candlelight reflected in his dark glasses. The steel frames were like sections of a black greenhouse, maybe for poisonous plants. "Don't talk to me about impatience, Victor Renquist. I have been very patient. Infinitely patient, you might say. I have known about the Urshu sleeping in the barrow at Morton Downs for over a hundred years.

I was aware of its existence since before Columbine Dashwood so much as moved into Ravenkeep."

When Marieko semi-predicted that Destry and Julia would be hunting together, she had neither imagined the peculiarity of the circumstances nor that she and Columbine would be hunting with them. They had decided before leaving Ravenkeep, aside from a dozen packs of whole blood in an ice-filled cooler for emergencies, they would live off the land as far as possible. They'd feed where they could, working on the assumption that, since they were moving fast and leaving as many false trails as possible, their depredations would be blamed on misadventure on the part of the victim or on some unknown human psychopath. Marieko had assumed, when the decision was taken, feeding would be a private and personal matter, with each female satisfying her needs as she felt fitting, and in her own way. She had certainly not expected Julia would both attempt and succeed to turn basic survival into a group social activity or that she would act as a kind of cheerleader for a collective blood-orgy.

Destry, as seemingly befitted their ongoing bonding, had elected to sleep in the room that connected with Julia's, and Marieko and Columbine had gone to the other two single rooms, where they could depart from the day in undisturbed isolation. Certain preparations had to be made before they could enter the dreamstate, primarily the covering of all windows with tape and aluminum foil, but Marieko herself had made sure they'd come prepared with all the materials for that eventuality. Some, probably Victor among them, claimed the undead traveled fast. Others subscribed to the opposite. Like certain fine wines, nosferatu didn't travel well at all. She felt the current outing conformed to the latter maxim. When finally alone in her room, Marieko had wondered if Destry and Julia might end up sharing the same bed. Neither could be truthfully described as masculine, but

they were both nosferatu females-of-action, and it looked
to be a case of like attracting like. Marieko had noticed
the unmistakable traces of a studied and mutual, quasi-
sexual heat in their auras when they were together and
thought they weren't observed.

The arrangement had been, once sunset had come and
all four had awakened, they would gather in Julia's room
to prepare for the coming night, and then journey on to
the Highlands and Fenrior. Marieko woke with an auto-
matic punctuality, and found that she was the first to
arrive at Julia's door. She knocked, and after a short
delay, Julia answered. Marieko was surprised Julia was
not dressed for the north of Scotland, but for cocktails
and seduction. In the background, Destry was similarly
in party rather than traveling mode. Marieko found herself at something of a loss and stood rooted until Julia
hustled her inside. "Don't just stand there in the corridor
like a bellhop waiting for a tip."

Marieko looked from Destry to Julia and back again.
Behind Destry, the connecting door between the two
rooms stood open. Marieko saw that Destry's bed was
unconvincingly messed up, as if in a last-minute attempt
to make it appear slept in when, in fact, it wasn't. Had
the pair sidetracked each other already? Both showed
signs of a definite dark-eyed, heavy-lidded satisfaction.
Nosferatu could suffer from a shortness of attention
span, but this was absurd. "What the hell do you two
think you're doing? We've got a long drive in front of
us."

"We also have to feed, my darling."

"I though we'd attempt to pick up victims on the run."

Julia shook her head. "First we feed. Then we travel.
We have to be on top of our form for what we are about
to do, and need all the fresh energy we can acquire."

Julia's white silk evening dress, which all but exposed
her breasts each time she leaned forward, was a perfect
match for her straight white-blond hair. Destry was
wearing the same man's dinner jacket she had worn to

greet Renquist. "The plan is that we hit the happy hour in the motel bar, glut ourselves, and then leave around nine. That should give us plenty of time to be at the gates of Fenrior well before dawn."

"Does Columbine know about this?"

Julia nodded. "Destry called her in her room. She's dressing."

By now Marieko was experiencing a definite foreboding. She stared at Destry. "So why didn't you call me?"

Destry avoided looking directly at her. Her aura had a certain blush. "I knew you'd be on time."

"I could also have dressed."

"You look fine as you are."

Marieko looked down at her faded blue jeans, T-shirt, and motorcycle jacket. "We look like lesbian humans."

Destry's aura-blush deepened, but Julia merely laughed. "All the better to reach our objective speedily without undue entertaining of the prey. You know how both human genders are fascinated by attractive lipstick lesbians."

"I'm just not sure I wanted to be cast as the butch tomboy."

Julia laughed dismissively. "You'll adapt, my dear."

Further discussion was interrupted by a curt rap on the door. Destry opened it and let in Columbine, who was also, literally and figuratively, dressed to kill. Marieko felt completely isolated, totally left out of this plan to collectively vamp the motel bar. How dare Julia dismiss her with "you'll adapt"? Columbine was a retrovision in flowing antique sequins and embroidery to a color scheme of white and pale blue. A large sapphire was at her throat on a white velvet band. Her curls fell to her shoulders in contrived disarray, and a dark blue diamond beauty spot decorated her heavily powdered left cheek. On close examination, though, all about Columbine did not seem right. She looked drained and unhealthy, but no one else appeared to notice. Was Columbine continuing to dream, or had what Marieko firmly believed was her link with Merlin entered some new and more damaging phase? Whatever the problem, Columbine was manifestly determined to put the bravest possible face on it. "So, are we going to see what this place has to offer?"

The hunting party left the room and followed the signs to the nearest lift with a giddy and high-spirited girlishness, as if they were off on an adventure. If the sight, when the lift doors opened, of two silver-green aliens with oversize heads and huge ovoid eyes wasn't initially a shock, it was at least highly unexpected. A second take, of course, revealed the creatures were in no way extraterrestrial, but merely humans in not particularly well made fancy dress, but this didn't completely cancel the primary surprise. More strangeness waited when the four, plus the two ersatz aliens, exited the elevator and stepped into the lobby. The entire motel seemed to have been taken over by emotionally disturbed humanity, many seriously overweight, elaborately costumed as if in some projected make-believe future. The quartet's nosferatu senses were instantly struck by a confusion of thought that came at them as an uncouth, nonsensical, and highly intrusive babble.

"What the hell is this?"

Julia looked around. "I suppose this must be the convention that delayed my obtaining our rooms this morning. The desk clerk told me it was dedicated to a popular science fiction series on television, but I didn't imagine it would be like this. These people are nothing more than chronic obsessive-compulsives. I suppose they must be the fans."

On this subject, Marieko was far ahead of Julia. She was well aware of the TV show and the less-than-rational cult surrounding it. She could only assume Julia was one of those nosferatu who disdained the gross pop culture of humanity, and restricted themselves to Miró and Mahler. Four humans walked by in identical imaginary astronaut uniforms, white Pan-Cake on their faces, and false plastic hair. Marieko commenced to follow them, going with the flow, and the other three came after her by default. The four nosferatu may not have conformed to the theme, but they were certainly not out of place. An entire section of the motel had been specifically set aside for the convention, designated banqueting and conference rooms on the ground floor where they held their seminars, watched their films and videotapes, bought and sold their artifacts, and would later indulge in painfully awkward drinking, disco dancing, and attempts at hedonism.

Before they could enter this reserved area, the quartet was accosted by a convention organizer in the costume of a warrior from some alien military culture. They might not have looked out of place, but they apparently lacked credentials. The faux warrior demanded to see their badges. Seemingly a badge indicated one had paid one's money and was entitled to partake of the convention. Marieko was tempted to use the immortal movie line from *The Treasure of the Sierra Madre*, but she decided the pretend-alien warrior wouldn't even get the joke, and she reduced it to "we don't need badges" accompanied by a brain-smack of sufficient force to ensure the young man would never bother them again. Just to cause him future remorse, she also left him hopelessly in love with her. If nothing better presented itself, he would be hers at a snap of her fingers.

Marieko made the mistake of allowing herself to be distracted by the convention itself. The way in which the humans were prepared to treat their passing amusements with such a quasi-academic seriousness was the source of a definite anthropological appeal. From Godzilla to Pokémon, Japan had served as ground zero for this kind of collector-cult behavior, and she felt patriotically obliged to keep abreast of developments in the field wherever she might find them. Some of the costumed participants seemed consumed by their fantasy cravings to the point of a wistfully neurotic melancholy that it all

couldn't be real all the time. After browsing a number
of random minds, Marieko commented to the others
without actually speaking.

*"I swear if we were to reveal what we really were
and our true intentions to some of these freaks, they'd
willingly give themselves to us."*

She turned and discovered no one was there to hear
her. Julia, Destry, and Columbine had wandered off,
more interested in the quest for prey than the weird cultural fringes of human sociodynamics. She supposed she
also should be taking care of the task at hand, rather
than wandering like a predator tourist. She decided the
bar might still be the best place to snag a fast and effortless victim. Her first glance inside confirmed Destry
and Julia had either come to the same conclusion or had
opted for a certain alcohol content in their feed. The
convention had thoroughly infiltrated the conventional
motel happy hour, and they were in deep conversation
with a pair of young humans in matching, somewhat
revealing. The minds of the two girls revealed they used
these conventions as a release for exhibitionism and a
limited perversity unavailable in their drably mundane
lives. Gatherings of this kind offered them an immunity
from shock, guilt, and inhibition in that they could always tell themselves afterwards they had only been playacting rather than acting out, and nothing that transpired
was really real. Under the screen of vodka martinis and
small talk, Julia and Destry were reinforcing this idea,
mentally conditioning them into the illusion that fantasy
could be elevated to far greater heights, and their limits
should be extended infinitely and unconditionally. At the
same time, they fed them a line of seductive suggestion
tailored precisely to the desires revealed in their purple-
tinged auras. Unfortunately these quasi-images were being broadcast on an indiscreetly wide band, and many
of the human males in the bar were becoming warmly
uncomfortable, but not sure why.

Marieko knew what Julia and Destry were up to, but this break for a roadside diversion hardly seemed appropriate. She would normally have no objection to playful bonding games, but they were supposed to be on their way to rescue Victor, and surely that was worthy of everyone's full concentration. She decided to take it upon herself to move matters along and remind them of their primary objective. She pushed her way through the crowd of space crew, extraterrestrials, and traveling salesmen. "Ladies."

"Marieko." They didn't seem overly pleased to see her, but the two humans, who, up close, were really showing too much of their thighs and cleavage for a sci-fi convention, seemed to find her oriental and exotic.

"I'm Epiphany."

"And I'm Devora."

Of course, these weren't the girls' real names. They'd taken them from a book they'd both read. While smiling politely at the humans, Marieko mentally hissed at Destry and Julia. *"This is not the time for games."*

Julia gleamed angrily and seemed poised to tell Marieko to fuck off and leave them alone, but Destry accepted the chiding. *"Yes, yes, we'll move it along. Do you have one of your own picked out?"*

Marieko decided she'd settle for the warrior checking badges. *"Yes. It'll take me just a moment. I'll meet you in the elevator."*

A snap of the fingers was literally all it took. The young man fell into step behind her. In the elevator, which they mercifully had to themselves, Julia produced a bottle of vodka. More alcohol was always a good and simple way to keep humans distracted without the need to lock down their minds. It was all too plain to Marieko that Destry and Julia, in their new role as soul-mate hunters, wanted their prey to be helpless but fully conscious, aware of what was being done to them but unable to resist. Marieko doubted Epiphany and Devora would resist anything. So many pleasure centers had been teased and tantalizingly fondled, they were all but beside themselves, surprised by the uncharted depths of the scary-strange, dark lust in which they found themselves. The young man was fully beside himself. He couldn't believe what was happening to him. Ever since he'd been coming to these events he had dreamed and even masturbated to a scenario of this kind. Alone with no less than five drunken and apparently bisexual women? His cup was close to running over, and Marieko knew she would need to keep him partially folded down in case, at the last moment, he panicked and bolted. Humans often found it hard to confront the flesh of their fantasies.

The party of five came out of the lift and stumbled down the corridor—Destry and Julia maintaining a pretense of drunken, human bonhomie as they let themselves into their room. Marieko ushered the young man in behind them, and then immediately wished she hadn't. The spectacle confronting the five of them would have been disturbing to any human except perhaps for the most intensely and suicidally depraved. In the middle of the king-size motel bed, Columbine was on all fours, clad in nothing but shoes, stockings, silk French knickers, and a sapphire, mouth to the throat of a blandly handsome and quite naked young man. She looked up with her fangs extended, blood on her lips, and a single trickle running down her chin. "My dears, you're back so soon."

Marieko felt shock course through her young man and immediately killed his conscious mind. She would have expected Julia and Destry to do the same with Epiphany and Devora, but they were still playing the game. They allowed the girls an exchanged look of mutual horror, and then swamped them with the illusion they had passed the portals of some dangerous but infinitely rewarding fantasy. The action risked them lapsing into full and screaming hysteria that might be easily noticeable in the motel full of humans, but Julia and Destry pulled

it off with almost unbelievable finesse, a finesse Marieko
suspected had more to do with Julia than Destry. Epiphany and Devora's faces grew slack and depraved, and
they swayed on their fetish heels with the expression of
evil children in purple eye shadow and loaded on opi-
ates. Julia and Destry assisted one apiece through the
door into the connecting bedroom. The last thing Marieko saw before she sank her fangs into the throat of the
young man in the warrior costume was Destry and Julia
on either side of Devora and Epiphany, kissing each
other while they undressed the two humans, stripping
and unlacing their pathetic latex and vinyl.

When she surfaced from the mindless animal bliss of
feeding to the death, Marieko rose from the corpse and
looked again. The two girls were drained and dead, and
Julia and Destry held each other. Destry was shaking
slightly as though she had just undergone a powerful
emotional experience, and the room resembled an untidy
abattoir. Columbine's boy lay dead on the bed, but there
was no sign of Columbine herself. Good manners should
have dictated Marieko not intrude on Destry and Julia's
moment, but as far as she was concerned, their self-
indulgence put them beyond normal considerations.
Marieko had set out on what she considered more of a
commando raid than a meandering pleasure outing. She
walked past them and opened the window at the far end
of the room, letting in the night air. The curtains billowed as if some kind of vacuum had been created.
"Does anyone have any suggestions?"

Julia and Destry languidly disengaged. "Suggestions
about what, darling?"

"About what we do with these leavings?"

Although Marieko was clearly very angry, Destry suddenly giggled. "We leave them."

This was finally too much for Marieko. She'd expected better of Destry. "Pull yourself the fuck together,
will you?"

Julia began to gather her scattered clothes. "She's

right, actually. We should simply leave them. I mean, who will remember us among a hundred demented humans masquerading as alien life-forms. The police will assume the obvious insanity of the one of the conventioneers and spend all their time trying to deduce which one. As the song says, we'll be in Scotland before them."

"That's madness."

"Is it? We can't get them out of here without being seen."

Marieko shook her head. Much as she might not want to admit it, Julia was right. It really was the only course they could take. "It's so damned messy."

"You worry too much."

"I worry to survive."

Julia looked at Marieko thoughtfully. "I've been noticing, you really are a lot like Victor."

"I'll take that as a compliment."

She looked down at the corpse of the boy in his bloodstained fancy dress. To simply leave him there went against the grain of all her training and upbringing, not to mention her innate orderly neatness, but she knew she had no choice. "I'll go to my room and get my things. We should leave as soon as we can."

Outside in the corridor she decided, before getting the bag out of her room, she should first check on Columbine. She rapped on the door of her room. After a few moments the door opened, and Columbine, still in her bloody lingerie, stood in the doorway, leaning heavily on the frame, a half-burned cigarette in her left hand. One look told Marieko something was very amiss. "You look sick."

Columbine nodded. "Don't say anything to the others—I think there's something wrong with me."

"Was the boy's blood tainted?"

Columbine shook her head. "It's as though all the energy is somehow being drained out of me."

"But you just fed."

"I know, and it doesn't seem to have made any difference."

"The chained were the lucky ones."

"How so?"

"The chained knew to the second when their existence would end. The ones who were simply turned loose and locked out prolonged their own agony. They squirmed, they tried to hide, they cowered in the very last patch of shadow as their flesh singed and smoked. Of course, there were others who simply jumped."

Fenrior had led Renquist up innumerable flights of spiraling stone stairs until they came out of a section of flat roof between two much taller towers, and the roof turned out to be a place of execution. A charred and rusting cage of upright iron bars, steel bands, and chains, all bolted down to a solid block of granite, stood in the middle of the otherwise open area, clearly designed to hold a kneeling nosferatu. "You chained the condemned out here to wait for the coming of the sun?"

"Every community needs its supreme sanction. Even among the Children of the Mist, there have been those who became dangerous and unmanageable. Don't tell me you haven't done the same."

"Most times it was in single combat. I never held organized executions."

"In a clan of this size, I could spend all my time in single combat if that were the only way to maintain order. Fenrior grew large enough to require its own code of enforcement."

Renquist walked to the edge of the roof. The drop to the rocks beneath, at the edge of the lake, was at least 150 feet. "The fall might not be enough to destroy a strong nosferatu."

"No, but it broke their bones and made it hard for them to move. And even if they should land in shadow and recover the strength to run, where would they go with the sun all round them?"

"Into the waters of the lake?"

"The waters of the lake are relatively shallow around the island. The sun would penetrate, and the condemned would slowly cook. That's why I say the chained were the lucky ones. They did not have to meet their end pursuing pointless choices that only delayed the inevitable."

As he looked into the abyss, Renquist wasn't sure why Fenrior had felt the need to show him his personal Tyburne. Was it to counter his warning of what might happen if Lupo came, or was it a simple reminder of the lord's authority? Either way, he really didn't need to have bothered. Enough of an abyss was already yawning in front of Renquist. When Fenrior had announced he had been monitoring the sleeping Merlin for more than a century, a whole new depth to the situation had opened up. "What I don't understand is, when you knew the Urshu slept beneath Morton Downs, why didn't you tell anyone?"

"Aside from the natural undead inclination to cling to secrets?"

"Aside from that."

"I suppose I could have told others of our community, but to what end? While the Urshu slept, there was nothing to be done, and if others knew, inevitably curiosity would get the better of one faction or another, and a move would be made to dig the thing up. I knew, in its own good time, it would eventually waken. That seemed to be the time to contact someone like yourself. Unfortunately the process of waking turned out to be much faster that I ever anticipated. I believe the humans disturbed it. I had no warning that damned Campion and his people would start digging into the mound."

"But you'd been regularly observing it."

"We had made a tradition of it. On the eve of every quarter day, either Gallowglass or I would formally use our vision to make sure it was still sleeping. We also paid very special attention when anything unusual happened near Morton Downs. I was especially concerned when Dashwood moved into Ravenkeep, first with her human husband, and then with her companions. At first I was convinced she knew something and had plans for the burial site, but nothing happened. It was only later I discovered that Columbine wasn't capable of anything as coherent as plans, and was too self-absorbed to notice a sleeping Urshu only a few miles from her."

"And all that time, the Urshu slept unchanging?"

"I thought I detected a slight change when de Richleau was conducting his experiments during the War against the Nazis, but it passed quickly and then returned to normal, so I was never sure." Fenrior smiled. "And I also observed you, Renquist, skulking in the bushes, watching de Richleau for the Undead Cartel."

Fenrior was very well informed, but Renquist refused to be awed by what the lord was telling him. Instead he focused on what he was not being told. "You still haven't explained why you think it necessary to kill the Merlin."

Fenrior paused before answering. He began ushering Renquist away from the execution site and back inside the castle. "It's hard to explain an instinct."

Renquist was as gentle as he could be with the lord. His hesitation told of a deep-seated fear. "Perhaps not to me. I don't demand a rational reason for everything."

Fenrior indicated they should continue to climb. "There is a high turret where sometimes I go to watch the approach of the dawn, just to see how long I can stand it.

Was that what had happened to Fenrior's eyes? Had he stood it for too long? Renquist had heard of other nosferatu who had developed a fixation about trying to see the sun—and finished up blinding themselves. Fenrior could obviously still see, but had he so damaged his eyes he felt the need to hide them? For a while they climbed in silence before Fenrior finally spoke again. "On one level, it's simply self-preservation. We live well here, Victor Renquist. For how long I don't know. The modern world encroaches, although we pretend it doesn't."

They reached the top of the last flight of spiral steps and came out onto the flat roof of a circular tower. Fenrior gestured to the moonlit lake and the majesty of the surrounding mountains. "Would you want to give all this up?"

"Of course not."

"Sooner or later it will end, but I would rather it were later than sooner. I am convinced Taliesin is a threat. Any disturbance is a threat, and I believe he will be a major rupture in the world in which we both dwell. Certain texts in history bear me out. All my reading would seem to indicate conflict has always broken out between Urshu and nosferatu wherever they have been in contact with each other."

Renquist nodded. "The obvious example is the confrontation between Tezcatilpoca and Quetzalcoatl when Quetzalcoatl was driven out of Mexico. There's little doubt Quetzalcoatl was Urshu and Tezcatilpoca one of our kind. Tezcatilpoca quite literally means the 'smoking mirror,' and has always been portrayed in human accounts as a malevolent god who demanded blood sacrifice."

"He has certainly always sounded like one of ours."

"In the Chinese writings of the Hung League we also find the *kiang-shi*, fully identified as nosfertatu constantly at war with Urshu-like beings who stand as the protectors of humanity."

"The Urshu have always taken the part of the humans, usually to our cost, and I mean to see it doesn't happen here."

"But you will observe him first."

"Of course."

"There's something I think I'm obliged to tell you."

"What's that?"

"I believe an unfortunate link may exist between Columbine Dashwood and the Merlin."

Fenrior had apparently been there already. "We detected the establishment of such a link soon after Campion began his delving. We've been monitoring it ever since. It would seem to have grown progressively stronger. You have a theory?"

"Miss Dashwood believes she has been selected as his consort for this period of his waking. She sees herself as his modern Morgan le Fey."

Again Fenrior's glasses glittered. "And do you agree with this hypothesis?"

"Not in the least. For an Urshu to select Columbine as a consort would reflect very poorly on the taste, intelligence, and perception of the Urshu in question, and Taliesin is not remembered in legend for his stupidity. I believe, as the waking process began, he unconsciously cast around for something genetically familiar, something from his heritage, something other than human, a trace, no matter how diluted, of a Nephilim legacy."

"And she was the first he found as he extended the radius of his search?"

"Exactly."

"So what would be the purpose of such a linkage?"

Renquist shook his head. "It's obvious an exchange of energy of some kind, but beyond that, I don't have a clue. My feeling is, however, that she is somehow intimately connected with Taliesin's waking."

Fenrior smiled. "Then maybe it's just as well she appears to be on her way here?"

Renquist wasn't surprised. He'd had a feeling Columbine might follow him to Scotland. "Right now?"

"Gallowglass is observing her progress. She is traveling by road with three companions, three nosferatu."

Now Renquist was surprised and also puzzled. Three companions? Who was the fourth? He could hardly believe Lupo would chose to throw in his lot with Columbine's troika. Indeed, it was so out of character, it scarcely seemed possible. Had someone else come from California? Julia? Renquist shuddered to think what havoc Julia might contribute to this already complicated cat's cradle of tensions. He was about to question Fenrior about this extra nosferatu when, with Shakespearean timing, a messenger called from below. "M' lord! Word is come from Gallowglass. Something is happening to the Merlin."

Chapter SEVEN

Renquist didn't know if he was amazed, aghast, or wanted to laugh out loud. After following Fenrior down endless steps and through a network of tunnels—in which each turn and intersection was crowded with an increasing security presence of armed Highlanders—he found himself in what resembled a perfect amalgam of the laboratories of all the Hollywood mad scientists of the previous eighty years. If Fu Manchu, Frankenstein, Auric Goldfinger, and Fester Addams had conspired to design the playroom of their dreams, inside a set supplied by Rotwang from Fritz Lang's *Metropolis*, they might have come up with something very close to the complex Fenrior had devised to accommodate the waking of Merlin. As Fenrior and Renquist entered, followed by the messenger and a number of Highlanders, the lord gestured with hasty pride to the intricate systems of electrical circuitry, oiled machinery, dancing needles on VU meters, and at least three generations of computers.

"You can doubtless see I have applied myself to this problem for some time."

The dungeon he had entered was, as far as Renquist could tell, deep beneath the castle, and the massive pillars that made the spacious interior resemble a stone forest seemed to support the weight of the entire building. Renquist decided the most diplomatic reaction was to act as if awed while quietly attempting to discover if all around him made any sense, or was just the product of an advanced undead madness. Fenrior had obviously had a very long time to think about this moment, and Renquist knew he had to take care not to confuse an understandable obsession with out-and-out insanity. The laboratory was nothing if not impressive. Great induction coils ran from floor to ceiling. Purple arcs of static electricity crackled between the poles of massive circuit breakers. Tall vacuum tubes, the size of wine casks, glowed in the confusion, and lights flashed on control panels dating back to the 1940s and the Manhattan Project. Overhead, cables drooped from ceramic insulators, looping between the stumpy stalactites created by centuries of moisture seeping down through the stonework, while more thick powerfeeds, with heavy-duty rubber sheathing, snaked across the floor. Cranks turned and gears engaged, and two thralls worked behind a concrete and cinder-block radiation screen, powering up an elderly X-ray machine. With the kind of incongruity typical of all of the Castle Fenrior, the scene was lit not only by electric bulbs and neon tubes, but also burning torches set in cressets in wall and pillar, which lent a certain flavor of an alchemist's lair from the fifteenth century.

Despite his obvious pride in his accomplishments, Fenrior allowed Renquist no time to linger or observe. He hurried to the epicenter of all the towering hardware, where, in the blaze of banked floodlights, the Urshu cocoon reposed on a raised rectangle of flat steel, which could have been an operating table or an advanced instrument of torture. Gallowglass stood looking down at the cocoon, as did two other undead with the distinctive Fenrior red hair, but dressed in contemporary clothing and white lab coats, who flanked a small, completely bald nosferatu with poached egg eyes and an Austrian accent. Fenrior didn't have to ask the nature of the problem. It was immediately obvious. The hairline cracks on the cocoon that Marieko had originally noticed inside the tomb were now gaping fissures, and viscous colorless liquid was oozing from them. Fenrior looked first to Renquist. "What do you make of this? Is this part of the process, or do we have a problem?"

Renquist was at a loss. "I'd hesitate to guess. If the cocoon was simply fragmenting, like a breaking egg, I'd say Taliesin was well on the way to some kind of consciousness, but this glop would suggest that it was trying to reseal itself. We have to face the possibility that it was damaged in transit, or even when Duncanon and his lads broke the spikes off so they could get it down the tunnel at Morton Downs."

Fenrior's aura flashed angrily. "Are you telling me I was wrong to move it."

Renquist shrugged. "I didn't have to make that judgment call. Ideally it should have been left where it was, but that would have meant leaving it to the humans, and they would definitely have moved it. On the other hand, it could merely be some kind of amnionic fluid, and the waking is proceeding quite normally. What do either of us know, after all, about the finer metamorphic details of the Urshu? I fear all we can do is once again wait."

"I've waited a long time for the Merlin to wake."

Renquist looked round at the strangely assorted technology. "How long has this place been under construction?"

"I first discussed the possibility of the wakening of an Urshu with Nikola Tesla in the early 1920s. He was still depressed at the time. His deathray experiment had blown up the Tunguska region in Siberia, the U.S. Navy had refused to believe in his robot submarine, and the electricity cartels had crushed his plans for free broadcast power. He was, however, able to design a device to draw off any surplus psychic energy."

Fenrior gestured to a tall, cylindrical, stainless-steel column topped by a perfect sphere of the same material. Renquist moved a little nearer to better see the thing and noticed small sparks of static running up and down its smooth milled surface. Fenrior spoke warningly. "Don't touch that. It carries a massive positive charge."

"You explained everything you were doing to Tesla?"

"He could hardly apply himself to the problem without knowing the facts."

"I'm surprised you confided in a human."

Fenrior laughed. "What makes you think Tesla was human?"

Renquist smiled wryly. "I often wondered."

"Of course, Wilhelm Reich was human, and he was also extremely helpful. All the work he did for me, though, was totally based on his theory of orgone energy, which I thought put too much stress on a single and not totally proven idea. I also corresponded with Fermi, but it came to nothing. Among the humans, Einstein was the biggest disappointment. He refused even to respond to my letters. I think he still felt burned in the matter of the Philadelphia Navy Yard Experiment. I would also have gone to Oppenheimer, but the FBI was so busy trying to prove him a Communist, and it seemed wise to keep away."

Fenrior led Renquist to a part of the complex where the equipment was more contemporary. "I recently had a number of lasers installed, so if the thing turns out to be uncontrollably monstrous, it can rapidly be cut to pieces."

As Fenrior continued to give Renquist the VIP tour, he began to see the undead laird in a somewhat different light. Although continuously surrounded by his Highlanders, advisers, and retainers, Fenrior was peculiarly isolated. From what Renquist had seen, few in the castle could match his education or intellect. Gallowglass was far from stupid, but academically lacking, and Renquist could hardly see the two of them talking philosophy far into the morning. Perhaps Gethsemany and others of the Seven Stars, and maybe the small Austrian filled these needs, but he still appeared gratified to have another there with whom he could discourse as an equal and demonstrate all his wonderful toys.

Renquist didn't care to guess how long the discourse and demonstration might have gone on had events not suddenly violently caught up with them. A loud crack was followed by the sound of a small moist explosion, and a piece of the cocoon's shell, about the size of a dinner plate, flew up into the air and about ten feet across the room. The first reaction by both Renquist and Fenrior was to duck for cover. Both had, in their time, been the potential targets of assassins. Half crouched, they found themselves facing each other. Renquist's mouth twisted into a rueful smile. "I think, my lord, the fireworks have commenced."

Julia drove, and Destry sat beside her. Marieko and Columbine were in the back, leaning away from each other, and with their heads resting against the interior fabric. After the feeding, everyone was naturally quiet, so it took Marieko some time to realize Columbine's eyes had, at some point, fallen shut, and she scarcely seemed conscious. Remembering her promise to Columbine not to say anything, and also not wanting to unduly alarm the two in the front, Marieko placed a soft hand on Columbine's leg. Normally a move like this would have produced an immediate reaction. Nosferatu were a cold breed who did not like to be touched without a definite purpose to the contact. To her dismay, Columbine only let out a soft, whispered whimper and failed to so much as open her eyes. Marieko shook her a little harder. This time the effect was more dramatic. Columbine groaned, opened her eyes, and suddenly sat bolt upright.

"Where the hell am I?"

Without waiting for an answer, she groaned again, and then collapsed forward with her head all but between her knees. Marieko put a hand on her shoulder, but Columbine shrugged it off as though the touch caused her pain. "Just leave me the fuck alone."

"What's wrong?"

"Something's happening to me."

"What kind of something?"

Destry glanced back. "What's going on?"

"Columbine seems to have a problem."

"Again?"

"I think this is real and serious."

Julia kept her hands on the wheel. "Shall I pull over?"

Marieko shook her head. "No, keep on driving. Stopping won't help."

"I think I've been dreaming."

"Dreaming about what?"

"I don't know. Darkness, pain, a feeling like being crushed, or drifting deep underwater."

"Do you think this is coming from the Merlin?"

"I don't know. I told you already. I don't know." She suddenly gasped. "Oh shit—"

"What?"

"This pain. It hurts—"

Destry turned in her seat. "Columbine, if this is a game, I swear I'll push you out the car."

"This game . . . as you call it . . . is fucking tearing me apart."

Marieko was as gentle as she could be. "You have to tell us what's happening to you so we can try to work out what to do."

"I don't know—that's what scares me."

Destry decided to play bad cop, even though Marieko tried to wave her off. "If you don't tell us what's wrong, we're going to look inside your mind."

The Dashwood belligerence resurfaced for a moment.

"Try that, and you won't have enough brains left to regret it."

Although Marieko disapproved of Destry's approach, she knew the fastest way to find out what ailed Columbine was to penetrate her thoughts and see for herself. "Destry's right. This all too weird. Your aura is unraveling. One of us has at least to see the surface levels."

Columbine's hand suddenly and completely unexpectedly flashed out like a talon and gripped Marieko's. "You want to see it, do you, my dear? Then taken a good look. How much of this do you think you could stand without a little unraveling?"

Marieko showed no reaction for almost a full minute; then her jaw dropped, her eyes widened, and she tried to pull away from Columbine. "Oh, no . . . no . . . no . . . let go of me . . . I can't . . ."

Columbine was weakly triumphant. "You can't? Look at it from my side. I can't, but I have to. He's only leaving me one way out of this."

She let go of Marieko's hand, and the two of them fell back into the car seat. Marieko's aura registered extreme, undisguised shock.

A second and third fragment of the cocoon had blown off with a noisy crack, and more of the clear slimy liquid was seeping from the holes. The underground laboratory was now at full function, reminding Renquist of a submarine going to action stations. Only a honking Klaxon was missing. The hairless Austrian looked urgently at Fenrior. "The readings on the orgone accumulator are right off the board, my lord."

"I suppose that rather negates Reich's theory."

"Unless, my lord, the cocoon is giving off massive waves of energy that are invisible even to us."

"Is that possible?"

"We are entering the realm where all things are possible."

Fenrior glanced at Renquist. "Dr. Morbius was the

companion of the notorious Ruthven. He managed to escape when, during their final and fatal escapades in Greece, the Orthodox Church declared poor Ruthven a *vrykolakas* and burned him in the sun."

Renquist nodded. "I knew Ruthven."

"I thought you did."

"I seem to recall he had a alienist with him who claimed to be seeking a 'cure' for vampirism."

Morbius seemed to think he could speak for himself. "I was that alienist, Herr Renquist."

Fenrior laughed. "Dr. Morbius abandoned that project many years ago. When he underwent the Change, he came to realize the last thing a vampire needed was a cure."

Gallowglass picked up an antique black rotary phone, listened for a moment, and then called to Fenrior. "Th' lads on th' hill are seein' bands o' radiation comin' fra' th' castle, pale blue fire in' big concentric rings."

Renquist wondered if Gallowglass was able to predict incoming phone calls. He had seen other nosferatu do it in moments of high stress. Fenrior, however, was more interested in his opinion of the concentric rings. Renquist considered them, but he was starting to think the lord credited him with knowing more than he did. "I still sense he's looking for something."

"You think so?"

Renquist spread his hands. "As I said before, I'm only guessing, but I have this feeling . . ."

Morbius snorted, wordless exasperation. The ex-alienist seemed unduly threatened by Renquist's presence at Castle Fenrior. He had no doubt acted as Fenrior's Dr. Stangelove for some time and was now afraid that his privileged and highly recompensed position was in jeopardy. "I cannot see, Herr Renquist, how the Urshu can be conscious, let alone sentient at this early stage of the process."

Gallowglass surprised Renquist by taking his side.

"Th' chick is conscious when i' pecks its way oot th' egg, isn't i'?"

"One can hardly equate the waking of an Urshu with the hatching of a common fowl."

Morbius was beginning to irritate Renquist. "I don't see why not. The principle is very similar."

Morbius decided to ignore Renquist and direct his next remark to Fenrior alone. "My lord, perhaps we should consider removing some of the outer casing ourselves?"

Fenrior turned to Renquist, and Renquist shook his head. "I think that's a very bad idea."

Morbius's sneer came with a heavy layer of accent. "From the man who opened the door of the burial chamber without a clue as to what might happen?"

"That's exactly why I would urge caution. I've had my fingers burned once, which makes me circumspect about sticking my hand into the fire a second time."

Morbius's tone was close to snippy. "It's easy to be knowledgeable after the fact."

Renquist's irritation boiled up into anger. "Listen, little man. When I'm asked for my opinion, I give it, strictly for what it's worth. I'm not here to debate each point with an individual who once believed in a cure for vampirism."

Fenrior intervened. "Gentlemen, gentlemen, no rancor, please. We are all working in the dark here, and all suggestions are welcome, and must be entertained, both the mundane and the outlandish."

If Fenrior wanted outlandish, Renquist was quite prepared to give it to him. "Are Columbine Dashwood and her companions still being monitored?"

Gallowglass answered. "Aye, tha' they are."

"And are they still on their way here?"

"Aye."

"Would it be possible to intercept them and bring them here as fast as possible?"

"Aye."

"Then I suggest we do exactly that. If I'm wrong, no harm will be done, but if I'm right, it could have a profound effect on the Merlin's waking."

Gallowglass looked at Fenrior. "Master Renquist ha' a point there, m' lord."

Another piece of the cocoon's outer shell came loose and crashed to the floor.

Columbine was shaking like a human. Julia gripped the steering wheel of the Range Rover with tense hands. "I think it might be best if we pulled over."

Marieko had recovered sufficiently to speak. "Just keep driving. I think Columbine's only hope is to get to the Merlin as soon as possible."

"What did you see in there?"

"It's impossible to describe. A vast sucking blackness, lights drifting but illuminating nothing, and casting no shadows. This terrible, crushing need to escape, and a feeling like falling. I swear the Urshu is pulling her to him."

Destry was leaning back, doubled over the front passenger seat. "Are you sure you're not projecting?"

"I'm sure."

Julia took her eyes off the road and glanced back. "How do we know, by going on to Fenrior, we're not just rushing into a trap?"

"We don't."

"Could you go back in there, and maybe look for something a little more concrete?"

Marieko's jaw was set. "I'm not going in there again. I've already seen enough. She's become an integral part of the Merlin's waking. I can't explain how or why, but she feels she either has to go there or perish. I think it's this link with the Merlin causing her progressively deteriorating behavior. I think he's using her as a source of energy."

Destry wasn't quite ready to buy the last part. "Columbine's always been a pill."

"But never as bad as recently."

Julia glanced quickly at Destry. "Do you think we should still go straight to Fenrior?"

Destry slid back down into her seat and nodded. "If that's what Marieko says, it's good enough for me."

"What about the horse? What about Dormandu?"

Destry cursed, but Julia was ahead of her. "The meeting place with the horse box is on the way. We proceed according to plan. If it's already there, we take it and one of us drives Dormandu to Fenrior."

"What about the driver?"

"We kill or incapacitate him."

"Simple as that?"

"Simple as that. I mean, we've hardly been covering our tracks in this trip. What's another body, more or less?"

The outer shell of the Merlin's cocoon was halfway broken away, exposing a translucent membrane, beneath which it was just possible to make out a man-shaped form. The viscous liquid had ceased to flow, and now only moisture coated the surface of the membrane. Fenrior stood close, and for the first time, Renquist saw the lord succumb to visible anxiety. His aura was suffused with worry, and he wasn't bothering to hide it. "If any record existed of an Urshu waking, we might have a clue if it was all supposed to be like this."

Morbius waxed pompous from a distance. "We all go blindly into the unknown. Such is the nature of exploration."

Fenrior snarled. "Shut the fuck up, you dwarf."

Renquist was equally at a loss, and didn't mind admitting it. Both males were totally accustomed to being both well informed and in control, but the current circumstances were beyond even their extensive experience. Those observing the waking of Taliesin had now divided into two distinct factions. Fenrior and Renquist stood alone, while those who were not monitoring the

curious assortment of instruments, were grouped around
Gallowglass. Morbius fumed because Renquist had
usurped his access to the lord, but there wasn't a damned
thing he could do about it. If he dared speak, it only got
worse. The shadows of the two groups constantly shifted
and shimmered, as bright radiation alternately surged
and faded through the underground chamber. At a fairly
regular rate, the surface of the membrane would emit a
ripple of static that would grow increasingly powerful,
until it arced off, snapping in a jagged curve to the
sphere at the top of the Tesla column. At the first of the
these, Fenrior had remarked dryly, "So Tesla was correct, even if he claimed to know less than we did."

When the cocoon had started to shed its outer shell,
the ripples had appeared completely random, but then
Gallowglass had the initiative to start timing them on his
large pocket chronometer. At first the pulses of power
had been twenty minutes apart, but then the intervals had
progressively dropped to fifteen, ten, and finally five.
The obvious correlation was that of being present at a
birth. The birth, however, was taking place in what was
rapidly becoming a sauna. The energy flow had produced a damp heat in the chamber. Renquist had removed his jacket, and Fenrior was down to his waistcoat
and jeans.

"I can't shake the feeling there's something missing.
The Urshu is throwing off this vast flow of radiation,
but is taking nothing in. Can a change of state occur
without some kind of energy intake?"

Renquist was too tired to be anything but blunt. "After
her dreams and the link your lads tracked from Morton
Downs to Ravenkeep, Columbine has to be the missing
factor."

"I'm sending out a Hummer to bring them in."

"The Hummer isn't much faster than their Range
Rover."

Fenrior smiled for the first time in a while. "No, but
my lads know the way."

"I though you'd sent them already."

"I was going to send Duncanon, but then I thought this might cause you a problem."

"It would. The lad doesn't like me."

"So I sent Shaggy Lachlan instead." Fenrior hesitated. "There was one thing I thought I should check with you first, though, Renquist."

"What's that?"

"You're saying the purpose of having Columbine here would be for the Merlin to take something from her?"

"That's precisely what I'm saying."

"Did you consider that although it might well be a benign and symbiotic exchange, it could also be completely one-sided and highly destructive to Miss Dashwood?"

Renquist's nodded. "I considered that."

"And it doesn't create any ethical issue?"

Renquist'd shrouded his aura. "I think we have to take the calculated risk."

"Even though the risk is actually incalculable?"

Renquist's voice was soft and chill. "Let's just get her here and see what happens."

An ancient nosferatu with clan tattoos covering his badly scarred face was leaning out of the passenger window of the black Hummer yelling furiously at Marieko, but his accent was so impenetrably thick, she was at a loss to know what he was saying. Then the Hummer, headlights blazing, got in front of her. It speeded up and she realized the driver was making it possible for her to go faster. He completely knew the road and could take it at a much higher speed. All Marieko had to do was follow in the after-images of his taillights. An element of danger was present, but Marieko's nosferatu reactions made it possible to follow in a way that would have caused a human to spin out on a turn or plow fatally into the back of the lead vehicle. Although she still had no idea exactly what the old Highlander had been yelling, the gist of the message seemed to be that someone in Fenrior wanted Columbine at the Castle as badly as Marieko wanted to get her there. She was, of course, leaving the horse box far behind. No way could the tall, swaying trailer-truck match the speeds of the Range Rover and the Hummer. The brief alliance of the four females was sundered into separate pairs with no means of communication between them.

Marieko, Destry, Julia, and Columbine had made it into Scotland fairly uneventfully after the bloodbath at the motel, except, of course, for Columbine mentally and physically deteriorating in the backseat. They had reached the appointed meeting place to discover the horse box carrying Dormandu was already there and waiting. The horse was decidedly put out after what he considered a swaying incarceration, but beyond that, all appeared to have gone to plan. The driver, of course, had to be incapacitated, which seemed less than strictly fair to Marieko. He was a superficially reasonable and trustworthy human who would have a great deal of trouble explaining to his employers how he had managed to mislay both horse and vehicle, and have absolutely no idea or memory of how such a thing could have happened.

Even before the rendezvous, they had decided, once they had Dormandu and the horse box, they would split their forces. Marieko knew it was against the classic tenets of strategy, but there seemed to be little choice. Bringing Dormandu had been an impulsive flourish on the part of Julia, which, so far, had proved a total hindrance, but what was done was done, and they had to live with it. Marieko, and the now sweating, shaking, and completely incoherent Columbine, would drive in the Range Rover at all speed to Fenrior and, once there, demand that she be taken immediately to the Taliesin cocoon, or whatever state of his metamorphosis the Merlin might currently occupy. Thus Marieko wasn't too concerned when, in chasing the fast-moving Hummer, she completely left the horse box behind.

The moment she had seen the Hummer coming toward her, she'd known it had to be from Fenrior Castle. Few enough of the U.S. military vehicles were on the roads of England. Tinted windows made it impossible to see inside, but her deep vision revealed four male nosferatu, and in all probability they'd been sent to intercept her. Marieko had decided not to slow the Ranger Rover as the truck approached. The encounter could only go two ways. Either these Highlanders had been sent to bring her to Fenrior as fast as possible or to prevent her from getting there. If it was the latter, slowing down would only make it easier for them, and if the intention was the former, speed was actually of the essence. The two vehicles passed close on the narrow two-lane road, each doing at least seventy. Marieko kept on going, but the Hummer immediately executed a wheel-spinning, three-point turn and came after her, placing itself neatly between the Rover and the horse box.

At first the Hummer followed her, fast, crowding her, forcing her to put the hammer down and press on the speed to prevent herself from being rear-ended. Now the speedometers of both vehicles were well into the eighties. Then, with one set of wheels on the grass verge beside the road, the Hummer had pulled abreast of her. Only advanced nosferatu driving stopped the two trucks from smashing into each other in the darkness. The confused and one-sided conversation had followed, but even though that communication failed, all had at last become clear. The Hummer was there to speed her progress, not stop her. They apparently shared a common objective.

Despite her undead skill behind the wheel, Marieko all but lost the road when she followed the racing Hummer over what turned out to the last ridge, and she had her first sight of the castle. The moon was a white-blue, blind wolf's eye in the sky, and it reflected in the still waters of the loch, from which the castle itself reared blackly on its own small island, as implacable and seeming permanent as the bedrock of its foundations. Her hands momentarily froze on the steering wheel as she felt herself transported back in time to when she'd been fresh from the Change, with a novice's angry hunger and razor energy. The Japanese fortresses of the nosferatu lords were architecturally very different to Fenrior, but the atmosphere couldn't have been more similar. Fenrior was shrouded in a cumulative psychic haze created by the presence of a large community of the undead. Such collective auras were now a rarity, largely a remembrance of the past, as the large communities of the undead vanished one by one.

The strange, lava-lamp bubbles of psychic plasma that rose lazily from somewhere under the lake to burst silently on the surface were not at all familiar, although she had seen enough at Morton Downs to know their source had to be Taliesin the Merlin, and by their color and the spasmodic way they surfaced, they left Marieko with the distinct feeling the Merlin was not in good shape. Then, as if to confirm all her theories, the same glow appeared in the backseat of the Range Rover like a sympathetic vibration, soft at first, but growing in intensity. Columbine moaned, trying to speak. Marieko could do little to help her if she was to continue driving, but she made her voice as hypnotically comforting as she could.

"Try to hang in. We'll be at the castle in a matter of minutes."

Columbine's words came out as a feeble and rasping croak. "I hate . . . to say this . . . my dear, but . . . I think I'm . . . being . . . slowly . . . destroyed."

"It's as though he can't close the final contacts, like he can't trip the last circuits . . . I don't know how to describe it . . . he's hit some obstacle that stops him from achieving full consciousness."

The outer shell had now entirely fallen away, and the

humanoid figure under the thick membrane was attempting to move, but with a feeble and uncoordinated lack of success. Even as Renquist and Fenrior watched and discussed it, the figure they all assumed was the Urshu Taliesin raised an arm, attempting to push at the membrane, as if trying to puncture or penetrate it. After about thirty seconds, the limb dropped impotently back, clearly drained of strength by the exertion. Fenrior faced Renquist. "Are you still against cutting it free?"

Renquist's experience at Morton Downs had left him convinced that to meddle with the Urshu was courting disaster, but he might well be placing too much reliance on the key to the Merlin's successful resurrection being the link with Columbine. Maybe Fenrior was right and they should try the direct and obvious approach. Without some kind of outside intervention, it was starting to look very much like Taliesin would perish in the effort of freeing himself from the cocoon. "I'm damned if I know."

"We have to do something. We could lose him."

"Perhaps if we waited until Columbine arrives. If nothing happens then, tell your lads to cut that membrane and pull him out of there."

Fenrior slowly nodded. "If nothing occurs when we bring her in, we get him out of that thing as fast as we can."

"Agreed. One chance—then you get no further argument from me."

Fenrior looked round at his Highlanders. "Do you all hear that? The moment I give the word, cut that thing free."

A few of the Highlanders looked nervous, and they touched their swords for reassurance. All in the laboratory were dealing in their own way with something well beyond the limits of their understanding. Renquist looked round at the lights and meters and discharge tubes, all the science and alternative science that had been Fenrior's contribution, and reflected on the irony that, when the chips were down, the resort was to cold sharp steel to solve the problem.

Gallowglass suddenly reached for the black rotary phone. He listened for a moment and then nodded. "Aye. I'll tell him."

"Tell him what?"

"Tha' were Shaggy Lachlan, m' lord. Th' Dashwood lass is i' th' castle."

Fenrior turned to Renquist. "Now we shall see."

Columbine seemed to recover with an unbelievable rapidity the moment she set foot inside the castle. She and Fenrior might be neither friends nor allies, but she seemed to find strength from the walls that had protected so many undead for so long. Marieko was relieved at the recovery, but not merely out of concern for Columbine. Such a marked improvement after simply entering the confines of Fenrior did a lot to confirm Marieko's theory that Columbine's collapse, and even her increasingly erratic behavior over the past weeks, were inextricably linked with the waking of the Merlin. To be proved right did a lot to offset Marieko's natural fear of entering the enclosed and ancient with little idea of what might happen next.

The Hummer and the Range Rover had roared through the village on the shore of the loch so fast, Marieko had no chance to observe Fenrior's preserve of domesticated humans. Just an impression of buildings, and then over the causeway and onto the bridge. Rings of blue iridescence rose to welcome or perhaps scrutinize the Hummer as it approached the castle's great main gates. The same thing happened to the Range Rover, and Marieko was both relieved and encouraged that she and Columbine were not immediately rejected by the fortress's radiant, defensive magic. The tall iron reinforced gates swung wide to admit the Hummer and remained open until Marieko was also inside. She found herself in a large central courtyard with high granite walls rising on all four sides. She brought the Range Rover to a stop beside the Hummer and wondered what her next move should be. A line of Highlanders was drawn up facing the two trucks, and Marieko thought she recognized two or three of those who had come to Ravenkeep with Gallowglass to kidnap Renquist. For a force so hard, wild, and unkempt, they maintained a fairly strict formation, suggesting they might be an honor guard instead of simply just a guard.

The ancient Highlander with the scarred and tattooed face dismounted from the Hummer, and Marieko wondered if she should do the same. Before she could make that decision, Columbine made it for her, opening the rear door, climbing swiftly out, and facing the rank of Highlanders with an air of impatient authority and a complete lack of any visible fear or trepidation. He voice was clear and strong in the night air, in total contrast to the enfeebled whisper of just minutes earlier. "I don't know who's in charge here, but I demand to be immediately taken to Taliesin the Merlin, or failing that, the Lord Fenrior himself."

A Highlander somewhat shorter than the rest stepped forward from the line and advanced on Columbine. "I am Goneril o' th' Seven Stars, an' delegated Captain o' th' Nightwatch. M' orders are exactly tha'. You will be conducted straight t' th' Lord."

Hearing her voice, Marieko realized the guard captain was female, and was somewhat gratified that Fenrior not only included females among his sword bearers, but had also elevated at least one to a position of command. Two taller Highlanders moved to flank Goneril. They carried burning torches that cast menacing shadows, but Columbine refused to be intimidated. "The Lord Fenrior should know me."

"Indeed he does, Mistress Dashwood."

"And my companion, Mistress Matsunaga?"

"She is also expected."

*   *   *

Renquist and Fenrior both turned as the party of five entered the chamber. Goneril, boots ringing on flags and hand on the hilt of her claymore, led the way, with Columbine and Marieko behind her, and two Highlanders bringing up the rear. Columbine advanced, brisk and businesslike. "Fenrior, Renquist, I would not have forced myself into your—"

Then Columbine saw the Merlin, bathed in light, beneath the so far unyielding membrane, and the sight left her, both figuratively and literally, gasping for breath. For a moment she seemed to regather herself. ". . . I would not . . ."

Again, though, her emotional footing was lost. "I . . ."

A flash of static fountained up from the Merlin, as if, as far as Columbine was concerned, their eyes had met across the legendary crowded room. For her, a love of the strangest kind filled the chamber of technology with a roseate psychic flush, and the illusion spilled over to all who were present. Sparkling plasma particles performed a drifting waltz before being drawn either to the Tesla coil or the orgone accumulator. Fluttering, birdlike hallucinations wing-whispered in the arches of the chamber roof. Lilting combinations of harps and flutes were indistinct but audible, until a second eruption of energy rose from the Merlin. Instead of drifting aimlessly, this one circled Columbine with a deliberate sense of purpose. As Renquist noticed this new control of the energy flow, the hallucinations vanished and the musical sounds ceased, as though whatever synergy was present had tightened its focus so the flow was strictly between Columbine and Taliesin.

She swayed for a second as though about to fall, but Marieko moved quickly forward and placed a steadying hand on her arm. The touch instantly brought her back from wherever she had been, but during her absence, an unmistakable change had taken place. She snarled at Marieko. "Get your Jap hands off me!"

Her eyes had turned piggy. She was greedy, and she

wanted it. She wanted it worse than any want she had
experienced, even if she had no clear idea of what *it*
might be. Somehow the Merlin had infused her with an
overpowering, and, Renquist guessed, a very unhealthy
desire. She moved toward the membrane that shrouded
the Urshu with both the longing and hesitation of a virgin bride. If Renquist hadn't seen it, he would not have
believed it. She stretched out her arms as though to her
long-awaited lover. Renquist quickly shouted a warning,
reinforcing it with a strong mental command. "Wait,
don't touch it!"

Columbine halted and turned. She was angry. "Don't
use the voice on me, Victor."

"You must not touch that thing."

"It's not a thing, Victor. It's Taliesin. And why
shouldn't I touch him? Soon he and I will be one."

"You know nothing about it."

Columbine's aura was drifting and indistinct. Her eyes
had become peculiar—unfocused and distant. "Oh, yes,
Victor, I know, I know. Soon I will be the consort of
the Merlin, and you will no longer be needed."

Fenrior took a step back, deferring to Renquist. "I
think I'll leave this one to you."

Marieko was also staring at Columbine, amazed and
disturbed that, at such a momentous instant, she could
take time out to play Victor against Merlin. Her mind
had to be crumbling. Meanwhile Columbine glared vin-
dictively at Renquist. He knew she could be both vicious
and infantile, and at times unstable, but contact with the
Urshu appeared to have sparked a dangerous and overwhelming insanity. "That's why you don't want me to
touch him, isn't it, Victor?"

"Try and detach from this, Columbine. You're putting
yourself at great risk."

Columbine merely laughed. "Does it bother you that
the Merlin is now the object of my attention? Or that he
should chose me as a mate and partner, Victor?"

"That's ridiculous."

"Is it?"

"Patently so. The Merlin is not even one of us, Columbine. You can't be his consort because you and he are not of the same species." He glanced at Fenrior. "We have to stop her."

Fenrior's expression was bleak behind his dark glasses. "Do we, Victor? She's gone this far, let her take it to the conclusion. You've warned her. That's all that can be expected of you."

Columbine laughed. It was definitely the laughter of madness. "You don't want me to touch him because now he has the hold on me and you don't."

And at that point, Renquist gave up. Fenrior was right. They had come that far. Let her take it to the conclusion. "I never had a hold on you. I wasn't even interested in you. Go ahead, Columbine, embrace your Merlin."

Columbine took one more step and it was as though a trap had been sprung. No fireworks and no radiance. Columbine's very being was simply drawn into the Merlin. At first it was as though all pigmentation had been leeched out of her body. Her clothing retained its color, but her flesh turned to a greyshade monochrome. Second to go was all trace of moisture. Her body took on the dry and fragile rigidity of a plaster statue. Finally what was left of the physical form of Columbine Dashwood gave up its structural integrity. It was no longer able to support itself. The weight of her ring snapped a dead finger—the ring with the large single ruby in the elaborate art nouveau claw setting. It hit the stone floor, bounced twice, and then rattled to silence. The fabric of her dress pulled down on her shoulders. Collar bones snapped like petrified twigs. Skin cracked and powdered. An arm fell loose. Her head sagged forward, her neck fragmented, and the head rolled and fell, striking the flagstones with a thud of soft horror, and a final disintegration left nothing but dust and ringleted hair. The large bones in her legs were the last to go, but then they, too, gave way, and her dress and underthings deflated to the floor, leaving nothing but grey powder and discarded clothes.

Marieko let out a short gasp of a kind that required immense control not to be a full-blown scream. Goneril's eyes widened in a way that suggested her mind was completely out of its depth. The other Highlanders demonstrated the same reaction as jaw muscles tensed and knuckles whitened on the hilts of their swords. The experience had temporarily paralyzed everyone in the chamber, and although it may have been an illusion, even the grind and crackle of the electronic and mechanical hardware seemed to drop to little more than a soft hum. When he finally broke the silence, Victor managed, with a great effort, to sound almost detached. "I didn't expect it to destroy her."

Fenrior was in immediate agreement. "None of us did."

But Marieko knew, from the way they avoided looking at each other, Renquist and Fenrior had suspected and maybe discussed the possibility of Columbine's destruction, if only as a worst-case scenario. Otherwise what had that final exchange been all about letting her take it to the conclusion? "You're a pair of elevated immortal hypocrites. You knew what might happen. She was one of my troika, damn you both!"

Before either could answer, Morbius created a much needed distraction by darting forward to collect a sample of the powder that had once been Columbine Dashwood. Fenrior cuffed him hard across the side of the head with his clenched fist. "Be still, you creature!"

The blow sent the small nosferatu sprawling across the flagstones. One of the Highlanders bent down and, grasping Morbius by the collar, hauled him to his feet, and maybe the judgment of his lord, but while he was nursing the pains in his head and hip, he, too, was blessed with a saving distraction.

Taliesin ripped the membrane.

Fingers split the sticky elastic film, and a seemingly human right hand thrust itself free, glistening wetly in the concentration of light. The body inside the glutinous sac summoned up a mighty heave, and an entire arm and shoulder burst free. Fenrior looked quickly to Gallowglass. "Bring the lasers up to power."

"They a'ready are, m' lord."

"What would I do without you?"

"Sometimes I wonder."

The Urshu's left hand had now reached around and tugged at the hole created by the right arm and shoulder. Ducking and butting it pushed its head loose. The membrane, once breached, seem to tear more and more easily. Marieko had heard the word *lasers*, but hadn't understood what Fenrior meant. The Urshu was now up on its knees clawing the membrane down over its chest. Fenrior gestured to Gallowglass. "Fire on my signal, but not before."

Gallowglass. "Aye. I hear ye."

Enlightenment dawned on Marieko, and it was immediately followed by an intense anger. Fenrior intended to use lasers to destroy the Urshu, presumably if he decided it was dangerous or unmanageable. The idea of casually cutting up so unique a being on nothing more than some antiquated feudal lord's order struck her as so fundamentally ignorant and immoral. "You fool, you can't kill him!"

Marieko had little or no idea what she intended to do when she launched herself at Fenrior. She only knew she had to stop him from killing the Merlin. That Goneril was able to block her was probably her salvation. As she staggered to one side, Fenrior spun round. "You dare to call me a fool deep inside my own castle?"

Marieko leaned on a pillar and pushed herself upright. Fenrior loomed over her, but she could only point at Taliesin. "Just look at it! It's beautiful! He's more than all of us put together."

*   *   *

"Fahg alsi hudi ilanit ilani ill-ia. Salalu kallatum rabuti, Tezcatilpoca-he?"

Renquist stood stunned at the silent center of chaos. He had become the eye of the storm. On his left, Fenrior and Marieko wrestled and screamed at each other. Gallowglass stood at the laser controls ready to slice the Urshu into superanimate fillets, while on his right, the Merlin spoke demandingly to him in a language he couldn't understand.

"Salalu kallatum rabuti, Tezcatilpoca-he? Tezcatilpoca-he?"

Only he *could* understand it! He was hearing a mutilated version of the Old Speech, more complicated, a larger vocabulary, more intricate verb and sentence structures. He knew in an instant what it was. The nosferatu Old Speech was the military form, tailored to the Original Beings. Taliesin was speaking the version of the Urshu. Most probably the purist form of the language the Nephilim had imposed on their creations. Feeling uncomfortably like an unversed hick, Renquist attempted to reply. No, the Merlin had not woken among the followers of Tezcatilpoca, but perhaps their distant descendants.

"Mensushu kalatum alsi adani-ia rabuti, Tezcatilpoca. Nee habbi nabbut sallalkm."

He hoped from the Merlin's response to glean how much had been retained and how much had been lost in the translation. Unfortunately, at the same time, Fenrior had hurled Marieko to the ground, and was simultaneously signaling to Gallowglass at the controls of the lasers. Renquist's only option was to scream. "Don't fire! I can handle this! Whatever you do, don't fire!"

Fenrior ignored him. "Are you ready, Gallowglass?"

"Aye."

"NO!"

Renquist's shout was enough to stay Gallowglass's hand despite the orders of his laird, but Taliesin speaking immediately afterwards, in perfectly modulated English, also had its effect. "Don't kill me yet, Lord Fenrior. Believe me, there is much I can teach you."

The Merlin stood upright, naked, superior, and proud. He was slim, slight, beautiful, idealized and golden, and Renquist realized to his amazement that what he was seeing was an idealized version of the young David Bowie. Where could the Merlin access not only a memory but a highly romanticized memory of a performer of the 1970s? It made no sense, and apparently made no sense to the others in the room, except he could see some of the Highlanders were fighting down a primitive fear. That the Urshu was speaking English completed the puzzle for Renquist. The Merlin had swallowed Columbine Dashwood whole. He had her language centers, her memory, and for all Renquist knew, a huge amount of extraneous nonsense. Taliesin had used Columbine to power himself up, and this also may well have meant the Merlin had treated himself to a major inoculation of the imprecise, the greedy, the shallow, and the pragmatically devious. The David Bowie figure gave it all away. It was one of the outward appearances Columbine favored in her young human playthings, and Taliesin could only have taken it directly from whatever might be left of her.

The Merlin must have somehow sensed from Renquist or one of the others that he had chosen the wrong disguise. What might be appealing to the last shards of Columbine Dashwood's taste and personality would hardly pass as plausible with Renquist, Fenrior, Marieko, or the Highlanders. The gold tarnished to a more realistic aura. The body broadened and the look quickly became less than narcissistically perfect, character built quickly in the face, until it was aged, wise, all-knowing, and yet infinitely compassionate. The hair grew long and white and cascaded down the Urshu's back. Bushy eyebrows formed as a thatch above tired eyes that had seen it all, and the hands grew larger and more capable. All in all, the Urshu had redesigned and transformed himself into something very close to what he'd been previously: the Merlin of lay and legend, folklore and the classics, Tennyson, Malory, and Marion Zimmer Bradley. With this one initial error, however, he had demonstrated, at least to Renquist, the surface had very little to do with what lay beneath.

Taliesin's conversion to his more traditionally accepted outward appearance also brought an infusion of calm to the room. The Highlander's released Morbius, Goneril lowered her sword, Marieko crawled to a safe distance from Fenrior and got back to her feet. Fenrior himself turned and faced the Merlin. "You are Taliesin the Merlin?"

"I was once."

"I am Fenrior of Fenrior."

"That much I already know."

Renquist felt it was time to interpose a question, and also that he should formulate the question in a way that told the others something of the nature of the being with which they were now dealing. "You have read our memories already?"

The Merlin stared at Renquist, smiling indulgently, but at the same time, Renquist could feel himself being assessed as a potential adversary. "Only that of Columbine Dashwood."

"Are you aware you totally destroyed her? You reduced her to ash."

The Merlin looked mildly regretful. "That was unfortunate."

Marieko was unwilling to let the Merlin off so lightly. "Unfortunate? Did you hear what Victor said? You destroyed her. You destroyed her immortality."

The Merlin tried for a little more sincerity in his regret. "I wasn't aware I was dealing with the more than mortal. As I said, that was unfortunate. But there must always be at least one sentient being sacrificed each time I wake. It's an unavoidable dictate of my survival. The kindling spark that empowers me has to be taken from

another. You people . . . what do you call yourselves?
You nosferatu? You should fully comprehend that kind
of need."

The Highlanders and technicians had now mostly recovered from the shock that had started with the rising
of the Urshu and culminated in the wasting of Columbine. They didn't, however, return to their posts, but
continued to stand and stare at the principal players.
Only Gallowglass still manned the bank of lasers that
were Fenrior's fail safe. "D' ye still wan' me t' use these
m' lord?"

Fenrior quickly shook his head. As far as Renquist
could tell, the laird had done a complete about-face in
his attitude to the Merlin, and now only acted anxious
to please. "No, Gallowglass. You can power down. For
now, Taliesin the Merlin is the guest of Fenrior and will
be extended all the formal courtesies."

The Merlin gestured to his total state of undress. "Perhaps the formal courtesies should start with giving me
something to wear. I know we come into this world naked, but I feel at something of a disadvantage."

"Damn me! Will you look at that?" Without thinking,
Destry had slammed on the brakes of the horse box.
Both she and Julia were tossed forward, and from behind
them, Dormandu protested angrily. The great Uzbek stallion had been cooped up for far too long and was building a head of wrathful steam. Right at that moment,
though, her prized mount was not her first consideration.
The loch on the far side of the Castle Fenrior seemed to
be on fire from beneath. The valley was lit up with a
submarine aurora glowing from the bottom of the loch;
indistinct hallucinatory objects and shapeless hostile
things swam around it, and in the middle of the bright
but sluggish vortex was the unique emptiness left by the
passing of a nosferatu. "I think something's happened to
Columbine. I can't feel her anymore."

Julia continued to stare at the psychic flares in the

depths of the loch. "I think we should leave the horse box right here."

Destry bridled. "I'm not leaving Dormandu."

"I didn't say anything about leaving Dormandu. Just the horse box. I don't want to drive up to the gates of Fenrior with everyone inside alerted and waiting for us. We'll go the rest of the way quietly and on foot."

"We're going on?"

Julia sighed. "Do we have any choice?"

Moving the horse box off the road, calming and then saddling Dormandu, and selecting essentials from their luggage that might be easily carried without making either themselves or the horse unwieldy beasts of burden consumed ten or fifteen minutes, and then Destry and Julia set off on what surely had to be the final leg of their journey. The narrow road zigzagged down the side of the glen leading to a village on the lakeshore before it turned into the causeway and bridge that would bring a traveler to the castle. Destry sniffed the air and used her deep vision. "Humans in the village?"

"We knew Fenrior maintained a reserve of humans. Did you think he kept them in hutches like tame rabbits?"

"Do you think they pose any kind of problem?"

Julia laughed. "Everything else we encounter seems to pose a problem, but logically they shouldn't be a source of trouble. They should be accustomed to the nocturnal comings and goings of nosferatu. Unless, of course, Fenrior has trained them as watchdogs, the way some cultures use geese."

Destry managed to smile ruefully. "But the only way to find out is to keep going and see what happens?"

"You said it, sweetheart."

And so Destry and Julia continued on down the hill, two females leading a huge black horse.

"You say Arthur died in 539?"

"As the Christian priests calculated time."

Gallowglass sniffed. "They still calculate i' th' same
way. Th' bastards ha' a lock on th' calendar, an' tha's
not all, by a long sight."

Taliesin looked shocked. "Christianity still survives?"

"It not only survives. It grows and prospers and be-
comes more blasphemously absurd year by year."

The Merlin shook his head. "I never understood how
Christianity managed to take and maintain such a hold.
As a religion, it seemed so damned . . . nebulous."

Renquist laughed. "Its strength has always been in its
nebulousness. The Christians have been able to adapt to
anything, most recently they began to use television to
spread their poison. They're also able to justify any
atrocity in the name of their God, from the Crusades to
the Inquisition and witch-burning, to the military-
industrial complex and nuclear weapons. When a priest
can bless an atom bomb, you know he'll bless anything."

Marieko felt the need to interject. "Of course, we are
maybe not the most objective observers of the Christian
religion. It is, after all, totally dedicated to our complete
annihilation."

Taliesin rolled his eyes as if it were all too much for
him. "I have a great deal of history to learn."

He was now comfortably dressed in a white kimono
with gold trim, and Turkish slippers, and had started to
look a little priestly himself. Dressing the Merlin had not
been easy. He had refused a plaid to which he was not
entitled. He appeared under the illusion that the whole
world operated on the same principles as the Castle Fenrior, and plaids had a universal significance. He obviously knew nothing of golfers, grunge rockers, soccer
hooligans, or horse blankets. The net result was that
none of the Highlander's clothing was acceptable. The
Merlin was approximately the same height as Fenrior,
but his broader chest and greater girth precluded very
much borrowing from the lord's extensive wardrobe. After some searching and assistance from the Lady Gethsemany, the kimono had been brought out, a gift from

some visiting Japanese undead, descendants of the
Kenzu, Marieko suspected.

When no longer naked, the Merlin had changed his
tune and commenced to complain about the cumulative
hunger of the past fifteen hundred years, and it was discovered that both his needs and tastes were so close to
those of a human, the difference hardly deserved comment. Lacking anything that even approached a repast
from Camelot in its prime, the larders of the darklost
were ruthlessly raided, and Taliesin was presented with
a tray of delicacies all of which were completely unfamiliar to him. In the matter of food, Columbine's memory was of very little use to him, and he consumed
canned sardines, picked pigs' feet, angel cake, salami,
jelly doughnuts, pork pies, all washed down with beer,
Coca-Cola, and strong black coffee, with the complete
lack of discrimination of the wholly ignorant. It was
hard, though, for Renquist or any of the other nosferatu
to know just how ignorant. Taliesin, after dressing, revealed no aura.

The challenge of finding a suitable outfit and acceptable victuals for Taliesin had caused the party to adjourn
from the underground lab with its monster mechanisms
to a spaciously elegant but windowless room in Fenrior's
private suite. Those invited to follow Fenrior and Taliesin were kept to a short list, just Renquist, Marieko,
and Gallowglass. Morbius had again been excluded. The
Lady Gethsemany joined them during the search for
clothes, but remained for the ensuing discussion and
proved herself the best read in the subject of England in
the fifth and sixth century.

"So you retired to hibernate after the death of Arthur?"

The Merlin munched greedily on a Cadbury's Chocolate Flake, an act that caused a certain queasiness on
the part of some of those present. Some undead simply
could not stand to watch a human eat. "That's how it
worked out, but the fall of Arthur wasn't the direct

cause. My natural time was, of course, close. We Urshu do not just curl up and slumber for a few centuries because our plans have been reversed or the going is rough. I doubted I would survive the Rain of Western Fire and the Dark Skies."

Fenrior frowned. "The what?"

The Merlin stared at the lord in amazement. "You ask what? The comet was probably the most important event of the entire millennium. More significant even than the fall of Rome."

Comprehension dawned on Gethsemany. "The comet impact? The one that supposedly struck the Earth in A.D. 540 and compounded the darkness of the Dark Ages?"

"You do know about it?"

"Human archaeologists have only just presented the first evidence in support of the theory, and it's still opposed by the majority of the archeological community."

Marieko scowled. "That's because the majority of the archaeological community is composed of individuals like William Campion."

The Merlin looked puzzled. "I'm sorry, but who is William Campion?"

"He's the one who started digging you up in the first place."

"So what would this William Campion say about the comet impact?"

This time Gethsemany supplied the answer. "He would deny it happened because no factual record exists."

"How could records be kept when there was no one to keep them?"

"Campion wouldn't see it that way."

Gethsemany leaned forward with the intensity of a true student of history. "So what did happen after the comet impact? What exactly were the Rain of Western Fire and the Dark Skies?"

The Merlin sampled a slice of salami, dipped it in orange marmalade, and leaned back in his chair. "You have to realize that, after the fall of Rome, European civilization was shaky but still basically viable."

As the Merlin spoke Renquist noted in passing how quickly the outlandish could become cozily urbane. Was it yet another paradox of nosferatu changeability, or did it go deeper? Was this what happened when the potentially immortal got together? One minute they would be issuing orders to cut each other to pieces with lasers, and the next, they were discussing European prehistory with extreme gentility. To say the company was an unparalleled mixture in an unprecedented environment was an understatement of apocalyptic proportions. Five nosferatu and a Urshu, all products of ancient alien genetic experiments, sitting in comfortable late Victorian leather furniture amid hanging lamps and art nouveau decor could never have happened anywhere or at any time previously. The scene had to be unique in infinity.

"Then the comet came, all remaining viability ceased. The humans called it the Rain of Western Fire. A dust cloud enveloped the Earth for a full seven years. That was the Dark Skies. Crops failed, wild and domestic animals died. Humanity was gripped by a paroxysm of kill or be killed. Famine and disease were all powerful. All across Europe and Asia, armed bands from starving and disintegrating armies roamed the countryside, preying on the weak and burning all that wasn't edible. It was a time of unconcealed horror, when the worst excesses of desperation became the basics of survival. Cannibalism was rife, and it was then I decided to repair to the bolt-hole I'd prepared for myself at Morton Downs and wait for a less disastrous age."

Marieko avoided looking at the Merlin as he followed the chocolate with a spoonful of Stilton. "Those were Columbine's dreams. Were you sending them to her deliberately?"

The Merlin wiped crumbs of cheese from his mouth. "I may have been sending those memories, but not deliberately. My contact with the unfortunate Miss Dash-

wood was purely random. She just happened to have
been at hand."

Marieko's mouth became very small. "It's that word
again. *Unfortunate*."

Renquist intervened before Marieko could start on
Taliesin about the destruction of Columbine. "And I suppose you know nothing of what has transpired in the
world since the sixth century?"

The Merlin nodded. "As I said, I have a great deal of
history to learn before I can tell what my new purpose
will be here on this planet."

"Purpose? What do you mean purpose? We nosferatu
have no purpose. We simply are. Humanity definitely
has no purpose. In fact, recent models have suggested
human behavior patterns here on Earth conformed more
to those of a highly destructive virus than any ecologically integrated species. Why does an Urshu need a purpose?"

"We were designed by Marduk Ra as the guardians
of humankind. Their shepherds, if you like. Back before
I slept, I was restricted to working within the very narrow confines of the time. I was primarily concerned in
supporting Arthur Pendragon against the invading Saxons and slowing the spread of Christianity by aiding the
Druids. In this age of mass communication, I believe I
can work on a much broader, a much more global canvas, as was first intended."

Renquist began to grow irritated with the Merlin's absolute certainty in the supposed infallibility of himself
and Marduk Ra. "How can you be so sure such an intention is still valid? Marduk Ra made a great many
mistakes, including coming to Earth in the first place.
The ancestors of the nosferatu were such a grievous error, he attempted to eradicate them with every advanced
weapon at his disposal. Human beings are a mess of
defects. To say the least, the God King tended to fuck
up."

The Merlin's face became prim, bordering on angry.

"In the case of the Urshu, Marduk Ra made no mistake."

The nosferatu in the room exchanged significant glances, and Renquist felt that perhaps, if he'd been a little less sure of himself, Marduk Ra, and the manifest destiny of the Urshu, the Merlin might have taken the note of warning.

Aside from appearing somewhat shabby, the village of Fenrior was nothing out of the ordinary and, in the dead of night, showed no signs that it was under the absolute control of an undead overlord. The village pub, The Red Hand, seemed perfectly normal, as did the red phone box and the general store. Advertisements for cigarettes, soft drinks, frozen foods, and photographic film covered its frontage, and were only remarkable in that they seemed a trifle out of date. All that appeared to be missing were any of the usual signs for newspapers—the *Sun*, the *Mirror*, the *Glasgow Herald*, and the *Scotsman*—which ordinarily would be on sale in a village shop of this kind. Perhaps the laird discouraged too much news from the outside world. Destry glanced up at the roofs of the two-story terrace houses in the main street and saw no TV aerials or the small satellite dishes that now covered most of residential Britain. The village apparently existed in a state of enforced isolation.

The slow clop of Dormandu's hooves echoed back from the silent walls of the buildings, and Destry looked round for any sign of movement at the curtained windows. "It's so damned quiet."

"I doubt Fenrior likes his thralls to be roaming the night."

"It seems scarcely possible such a place could exist in this day and age."

"It's that very impossibility that allows it to survive. The truth is so fantastic, no human from the outside would ever believe it." Julia softly grasped Destry's hand. "Isn't that what saves us all, my sweet?"

"I suppose so, but you have to admit this place is well

beyond the unconventional. Do you think they ever come here?"

"Who?"

"Humans from the outside. Tourists, travelers?"

"I'm sure they do, now and again. Every so often a busload of Japanese probably takes a wrong turn and finishes up here. They find the place quaint, take their inevitable photographs, and move on. They probably even take pictures of the castle, assuming it's a picturesque abandoned ruin."

"And what about mailmen, and government officials, and delivery drivers? What the hell do they think?"

"I'm sure Fenrior has all that under total control. In Los Angeles, we even live on a road that's no longer marked on the maps. Victor is very clever about things like that, and I'm sure Fenrior is just the same. I sometimes think males make too much of secrecy and security. It's been my experience humans will believe pretty much anything if you give them half a chance."

Destry suddenly let go of Julia's hand. "But I don't believe this."

On the final stretch of the main street of the village, with its pub and its shop sloped quite steeply down to the shore of the loch, and coming up the incline toward them was what could only be the Fenrior village constable. The man was fleshy and audibly out of breath, and wore a flat Scottish-style peaked cap with the checkered band rather than the English-style Victorian helmet, but he was pushing a bicycle, and his uniform looked to be fifty years out of date. At the sight of Destry, Julia, and Dormandu, he stopped dead in his tracks and stared at them in amazement. Destry leaned close to Julia. "Do you think he knows what we are?"

"I don't think so. And he doesn't need to know unless it's positively to our advantage."

The constable took almost a minute to recover from his initial shock and find his voice. "So what do we have

here, wandering about in the night? Are you lassies
lost?"

Julia shook her head. "No, Officer, we're not lost."

"Is that an American accent?"

Julia wasn't ready for this. "Is that a Scottish accent?"

The constable seemed to miss the slight mockery.
"I've heard Americans talking at the picture show."

The picture show? In what century did Fenrior keep
his thralls? "Then you probably recognize us for what
we are?"

Destry looked sharply at Julia. What was she up to?

"I'm sorry, miss, I don't know what you're talking
about."

Julia giggled, a parody of a flighty human. "We're
two gal-pals on a horseback vacation."

"My best advice to you is to turn yourselves around
and go back the way you came. This street goes to the
water and stops. It's a dead end here."

"What about the castle? It was our intention to spend
the day at the castle."

"No, miss. No one goes to the castle. It's not safe."

"It will be safe for us."

"Don't make me have to take action, miss. No one
goes anywhere near the castle. That's the law."

"The law doesn't apply to us, Constable."

"I'm warning you, miss, I don't want to—"

Julia silently gave Destry the signal. "It's time to let
him have it."

Destry and Julia revealed what they truly were. To the
constable, their eyes would appear to glow a deadly and
hellish scarlet. At the same time, Dormandu snorted and
tossed his head. The constable didn't fall to his knees,
but, in every other way, he groveled. "I—I—I—I—"

"Yes, we know. You're sorry and you're scared, but
we won't harm you if you just get out of our way."

"I—I—didn't know."

"Just let us pass, and we'll say nothing to the lord."

The constable scuttled to one side and then watched,

stunned, as Julia, Destry, and the huge black stallion walked past him, ignoring his very existence.

"Although we are in no position to dictate what you should do, I would strongly recommend you remain here as our guest for a time. At least until you've caught up with all the changes in human civilization."

"You think there's a great culture shock waiting for me out there?"

Fenrior nodded emphatically. "I do, indeed."

Marieko was taking an increasing dislike to Taliesin, and she hardly bothered to conceal it. "Perhaps you should have consumed a being who was more informed than Columbine. It might have better prepared you for the changes."

The Merlin was using his fingers, stuffing Heinz Baked Beans into his mouth with a determined gluttony. Red-brown sauce had dripped on his previously white kimono. Sucking his fingers and wiping his chin, he ignored Marieko and nodded toward Renquist. "Will he also remain?"

"Of course, if I'm needed."

The Merlin laughed and washed down the beans with a local soda pop called Tizer. "If you're needed? Of course you'll remain. You wouldn't miss a chance to study a real live Urshu. I understand you, Victor Renquist."

Renquist might have imagined Taliesin as a pig, but he was carefully editing his imagination. He was rapidly becoming convinced that Fenrior and the others were seriously underestimating the Urshu, with the possible exception of Marieko, who was positively simplistic in her undisguised loathing. The Merlin might be busily creating the impression of an uncouth slob on the far side of disgusting, but Renquist still remembered when he had first woken and assumed the golden Bowie form. The Urshu was as immortal as any nosferatu, and certainly as powerful, if not more so. He might even be able to read minds. Renquist was quite convinced the thing swilling soda pop and spilling beans on itself was just another illusion designed to keep them collectively off balance. The only advantage the five nosferatu had was that Taliesin knew next to nothing about the world into which he had awakened, and the only deception open to them was to keep him convinced they were buying his act.

The Merlin was again pawing through the platter of assorted snacks, seeking an even more gross combination and supposedly considering Fenrior's suggestion he remain at the castle until he was prepared for the complexities of the outside world. "You have books and things that I could study?"

Renquist knew Fenrior was about to boast of the size of his library, but Gethsemany preempted him. "We not only have books. Since I prevailed upon my lord, we also have television."

"Television?" The Merlin spoke the word experimentally, as though there might be danger even in uttering it. "What is television?"

"Descriptions are pointless. You need to see it for yourself."

"When can I see one?"

Gethsemany smiled. She was able to play the charming hostess under just about any circumstances. The party seemed about to move, taking Merlin to the nearest TV set, when a discreet knock on the door caused them all to turn.

"Enter."

Goneril stood in the doorway. "I'm sorry t' disturb ye at such a crucial time m' lord, but there's a problem on th' causeway."

"A problem?"

"Duncanon has detained two foreign nosferatu."

Marieko stood up. "That will be Destry and Julia."

Renquist was gripped by a feeling of rapidly sinking. "Julia?"

"She intends to rescue you."

"The last thing I need right now is to be rescued by Julia."

A dozen Highlanders, strung out across the causeway with drawn claymores, were clearly no coincidence. They were waiting for something, and Destry had little doubt they were waiting for her and Julia. The constable may have groveled and scuttled, but he must also have relayed word to the castle of the strange nosferatu on their way through the village with their black horse. "I don't like the look of this at all."

Julia concentrated. "I can sense Victor and Marieko inside the castle, but not Columbine."

Destry scanned the sky. The moon was setting behind the mountains. "I fear we have less than an hour before dawn."

Julia took a deep breath. "It would appear we have three options. We confront them, we surrender and throw ourselves on the Lord Fenrior's mercy, or we flee."

Dormandu whickered, and Destry quieted him. Perhaps he remembered the Highlanders from the confrontation at Ravenkeep. "I've never thrown myself on anyone's mercy—neither human nor nosferatu."

Julia was staring at the wild Highlanders, and Destry realized this was the first time she had ever seen them in their rough barbarian glory. "And how would you categorize these creatures?"

"Oh, they're definitely nosferatu. They may be uncouth, unkempt, and some are downright filthy in their personal habits, but they are definitely our kind."

Julia looked grimly down the causeway. "I find that hard to believe."

"You'd better believe it. It would be a big mistake to dismiss them as just crude or stupid."

Julia and Destry were both unarmed, something they not only regretted, but also for which they had only themselves to blame. Columbine had insisted on packing a selection of steel, but it was still in the Range Rover. No one had thought to place even a pair of weapons in the horse box when the four had parted company. Even so, to match swords with so many Highlanders would have been nothing short of suicidal.

"You had better mount up."

"What?"

"You said you didn't care to surrender, and I am not about to turn tail and run, so you'd better get on that horse of yours. If we're going, we might as well go in style."

Destry again had to gentle Dormandu, who sensed trouble on the wind. "And where exactly are we going?"

"The only place we can go. Into the castle."

Destry glanced back at the village. "Maybe we could hide in one of the houses until sunset comes again?"

Julia sighed. Destry really wasn't thinking. "And wait for Fenrior's thralls to search us out and drive stakes through the pair of us while it's still daylight?"

Destry slowly nodded. She placed one foot in the stirrup and swung herself up into the saddle. "So what exactly is our intention?"

"To bluff or brazen it out. That's all we have left."

The two of them moved slowly out onto the causeway, Julia walking slightly in front of Destry on Dormandu. A single Highlander, clean shaved and slightly neater than his fellows, stepped out in front of the line, but otherwise the Highlanders didn't move. "Let's hope we look sharp enough to make an impression. It's always been claimed that courage impresses the primitive. Although I have observed it sometimes pisses them off."

Julia quickened her pace, and Destry urged Dormandu forward. The young Highlander in front of the others allowed them to come about fifty paces, and then he held up a hand. "Tha's quite far enough, lassies."

Julia didn't stop, and Destry took that as her cue to keep Dormandu moving. As a measure of command came into Julia's voice, her German accent also deepened. "And who might I be addressing?"

"Ye're addressin' Duncanon o' Fenrior, an' I just told ye both t' stop where ye are."

"And I am Julia Aschenbach of California, and this is Destry Maitland of Ravenkeep, and we have business with the Lady Gethsemany."

Duncanon seemed to think about this and then dismiss it as unimportant. "Tha's a fine horse ye ha' there."

Even in the tension of the moment, Destry could not control her pride. "He's a Uzbek."

This impressed even the unpleasant Duncanon. "A Uzbek? I'm damned if he is."

"Then you are certainly damned, my friend."

"Order Duncanon to back off."

Goneril shook her head. "He willna', take i' fra' me, m' lord. He's th' Captain o' th' Bridge, an' I only command th' Nightwatch. He figures he's taken two nosferatu captives, an' ye know wha' he's like when th' bit's between his teeth."

"He's an arrogant, undisciplined little bastard." Fenrior rose and snapped his fingers at Gallowglass. "I will have to correct his manners myself."

It was the first time Fenrior had rolled his *r*s in Renquist's hearing. He seemed to enjoy the word *correct*. The Merlin looked around, surprised he was no longer the center of attention. "Is something amiss?"

Renquist and Marieko were also on their feet. Only Gethsemany remained seated. Now the Merlin seemed quite put out. "Is everyone leaving?"

Gethsemany smiled sweetly. "Don't worry, Taliesin. I'll keep you company until they've resolved this small problem."

Once out of the room, Fenrior, Gallowglass, and Goneril descended flights of winding stairs with both a nosferatu speed and surefooted accomplishment of long practice. Fenrior snapped orders at Gallowglass as he went. "How long is it to dawn?"

"Under an hour, m' lord."

"Then the first thing you'd better do when we get down there is lay some mist. Thick enough to hold off the sun if need be."

Renquist and Marieko were left to follow as best they could and listen while Goneril filled in the details for the lord. "In addition t' th' pair o' undead captives, I think Duncanon also fancies th' horse as a prize."

Fenrior glanced back "Horse?"

"Aye, m' lord. A big black stallion. The female riding claimed i' was a Uzbek."

"Nonsense, the breed died out years ago."

"I'm only repeatin' wha' th' female said."

Renquist called down the stairs to Fenrior. "As a matter of fact, it's true. I've ridden the beast. It really is one-quarter Uzbek."

Fenrior was adamant. "Then that's all the more reason to hurry. Even a quarter Uzbek must be protected at all costs. A stallion, you say?"

Apparently Julia and Destry might be expendable, but the Uzbek was a prize beyond price.

"Tek 'em, lads, but din'a harm th' horse."

Destry had seen troops of all kinds charging through the night. She had seen North Vietnamese regulars charging the wire at Khe San, and faced the MPLA in Angola, but she could recall nothing as fearsome as the silently running Highlanders. She'd heard their human counterparts had attacked with full sound and fury, but these undead clansmen uttered no howls or cries, and even their footfalls were close to soundless. An extra eerie dimension was added by a strange mist that rose from the loch, rearing over the bridge and causeway in climbing tentacles. Dormandu snorted and reared, and Destry struggled to keep her seat. Julia, on foot, was quickly surrounded, with a ring of gleaming claymores leveled at her. Destry, still in the saddle, would have been similarly helpless, had not an overeager Highlander grabbed at Dormandu's bridle, thinking it would be easy to take the horse from its unarmed rider. To his surprise, Dormandu reared again, lashing out with his front hooves, one of which caught the man squarely between the eyes. The Highlander staggered back, blood streaming down his face.

Duncanon let out a roar of fury. "Wha' did I tell ye, ye damned fool? Harm yon beast, an' I'll ha' y' fuckin' head!"

Duncanon, however, had another problem. Blood was in the metaphoric water, and while he might be able to command Highlanders defending a castle that hadn't been under attack for nearly two centuries, the young nosferatu had neither the experience nor the authority to maintain discipline in the face of free-flowing blood, and the possibility of his company lapsing into an unnatural frenzy. To further complicate matters, Dormandu decided to go on an offensive of his own. He bucked and snorted, eyes red-rimmed and furious, now lashing out with his back hooves, as the warhorse DNA of generations of selective breeding by Pathan Gash (the Merciless and Eternal) came to fore. This time, two Highlanders went down, and more undead blood was flowing. At the same time, Destry rolled from the saddle. If the Uzbek was going to do battle, she could only be an encumbrance by remaining on his back. As Dormandu kicked front and back, she went down on one knee, to avoid being the accidental recipient of a flying hoof. Four Highlanders were immediately on her, sword points poised at heart, throat, and eyes.

Dormandu continued, on the other hand, to hold his own, he moved in tight circles, lashing out each time a knot of Highlanders gathered to attempt to subdue him. Duncanon himself tried to make a grab for the Uzbek's bridle, and only avoided being severely kicked by throwing himself flat on the cobbles of the causeway. Infuriated, he yelled at one of the Highlanders who had Destry on her knees. "Decapitate th' bitch. Maybe th' beast'll calm down, if i' has no mistress t' protect."

The Highlander swung his claymore back ready to take Destry's head clean off, but immediately a terrible roar came from the gates of Fenrior.

"DON'T YOU DARE!"

The Highlanders froze in their tracks. Dormandu bucked and pranced, but didn't lash out at any of his now motionless foes. Destry scrambled to her feet and ran to the horse, attempting to soothe and pacify the angry stallion as five figures came out from the gates and strode toward the horse, the Highlanders, and Julia and Destry.

"Marieko?"

"Victor?"

Julia dusted herself off. "I came here to rescue you, Victor."

Renquist looked Julia up and down with a certain degree of amusement. "Perhaps you should have checked with me first. As you can see, no harm has befallen me."

"I understood you'd been kidnapped."

"I was, but that situation has been rectified. Julia, I'd like to present Fenrior of Fenrior."

Fenrior made a courtly bow to both Julia and Destry, while Gallowglass and Goneril looked on and Duncanon and his Highlanders stared in both amazement and trepidation. "Mistress Maitland, Fräulein Aschenbach, welcome to Fenrior."

Chapter Eight

Renquist was in the great spaceport of Baalbeck, but it was as he'd never dreamed it before, and he wondered why the Merlin was sending him this glimpse. The sliver of rational thought that remained with Renquist even in the dreamstate, the part that would always tell him he was only dreaming if the imagery or content waxed too outlandish, had few doubts that the ancient epic now decorating his sleep was coming straight from Taliesin, and might actually be an unedited slice of Urshu memory. In the fourteenth century B.C., all chaos seemed to rule. Parts of the spaceport were burning, and the obelisks and trilithons around the central landing ziggurat were shrouded in a pall of oily black smoke. The sparking blue tracer of particle weapons cut through the gloom and ricochetted off the marble, gold, and black titanium facings of the power stones in lethal energy splashes. Attack disks hurled low overhead, pounding the ground with their deathrays. Crumps like the rumble of thunder, and regular tremblings from the ground under his feet, indicated, somewhere in the distance, huge explosions were being detonated as Nephilim-loyal sappers demolished the Baalbeck infrastructure. Without being told, Renquist knew he was seeing the final days of the Nephilim. They were pulling out, abandoning the colony as the rebellion swept over them and the Earth became unmanageable.

The revolt was first instigated by the genetically engineered military class, Renquist's own ancestry, the Original Beings, but it had quickly spread through the large and constantly growing human population, and even to some of the Urshu. Tampering with monkey genes, it turned out, had been a grave error by the alien Nephilim. All around him, crowds were in advanced states of refugee panic or lynch-mob hysteria. Some simply wanted to get away, while others sought to destroy. Bodies of the dead and wounded lay where they fell. The great flowing flags and banners that had once streamed in the backwash of the rising and descending shuttles were now burned, torn, or trampled underfoot. The vents in the lower levels of the ziggurat, that, in better and calmer times, had jetted decoratively imposing gushers of brightly colored vapor, were now dead— smashed by rioters or clogged with debris. Only the massive iron wind chimes in front of the primary trilithon clashed and clanged, and even their tone seemed to have changed. They now tolled the passing knell of an era.

The crowds milling across the landing and launch sites at Baalbeck were primarily human, but by no means exclusively so. Dozens of the small grey bioentities scurried, scuttled, and tried to hide before they were trampled underfoot. A number of Urshu could also be spotted amid the tumult, doing their best to avoid the hostility they naturally seemed to evoke as the Nephilim's key administrators. The only group manifesting a defined sense of purpose was a flying wedge of Original Beings who had fought their way to the foot of the landing ziggurat. Their intention seemed to be to board and cap-

ture the single spacecraft that floated over the apex of
the ziggurat and continued to load a select passenger list
of those who would return to the stars and continue to
live in the golden sunland of an advanced culture and
technology. The Original Beings had a few beam weapons, but they were seriously outgunned by the loyalist
humans in blue battle armor maintaining a perimeter
partway up the structure.

Renquist didn't have to be told he was not only looking at the very last ship out, but the command vessel of
Marduk Ra, as well. It came to him as one of those
innate pieces of given intelligence that come only in
dreams. He had seen ships like it before in the dreamstate. More organic than the geometrical machines to
which Renquist had become accustomed in the twentieth
century, they gave the impression parts had been grown
rather than built. The long threatening spines that extended from the underside and the outer edge of its con-
vex, saucer-shaped structure seemed more akin to
something that might be found on a creature from an
extremely hostile marine environment. The sense of the
aquatic was reinforced by fringes of waving tendril-like
projections that undulated between the spines. Even the
very fabric of the craft's main hull was composed of
formidable overlapping scales, like those of a mytholog-
ical dragon or sea monster. He could imagine how effective these craft must have been in putting the fear of
the gods into primitive mankind when they had first arrived. Now that the last ship was leaving, the Earth
would undoubtedly revert to the same primitivism that
had held sway before the Nephilim had arrived, except
it would be complicated by the products of their failed
experiments. The newly modified humans, the Urshu,
and the nosferatu would roam the planet, having their
own influence on all the history to come.

A commotion broke out at the foot of the ziggurat. A
small force of loyalist troops were fighting their way up
to the ship, acting as an escort to something that, at first,

Renquist was unable to see. Then, in a flurry of movement, as the escort struggled up the main ramp of the
ziggurat, he had a brief glimpse of a face. Malevolent
and wholly nonhuman, it had two black, sharklike eyes
and a bizarre, vertical, almost vaginal slit for a mouth,
beneath which depended a beard of moving tendrils, like
articulated feelers or fleshy sluglike probes. He recognized it immediately. It was either the Great Lord
Cthulhu, the soul-sucking, squid-headed god of human
legend, or one of his close, malignant, and alien kin.
Thousands of years later, in contemporary Los Angeles,
Renquist would all but lose his undead immortality to
Cthulhu, and although many among those who knew
credited him with having defeated the monstrous Old
One, he knew he had inflicted only a mild reversal, and,
indeed, finding himself so close to the being, or even to
one like it, so disturbed him that Renquist struggled des-
perately to wake.

Although neither would ever know it, at the same time
Renquist's dream took him to the ancient destruction of
Baalbeck, Marieko's dreamstate was also being invaded
by outside forces. As an accomplished dreamwright herself, Marieko instantly knew that she was being either
mildly tortured or rigorously tested. Her first assumption
was that, since she was deep within Fenrior's realm, it
was the lord or one of his retainers infiltrating her sleep,
but she had seen his handiwork when he'd introduced
his ninja into the dream she had shared with Renquist
back at Ravenkeep. This intrusion was entirely different
in its style, content, and the ambiguity of its meaning
and motivation. Fenrior's approach might have been violent, even intimidating, but it would also have been
direct and to the point. Whoever or whatever was now
gauging the vulnerabilities of her mind was subtle, devious, and so highly skilled it frightened her. What
frightened her more, though, was that each time she attempted to wrestle back control of the nightmare, the

author of the horror had the power to swat her helplessly away, as though it was scarcely any effort.

To start from a point of complete imbalance, the invasion of her dreams began by using her own memories to take her back to the single most terrifying episode in her existence. She found herself back, buried alive in the iron-bound Kenzu casket, with twelve feet of earth packed above her, at the very moment when, in reality, she had started helplessly screaming, before she was ultimately rescued by the thrall Katoh. In this new version, however, Katoh didn't seem to exist, and she had to rescue herself, chewing with her own fangs, like a man-trapped she-wolf, through the carved and lacquered pine of the confining coffin, and then clawing her own way to the surface, nails ripped, and fingers little more than bloody stumps, choking and gagging on the loose earth that filled her nose, mouth, and throat.

Even when she thrust through the subsoil, parting the damp, insect-filled grass on her grave, she found her troubles far from over. In one of those unquestioned and unquestionable dream transitions, she was suddenly a human child again, age seven or eight, the time when the Lord Vampire Daimyo and his noble undead companions, on their tall thoroughbred horses, had descended on the peasant home of her parents and feasted with casual brutality on the entire family with the exception of the single girlchild who would one day be Marieko Matsunaga. On a whim, Daimyo had taken her alive to be put through the Change at puberty and adopted into the Yarabachi Clan, first as a plaything, then as a concubine, a blade-maid, and finally, when she found elevation and favor, as a scholar and historian.

Again, the story differed from reality; instead of being taken by the Lord Vampire and set on the strange immortal path she had taken ever since, in another exquisitely executed transition, she found herself part of a parade of miniskirted street whores in some gaudy post-nuclear anime dystopia. Strange aircraft drifted over a landscape of slums and bombed-out ruins, and mutant cruisers leered at her from passing, futuristic automobiles, while the engines of lightweight motorcycles screamed as suicidal young men performed tricks on them for the benefit of the working girls. A figure in a voluminous Yakuza pimp-black overcoat approached her down the wet neon-reflecting sidewalk. She recognized him immediately, or, to be more exact, she recognized both of the pimp's alternating faces: Lord Daimyo and Taliesin the Merlin, one and the threatening same, in body and overcoat.

In Marieko's reading of the glimpse, the Merlin had just betrayed himself by a flourish of vanity. He hadn't been able to resist affixing his signature to this bout of Freudian assault. Had he remained anonymous, he would have been able to continue to mess with her mind long after the dream was finished. She would never have been sure who had been doing it to her, and she would have continued to guess and speculate. The Merlin was a fool, and she decided to tell him so. She opened her mouth and found herself screaming invective, and probably obscenities, in some imaginary dream-tongue even she didn't recognize. The other prostitutes on the street were nosferatu to a sister, but once she had opened her mouth in defiance to Daimyo/Taliesin, they turned on her, fangs extending, hands morphing to talons, eyes glowing with the menace of bloodlust, advancing on her like a pack, edging to circle, building their rage to rip, rend, and mutilate. At the selfsame time Renquist was fighting his way out of the dream downfall of Baalbeck, Marieko decided she'd had more than enough of this pointless and unpleasant game and kicked upward with all her strength for the surface of wakefulness.

Renquist exited the dreamstate both angry and mystified. His distrust of the Merlin was also greatly intensified. Taliesin had fed dreams to Columbine—and look what had happened to her. He had no idea of the extent of the

Merlin's powers or his objectives, and he knew there was no easy way to learn. The only purpose Renquist could see behind invading his much needed sleep with a graphic dream projection of the fall of Baalbeck was to implant the idea of a kinship between the nosferatu and the Urshu. Of course, the destruction of Baalbeck could have come either from his own genetic memory or that of another of the undead, except he absolutely knew it couldn't be.

The destruction of Baalbeck was not encoded anywhere in the DNA memory of any contemporary nosferatu because that very destruction had been total and all consuming. That last spacecraft, with its scales and spines, had dropped the final sunbomb as it rose through the stratosphere. The fusion-plasma device had incinerated the spaceport from which the vessel had, moments before, departed. All were obliterated, loyalists and rebels alike, nosferatu, human, Urshu, and bioentity. No place remained in the double helix for any legacy of the ones who perished in the spaceport holocaust. All trace of them had been permanently erased. Modern nosferatu were exclusively descended from the Original Beings who had taken part in the earlier escape bid, the Flight. The logic was irrefutable. The dream was a manipulation by the Merlin, and the invasion angered Renquist to the point that he knew he must confront Taliesin immediately. The game must be stopped.

He rose from the bed and from his precious fur rug. He knew the sun had yet to set, but it hardly mattered. Both his room in the castle, and the one where the Urshu was lodged were closed and without windows. Inside the confines of Fenrior, day and night were one. After the arrival of Julia and Destry, Renquist's quarters had been upgraded from the high-end dungeon to a fairly luxurious guest room as merited by the understanding, not to say friendship, being established between him and the Lord Fenrior. Although he by no means had anything

more than the most vague impression of the general layout of the castle, he knew the Merlin occupied similar
guest accommodations two landings below him in the
same tower. He would face the Merlin immediately,
while his anger was still hot. He knew to confront Taliesin while still incensed would probably be the best
kind of psychic smoke screen. The Urshu would be
forced to cut through a tangle of outrage before he discovered Renquist's real thoughts.

He dressed quickly and left the room. For a moment,
as he closed the door behind him, he contemplated
taking a sword with him, but decided against it. The
occasion called for tactics and intelligence, not cold
steel, and carrying the blade, even for the sake of sym-
bolism, was too much of an implied admission that he
didn't know if he could handle the situation without resorting to violence. With the Merlin, recourse to even
the threat of violence was the very last thing Renquist
desired. Aside from any other considerations, he was
certain the Merlin was more than capable of handling
anything physical.

As he descended the stairs to the level that included
Taliesin's quarters, he met Theda dressed in an ankle-
length leather skirt with a hobble, and a starched white
shirt, which together lent her a look not unlike a fetish-
istic Edwardian governess. Her face was a pale thunder-
cloud of undisguised frustration. "You wouldn't have
happened to see a lazy slut of a house thrall would you,
Victor?"

Renquist shook his head. "I'm afraid you're the only
person I've seen at all since I woke."

"Never mind. I'll find her."

Short black bicycling gloves covered Theda's hands,
and between her fingers she snapped a leather strap, what
Renquist believed was known as a tawse, a punishment
implement once used in Scottish schools as a substitute
for the cane favored by the English. From this, he de-
duced the thrall would undoubtedly suffer once she was

located, and dragged from wherever she was hiding, but Theda and the punishment of her domestics was absolutely none of his concern, and after the courtesy of a curt half bow, he hurried on down the stairs. As Renquist strode along the landing, a part of him felt like bursting in—throwing wide the Merlin's door—with full nosferatu dramatic effect, but, like the sword, it was both too uncontrolled and predictable. Instead, he simply rapped firmly on the door and waited for an answer. An agonized female shriek echoed down the stairwell. Theda had clearly captured her errant thrall, whose howls all but drowned out the voice from within.

"Enter."

Yes, my Urshu friend, indeed I will enter.

As Marieko left her room, she heard a drawn-out series of slaps, leather on flesh, each strike followed by a sobbing wail. She glanced up and saw, on the landing above, the Lady Theda had a thrall bent over the banisters, buttocks bared, and was thrashing her with slow, deliberate strokes. Similar scenes and worse had been acted out in the great castles of Japan in the old days, and even the poor departed Columbine had her moments, so Marieko thought nothing of it and continued on her self-imposed mission. After much consideration, she had decided the effrontery of Taliesin to pervade her dreams, unasked and unwanted, could only be faced head-on. Her connection with the Merlin, as long ago as when he slept beneath Morton Downs, had been through Columbine's dreamstate. Perhaps it all must also end in the dreamstate. When Columbine had first complained of her dreams, Marieko had treated the matter with a certain lack of gravity. Now that she herself had experienced the Merlin forcing his way into her sleep, she regretted not having taken Columbine more seriously. The process was both humiliating and enervating, and it had only happened to Marieko once. Columbine had suffered it day after day, week after week. She knew, if she was to retain her honor and her self-respect, she had to go to the Urshu and demand that he cease this violation and trespassing in her unconscious.

"Inundated with all this television, they cannot dream. This Hitler, did you know him?"

"Only his henchman."

"Was he human?"

"I believe so. I think he may have been a product of environment. After trench warfare of the kind he experienced as a young man, many things might seem possible. Unprecedented mass slaughter being among them."

The Merlin was watching four TV sets simultaneously and appeared to be speed-reading at the same time. His eating had diminished a little from the obscene gluttony for human food he'd exhibited during the first few hours after his waking, but as Renquist had entered, he'd been spooning breakfast cereal into his mouth, only he'd substituted Guinness for the more usual milk and sugar. Whether this was truly how the Merlin was, or simply an elaborate piece of lifestyle playacting was debatable. What couldn't be questioned was that he was learning at an impossibly fast and furious rate. Already he was fluent in half a dozen languages, and he had a firm grasp of contemporary world politics and the events that shaped them, but his opinion of human civilization appeared to be diminished each time Renquist spoke with him. Though he devoured all the videotapes Fenrior could provide for him, plus sampling every channel that could be pulled down by the castle's satellite dish, he seemed to blame a great deal of the world's current ills on the invention of television, which he considered a more dangerous piece of machinery than the atom bomb. "Their collective span of attention grows so short, I swear they'll soon be unable to feed themselves. They are sheep governed by charlatans."

"Hasn't it always been like that?"

"Yes, yes, but in this new world it all moves so fast.

The Roman Empire lasted five hundred years. The British Empire less than two hundred, the Soviet Empire didn't make it through a century. How long do you think the American Empire will last? And then what will come? It moves so fast, it scarcely bears thinking about."

Renquist allowed himself a smile, even though he knew Taliesin's generalized tirade was only designed to defuse his anger. "I confront that by mostly not thinking about it."

"How is it that you nosferatu couldn't intervene and halt some of the humans' worst excesses?"

Renquist shrugged. "We are few in number."

"The Urshu were even fewer in number, but it never stopped us."

"We also can't walk in the sun."

"That I will concede is a definite disadvantage."

"Primarily, though, we didn't give a damn. Sometimes we manipulate human illusions in our own interests, but we seem to court disaster when we play at God. We learned that the hard way in the upper valleys of the Indus ten thousand years ago."

The Merlin chuckled and drank the last of the cornflakes and Guinness straight from the cereal bowl. "I heard about that. A nasty business. So what exactly do the nosferatu care about?"

"Mainly our food supply and our privacy."

Renquist wasn't sure if the Merlin's expression was a sneer or not. "Is that an oblique way of telling me you didn't appreciate the little glimpse of the fall of Baalbeck. I thought it might be educational for you. Obviously your own DNA memories cannot encompass that epic moment that left your kind and mine stranded on this miserable and backward planet."

Renquist's spine stiffened. He was not going to permit the Merlin to laugh the whole thing off. "The nosferatu care that their minds should remain inviolate. We respond badly to psychic intrusion, whoever or whatever the intruder."

"Is this what you came to tell me?"

"It is. Putting it succinctly, the message is 'Stay out of my mind, Urshu.' "

"That's a warning?"

"You could take it as such."

"A warning backed by what, may I ask?"

Before Renquist could answer, he was interrupted by a soft tapping on the door, and, since he had no answer with any conviction to it, it could not have happened at a more opportune time. The Merlin smiled as though he already knew this. "It seems everyone wants to spend time with me."

"Have you been invading all their dreams? I wouldn't recommend trying it with some of the Highlanders. I've only seen them when they're having fun. I shudder to think what they're like when they're angry."

Taliesin ignored him. "Enter."

The door opened. The caller was Marieko. Her attitude was formal, and she wore a kimono of Yarabachi, but Renquist noted her mouth was exceedingly small, a sure sign she was exceedingly angry. The Merlin put aside his cereal bowl and used a remote to lower the sound on the TV sets. "*Konnichiha,* Marieko-san."

As if she'd been steeling herself for the ordeal for some time, Marieko delivered a lengthy complaint in Japanese. Renquist's Japanese was good, but not that good. He couldn't match Marieko and the Merlin in nuance and subtlety. The gist was that Marieko's dream-state had also been violated by Taliesin, and she had come to complain about it. Perhaps not as forcefully as Renquist, but complain all the same—but for Renquist to be excluded by language was clearly another of Merlin's ploys. "Could we please continue in English. This kind of thing makes me nervous."

"Nervous, Victor? To be excluded from the conversation makes you nervous? Surely I should be the one who is nervous."

Marieko switched to English. "And why should you be nervous, Taliesin-san?"

"Am I not alone in a remote castle full of vampires?"

This was nonsense, and Renquist didn't hesitate to say so. "You have no fear of us. You walk in the sun, and as far as I can observe, you don't sleep."

"I am watched constantly."

"Could you expect otherwise?"

"And Fenrior plans to kill me."

At this, Renquist said nothing. Marieko looked stunned. "Is this true?"

Still Renquist said nothing. The Merlin laughed. "So tell the lady, Victor. Is it true or isn't it? You don't mind if I call you Victor, do you?"

Marieko had never seen Renquist so uncompromising. "So when we really descend through the levels, you're actually seeking my support."

The Merlin was more than his equal, however, in a lack of compromise. "Of course, why else should I have gone to so much trouble?"

"You believe Fenrior plans your death?"

"Indeed I do."

"Why tell me this?"

"Because you have yet to make up your mind. You don't know if you want me alive or dead."

Renquist's eyes were even harder than before, and Marieko was glad such a gaze wasn't directed at her. Victor knew the Merlin was reading his mind, and he both loathed and resented it. "I've discussed this with no one."

"But it shows. Even you cannot conceal everything, my excellent Victor."

"So it would seem."

As the Merlin slowly smiled, Marieko realized the Urshu were truly a very different species both from nosferatu and man. "And your answer?"

"Do you really believe I'll assist you to survive when

you as good as tell me my mind is an open book anytime you care to read it?"

"What makes you think I need your assistance to survive?"

"What else could you want from me? I have little else to offer. You either want me to dissuade Fenrior and his Highlanders from chopping you to cutlets, or at least buy you some time until you have fully prepared yourself for whatever you intend to do."

The Merlin stroked his chin. He didn't shave, but apparently he needed to. Stubble was graduating to the start of a full beard. "You're not stupid, Victor."

"No, I'm not."

"Could I command your loyalty if I were, for the sake of argument, to show you the future?"

Marieko made her skepticism as obvious as possible. "You have gained the gift of prophecy?"

"Of course not. We both know that the future isn't stacked, immutable, just waiting to unreel like one of your motion pictures. I can show you the future because the Merlin has returned, and from here on in, I will be shaping by far the greater part of that future, all in fact that is not purely random. I would show you the way to exploit coming events to both your benefit and to the benefit of your kind in general. Indeed, if the nosferatu as a species might compromise a little, I could bring them to their very own paradise."

Marieko expected Renquist to have a response, possibly a violent one, to the idea of nosferatu compromise, but instead, he remained silent. Taliesin looked at him questioningly. "You have nothing to say, Victor."

Renquist shook his head. "I would hear more first."

The Merlin looked at him hard and then picked up a bottle of peppermint schnapps from his litter of supplies, and drank from it. "As I tried to tell you when I first woke, we Urshu have a genetic imperative to interfere in the business of humans. We are also immensely powerful, as you may be beginning to learn."

"You also told us you had yet to formulate your plans, but you were looking forward to working on a more global canvas."

"And now I'm working on it."

Marieko frowned. "Are you saying you've already formulated your plans?"

"In a broad sense. I have at least drawn my conclusions."

Renquist's voice was careful and measured. "And these conclusions are?"

"Without exception, all contemporary problems stem from there being far too many humans—by quantum proportions, there are too many humans. Their breeding puts rabbits to shame. They are ecologically unsound and their reliance on technology is precipitating them into devolution."

Marieko looked at Renquist. "I can have no argument so far."

Renquist smiled at her. "Nor I. That's why I have nothing to say."

Merlin continued. "The only answer, as I see it, has to be a major cull of the herd."

"A cull?"

"An extremely large reduction in the human population. I have considered various means that could be employed, and I tend to favor political manipulation toward what would at first be a limited nuclear conflagration. Let's say between India and Pakistan, escalating to more of the smaller and less stable nuclear powers, Iran, Iraq, Ukraine, Argentina, Chile, and stopping just short of Russia, China, and the USA from going into total overkill. That would give us a modest nuclear winter for some six or seven years, during which the other well known Horsemen of the Apocalypse—Famine, Pestilence, and Death—would naturally follow where War was to lead, but not to actual extinction. It would be a new dark age in which the nosferatu, if forewarned and forearmed, could stake out their own territory, fully defensible against all humanity, humans having mainly reverted to the primitive. You could have your own world, or, at least, your own continent."

As the Merlin spoke, he also wove a seductive visual picture in Marieko's mind of a dark wasteland where the nosferatu ruled. A dominion of sere and leafless lands, haunted trees, scorched earth, and the skeletal ruins of abandoned cities, some with perpetual fires burning and others that glowed radioactive in the dark. Such meager life as could survive the breaking of the food chain, and the extinction of tens of thousands of species, lived according to a cycle of black, starless nights, and shroud-sheeted days of windswept gloom, black rain, dust storms, and dirty snow. Such humans as remained, ragged and wide eyed from the trauma, died at the side of the cracked ribbons of what had once been highways as the scavenger pickings of the vanished civilization were rapidly exhausted.

"Dig deep, Victor. Hoard the power and the technology. Wait out the storm and then emerge, dominant and victorious." The Merlin swilled a little more schnapps and grinned like a jovial conspirator. "Doesn't it all seem tempting?"

In the country of death, the undead rode on hard iron as modern lords in gleaming armored vehicles, sweeping past the remnants of self-destructed humanity, with feudal banners flying and a thousand years of institutional dread and imposed terror to contemplate. The only well-fed and healthy humans were those in the underground pens, and, to a lesser degree, the slave laborers in the Urshu/nosferatu-controlled reconstruction camps.

"I'm offering you a world for nosferatu, by nosferatu, without the need to ever again hide from humanity because humanity has been completely and permanently reduced to the subservient role."

Marieko was suddenly repulsed. Not so much by the concept but by the brutish and totalitarian ideas of implementation. "I'm sorry, Merlin-san, but you have gone too far. The Nazi flags and Stalinist banners are redundant. Such images will only play as retro kitsch and nothing more. My own people, the Japanese, learned that lesson in the atomic fire. You still haven't watched enough television. You're bringing too much of the fifth century—and what you saw in the aftermath of the comet—to your seductive little vision. Times have changed."

"Are you telling me humans have improved in the last fifteen hundred years?"

"Not in the least, but they're different. They move so much faster."

Renquist nodded in agreement with Marieko. "For a full half century they lived under the threat of mutually assured nuclear destruction."

The Merlin still seemed fully convinced he was right. "It matters not what they might live through or under, or at what speed they live it. They still have the same desires, don't they, the same susceptibilities? You can attest to that, can't you, Victor? You've lived among them for almost a thousand years. Have humans changed so radically?"

"It's hard to say how much they've changed, since I have naturally had to adapt to those changes."

"But you would agree there are far too many of them?"

Marieko was surprised to see Renquist all but smile. "Oh, yes. There are far too many of them." She was even more surprised when Renquist quickly rose to his feet. "But on that point of agreement, I think it's a good time for me to leave you. I think we've exhausted most avenues of discussion for this night."

Renquist started for the door, and this seemed to be a surprise even for Taliesin. "But I don't have your answer."

Renquist turned in the doorway. "Of course you have my answer. You already know it. The only reason you wanted me here was to confirm what you already knew."

Renquist paused, and a momentary and demonically teasing grin flickered behind his eyes. "If you don't know, Old Merlin, then your bluff may very soon unravel. You don't mind me calling you 'Old Merlin,' do you?"

"What was going on in there?"

Renquist adamantly shook his head. He was attempting to make his mind as blank as possible, to exclude the Urshu from his thoughts, and Marieko had to do the same. "We shouldn't talk about it. We shouldn't even think about it. I don't know from what distance he can read our minds."

"If he's so powerful, he will know everything anyway."

Renquist interrupted her. His manner was less than kind. "Listen carefully, Marieko, because this is all I'm prepared to say. When Fenrior first told me he intended to kill the Merlin after he had studied him, I was shocked. I protested. The Merlin obviously knows this, and that's why he wants to win me to his side. The only thing he reveals by this is that he may not be as invulnerable and all perceiving as he wants us to believe. That is why I still maintain my silence. It may be hopeless, but I don't think it is."

"And what about me? Why does he interfere in my dreams and bring me running to him?"

"Maybe he thinks we have some kind of bond or coupling."

Marieko's mouth grew very small. "That's a highly patriarchal attitude."

"Taliesin is a high patriarch, even if he is sterile. It could be another weakness. As far as possible you and I have to think in paradox and disinformation. If the Urshu is using us as his window on a particular facet of the world, we have to afford him the most distorted possible view."

They had reached the point on the stairs where, if

Marieko were going to her room, and Renquist to his, they should have parted company. A sudden impasse imposed itself. Renquist, when leaving his room to confront Taliesin had given no thought to what he might do after that, and it appeared Marieko had been just as narrowly focused. Renquist had assumed he would probably seclude himself with his thoughts. Even having complete freedom of action after so many alarms and excursions, down the full length of the British Isles was something of a novelty. Fortunately, Marieko was bolder than he was, right at that moment, and he was spared everything but a simple decision. "Perhaps I could come to your room. We could summon a thrall and we could feed."

Renquist slowly nodded, commencing the game. "Perhaps you should."

Marieko shrugged, equally offhand, continuing the game. "One way to thwart a mind reader is to turn off the mind and let the flesh and its needs hold sway."

Marieko prided herself on her reactions, but even she wasn't sure for a moment how she came to be seeing everything from an unhealthy vantage point, sprawled in a corner and twisted up against the wall, while Renquist scuffled with three nosferatu in the middle of the room. The only thing she remembered prior to that was Victor opening the door to his room for her and ushering her inside. She had been violently slammed sideways and out of the way. Once again, it appeared Victor was the elected target of Highland skulduggery. The three assailants might well have taken Victor completely by surprise had they not expected him to return to his room on his own. That Marieko had walked in first had upset their deadly applecart. No sooner had Marieko managed to straighten up than she both recognized the attackers and saw the full unpleasantness of their intentions. Duncanon and a brawny Highlander wrestled with Renquist while the small bald Morbius from the laboratory danced round them, keeping his distance. Apart from his size,

Morbius took no part in the fight because he was clutching a mallet and a foot-long iron spike. The plan had obviously been for Duncanon and the Highlander to seize the unsuspecting Renquist, hurl him to the floor, and before he could gather his wits to put up a fight, drive the spike through his ribs and into his heart. Marieko coming into the equation had, however, spoiled all that, and the deadly trap had degenerated into a staggering, snarling free-for-all.

Marieko decided to upset the plan still more. The onetime sword of Hideo Matsutani lay on top of a dresser in its ivory sheath, next to a large Jacobean glass jug. Victor's damned water. Duncanon, Morbius, and the Highlander were so focused on Renquist, they failed to notice when Marieko commenced her move. Loath as she was to touch a blade that had once been Kenzu, need dictated, and the sword was already unsheathed and describing a precise arc that terminated in Morbius's throat as the small nosferatu, the alleged accomplice of Ruthven, turned and realized his last moment was upon him. Marieko had swung with all the grace and tidy style of a French executioner of the sixteenth century. Morbius's head remained in place for a full second until it toppled, freeing a short fountain of dark blood and noxious spray. The head rolled for about two feet across the floor before it came to a halt. The body attempted to crawl toward the head, feebly trying to reunite the two for recovery and reconstruction, but Marieko put a stop to this by bringing the sword firmly down into his heart.

The slaughter of Morbius caused a sharp, shocked freeze in the action, which Renquist used to break free of Duncanon and the Highlander and snatch up his walking cane. A twist and flick, and the secreted blade was a naked eighteen inches of Milanese steel. Without hesitation, while the hollow wooden shaft was still falling, and Marieko had yet to pull her own blade out of Morbius's back, Renquist had driven the point unerringly into the Highlander's left eye. Ultimately the eye would recover, although a new one might never grow, dependent on the extent of the damage, but this didn't minimize the bleeding or the agony. The nosferatu dropped his claymore and pressed both hands to his face, but blood still flowed between his fingers as he staggered from the room. To Marieko's eternal wonder, Renquist actually let out a short laugh of delight. In far less time than it took to grasp what had happened, the tables had been immaculately turned on Duncanon. His trap had reversed itself, so he now found himself facing Renquist one-on-one, but with Marieko at his back with the Bushido sword ready to take him.

His head lowered and claymore held level, Duncanon retreated, seeking to protect his back, but the room wasn't large enough to give him the space he needed. Marieko also began to circle, but Renquist stayed exactly where he was with his back to the door. "So who gave you your orders, boy? Was it your laird, or did you make this little adventure up all by yourself?"

"I can spot m' own enemies."

"Can you now?"

"Tha' I can."

"Can you also spot when you're beaten, and ask for quarter?"

"I ask quarter from no man."

Renquist raised his blade slightly. "Then I'd commend you to make the most of your last few moments."

"Ye're powerful big wi' th' talk when it's two on one."

"I seem to recall you thought you needed three to take me."

"An' where would ye be if ye din'a ha' th' lassie t' back y' play?"

Renquist's lip curled. "So now the ruse has failed, you have the audacity to appeal to honor?"

Marieko took a step forward. "Defend yourself, Duncanon. I'll take you."

Renquist shook his head. "Give me the sword, Marieko. This one is mine, by right."

Marieko would have been profoundly pleased to have thrust Victor's sword straight through Duncanon and be finished with the arrogant little whelp, but Renquist was correct. He did have the right, the prior claim on Duncanon, and after just the slightest hesitation, she tossed the sword of Hideo Matsutani over Duncanon's head to Renquist, who caught it deftly. Duncanon glanced at Marieko. An evil smile was spreading across his face, and his fangs were slowly extending, exceptionally long and gleaming white. "Ye made a mistake there, lassie. Ye should'a kept y' sword. Now all ye can do is watch while I gut y' fancyboy."

Duncanon's breath was in Renquist's face. It smelled of whisky, and bloodshot eyes told of recent feeding. Was the young one hyped on microfungi and a fresh kill? He might maintain the pose of fearing nothing, but even a fresh, wild, young one like Duncanon might need to steel himself before he actually did away with another of his kind. Particularly when the method was to be the hammered stake, an end that not only terrified most undead, but also disgusted them as a gruesome and degrading way to go. After catching the sword tossed by Marieko, Renquist had shifted blades into opposite hands. The Bushido blade was in his right and the thin straight blade of swordcane in his left. As he made the exchange, Duncanon saw a chance to rush him and took it, but Renquist was able to block the downward swing of the claymore, intended—had it struck home—to cleave his skull clear to the jawbone. He caught Duncanon's single blade close to the hilt between his two, and after a short trial of strength, was able to push him back and away. Without making a big thing of it, Renquist also took a step back so he was halfway out the door of the room. "You were already bested by a horse."

Duncanon snarled at the taunt and again rushed Ren-

quist in the hope that a second furious downward slash
would succeed where the first one had failed, but Renquist was able to block it and again take a step back,
out the door. Using the two eccentrically matched
blades, Renquist found he was having to quickly evolve
a highly unorthodox and ad hoc style, a hybrid of formal
Japanese and the hard Italian art of rapier and poniard.
He jabbed at Duncanon with the point of the samurai
sword. "Did you ever hear a blade sing, boy? Ever fancy
you sensed an elusive metallic purring as though the
steel were anticipating the strike? Did you ever feel a
kinship of soul with a weapon?"

In addition to an eclectic and fabricated style, Renquist also had a strategy. His goal was to lure Duncanon
out of the room and into the narrow corridor, where he
would find himself at a distinct disadvantage. To swing
the long, cumbersome claymore required space. It was a
weapon of the outdoors, the battlefield, and the crossroads at midnight. It did not serve its master well in the
nooks and crannies of an architectural rabbit warren like
Fenrior. The ploy depended on keeping Duncanon angry,
and burning his energy by forcing him to bring the fight
to Renquist. His youthful fury and nosferatu bloodlust
would distract him from noticing he'd been effectively
confined until it was too late, and to feed that fury, Renquist went right on talking as he repeatedly jabbed with
the Matsutani. "This has the reputation of being an 'evil
blade.' "

The antagonists were now facing each other on either
side of the doorway. Duncanon looked to strike, but
found he was impeded by the door frame. He lunged
clumsily at Renquist, who parried easily. "The previous
owner used it when he assisted in the ritual suicides of
three of his friends."

Renquist parried two more of these lunges. The claymore offered its user very little control of the point, and
Duncanon had almost none. He relied entirely on the
wide and flamboyant forehand swing. "After that, he

handed it to a fourth knight who used it on him."

Renquist retreated two more paces, and Duncanon had to follow to get to him. Renquist feinted with the sword and then went for Duncanon's ribs with the swordstick blade. "Perhaps perversely, it has changed its character since coming into my care. It's proved itself little short of a good-luck talisman."

Duncanon hauled off for a horizontal swing intended to finish Renquist, if not actually cleave him in two, but the blow was spoiled when the blade hit the stonework of the narrow corridor. Duncanon cursed as Renquist nicked his left upper arm and danced back. "First blood, boy. Do you believe evil seeks out evil?"

Duncanon drew a dirk from his sock. Now he at least matched Renquist by having a blade in each hand. He rushed him, flailing with the claymore while trying to inflict a stomach wound with the dirk. Now Renquist had to use both blades to full and fast effect to fend off the wild flurry of blows. Duncanon had finally understood how he'd been suckered, and that Renquist was a skilled and experienced swordsman who would not fall beneath a confusion of aimless slashing and brute bravura. He was finally working according to what was possibly the only tactic left to him. Behind Renquist, at the end of the corridor, was the tower's central stairwell. If Duncanon could load on sufficient berserk pressure, he might be able to force his older adversary all the way down there, and into the more open area where he could properly use the weight and single edge of his claymore.

Renquist knew it was time to stop taunting and go to work. He beat off one more rush by Duncanon, giving a little more ground. He could see Duncanon calculate the distance to the end of the corridor. The young one was telegraphing his every move before he made it. Renquist braced for the next rush. When it came, two blades flying, hungry to connect, Renquist sidestepped like a matador, feinted left, struck right, pierced Duncanon's thigh with the swordstick, and, with his leg already weakened, tripped him so he fell heavily. The claymore was lost to his grasp and clattered along the flagstones of the corridor. Duncanon might have lacked forethought and finesse, but Renquist couldn't fault the young one for courage. Even though bleeding badly, he came back up on his uninjured knee with the dirk still in his hand. He thrust at Renquist but failed to connect. Renquist stood quite still. "I'd recommend you don't do that again. Surrender now and maybe I'll let you survive."

Typically ignoring the advice, Duncanon again stabbed at Renquist. This time the Bushido blade really did seem to sing, as, in a single stroke, it severed Duncanon's left hand just above the wrist. "I warned you, boy, and I only give one warning."

Duncanon stared in disbelief at the way his arm now ended in a bleeding stump."

"So what is it now? Shall I take your heart or shall I take your head?"

The raised voice of the Lord Fenrior came from somewhere down the stairwell. "I would recommend you do neither, Victor. I still have uses for Duncanon."

Marieko hurried to Renquist's side as Fenrior and his entourage reached the landing and started down the corridor toward them.

Renquist lowered his swords and stepped back from the kneeling Duncanon. "You want this thing, even with a hand missing?"

Fenrior brushed the question aside. "He's undead. It'll grow back in time. The more important question is what am I supposed to do with you?"

Duncanon dragged himself, using one arm and one leg, to the feet of his lord like a maimed dog seeking its master's protection. The laird had a quite formidable force behind him. He was flanked on one side by Gallowglass, and Julia Aschenbach on the other. What game had she embarked on now? Julia looked down at the crippled Duncanon and then up at Renquist. "What have

you been up to now, Victor? Aren't you a little old for
swordplay with the youth?"

Renquist leaned forward on his sword. He looked suddenly tired. First the Merlin and then the fight had obviously taken their toll. "Why don't you ask the Lord
Fenrior? I can only assume he ordered my murder."

Julia stepped away from Fenrior. "Murder? You said
it would only be a distraction."

"Does Victor look murdered?"

Behind Julia and Gallowglass were a guard of a half
dozen Highlanders, armed with pikes and claymores, led
by Angus Crimmon, the laird's piper, and including, yet
again, the diminutive Prestwick with his axe. One look
at the auras, heavy with suspicion, paranoia, and distrust
were enough to tell Marieko that Renquist's problems,
and by association her own, were far from over. All
present were doing their best to screen their thoughts and
emotions, and achieving varying degrees of success, but
the general tone and the militant formality of Fenrior's
arrival didn't bode well. Crimmon and the guard halted
a few feet behind Fenrior, Julia, and Gallowglass—close
enough to give aid, but far enough back not to be part
of the conversation. Fenrior looked Renquist up and
down. "So you've started cutting up my people now,
have you, Victor?"

"There's another back in my room separated from his
head and a third wandering the halls somewhere, lacking
an eye and feeling very sorry for himself."

Marieko refused to be sidelined as an innocent by-
stander. "The one in the room is mine. The one called
Morbius. I took his head."

Fenrior treated her to a hard look. "Dr. Morbius was
my chief scientific adviser."

"Dr. Morbius was a self-serving charlatan, my Lord."

"And that's why you beheaded him?"

Marieko shook her head. "No. I beheaded him when
he attempted to drive an iron stake into Victor. I presume
that was on your orders?"

Renquist stared intently at the Lord, seemingly curious to hear the answer to this question. Fenrior looked away. "Duncanon was of the firm opinion you had made a secret agreement with the Merlin, to side with the Urshu against me. I believe it was Morbius who sowed the seeds, however. He seemed to take an instant dislike to you when the Merlin first awoke, and it's been festering ever since."

Renquist handed the swordcane blade to Marieko and pushed his hair back out of his eyes. The guards stiffened warily, but they relaxed when no further move followed. "But you didn't order my assassination?"

"Shall we say I simply reserved judgment and let events take their course? You could look on it as an old-fashioned trial by arms."

"And what exactly was I on trial for?"

"Morbius had accused you of betraying us to Taliesin. He had seemingly observed your comings and goings, and the secret meetings between the two of you."

Marieko's face contracted in anger. "We weren't supposed to study the Urshu?"

Renquist gestured for her to contain her outrage. "There was the faintest germ of truth in Morbius's conspiracy fantasy. Already tonight Taliesin has solicited my aid and support against you."

Fenrior blinked. "Did he now? And did you give it?"

Renquist turned to Marieko. "You were there. Did I pledge myself in any way to the Merlin?"

"No." Her reply was true to the letter. Renquist had given Taliesin no answer, but that was hardly the entire story. "Victor gave no reply at all."

Julia knew Renquist well enough, and perhaps Marieko as well, to suspect they were maybe telling the truth, but not the whole truth. "The woman is hardly an unbiased witness. She would obviously do just about anything for Victor."

Marieko would have happily driven the blade of the swordstick into Julia's eye just as Victor had done with

Highlander. She clearly was prepared to totally court disaster to thwart anyone who might be a rival for Victor's attention. Also Julia wasn't finished. "As we all well know, she was quite prepared to sacrifice one of her own troika to ensure that the Merlin awoke."

Marieko took a step toward Julia. "You know it was nothing like that, damn you."

"It wasn't? You brought her here, and where is she now?"

"We all know she met the true death when the Urshu lured her to him and drained her energy."

"You have a lot of nosferatu bodies around you, Marieko Matsunaga. First Columbine and now Morbius. How many more will perish at your hands before this is over?"

Renquist's aura flared with anger. "If you can't see the hand of Taliesin in this confusion, you're all fools."

Fenrior's hand went to the hilt of his sword. "Do you call me a fool, sir?"

"You're worse than a fool if you can't see what's happening in your very own domain."

For a moment it looked as though the Lord himself were going to raise steel to Renquist, but instead, he gestured to Gallowglass. "Have the lads take him."

Gallowglass nodded. "Aye m' lord." He glanced back at the guard. "Lads . . ."

Pikes were lowered and claymores raised. Fenrior stepped to one side to give his escort free access to Renquist, who raised his sword, obviously unwilling to be taken by the Highlanders without a fight. Then, out of nowhere, Lupo was there. Although certainly part of an illusion, he appeared to rise from the floor right beside Fenrior, but then assumed a solidity and strength far beyond any apparition. Marieko, although she had only spoken to Lupo on the phone—and very briefly—knew it could only be him. The broad back and shoulders, the prominent nose and bull neck, the swarthy complexion, black unknowable eyes, and aura of total and uncompromising invincibility. Having now seen him, Marieko could easily believe he had been created by the Craft, and, indeed, that all the other legends about him were absolutely true. And better than just being there, Lupo held what had to be the complete, state-of-the-art, high-tech, ergonomically balanced, butterfly Solignem fighting knife, undoubtedly with a honed and razor edge, to Fenrior's throat, and with Lupo's inhuman strength behind it, the weapon could certainly all but sever the lord's neck.

"Should I finish him now, Don Victor?"

Renquist wanted to laugh out loud. Lupo! At the moment when all seemed about to unravel violently and fatally—Lupo! His very presence was both a comfort and a delight, and Renquist felt irrationally buoyant. From there on in, all problems were reduced by at least fifty percent. "Where the hell did you come from?"

"I've been in this place almost as long as you have, Don Victor. It finally seemed the time to reveal myself."

"I'm very pleased you did."

Fenrior's head was twisted away from Lupo and the knife at an odd and probably painful angle. "Would you please ask your friend to take the dagger from my throat, Victor? I feel very uncomfortable like this."

"You better let him go, Lupo."

Lupo didn't immediately release Fenrior. "He has already committed one assault on your person, Don Victor, and was seemingly about to commit another. Letting him survive could set an unfortunate precedent."

Fenrior attempted to placate with actually groveling. "Believe me, this is not something I'd want made public either."

"I think we can allow for extenuating circumstances here, Lupo."

"You mean Taliesin the Urshu?"

"You know about the Merlin?"

Lupo gave his don a dark look. "My greater concern is whether he knows about me."

"I think we all share some variety of that concern."

Fenrior was becoming about as impatient as was possible for a man with a knife at his throat. "Please, Victor."

"Let him go, Lupo."

"You're sure?"

"I believe so."

Lupo stepped away from Fenrior, at the same time folding the knife away with a single deft and oft-practiced movement into a concealed sheath strapped to his forearm under his black combat-style jacket. Fenrior touched his throat with exploratory fingers in search of blood or broken skin, although all that showed was a faint red mark where the cutting edge had been pressed against the flesh over the jugular. Then he turned away and removed his dark glasses to wipe his face, but he replaced them before anyone could see his eyes. "I take it we talk?"

Renquist nodded. "Bearing in mind the Merlin is probably eavesdropping on every possible word and thought."

"We will meet. In an hour. In the Great Hall, to finally settle the fate of Taliesin."

Renquist's laugh was short and ironic. "Or for him to settle our fate?"

"He won't be there."

"He doesn't need to be there. It's my opinion that he's playing us like puppets."

Fenrior looked from Lupo to Marieko and finally to Renquist. "It's been a very long time since anyone held a knife to my throat under my own roof."

"And, for the first time, you have an Urshu under your roof. These happenings would appear to beg for correlation."

"This is what we must discuss in the Great Hall."

"In an hour?"

"In an hour." Fenrior gestured curtly to his escort. Two of them picked up the bloody, incapacitated, and now barely conscious Duncanon. The others turned smartly and proceeded down the corridor, back the way they had come. For a moment, Julia seemed uncertain of what she should do, almost as though she wasn't sure which side she was on. Then she appeared to make up her mind, and she followed Fenrior and Gallowglass. As they moved off, Gallowglass turned back for a last consideration of Lupo with an aura of kinship and awe. Renquist let out a long weary sigh. Julia's apparent problem with allegiances would assuredly create more upheavals before it played itself out, but in the meantime, he had Lupo with him, and his previous grim uncertainty was hard to maintain.

"Lupo."

"Don Victor."

"Once again you burden me with a debt of gratitude."

"Isn't that my primary function?"

Renquist had no answer to this, so he gestured to Marieko. "Lupo, this is Marieko Matsunaga. She has been a great help to me since I came to Britain."

Lupo bowed. "I'm honored to meet anyone who fought with the Yarabachi."

"You are very well informed.

"I recognized the symbol on your kimono."

"You've been in Japan?"

"Alas, no—but the fame of the clan was not limited to the shores of the Rising Sun."

Marieko responded to the flattery with pleasure and a certain discomfort, and the body language of a reluctant coquette. Lupo could be strangely charming when the mood took him, and outwitting Fenrior and his entire clan had obviously put him in a very good mood. Not to prolong the moment, Renquist decided to move the conversation along. "So the Highlanders had no idea you'd penetrated their fortress and were lurking in its passageways and on its stairs?"

"I fear these Scots can't see beyond their noses. They may once have been among the foremost guerrilla fighters, second only to the Apache, but life has been too easy for them for too long. They have grown lazy and careless in their unchanging sanctuary, and they lack a sufficiency of foes to keep them sharp."

"A pity we can't claim the same."

Lupo eyed his don knowingly. "Would you really have it that way?"

"A quiet life? I don't know. It would make a change. How long did you manage to fool them?"

"I was present at the Lord's feast and his 'entertainment.' "

"You partook of it?"

"No, Don Victor. I felt the risk of discovery was too great. I did, however, encounter a young woman called Annie Munro. She wanted me to Change her."

"And did you?"

"I thought about it. She might have provided a diversion, but I calculated it to be too much time and trouble."

Three thralls appeared and went into Renquist's room. They quickly reemerged, two carrying the body of Morbius by the arms and ankles and the third lugging the head. Lupo looked curiously at the head and then at Renquist. "Morbius?"

"Morbius."

"He won't be missed."

"You knew him?"

"He was a nuisance all over Europe after he went to Greece with Ruthven on his final trip." As the thralls departed, Lupo stared around and frowned. "Don Victor, we do seem to be standing in a corridor."

"Indeed we do." Duncanon's blood was on the floor at their feet, but Renquist knew even more gore was splattered over what had formerly been his room. "The problem is I'm not quite sure what to do about it."

Marieko was pleased to have the answer. "I have a room in which no one has recently been killed. We could go there while we prepare for Fenrior's meeting. It's just one flight down."

As they descended the stairs, Marieko made conversation with Lupo. "Is it true Lupo-san that you were contracted to kill Benito Mussolini?"

Lupo laughed. "Unfortunately I had to turn the assignment down. The logistics of traveling from Havana, where I resided at the time, all the way to Rome in the middle of World War Two was beyond even my contacts and resources."

How Fenrior had been able to completely transform the castle's Great Hall in time was a mystery Renquist would never solve. Had thralls been beaten bloody to prepare the place in a single hour, or had Fenrior been planning a meeting of this kind all along? The dais and the high table had been removed, and now just one long table, cleared for a conference and lit by electric spotlights, ran straight down the middle of the room. Fenrior's throne had been moved so it now presided at the head of the table. Long clan banners were unfurled, draping the walls and streaming down from the rafters, lending the hall a majestic feudal dignity. The fire in the huge hearth was cold, nothing but swept ashes, as though the dancing flames of the feast would detract from the solemnity of this occasion, which, from the elaboration of its staging, was intended as a grand and formal hearing on matters of great import before an autocrat assured of his own ultimate power.

A single plain chair was set at the end of the table opposite, back somewhat, so it reminded Renquist of the seat of the accused at the courts of the Inquisition. When Renquist saw the efforts made to overawe with a display of pomp, and circumstance, he had to take a deep breath. It was predictable, but totally the wrong approach. The Lord plainly had yet to grasp what kind of being the Merlin really was, and what he might do if pushed. The lone chair seemed to indicate he meant to subject Taliesin to some kind of inquiry or interrogation. Fenrior appeared to have missed the crucial point that, for such a thing even to take place, it presupposed those conducting the interrogation actually wielded the power. Fenrior's secure certainty in his own power was understandable. He had lorded it over his clan for centuries, overcome all challenges, and was obviously accustomed to never having his authority questioned. Renquist could hardly blame the laird for what he feared might be an excess of confidence and a severe underestimation of the power of the Urshu. Nosferatu in general had been corrupting and confusing the minds of humans for so long it would be hard to accept the seemingly impossible: a being might come among them who could corrupt and confuse theirs.

"You look worried, Master Renquist."

Lost in his concern, he turned quickly, taken completely by surprise, and found himself facing the Lady Gethsemany. The blue eyes fixed on his were arctic, and they challenged him not to make diplomatic small talk. Gethsemany wanted to know why he was worried. In a snap call of judgment, he decided to be as open as he could with Fenrior's consort. "I wonder if the right approach is being taken here. The Merlin's legend tells of his being able to bend flag-decked halls to his will and freely manipulate monarchs. Arthur Pendragon did not, by the old accounts, die well. They did more than just throw his sword into the lake."

The blue eyes didn't waver. "You don't equivocate, do you, Victor?"

Renquist smiled in an attempt to mitigate what threatened to be a stifling gravity. "I frequently equivocate, my lady, but this is not the time."

"We will not deflect Fenrior from his course this late in the day. You do realize that, don't you?"

Renquist had obviously made the right choice. The use of the word *we* could only be a signal that Gethsemany shared his misgiving of Fenrior's methods. "I'm very aware of that."

"And?"

"And I hold myself ready for what may come next."

Gethsemany lightly brushed Renquist's hand. "I'm glad to hear it, Victor. It's a pity we haven't had time to know each other better." She hesitated. "Out of interest, how would you deal with the Merlin?"

"With stealth and silence, my lady. The twin touchstones of the predator."

"Thank you, Victor." And the lady was gone, leaving a waft of perfume, and Renquist again wondered about the dynamic between Fenrior and the females around him.

Renquist, Lupo, and Marieko had not been the first to arrive, but they were also far from the last. As the increasing number of those summoned waited for Fenrior, conversation was sparse, and even Theda was subdued, with her purple hair pulled back into a severe bun. Those summoned to the function struck Renquist as a strange assortment: Shaggy Lachlan and other elders of the clan, five of the Seven Stars, some outsiders he had seen previously at the feast, the corporate moderns in their dark suits and tinted glasses, the exquisite in the powdered wig, the obese kaftan-draped grotesque, even the irritating Henri Brazil. It was, however, fairly typical of nosferatu democracy, in which a leader might solicit the opinion of the many, and then do exactly what he'd decided to do in the first place. Surveying the exotic mixture that seemed already to have been given a voice in the debate, he wasn't surprised when Julia and Destry walked in together. He hadn't expected them to be holding hands, though, or wearing matching borrowed plaids. Renquist suppressed an inward groan. He had seen Julia's attempts at bonding with other young powerful females—and remembered how they always ended in some display of lovelorn violence or worse. The groan was repeated when the pair came directly to him. "I need to speak with you, Victor. In fact, Destry and I need to speak with you."

"I don't have time now, Julia. Much more pressing matters are bearing down on us."

"That's a little offhand isn't it, after I came all this way to rescue you?"

"So far I haven't seen much rescuing going on, my dear. In fact, I seem to recall you had to be rescued from Duncanon and his Highlanders on the bridge."

"I'm serious, Victor—"

"So am I, Julia. I'm very serious. In fact, I cut off Duncanon's hand to express my displeasure."

Julia's tone became exasperated. "If you're in that kind of mood, Victor, we'll have to take this up later."

"I'm sure we will."

About the only ones in the room who seemed to be taking the situation in absolute stride were Gallowglass and Lupo, who had greeted each other with great and dignified enthusiasm and were now conversing with more animation than he'd recently seen exhibited by either. Standing a little way off, he focused on the two of them, shamelessly eavesdropping. Gallowglass wanted to know how Lupo had managed to come upon Fenrior so completely unawares.

"How d' ye do that'?"

"It's a trick of merging one's aura with the prevailing mood. It can make one virtually invisible to other nosferatu if they're in a sufficiently heightened state. It works particularly well at times of conflict and confrontation."

"So ye're no shape-shifter."

"There are no shape-shifters left, my Highland friend."

"There are those who swear th' Craft-workers are all gone, but look yonder."

The pentacle coven of the Craft-workers in their ceremonial black robes and cowls had just entered. It was the first time Renquist had ever observed Lupo less than

fully in control. His jaw dropped, and he performed a
complex and seemingly half-remembered genuflection
with his right hand. Gallowglass was about to comment,
but a small thrall dodged around the coven of Craft-
workers and hurried up to him. The lanky Scot bent
down to hear what the thrall had to say; then he straightened up and clapped his hands.

"Everyone take y' seats. Th' lord is on his way."

No one had indicated to Renquist where he was supposed to sit, and he wondered if some arcane protocol
governed meetings of this formal kind. He feared it
would be explosive enough with so many nosferatu set
to arguing. He didn't want to court trouble before the
proceedings had even started over a matter of seating.
To his relief, Gethsemany took him by the hand. "Sit
next to me, Victor. We may have need of you."

This positioned him on Fenrior's right, just two seats
down from the lord. The Lady Gethsemany's action
didn't pass without comment. Some further down the
table had in their auras the unmistakable resentment of
those who feel passed over. Some may even have believed, like Duncanon and Morbius, that Renquist was
the creature of the Merlin. Marieko also looked decidedly put out, as though she had expected to be seated
next to him, instead of a long way down the left side of
the table between Goneril and a modern.

Fenrior came in fast and businesslike. No piper (although Angus Crimmon was present in the hall), no
dwarf with wolfhounds, and just two guards at his back.
He went directly to the throne without speaking even to
Gethsemany, unhooked his dress sword from his belt,
and tossed it with a clatter onto the table.

"My friends and followers, Clan Fenrior, and distinguished guests, we face a circumstance of great gravity."

He stared slowly round the assembled faces to see
what effect his words might have had. Total silence ruled
in the Great Hall, laying over those present like an uncomfortable blanket of anticipation, and for some, a

slight chill of fear. Aside from the unique enormity of the concerns at hand, the very size of the gathering had the weight of potential history. It had been a very long time, even by nosferatu calculations, since so many of the undead had convened formally to confer.

"We face a challenge of a proportion we have not witnessed in recent times. As many of you already know, Taliesin the Merlin of old, possibly the last of the Urshu race on this planet, currently resides within the walls of Fenrior." For those who didn't know, he proceeded to recount the waking of the Merlin and give a brief résumé of the problems the Urshu's presence appeared to be creating. "I have to take responsibility for initiating all this. My only excuse is that it was done under the innocent auspices of scientific research. In our eagerness to learn, we failed to appreciate what we might be bringing back to life."

"Wha' does he do right now, th' Merlin, m' lord? Is he passive? Is he liable t' turn dangerous?"

"He eats, he drinks, and he learns. He stuffs his face and studies all there is to know about what came to pass while he slept. The Urshu is definitely catching up for lost time. In the matter of is he dangerous? That may well be what we've gathered here to discuss."

Fenrior paused and glanced at Renquist long enough for all present to perceive the message. "Some here believe he is a danger already. Maybe from the very moment he awoke. That was certainly the conclusion of Dr. Morbius, who played a major role in the entire experiment. Unfortunately, Dr. Morbius cannot be with us to state his own case since he was just presently beheaded and stabbed through the heart."

A number of Highlanders were instantly on their feet, ready to mete out honorable revenge at Fenrior's slightest say-so. "Who did this thing, m' lord?"

Marieko remained seated, but her voice was high and clear. "It was I who killed him, gentlemen. For those of you who don't know me, I am Marieko Matsunaga, of the Ravenkeep troika, formerly of the Yarabachi, and the kill was legal and with honor."

All eyes were suddenly on Marieko, and Renquist understood he was sitting in a very devious, even dangerous, poker game, where what was to be lost or won had yet to be defined. Already hands were on sword hilts and Highlanders were looking for the license to hack. Fenrior calmed things somewhat as he treated Marieko to a courtly smile, but Renquist knew, behind the greenhouse sunglasses, a brightly insidious mind was at work. "Please, Mistress Marieko, I did not intend to imply otherwise."

"Thank you, my lord."

Renquist decided it was time to toss out his first card and take the pressure off Marieko. He now saw how deftly he and she had been physically separated, and at least they should close ranks tactically. Renquist let his voice and aura become almost languid, as thought it were a fine point, but one that needed clarification: "Perhaps it should be made clear, my lord, that Mistress Marieko was defending my life at the time."

"So I understand."

The Lady Gethsemany quietly interrupted. "Excuse me, my lord."

"My dear?"

"There's one thing I'm less than clear about. Why did Miss Matsunaga have the legal and honorable need to destroy Dr. Morbius in the first place? I don't quite understand."

Gethsemany glanced at Renquist. Beware the cold depths of those blue infinite eyes. The Lady Gethsemany had steered him to the seat at the head of the table, and now she seemed to be setting him up for Fenrior's next play. Let it never be said the Lord and Lady of Fenrior didn't hunt as a team. Now he needed to know if he was the quarry. "Perhaps I should answer that, my lord?"

"By all means, Victor."

"Dr. Morbius was attempting to extinguish me with a steel spike."

Gethsemany turned on her patrician smile. "But why should he do a thing like that? He knew you were our guest."

Renquist decided to go for broke. "Dr. Morbius held the considered belief that I was in league with Taliesin against the Lord Fenrior."

Murmuring began among the Highlanders as Gethsemany's patrician smile grew even sweeter. Renquist had underestimated her. She wasn't just a shill; Gethsemany was quite as devious as her lord, only she was happy to reveal her eyes because she knew they were one of her most powerful weapons. "And are you, Master Renquist?"

"Am I what, my lady?"

"Are you in league with Taliesin against the Lord Fenrior?"

The game was turning positively Elizabethan—robust and deadly twists of undead power brokerage, and hints of treason and plotting dedicated to keeping everyone off balance. Was Renquist being invited to place his head in the noose? "You make me feel as though I'm on trial here." He gestured to the empty chair at the far end of the table. "Should I take the seat reserved for the one under interrogation?"

The Highlanders were exchanging glances. Fenrior could either calm them down or let Renquist become the villain of the piece. They were happy to go either way, but he could do very little about it. Fenrior pretended to consider the situation. "You volunteered the information."

"Indeed I did, my lord. And I have had a number of conversations with the Merlin. Perhaps as many as you, my lord."

"And your conclusions?"

"I made a number of observations, but I'd prefer to wait before I present them."

"Wait?"

"I'm sure others have opinions to express. I'd rather hold off until we've heard from them. But, in answer to your lady's question, I have sealed no secret compact with Taliesin. When you made me a guest in your domain, my lord, I pledged my sword to your service in this very hall, and nothing has happened to cause me to renege on that pledge. Victor Renquist does not go back on his word."

The short speech seemed to have the right effect, in that it at least produced a silence, which was filled only when Cyrce surprised everyone by deciding to speak in public. Having eschewed one of her usual extreme fine-fetish outfits for a fashionable black evening dress that would have been acceptable at any cocktail party on the planet, she had so far spent the entire meeting writing notes in what looked to be a school exercise book. Now she half raised a hand to be recognized. Renquist, at least temporarily, was off the hook.

"My lord?" Her voice was a soprano purr that commanded all to listen closely.

"Cyrce?"

"Leaving the matter of Dr. Morbius and Master Renquist aside for a moment, I'd be interested to know how many of us have had our dreams invaded by this Urshu."

"Have you experienced this?"

"If I hadn't, I wouldn't be asking the question. My dreams have been violated by this thing, which I find both disturbing and offensive. As you, my lord, are well aware, I can create far more interesting scenarios for my dreamstate than being forced into gratuitous virtuals of fifth century England or the Nephilim occupation. As far as I'm concerned, this would indicate the Merlin intends us no good, and we should consider ridding ourselves of him. He is a boor and should be dispatched without delay. Of course, this may only be happening to Theda and myself, but somehow I doubt it. That's why I ask again, have more of you had these invasive dreams?"

It was one of those situations where, despite much muttering and exchanging of looks, no one wanted to be the first to make a public admission. Theda, still in her gloved governess outfit, metaphorically cracked the whip on the assembly. "Perhaps we could have a show of hands on this?"

Finally Shaggy Lachlan himself owned up. "Aye, lassie. I hate t' admit it, but th' bastard's been gettin' inta mine, an' no mistake."

"An' mine."

"Mine too, fuck him."

With Lachlan having broken the ice, other Highlanders felt able to make the same confession without showing weakness. After some delay, about half the assembled company raised their hands. Even Renquist was a little surprised. The Merlin appeared already to be deep into his game. Cyrce regarded Fenrior as if her point had been proved. "Thus we see the Urshu is making a bloody nuisance of himself all through the castle."

One of the coven of Craft-workers—who were sitting together halfway down the left side of the table like a row of black crows on a branch—spoke in a hollow voice from inside her cowl. "The imparting of dreams would seem a small thing on which to condemn the Urshu out of hand."

An elder Highlander grumbled. "M' minds m' own. No fuckin' Kings Cross Station on a Saturday night."

Up to this point, Destry and Julia had seemed to be contained in their own world of budding undead romance, but Destry suddenly and somewhat angrily detached herself and joined the meeting. "With all respect to the learned Craft-worker, how long will the invasion be confined to our dreams? Let's not forget the total destruction of my troika companion, the late Columbine Dashwood, began with dreams. The worst catastrophes can start small, but they grow to be uncontrollable before anyone realizes."

Shaggy Lachlan spat on the floor. "Not t' speak ill o'

th' dear departed, but th' Dashwood lassie was bloody mad fra' th' get-go. Remember aw th' trouble she caused before, an' tha' she had t' be run oot of' here wi' her fancy tail between her fancy legs?"

"And when she returned here, compelled by the Merlin, she was reduced to her fundamental ashes so the monster could wake."

Shaggy Lachlan appealed to Fenrior. "Let's be done wi' i' an' kill th' thing, m' lord. Then we can aw fall t' drinkin'."

This brought a roar of relieved laughter, but also a good deal of agreement. Fenrior raised a hand. "Then you'll be pleased to hear that before we gathered I placed a guard on the Urshu. Taliesin is now under close arrest."

Renquist was careful not to show how he felt. With Gethsemany right next to him, he knew his every feeling was being monitored. Fenrior still had to be in denial of the true power of the Urshu. Lupo had walked through Fenrior's Highlanders without any of them sensing him. How much more could an Urshu do? Posting some lads with pikes outside his door, even undead lads with pikes, would serve only to confirm for the Merlin that the wind had changed and he was no longer the honored guest. While Renquist gloomily hid his fuming, the Craft-worker nearest to the head of the table rose to her feet. One among the Highlanders muttered the word *witch,* but was ignored. Her voice was less hollow and more melodious than that of her companion, and since she sat nearest the head of the table, Renquist surmised she was the Mistress of the Coven, the Seventh of the Seven Stars who had sat on Fenrior's right hand during the feast and the entertainment.

"My instinct is to concur that, in allowing the Urshu to awaken in these confines, my lord, there is a strong possibility that you have unknowingly introduced a malignancy into your house and into the modern world. Such texts as have survived all led to the supposition of

a natural enmity and ill will between Urshu and nosferatu. The old accounts tell of battles fought and of strug-
gles for the most conclusive of tools of power. The
assumption among we of the craft has always been that
conflict would inevitably follow an encounter between
two creations of the Nephilim. If my lord recalls, we
urged you long ago not to assist in the waking of the
Urshu, but you were of another mind."

Fenrior glared at the row of black cowls. "I do not
need those of the Craft to remind me they told me so."

"I'm sorry, my lord. Should I continue?"

"Yes, yes, go on. You may be irritating, Mistress of
the Craft, but you're also usually right."

"Master Lachlan has counseled 'kill the thing,' and I
would assume others here, perhaps even the majority,
feel the same way. Before, however, passing a final judgment on anything, we needs must know whether we can
in fact impose the penalty demanded of that judgment."

"Could you put that a little more simply."

"To be blunt, my lord, saying 'kill the thing' is all
very well, but I'm not sure any of us have the means to
kill it at our disposal. There may be no way of killing
an Urshu. The death of one has never been recorded.
The remains of one have never been unearthed."

A Highlander was on his feet. "Aw things die if killed
right. When we were human we slaughtered th' English,
an' when we came t' nosferatu estate, we slaughtered
th' humans. Who tells us we cann'a slaughter one Urshu?"

The Mistress of the Craft pressed on. "Remember the
legend, my lord. In confrontation between Tezcatilpoca
and Quetzalcoatl it's recorded that Quetzalcoatl was
driven out of Mexico, not that he was killed. It is possible the Urshu do not suffer death as we know it. It
might seem impossible to us, who fear the sun and all
the other fatal weaknesses that beset us, to conceive of
a being to whom all forms of death are a mere abstrac-

tion—but think of how the humans are unable to understand us, the nosferatu."

The Highlander hardly seemed impressed with the Craft-worker's reasoning. "Hack i' t' pieces an' spread it's parts. Then burn i'. Tha' seems t' work f' even th' foulest o' fiends."

Gallowglass spoke for the first time, almost to himself. "Tha' or we find th' Green Kryptonite."

A number of those present looked at him in puzzlement. "What are you talking about?"

Gallowglass glared at those who seemed to question his statement. "Green Kryptonite, ye ken? Do ye no read th' comics, or watch th' moving pictures on t' telly? Green Kryptonite was th' downfall of Superman, a rock fra' his home planet tha' caused him t' lose his powers. Aw seemin'ly invincible bein's sooner or later reveal a weakness. Th' Persians say perfection's only wrought by God himself. Me? I obviously cann'a believe in God, but I believe th' Persians. I know fra' my readin' and fra' th' tales told that Marduk Ra never wrought perfection i' anythin'. Jus' look a' us. Th' Urshu has a weakness, mark m' words."

Without rising from his seat, Lupo spoke next. "Shouldn't we be asking ourselves if we have the time to go looking for a weakness in this thing? It already knows all of ours."

Before Lupo was answered by anyone, another of the Craft-workers was on her feet. "Before we seek a weakness in the Urshu, shouldn't we question our right to destroy it at all? It is not our food. It is not a kill. With the exception of Columbine Dashwood, it has not overtly harmed one of us. The moral burden of its destruction could prove a weighty one."

Again the Highlanders were muttering. The words "fuck the moral burden" were repeated at least twice, but it was impossible for Renquist to tell who had uttered them. He was more intrigued that the coven seemed to be arguing as one for the preservation of the Merlin, and he wondered what their agenda might be. He continued to wonder as the Lady of the Craft resumed. "It is one of the last of its kind. In fact, it could be the last. There may be no more. Far from destroying it, shouldn't we be seeking a way to safely preserve it? Once it's gone, it will never come again."

Taking a cue from Lupo, Renquist didn't stand, but he made his voice heard over the Highlanders' grumbling undertow. "The argument of the Lady of the Craft does have a certain merit. We would be destroying a crucial link with our own past and origins."

Fenrior turned and faced him, and Renquist wished to hell he'd take off the dark glasses. "So Victor, you do stand with Taliesin after all?"

The debate had come full circle, and they were back to the impeachment of his loyalty again. He let show some of his distaste for the turn of events. "No, my lord, I merely thought the point of our friend here was worthy of consideration."

Fenrior shook his head. "I fear, Victor, you are too much the historian. Can the Urshu really be considered a species? It does not breed like a human or perpetuate its kind in the way of the nosferatu. It's a relic, and I know you love relics, Victor. I would be the first to admit I share the same fascination, but I believe it is a dangerous relic, like an ancient toxin, an artifact that proves cursed or radioactive, or a disease suddenly flourishing again long after being thought eradicated. My instincts are that the Merlin must go. He is nothing but a sorry relic of Marduk Ra and the Nephilim who sought to enslave and destroy us. Let's hold the method of his going for the moment, and just consider how safe it would be to permit such a thing to continue. What say the rest of you? Gethsemany?"

Gethsemany didn't hesitate. "It must be destroyed."

"Gallowglass?"

"Aye, m' lord. It was a noble experiment, but put an end t' i'."

"Ladies of the Craft?"

The Mistress spoke for all of them. "We reserve our judgment for the present."

Fenrior didn't seem pleased. "So be it. Theda?"

"Kill it."

"Cyrce?"

"Kill it."

One by one, as Fenrior continued down the length of the table, the responses seemed unanimous. "Kill it."

"Kill i'."

"Destroy it."

"Kill it."

"Aye, kill i'."

"Kill i'."

"Kill it."

"Kill."

"Yes, kill it."

"Aye. Do away wi' th' bloody thing."

"Aye."

"Kill i'."

All seemed to be in agreement, and of the principal protagonists, only Renquist had yet to speak. "Victor?"

His would, by no means, be the deciding vote, but he knew the comfort of his immediate future would be seriously affected by his yea or nay. Yet he couldn't just be ensuring his own comfort. Too much was at stake, and in the ancient unreality of the Great Hall, of the Castle Fenrior itself, in the midst of this unprecedented gathering of the undead, he could all too easily be carried along by the prevailing mass consciousness of fear and threatened pride. And then there was the temptation of the Merlin. What had he offered? "A world for nosferatu, by nosferatu, without the need to ever again hide." Was that not a prize to at least be considered? If, of course, there was a word of truth in it, and if the Merlin was not simply playing him for a fool. And wasn't that a very strong possibility? How else would an Urshu view a nosferatu, descendant of intractable fighting machines—without wit or imagination? As an inferior. As a fool.

"You have a problem, Victor?"

With a sense of profound relief, Renquist made up his mind. "No, my lord, I have no problem. Kill the damned thing. It's an obscenity. It's a thousand times worse than we are."

"Kill the obscenity, Victor? Or is that merely for the benefit of Fenrior and his people?"

Taliesin was in the Great Hall, suddenly standing beside the plain empty chair. Marieko could feel a terrible nosferatu dread flowing in waves. They were children caught by an elder, ineffectually plotting the elder's downfall, and now they would have to suffer for their presumption. Some of the fear came from the gathering itself, but much more was being imposed. To be able to inflict such a massive and all-enveloping emotional miasma told her this Urshu had hitherto unsuspected reserves of power.

"Would you really reject the chance to be Lord of the Earth under me, Victor? Or you, Fenrior?"

Renquist and Fenrior stared at each other. They had both been offered the same contract with the Merlin? And as the Merlin laughed, the banner in the Great Hall billowed slowly and ominously, and he seemed to glow from within with a mesmerizing radiance. "There's no point in looking at each other like that. You will tell yourselves it was all lies, but you'll recall the rejection you made for the rest of your long, long time. The fields of absolute domination were laid out in front of you, but you turned your backs on them. Fenrior for the security of your crumbling castle and outmoded clan, and Renquist for your wholly spurious pride. And Gethsemany, and you, Julia—neither of you cared to be the Mistress of All? Where do your loyalties lie? What better could you hope for beyond the sensual luxury of unquestioned command and absolute authority? Could none of you bring yourselves to serve only the Merlin? Could none of you brave the truth? Accept the inevitable that Taliesin had awakened, and your sole superior was come among you?"

As he spoke, the Merlin also shifted shape. He grew taller, the merry girth disappeared. Golden robes flowed from his shoulders like wings at rest, and his countenance became all but divine. The humanoid resemblance at once more idealized and more tenuous. A god or monster? The choice was theirs. They could make of him what they would, the very undead who were themselves considered masters of the grand illusion. They, too, had been gods in their time, and monsters, too, but the Merlin had come, and their reign of night terror and blind day was at an end. The assembled nosferatu, Marieko included, sat paralyzed, helpless in the vise the Urshu was rapidly closing on their minds; Victor, Fenrior, the Craft-workers—none appeared able to stand against the Urshu. Some, including the grotesque, the exquisite, and Henri Brazil, had been permitted to flee.

"For shame, you sad and faithless vampires, shall I now seat myself in the chair of the accused and have you put me to the questioning? But, no—your votes were cast. Kill, kill, kill, kill, you cried. 'Do away with the bloody thing' was what one said. The Lady Gethsemany spoke so sweetly and without hesitation. 'It must be destroyed.' The one who offered all was to be hacked to pieces and the pieces scattered and burned, when all the poor Merlin intended was a place of perfection for the nosferatu. And how will you who rejected me think about this day when you see your world sere and scorched, the very finality of your kind close at hand? Will you curse the foolish pride that caused you to reject Taliesin, Victor? Will you weep your cold, dry, and bitter tears for what might have been, Gethsemany?"

Was this the kind of speech he had made to Arthur on the dirt floor of Camelot, shape-shifting and delivering dreams of a future golden and eternal? Was that the promise made to Pendragon? And yet Pendragon had himself been deceived. An idyll of less than a human lifetime, and then the great war harps had roared in the tempest, and Camelot had fallen to the fire, sword, and axe of the Saxons. And as Marieko had that thought, the glory of the Urshu seemed to diminish slightly. She thought perhaps it was only a matter of her own perception fighting back, but she was suddenly and drastically shown she was not alone. A Highlander hurled himself at the Merlin with a single scream. "Fenrior!"

The fine but futile gesture ended immediately as the Highlander, still nine or ten feet from the Merlin vanished in a blinding brilliance of silent lightning that left only clothing, grey ash, and a fallen sword. In the flash, however, some part of the irresistible, confining bubble somewhere burst. Taliesin's will was only finite. Fenrior was first on his feet, seizing his dress sword from the table and throwing off the scabbard, but Gallowglass and Lupo were a close second and third. Marieko knew she had to join them. She quickly fell into step beside Lupo. It seemed an intelligent place to be. Drive out the Merlin or let the creature take them. It had gone on too far for any other course. Highlanders joined them, Theda and Cyrce, Julia and Destry, Shaggy Lachlan with claymore drawn, a half circle of nosferatu, far beyond anger, in a state of mind where the only options were death or . . . Or what? At that point, no one quite seemed to have an answer. Lupo leaned close and murmured a low warning. "Be careful, he may not be here at all."

"He could do all this from at a distance?"

"Who can outguess an Urshu? Who even knows what an Urshu really is under all that illusion?"

Renquist and Fenrior were a few paces in front of the rest and a distance from the Merlin; Fenrior held up his hand, and everyone halted. Marieko watched as the two exchanged a single glance. Renquist, who was unarmed, turned and held out his hand. Immediately the hilts of a half dozen claymores were offered to him. He took the nearest one. It was no time for show. Taliesin immediately recognized their intent. "Oh, my boys, the two heroes come for me."

Renquist and Fenrior momentarily paused, black silhouettes against the larger-than-life luminescence; then together they hurled themselves at the Merlin. And the Merlin vanished.

The immediate result was uncontrolled undead panic. The hysteria couldn't have been worse. With the Urshu mind control instantly withdrawn, the nosferatu simply vented. Some screamed, some tottered, some sagged in their seats, and others went into a frenzy. One killed an unfortunate thrall and fed on the spot. Many tried to flee the Great Hall, wanting to get away but seemingly having no other aim in mind. Renquist and Fenrior stood looking at the place where the Merlin had been, as though dazed. Highlanders, equally confused, gathered around their lord, swords drawn, and moving according to their ingrained instinct to shield him, but again, hardly knowing from what. This instantly convened bodyguard was so unthinkingly protective, it almost got into an internecine fight when another squad, under the command of Goneril, ran into the room. Fenrior managed to get between them, and after some shouting, those who'd been in the hall and received the treatment from the Merlin started thinking again.

"We've been deceived by an illusion."

"Where's the Merlin?"

"Where's th' fuckin' Merlin?"

Goneril unhappily came to attention. "Tha's wha' we came t' tell ye, m' lord. Th' Merlin is gone. He ha' escaped."

"I know that, damn it. He was just here, and now he isn't."

"No, m' lord . . ."

Fenrior looked ready to strike her down. "What do you mean, 'no, my lord'?"

"I posted two sets o' guards as ye ordered, m' lord. Two inside th' Merlin's room an' two i' th' corridor."

"And? . . ."

"An' th' two i' th' corridor reported he never left his room, but when i' was time t' change th' guard, th' Merlin was gone an' th' two i' th' room . . ." She hesitated, at a complete loss and very close to being spooked.

Fenrior made his voice firmer but more gentle. "Steady, Goneril, you are not responsible."

"Th' two guards i' his room, m' lord, they were turned t' dust. Nothin' left o' them save their clothes an' their weapons."

Quickly, Gallowglass took control. He pointed to a Highlander at random. "You. Run an' see if any vehicles are missing." He selected three more. "You, you, and you. Secure th' castle. Order oot aw th' able-bodied. See tha' aw gates are locked an' tha' th' walls are fully manned. I want this place closed up tight as a drum, an' no excuses."

The ones so designated hurried from the hall. With a new sense of purpose, the clan began to recover from its disarray. The mystery of what the Urshu had really done, however, was far from being solved, and Fenrior was about as furious as a nosferatu could be without actually spitting blood. Lupo eased close to Renquist. "I doubt they'll find him, Don Victor."

Renquist nodded. "I doubt they'll find him, either. In fact, I think the Urshu was ahead of us from the moment he awoke. He has played us the way we might play a rabble of unsuspecting humans."

"You think perhaps we might make ourselves scarce? Before anyone thinks to blame us for what happened. I'm not sure the Lord Fenrior will be ready to accept he was simply outclassed by the Merlin."

"Me, too, Lupo. I was fooled right along with the rest."

"That may be true, Don Victor, but should we make a discreet exit?"

Before Renquist could answer, the Highlander who had been sent to check on the vehicles hurried back to Gallowglass. "Aw th' motor vehicles are accounted f'. No one had crossed th' bridge, an' th' thralls i' th' village claim no one has passed through."

Fenrior joined them as the Highlander finished his breathless report. "He must be in the castle somewhere, damn it! Goneril, form search parties. Find him!"

With orders given, the castle being sealed, and search parties organized, Fenrior had the time to turn to Renquist and Lupo. "Can you explain any of this to me?"

Renquist spread his hands. "No, my lord. I wish someone could explain it to me."

"We should never have meddled in this."

"Taliesin would have woken anyway. We only selected the time and the place."

Fenrior, Renquist, Lupo, and Gallowglass fell silent as an eerie sound echoed through the Great Hall. Somewhere a female was sobbing, a sound of bereft, inhuman desolation that was coming closer as they listened.

"Now what?"

As if in answer, Julia entered the hall supporting Destry on her arm. The dreadful sobbing was coming from none other than Destry, who had completely broken down.

"What happened?"

"Destry went to check on her horse, and it was gone."

A bad feeling overtook Renquist. "Gone? The Uzbek?"

Destry gathered her wits. "Dormandu is gone. His saddle and harness, too. That thing has taken him."

Fenrior's expression was grim. "So that would be how he got away."

Gallowglass was even grimmer. "An', m' Lord, th' sun is about t' broach th' horizon. Taliesin ha' well timed his escape. No pursuit can be staged until sunset."

*   *   *

The sun sank behind the mountains, marking the end of a long, tense, and sleepless day. Everyone in the castle seemed to have a reason to be in the courtyard inside the main gate before the sky was even dark. Vehicles were being manned and their engines started, search parties were organized, and little effort was spared to find the Merlin, but with almost a twelve-hour start, none but the most blindly optimistic expected to find him. Renquist and Lupo walked slowly through the sunset chaos of a delayed pursuit. They first encountered Marieko. Renquist took her by the arm and moved her away from possibly eavesdropping Scots. "Lupo and I are leaving under the cover of all this chaos."

"How?"

"Lupo has a way prepared. Will you come with us?"

Marieko reluctantly shook her head. "I must return to Ravenkeep. It's my home. With Columbine gone, there will be much to sort out."

"How will you get there?"

"The Range Rover has been commandeered by one of the lord's search parties, but I will go with Destry and Julia. They left the horse box in which they brought Dormandu beyond the village. Fenrior and his people don't know about it, and we will use it to travel south."

"Julia is going with you?"

"That seems to be her intention. Right now she and Destry claim to be inseparable."

"You must come to California as soon as you can get away. I will show you my library, and we will drink the blood of movie stars together."

"We will do that, Victor, but right now I have to go."

Lupo stared speculatively at Renquist as Marieko walked away. "A flirtation in the middle of all this, Don Victor? An attraction to the Yarabachi?"

Renquist ignored him except to project a certain concern over the three females traveling on their own.

Lupo looked at him as if he were insane. "Let them adventure their own way out of this, Don Victor. Now you travel with Lupo. We will go home. We will have no more trouble."

Epilogue

After what Lupo called "all his globe-trotting" Renquist had taken his time settling back into the simple routine of the Residence in Los Angeles, but bit by bit, he sank into the colony's essentially lazy ways. Evenings began in the big kitchen. Details of the day-to-day running of the house required his attention, as did the management of the financial complexity needed to materially support the small group of nosferatu. In the days after his return, he had explained to the others that Julia might not be returning for a while, and that they might expect a visit from a female called Marieko Matsunaga, late of the Ravenkeep troika and the Yarabachi Clan. The first piece of news was greeted with indifference. The other nosferatu in the colony, particularly Dahlia, considered Julia something of a loose and unpredictable cannon. The second item had caused a certain gossipy speculation: Was Victor through mourning Cynara and casting around for a new consort?

In the first few weeks after his and Lupo's return from

Europe, Renquist had earnestly taxed himself wondering
and worrying about the location of Taliesin and what
fresh games the Urshu might be planning. He had taken
the Merlin's declared plan to conduct a cull of the human
race at face value, and he had done a good deal of research into the best survival prospects in the event of a
limited nuclear war. With the sole exception of Lupo,
Renquist had kept his work secret from the others, lest
they accuse him of excessive paranoia. The months had
passed, however, and the Urshu failed to surface or in
any way manifest himself, and thoughts of him had been
pushed to the back of Renquist's mind.

On this particular morning, Renquist had arisen late,
drank his water, and dressed. He'd hunted the night before, feeding on a confused table dancer from a strip
joint near LAX. The girl had been so loaded on designer
drugs she had hardly recognized death even when it was
upon her. When he entered the kitchen, he was surprised
to see that everyone else was already out and about their
business—unusual, but hardly remarkable. The smell of
Sada's idiosyncratic coffee was in the air, and someone
had left the TV on. He eyed a report by Wolf Blitzer on
CNN with little interest. The subject of the report was
Mervyn Talesian, the U.S. president's new Special National Security Advisor, the one the media were lionizing
as the new genius of the current "tough line" in international diplomacy. An Armenian American, and previously a political unknown, he had apparently been a
cloistered academic at either Harvard or Princeton, but
the press seemed confused over which. He'd only
emerged from academic obscurity when the incoming
president had selected him to author the first draft of
NACT, the Nuclear Arms Containment Treaty. From
that point on, he had moved with almost uncanny swift-
ness into the very center of power, with his own staff,
his own office in the White House, and, some said, his
own private intelligence unit. Right at this moment, Talesian was in the very center of the nation's efforts to

defuse the growing nuclear-armed tension between India and Pakistan. Blitzer spoke into a hand mic as, behind him, Talesian disembarked from Air Force One, discreetly behind the president, as they returned to Washington from what was being called a "crisis summit."

Renquist had read about Talesian, and even seen photographs of the man. He seemed the capable, good-looking politician in the current cookie-cutter mode, but since he watched little TV, he had never seen him through that medium before. The moment Talesian emerged from behind the blandly smiling president, Renquist experienced a not inconsiderable shock of recognition. Talesian outwardly looked nothing like the Urshu he had encountered at Fenrior, but Renquist knew instantly they were one and the same. The deliberate and joking similarity in names should have been a clue, but Renquist had failed to make the connection. To paraphrase the Beatles, it was something in the way he moved: a mannerism, a gesture, an inclination of the head, the way he related to the humans around him. Mervyn Talesian was, beyond all doubt, Taliesin the Merlin, and he was the one attempting to broker a peace between the two fractious nuclear powers on behalf of the president of the United States. Perhaps it was time to dust off the files on survival and prepare the others for what might be the Merlin's worst-case scenario.

COMING IN OCTOBER 2002 FROM TOR BOOKS:
THE FOURTH BOOK IN MICK FARREN'S RENQUIST QUARTET

UNDERLAND

Victor Renquist meets his toughest opponents yet. He's been co-opted by a top-secret US agency to battle the remnants of Hitler's Third Reich, who have some very strange allies.

▼ ▼

Coulson laid a hand on the closed folder. He couldn't allow Renquist to completely run the encounter. "Do you mind if I take a turn and ask you some questions?"

"I need to know just one more thing."

"What's that?"

"My feeding requirements?"

Coulson had been wondering when the question would come up. When the plan to trap Renquist had been approved by Grael, Schultz, Lustig, Brauer, and a half dozen other company men had drunk themselves jubilantly stupid in a Washington bar later the same night. Netting the vampire was a much needed justification of their work in very uncertain times. A chant had even broken out. "We're getting a vampire! We're getting a vampire!" Coulson, as drunk as any of the others, but holding it better had, had at that point asked the same thing Renquist was now asking. "If you get a vampire, who's going to feed it?" By so doing, he had stopped the party in its inebriated tracks. Lustig had been the first to recover off handedly suggesting that Washington had enough junkies and crackheads to satisfy any vampire.

Coulson regarded Renquist with all the neutrality he could muster. "Mercifully that is not my direct problem or responsibility. Plans have, however, been made."

"An exclusive diet of drug addicts is not advisable. They make me sluggish and stupid, and eventually I sicken."

Coulson looked hard at Renquist. "I thought you agreed not to read my mind."

"I'm not reading your mind, I was just anticipating the obvious and pragmatic. Crackheads will make me ill."

"The nosferatu are that fragile?"

Renquist shook his head. "No, my friend. Humans are that toxic."